A Season of Mists

SARAH WOODHOUSE lives on a farm with her husband and two small children in Norfolk, and has been writing historical short stories since she was eighteen.

A Season of Mists is Sarah Woodhouse's first novel, and the story revolves around three or four families in a country village in Norfolk in the eighteenth century.

She is now at work on a second novel.

D0318550

SARAH WOODHOUSE

A Season of Mists

FONTANA/Collins

First published in Great Britain by Century
Publishing Co. Ltd 1984
First issued in Fontana Paperbacks 1985

Made and printed in Great Britain by
William Collins Sons and Co. Ltd, Glasgow

To my Mother

1

MISS PENNYQUICK hated washdays. Up to her scant eyebrows in filthy water she reassessed her foot-square view of the yard and found it as depressing as ever; and the sodden curtains in the tub looked still, in spite of her frenzied ministrations, like old dishcloths.

Of course it had been Hollin's idea: the house was shabby and neglected enough, he had said – and quite as if he himself had made no contribution to its shabbiness – without being further shamed by dirty curtains, grey counterpanes and yellowed cushions. He had stood bovinely in the middle of the unused drawing room, in vast outdoor boots, and had scowled round at the threadbare hangings and greasy upholstery, at the blackened candlesticks and the ashy grate; the place could do with a spring clean, he had suggested, and not without malice. After he had gone Barbara Pennyquick found his imprint on the faded Turkey rug, huge and muddy and reeking of the cattle shed.

A spring clean in December, the yard a sea of liquid mud and the wind rising and promising snow: it was impractical, absurd. She could see the naked trees that lined the steep lane already bending to a half gale and the sky above the Gorse was an unrelieved pewter, unhealthy, untrustworthy. The washhouse, attached somewhat haphazardly to the back of the great kitchen chimney, was always bitterly cold, however much water was heated and however much steam rose to curl about her reddening ears.

And all for that ... Her imagination failed for a moment and then reasserted itself: all for that sprat of a girl who had had the temerity to turn up on the tailboard of Pashman's cart with just two bags, boots muddied to their tops, and the hem of her plain dress draggled and frayed. For that object, deposited in the mephitic quagmires of Thorn, Miss Pennyquick had seen the household overturned and ten years of slovenly housekeeping end in an instant.

Ann Mathick had startled them all out of midwinter complacency, that was indisputable. Also indisputable was Ann Mathick's right to be mistress of Thorn now that old Francis's indigestible will had been swallowed after so much choking and spluttering. No-one could deny there was only Ann to whom he could leave the farm – such as it was – and his last twenty bottles of precious claret: she was the child of his dead sister, his last living relation; on the other hand his minor provisions caused untold speculation, a cynical jigging of eyebrows all over the county, a great deal of sly laughter behind fluttering fans. For instance, there was his splendid bequest of two hundred pounds to Miss Pennyquick – and all High Common knew what that was for – and his equally benevolent hundred guineas to Hollin, to old Ned Bushey, and to a mysterious Miss Prosser; there was also the small matter of the same sum for a Jenny Styles 'and child'. But the heavy odour of scandal was nothing to the fact, learned much later, that Francis Forsie had had no money to leave anyone at the time of his death, his account at Kerrison's bank standing at twenty pounds nine and fourpence, a sum which did not even provide a decent funeral and a headstone: the sale of the last farm horses, a silver tankard, and a pair of Manton pistols achieving these. His lawyer Savill, attempting to clear the debts, found himself confronted by a touchy Miss Pennyquick with a frightening list of articles in pawn, and later by a slovenly woman from a village the other side of Norwich who claimed to be the unknown Miss Prosser, strident on the subject of masculine vices. Underfed – Miss Pennyquick was an indifferent cook – unnerved, and clinging with difficulty to the shreds of his dignity, Savill fled back to London and the sanity and sanctity of his respectable office. His letter to Ann Mathick, informing her that Thorn was now ready for her possession, was chillingly formal.

Miss Ann Mathick was twenty-four, short, slight, brown, and unremarkable. She had not inherited the Forsie looks and nor did it seem she had inherited much, if anything, of the volatile Forsie temperament. Her mother, another Ann, had married a prosperous, conscientious Northumbrian parson; she had never returned to Thorn, had lived a cheerful, sociable life, and had died suddenly at forty. The parson had followed her within nine months, worn out by work and grief. For the next three years Ann coped alone, an elderly cousin of her father's acting duenna, a vague, skeletal lady by the name of Millington. The old house was far too large for them, though difficulties of communication were caused by more than damp stone walls and interminable corridors. It was a trying time. Ann's social life was patchy, her friends now miles away across bleak uplands, her position considered a little eccentric; and there were several young men and not so young a-dangle for her hand, her tidy fortune. For Ann Mathick had been left the very last of the Forsie money by her mother's settlement, a sum invested in funds which brought in about two thousand a year; on top of which there was twenty thousand pounds from her father and the vast grey house in which he had grown up.

It was a house that held no memories for Ann; how she regretted the loss of the sunny parsonage! It was crazily built, draughty, sprawling, inconvenient. She could spend a whole day and not meet Miss Millington, it had such twists and turns, such passages, such dim and useless rooms. The news of Francis Forsie's death had found her bored, besieged and lonely, occupied solely by the problem of how best to move the coal the half mile from the cellar to the drawing room. In an instant everything was changed. Once more she was active and decisive, glowing with hope, ambition; Miss Millington was sent home, the house was sold, and a survey of her wardrobe revealed that nine tenths of it disagreed with her taste and complexion – Miss Millington's sober influence? – and must be discarded. In a wild spirit of adventure, never before known in sensible Miss Mathick, she had forced everything she wanted into a leather portmanteau and a soft canvas bag, had bought a ticket on the London mail, and had travelled there, alone.

Savill had greeted her stiffly, taken aback. He found her reassuringly grave, however, where legal matters were concerned, disconcertingly attentive even. She seemed to have a head for figures, a grasp of the potential, the possibilities involved. She knew a little about farming – mainly sheep – a great deal about running large houses, recalcitrant servants, anything you like in that department, and had been on intimate terms for years with every conceivable sort of household account. She vexed and surprised Savill – travelling by herself, such odd baggage, no definite plans – and he found her physically unattractive. She was not his idea of a parson's daughter and privately he thought her a fitting successor to the unacceptable Francis.

It was early December, the weather atrocious: rain, sleet and high winds. Ann stayed for two weeks with Lady Copeland, a very old friend of her father's. London was dirty, disagreeable, busy, and indisputably smart. On the sixteenth she set out for Norfolk, travelling by the mail to Norwich and arriving in a downpour, the sky like lead. A letter from Savill, delivered to Lady Copeland's, had told her what little she had not known about the Forsie family, mentioned some obscure business about overdue rent on some land leased to the neighbouring Blackow estate: a recommendation to consult the 'Doctor' in High Common on this and sundry other odd matters. Why the Doctor? Why not? The Forsies had been eccentric, eclectic to a man, agricultural reformers at one time in the vanguard of the experimenters, the drillers and dibblers, the growers of lucerne; Francis himself had been one, before drink and women put an end to ambition in any direction but two. First and foremost the Forsies had been farmers: farmers before gentlemen Savill might have said, looking down his long, warty nose. They had husbanded the land about Thorn for generations and the graveyard at High Common was crammed with their dead. They had been reckless too, usually fair-headed and often fine-looking, more than likely drunk. The passing years had seen their acres squandered and their silver auctioned to raise cash for wild schemes, wild wagers, wilder women. Thorn was all that was left out of a sizable patch of Norfolk county that had once looked prosperous in their ownership and now, December 1799, had passed out of their hands for ever.

The mail was late into Norwich driver and guard mud to the eyebrows – and it was unheard of, shameful, to be a minute over the time. The post-chaise Ann had ordered set out for High Common boldly enough but after a while the lanes deteriorated to little more than tracks, the going was foul, rain in great swathes, persistent, penetrating. A swamp and a hidden stone did their worst and a wheel came off; there was a gentle and ignominious collapse into the mud rather like a ship heeling over on an outgoing tide, and the postboy predicted no help of any kind to be had for twenty miles, an amazing exaggeration. Five minutes later he departed for Norwich on the shivering horse, and God knew when he might return, if ever. Ann had refused to seek shelter – why, she would be soaked the moment she stepped out – suspecting he would think his duty done if he left her snug at some accommodating farmhouse. A two-hour wait in the tip-tilted chaise chilled her principles, however, along with everything else; she got down and began to walk, dragging the bags.

Pashman the carrier, fifty and sour and disobliging, but always on the lookout for a slender pair of ankles, offered her the tailboard and a piece of dry sacking when he passed her twenty minutes later. It was already dusk. He took her, in the dim light and with his failing sight, simply and incuriously as a servant girl, meek, well-mannered, probably grossly underpaid; certainly nothing in her clothes or her insignificant baggage suggested otherwise. Her face was a pale oval, dominated by candid, intelligent brown eyes, but there was nothing remarkable in it that he could tell, and nothing to raise suspicions that she was in any way related to the Torsies, swaggering like nabobs even when hand over fist in debt.

It was as well perhaps that Ann spoke little and Pashman, putting on airs, scarcely at all. He was mildly interested when she asked to be set down at Thorn, but not more than mildly, for maids were two a penny and that had long been a disorderly house; as for the expected heiress, whoever heard of heiresses walking to take up their inheritance? He left her at the yard gate, unwilling to bog himself down trying to turn his heavy cart inside, and he watched her squelch, skirts kilted up, towards the back door. Then he pulled his underfed horse in a tight circle and went back up the melancholy lane to the Gorse and his road to High Common.

Thorn, Ann found, looked what it was: a rambling neglected house set amid two hundred acres of weeds, boasting, for what they were worth, unstable Tudor chimneys, six indifferent cows, a flock of aged geese, and a barn of mouldy corn; she had read the inventory, absorbed every sorry detail, Mr Savill breathily apologetic over her left shoulder. And she was enough of a country girl to judge the extent of the neglect. The parsonage had brought with it forty acres and her father had turned them over to cultivation, to carrots, to clover and vetches, experimenting with the tough little hill sheep, crossing them with Leicesters, fattening them assiduously. Ann had taken an interest, bored with the duties of house and parish, tired of the social round her mother so adored, pursued by insipid young men she did not care for. She took great notice of the sheep – her mother declared it was unhealthy, unnecessary to be embroiled in such earthy matters – and, if the truth be known, found a strange solace in them.

And so to Thorn. What chances would be here? What might she make of it, and of herself? Or would she again find hers smiling at those she disliked, dispensing charity to many who no need of it, struggling impotently to bring it to those who m assuredly had? Her father had been a good man, clever, kind; wished she had his courage and his energy. She eased herself onto the doorstep and sighed, looking down at the vast tract of sucking mud. Her enthusiasm dipped and faltered. But nothing, she thought, could be worse than that damp mausoleum and Miss

Millington's vapid company, the perpetual domestic crises over trifles, the unconquerable smell, repulsive and all-pervading, of bacon and boiled cabbage. She felt a surge of resolution, of renewed strength. She took another step and then banged on the door with a little clenched fist and waited for results.

Results were Miss Pennyquick and Hollin, in that order, the one from the dairy and the other from the cowhouse and both swearing. In the near-darkness it was difficult to see what Fate had brought to the doorstep but some judicious swinging of a smeary-glassed lantern revealed a young girl in drab brown with two undistinguished pieces of luggage at her feet and her hand raised to knock again and even more imperiously.

Of course they had been expecting her but not until the spring, and quite what they had been expecting was never mentioned but Ann knew, smiling into her supper dish, that she was not the mistress either Miss Pennyquick or Hollin had intended. These two, she found, though often in violent disagreement, had ruled Thorn together since long before Francis Forsie died. Miss Pennyquick had been housekeeper twenty years, Hollin had wrestled longer than that with the decaying farm. He ate in the house as had always been the custom, though he lived in his own cottage down near the river, and because everywhere but Miss Pennyquick's spartan bedroom was shut up he ate in the kitchen at the vast elm table, his temperamental back to the blast of heat from the great open fire.

After the insipid rabbit, the chewy currant pudding, Ann spent a chilly night under inadequate blankets in the room Miss Pennyquick moodily assigned her. The four-poster was ancient: searching, with a sort of stifled hilarity, for secret cupboards in immense panelled back Ann found a piece had come away in hand. She was used to such minor disasters however, her other having been, perhaps in true Forsie fashion, a vague and uninterested housewife, happier at someone else's fireside raising money for charitable projects, leaving Ann to assume command at an early age. Disintegrating four-posters were nothing to Miss Mathick.

She was up early too, and quietly, casting a steely eye over the domestic arrangements.

"Never had any money spent on it as long as I can remember," said Miss Pennyquick, startled to find this insubstantial brown girl already inspecting the meal bins in the larder at five thirty in the morning and trying to subdue her sense of outrage.

"What it needs," Ann informed her pleasantly with a blank glance at the floury bricks underfoot, "is a scrubbing brush, not a fortune."

For a moment they assessed each other, the one indisputably calm, the other uncharacteristically defiant. Indeed, Miss Pennyquick gave a good imitation for some minutes of one of Rob Pashman's fighting cocks. Ann was tempted to laugh, but injudicious hilarity, she had found, was as troublesome as too much self-restraint. She suppressed all unruly emotions with an effort and met the hot blue eyes of her housekeeper without further comment.

How old? The question sprang to mind, made her take more careful notice. Miss Pennyquick was thin, almost impudently angular, a kind of anatomical aberration; her face was all stark bone, her thinning hair drawn back severely in a tight grey twist under her cap, her eyes deep-set and an indeterminate blue. She was the far side of forty, Ann decided, and had lived all her life at the beck and call of others which accounted for two thirds of her sourness; Francis Forsie's unwillingness to marry where he bedded might account for the rest.

"I would like us to begin friends," she remarked gently, leading the way back to the draughty and smoke-darkened kitchen. Her father had taught her that the unexpected often achieved commendable results, that battles were won by attack.

There was, in fact, only silence behind, but she had the feel Miss Pennyquick was choking over a reply. She stopped by table and ran a slim finger experimentally along its old grain. Something suspiciously like soot inserted itself under her nail.

"Breakfast first," she announced briskly, "and then we had better make a start."

"A start?"

"On this house," Ann was staring up at the shadowy ceiling, at a decade of cobwebs in the angle of a beam. "About time it was put to rights. And we can hardly live entirely in the kitchen."

They had done so perfectly comfortably for at least the last five years and she knew it. She saw Miss Pennyquick's badly-disguised rage, her grim, compressed mouth.

"Breakfast," she repeated. "Coffee, toast, bacon; I suppose there are eggs?"

A further silence. A log in the huge hearth fell with a hiss from the andirons and the ash glowed as red as Miss Pennyquick's face.

There was no coffee, no bacon; it was inconceivable, a farmhouse with no bacon. The larder held nothing of consequence, produced eggs but no marmalade, ancient tea in a locked box – and locked for quite fifteen years, Ann thought – but no meat of any kind. It began to look as though Miss Pennyquick and Hollin lived entirely on beer or grog – a bottle of antique rum was discovered behind the dough chest – and the tooth-rocking stuff humorously passed off as bread in this eccentric household.

And it was some hours later that Hollin stood lumpishly in the drawing room and made his idiotic and exacerbating remark about spring cleaning, hence the curtains in the washtub and Miss Pennyquick's rising bad temper.

The day drew on. Ann proved indefatigable, unanswerable, stubborn as Hollin's own notorious pony, a local byword for all the worst in horseflesh. She passed through room after room, examining, discarding, peering into cupboards and under cushions and at the back of dim alcoves no-one had bothered with for generations. Behind her rose a cloud of fine dust and the shrillness of Miss Pennyquick's justifications and denials. In the yard Hollin stamped up and down venting his frustration on the twelve-year-old lad who herded the geese and helped with the cows and was all the hired labour. Now and again instructions, carrying and clear in Ann's pleasant young voice, would issue from a flung-open casement. These heralded the demolition of some bodged-together cupboard or the removal of an offending pieces of furniture; in either case Hollin, the only man about the place, had to lend his slackening muscles and inconsiderable brain power. Thus the morning passed and lunchtime found them eating silently at the newly-scoured table, Ann swallowing what Miss Pennyquick ladled gloomily out of the pot and rising almost at once to continue the assault on the upstairs rooms.

The day was grey and cold, flakes of snow on the wind. Miss Pennyquick had a notion that by the time Pashman passed by again on his weekly trip to Norwich, or anyone else knocked on the door, it would be too late to make herself out a martyr; the house would be so clean she would be pleased to take the credit for it. But why, she wondered, did the girl dust and scrub herself? Why not pay others to do so? Ladies, Miss Pennyquick reasoned, should not let themselves be discovered practically afloat on a sea of greasy water, hair tied up in a towel and a yard of damp petticoat on view. It was not proper, not suitable. Opinions varied as to its size but Miss Mathick's fortune certainly existed; why, Mr Savill had told her so himself. 'A young woman and handsomely provided for' – his very words – 'Unfortunate circumstances, parents dead, dreadful shock. She must undoubtedly be the object of our sympathy.' And so she had been perhaps until that moment she had knocked on the door. If only, Miss Pennyquick thought furiously, Savill had warned her of this … this competence, this hell-and-damnation determination. The very light of battle shone in the girl's eyes and sometimes – surely she was not mistaken? – sometimes a great flood of something remarkably like out-and-out amusement washed across the plain, pale features of Miss Ann Mathick's face. But what could she be amused about at Thorn?

"You will take on more servants, men for the farm," Miss Pennyquick remarked as they all sank wearily into their places at the supper table and contemplated the stringy hen, the very one which had been found stepping delicately over the lately-washed hall floor and had not only been evicted instantaneously but hanged for the crime.

"I have no idea. Something must be done," Ann replied,

thinking that for a start a good reliable cook might not come amiss.

"There won't be no harvest next year if I don't have help," Hollin said, crashing down his fist and making all the plates jump. But if he had thought to frighten Ann he failed, she was aggravatingly unmoved – or so it seemed. Only she herself knew the courage she had to draw on to answer him, never dropping her eyes, all her muscles consciously relaxed.

"Everything will be settled in good time, I promise."

A mild reply, infuriating, unexpected; but then everything about this odd girl was unexpected. Hollin looked as though he longed to shake her but after a moment he returned to his meal, abashed, and the tinkling of the crockery subsided.

The hen was tough; a Miss Pennyquick of the poultry yard, Ann thought. She felt dispirited, bowed by the enormity of her task, unutterably tired, and lonely, lonely.

But: "That chimney smokes abominably," she said, and met two pairs of eyes, not hostile but considering, across the table.

"It always has done," Hollin sucked a chicken bone reflectively and then grinned his humourless grin. But a little later he cast a surreptitious and wondering glance at the fireplace, at the huge fire that leaped and settled in the raging, contrary draught, at the wicked billows of smoke; she would not make any improvement there, not unless she rebuilt brick by brick.

But she would do it, he thought; by God, she would do it!

"The world is so very wicked," the Doctor said amiably, "I sometimes suspect we are due for another flood. But look what small good the last one did." He mused a moment, swallowing some port, spilling a little, "And what hopeless navigation. Perhaps owing to the superabundance of animals. I cannot say I would care to steer a ship so perilously encumbered."

Lord Barsham, who had thrown off wig, coat, neckcloth and shoes in an attempt to counteract the heating effect of a good dinner, a rank overdose of burgundy, and the incomparable port, and was now lounging in complete dishabille in a shabby armchair by the ashy fire, gave a grunt of bewilderment. "Are

11

you supposed to take old Noah so literally? I cannot see the practical possibility of such a voyage. As to navigation, why, what point? How could he come to land? There was none. And speaking of land and landfalls ..."

There was a pause. The Doctor scratched his head slowly, contemplating his port, his past, the vagaries of middle-aged gentlemen with gout, a recent difficult confinement which had kept him from the house a day and a night, and a brute of a chest wound, ribs in splinters, that he did not expect to live. A country practice did not suit him; he had always known it. He had escaped four times, three to the army as a field surgeon, once to Dublin to teach fledgeling physicians the pleasures of anatomy. He had returned to High Common each time by choice or circumstance and applied his considerable talent to the same vaporous ladies and cat-bitten babies and agricultural accidents. He fiddled with the stem of his wine glass and frowned, and wondered why it should be so.

"Landfalls?" The present recalled him at long last, "What landfalls? You are not a seagoing man."

"No, no. Strictly metaphor. I heard Forsie's niece has ... ha, how shall we say? Beached on the shore of her grim inheritance?"

So that was it. The news had come and gone through High Common like a spring flood, and now lapped, it seemed, at the noble steps of Upgate Place.

"Very pretty," said the Doctor. "You are becoming charmingly poetic. And yes, it had been brought to my notice the young person — dare I say the most eagerly-awaited arrival for twenty years? — has come to pick up the Forsie remnants. It is certainly a sad piece of land, and a house like a mortuary, as cold, as grey, as ... bleak. Have you seen her?"

"No-one has. This infernal weather is part to blame. And rumour has it she is less than a lady, came from Norwich with the carrier, dressed like a kitchen girl, bare legs and clogs. I can hardly believe it. Understood there was money in her family."

The Doctor cast a baleful look at the slumbering fire. He got up and tried to revive its enthusiasm with great heaves of the poker, but it was mutinous and smouldered on regardless.

"Rumour grows, like phantoms, out of shadows and an idle mind. I had certainly supposed the girl to be an heiress. I met old Forsie's lawyer while he was here and he indicated as much. She has respectable connections, a great many influential friends. I should not put your faith in the carrier and the clogs, my friend, I should not indeed."

"She will need every penny she has to keep up Thorn. Disgracefully let go, by God. And Blackow no better. A foul stretch of country, gorse and bramble and bare sheepwalk; no proper husbandry for twenty years. And when I was a boy why, I remember the barley …"

"I daresay. It would be civil to call, yes? I must do so. Who knows what ills might not have accrued from Pashman's malodorous cart and the bare legs? More port? The last of the bottle. Come, a mere trifle. You will not sleep the worse for it."

"I thought," Barsham said heavily, with his slow, rare grin, "you disputed the bare legs?"

They were very old friends; everyone in the county knew it and yet it was still scarcely credible: they were too dissimilar, in shape, tastes, backgrounds. The Doctor had no place on the social scale, roved free and eccentrically wherever he wished, welcomed in the grandest drawing rooms, the meanest kitchens, carried a flavour of the one into the other, sometimes to the consternation of proud hostesses and sometimes to the confusion of the labourers' wives. Barsham was fixed of course, and at the top. He was a florid, jovial man, upright, sound, the largest local landowner and from a family rooted in the district fifteen generations, a man who cared for duty and knew what his was. He was a rich man but a frugal spender, a man who preferred to see his fields well marled rather than his wife fashionably dressed. He had had cause to consult the Doctor long ago, an old leg wound opening up, a distressing business and all the most expensive, educated men running in circles contradicting each other. In despair, in agony, he had sent for the new man in the village who performed miracles, they said, and charged nothing. How could any man live on nothing, Barsham had wondered, except perhaps in Paradise? And the Doctor turned out to be short, badly-dressed, astringent in manner, and under no illusion High Common was anywhere near Paradise. He probed, glowered, snarled; the nurse fled, terrified. A trifling amendment to diet, some blue stuff in a bottle – a placebo? – clean dressings, a half dozen applications of something vile smelling, and the thing was mended, the bill – certainly absurdly small – sent in.

After that Barsham called the Doctor to attend to his wife, to deliver a daughter, a son, two more daughters. A succession of minor ailments followed: measles, sore throats, broken bones, a severed finger. The Doctor became a familiar figure at Upgate Place, dining there frequently in his working clothes – bottle green frock coat and yellow breeches, a peculiar, reptilian combination – playing shuttlecock on the lawns with the children, stamping through the attics throwing open windows to blasts of invigorating winter air when called out to a feverish maid, picking oranges in the conservatories and leaving them absentmindedly all over the immaculate sofa in Lady Barsham's own drawing room. He was temperamental, difficult, cantankerous even, but he was revered. The family, the cohort of servants, the Upgate tenants took him to their hearts. Excuses were made for his odd behaviour: he had been an army surgeon, had dealt with rough soldiers, terrible wounds, unremittant savagery – he had been in the West Indies in ninety-three, had seen thousands die of tropical diseases. What was the measles to a man of such experience? Surely a trifle, almost beyond consideration.

Then, just as he seemed almost unbearable, ignoble, simply an irritant, he would startle them all by being on his best behaviour, urbane, unquestionably witty, a lover of music and intelligent debate. The children adored him, of course, saw nothing strange in him at all. And Lady Barsham had been heard to point out that she had never known children be deceived.

"This girl, this girl at Thorn," Barsham said suddenly, "I suppose I should get Louise to call."

"And have your carriage stuck in a bog? Have you been near the house since Forsie died? No, I thought not. It is a wilderness, a rank wilderness. Hollin has let it go to ruin, not that it is his fault entirely but with care they might have managed; and I would wager most of the men left because of Hollin's sour tongue and not because they had had no wages. There is hardly a sound roof on the buildings now. I would not dare compute the cost of setting it all to rights."

"She will not do it then," Barsham said gloomily, for he hated waste and wanton neglect. "No girl will care for tares and turnips over a yard of muslin and a handsome husband."

The Doctor eased off his shoes. His house was very peaceful; his cook had long ago gone to bed, his Lascar cook, acquired years since on some tedious, wallowing sea voyage cooped up with some hundreds of disgruntled foot soldiers. Yes, the house was quiet, not the slightest reverberation of domestic strife. This was why Barsham chose to dine with him so often, as he well knew. Upgate Place was charming, luxurious, but there was always some squabble, some echo of raised voices: servants, children, mother, daughters, visiting aunts.

"Miss Mathick may be a Venus, a Ceres, perhaps the two combined. You are such a pessimist and unfailingly unjust to women."

"I have a household full of 'em," Barsham said morosely. "That's why. And I cannot see what Venus has to do with anything."

The Doctor stretched and grinned. "Not much more than Noah had to do with convict transports, I daresay. It was transports we were talking about, was it not?"

The night of the twentieth brought a bitter cold, more flurries of snow. Barbara Pennyquick, thoughts turning to her narrow box bed and sweet sleep, crept through the drawing room only to find Ann curled in the tapestry wing chair by the dying fire, six old ledgers of accounts sliding off her knees.

"Why did he let the farm go so wild?" she asked, bending to retrieve them.

"Drink. Debts. How should I know?"

"But you must have known him better than anyone." It was a statement not a question, and oddly inoffensive in spite of what it might imply.

15

"It was not what you think," Miss Pennyquick's hands plucked at her old-fashioned bodice. "I was only his housekeeper."

It was not what you would hear in High Common or Upgate or Hackthorpe or anywhere along the Gorse; on the other hand it might quite possibly be the truth. For a moment defiant blue eyes met Ann's cool brown ones.

"You did not care for him much," Ann said; this was not a question either. "But you were loyal."

"He was not a bad man. He was a Forsie," as if that explained all.

The shadowed room was cooling, the logs subsiding to white ash. Miss Pennyquick stood stock still, remembering. She had been sent to Francis Forsie's service by a mother with too many children and no means of feeding them all, and she was perhaps the only female to come within range of his speculative eye whom he had not touched, not teased, not propositioned. They had even come, slowly and with setbacks, to a tolerable understanding.

"I am half a Forsie. Will you be loyal to me?"

Heaven help them, this child was always taking them by surprise! Miss Pennyquick swallowed, stuttered, took a few steps forward and then back. What was she to say? She had grown acid and old in Forsie service, fetching, carrying, turning a blind eye. If that bequest had been anything but a mockery she would have been away from here by now, snug with her unmarried sister at Lynn.

"You want me to stay on then?"

"That is up to you."

Silence. Then: "I'm fond of the old place."

"It is your decision, not mine. I would not beg you to stay in the circumstances. For myself I think it will be a long and bloody business rescuing the farm. You may be better off elsewhere."

Miss Pennyquick was no mistress of the delicate phrase but she felt this was too blunt, too masculine an approach. She frowned, blushing a little. She saw an impassive face, rather grey with fatigue and dust; she saw huge, impenetrable dark eyes looking back at her, through her, beyond; she also recognised that dashing resolution, that unquenchable resilience – it was in the tilt of the girl's chin, the set of her mouth.

Ann bore the scrutiny well – but she prayed. She felt she had exhausted half the prayer book before Miss Pennyquick spoke again.

"I would like to stay."

So it was settled.

2

CHRISTMAS PASSED almost unnoticed at Thorn, temporarily isolated at the foot of its hollow lane while the sleet blew over Blackow Gorse above, obliterating the roads, the scrub, the choked ponds, the dead leaves. Christmas dinner was salt bacon, a muscular goose of undoubted antiquity, sundry root vegetables diverted, Ann suspected, en route to the cowhouse, and an apple dumpling horribly redolent of rum. Hollin was moody, an inconsiderate shift in the wind had every chimney in the place belching smoke, and Miss Pennyquick, having drunk off two glasses of the late Francis Forsie's claret like water, proved incapable of the simplest tasks. Ann put on her best dress – high-necked, sober grey, unexpectedly loose on her diminishing figure – and celebrated by herself in the drawing room. In the end, obliged to throw open both windows to get rid of the smoke, she went for a cold and blowy walk around the stockyard, the rickyard, and the Home Field, passing Hollin's decrepit cottage and ending up by the turgid brown river, chilled to the bone.

In the new year she put on the grey once again, augmented by a puritanical sort of bonnet with a shy feather, this time for her first foray into High Common. She was gratified to find Miss Pennyquick had risen to the occasion with her best coat, a severe and unrelieved nautical blue, eminently respectable. A country trap was run out of the barn – where it had apparently lain undisturbed these many years – was dusted down perfunctorily and given over to the abuses of Hollin's pony, a squat, sour, grey creature which took its moods from its master and had a tendency to go every way but forwards. The yard gate was hardly reached before it stood like a stone, ears laid, head in the air, a graphic illustration of Disobedience. A peculiar gurgle somewhere behind suggested Hollin was still at hand, and laughing. Ann took the whip from its socket and applied it selectively, meaningfully; the pony bounded like a rabbit, shocked, and scuttled up the lane at a trot. At the top, buffeted by the full force of the wind, she turned him right on Miss Pennyquick's instruction and touched him up even more sharply. He fled, his ill-shod hooves scattering the powdery snow and the half-frozen mud beneath, the trap crashing and bouncing along behind. The road, even under as little as an inch of snow, was lost to view; on every side bleak waste, sheep-scoured, and the gorse bushes that gave the place its name. Here and there decaying, neglected woodland came into view, clumps of old, unsteady trees, and tangled copses. When the track eventually ran down off the heights and took a dive across some rich, well-tended land – part of Lord Barsham's Upgate acres – it was like entering a different world, orderly and civilised. Then they climbed again, reached a plateau, a vast stretch of unenclosed grazing surrounded by fields, and came all at once to the first cottages of High Common.

It was a large, elongated village, three or four substantial and distinguished farmhouses breaking up a general hotch-potch of lesser dwellings, most of them leaning on each other for support. Near the central church was a cluster of tradesmen's windows, and the road widened here to form a sloppy little square, churned by traffic. Hollin's pony swerved automatically towards an ale-house but was straightened with a ringing command to trot on and behave himself. He did so, much to the surprise of two old ladies, a farmer in immaculate gaiters, and a very small boy with a hoop, who were all standing near enough to hear. There was instant and considerable interest in what was obviously the Thorn heiress, a lady who had undoubtedly – if only temporarily – got the better of Hollin's dreadful pony.

"Lord, I shall be glad to pull up!" was Miss Pennyquick's cry as they rattled past the saddler's, the butcher's, and the grocer-apothecary, and veered abruptly towards another pot-house. "There, there it is, the last house beyond the pump, white, two steps, a holly bush."

Ann hauled on the stiff old reins and pulled up with a flourish. There was indeed a holly tree, a miserable specimen, planted in one of the two square patches of earth either side of the front door. On closer inspection the door was seen to bear a plate, quite undistinguished, to the effect that a Doctor Alexander French might be found somewhere on the other side of it. Ann secured the pony to a rail with a double knot – having taken his measure, or so she believed – and climbed the two unscrubbed steps to ring the bell. There was a long silence during which she could sense unseen faces staring from all sides, though not, she thought, from within the Doctor's house, which was tall, gaunt, and modern, and whose windows looked uncurtained. At last the door swung open and a tiny maid stood there who could hardly have been more than thirteen or fourteen. Miss Pennyquick, handy at Ann's elbow, murmured: "Susan Cowley's eldest. The Doctor took her in when Cowley was killed in the flood."

Susan Cowley's eldest gave them a frightened stare. After announcements and explanations she let them in reluctantly and left them in a dingy parlour saying she would "see if the Doctor was mixing his powders and say Miss Mathick from Thorn is come to pay respects".

"Heaven knows what garbled message he will get," Ann remarked, glancing round. The room was high-ceilinged, square, and bleak; there were no curtains, nor was there any carpet on the board floor, nor a cushion in sight, nor a live coal in the dirty grate. She sat down on a faded blue brocade chair and grinned.

"Do you think we have been shown into an unused part of the house? Have you ever seen such spartan furnishings?"

"It is all much the same. He lives very simply. He was an army surgeon, did you not know? There is only the maid Fanny, and Dolly Cushing to clean, and the cook – a brown man, an Indian, a strange quiet little thing – and only the cook lives in."

Ann considered. The room gave no sign it had ever been used for anything but to display the two brocade chairs and a hideous rush-seated sofa with a faintly eastern air. There was not even a side table, only one tarnished candlestick upon the mantelshelf, and no equipment for the fire except a poker thrust through the bars of the grate.

The door opened. A short man in some disarray entered. His brown coat was spotted and splashed with some white stuff, his wig was askew, and in his hands he carried, rather awkwardly, a brown animal with a pointed nose and bright, wicked black eyes.

"Miss Mathick, Miss Mathick, how pleasant to see you! But why are you here in such a chilly expanse, no comfort, no refreshment? Come! Ah, Miss Pennyquick, how handsome you look! No, don't mind the mongoose, he is only a little partial to petticoats. Fanny!"

His shout echoed down a dim passage. There was a distant scurrying of feet. A dark face bobbed out from a doorway on their right, a voice said: "The child has stepped out to the butcher," in tones of the greatest solemnity as if announcing the death of an eminent statesman at least.

"Then you must bring in tea ... Coffee? Biscuits. Some cake. Miss Mathick, do step in," flinging open another door, "do take the chair by the fire."

She did so, removed her bonnet. The Doctor gazed a moment with approval at her springing brown curls. Behind him the Indian cook carried in a huge tray on which steamed a silver jug of coffee and sat, smugly overloaded, three large plates of sweet, delicious pastries.

The mongoose besieged Ann for crumbs and had to be forcibly removed by the Doctor, who by this time had tossed off his wig completely and revealed a bristly, grizzled head of hair. He looked younger at once, though certainly more disreputable.

"I had a letter from Savill," he said when a decent interval had passed and they had demolished the greater part of the pastries. "He spoke of Blackow, the fifty acres leased to old Sir Harry etc., said I was to – how did he put it? – oh, I have it: 'furnish you with the facts'. Well, I shall do my best. But I am quite at a loss to know why he could not do so himself."

Ann gazed down at the carpet under her feet — another acquisition, like the mongoose, from distant shores — and then up at the lacquered cane furniture, the country-made table with its too-large legs, the litter of maps, bills, papers of all sorts, several dirty wine glasses and what looked like, though thankfully she could not be sure, a snake in a glass case.

"You have travelled a great deal," she remarked. There was a parrot cage in a corner, she noticed, but without an occupant.

"To very little purpose, I fear, except to learn what dread calamities man can bring down on fellow men. I spent a great waste of time on the lower decks of ships tossed up and down interminably or floating about waiting for a wind that never came; I spent even more time putting up tents and taking them down again, and packing and unpacking my instruments, and attending to an endless stream of young men with the pox."

Miss Pennyquick drew in her breath sharply; she could never quite forgive him his outspokenness. He should not make young women blush at the thought of unmentionable diseases over coffee and cakes.

Ann was not blushing. She was stepping across to investigate something jumbled in the corner with the parrot cage.

"The shell of a giant tortoise," said the Doctor, springing to lift it to the light. "We took him on board ship, fed him like a lord, but a wicked squall did for him — or so I have always believed, though it may have been a conspiracy, fresh meat being in such short supply at the time — everybody sick and not an inch of the ship dry or anywhere near it. I kept the shell, a memento of a real blow — we lost masts, spars, yards, oh, a great cat's cradle of rigging all over the deck."

They gazed in silence at the shell. Then Ann said: "Do you not find High Common a little dull? What can you do here to compare with eating tortoise in the middle of a gale?"

He caught her smile, the laughing brown eyes. She was plain — disappointing he had thought at first, certainly no Venus — but by God how her face lit up when she was amused ... And that way she had of turning her head, enquiring, defiant. He liked her, yes, he liked her, and anyone who showed no inclination to shrink from the mongoose and caressed the carapace shell so lovingly must be taken immediately to his heart.

"One day," he said, leading her back to her chair, "I may go once more to some intemperate climate to mop up and mend after the latest disaster perpetrated by ambition and politics; before I am too old, that is. I am very nearly too old, Miss Mathick, but I shall do it, I shall suffer the sea journey and the noisome orlop and the salt pork and peas and biscuit and then the tents or the native quarters and the sitting about and swatting flies, and maybe at the end of it half a day of action and some hundreds killed and hours of sewing up and sawing off. I assure you, I cannot think why I sometimes hunger to be away to such a living. I came to this village twenty — nineteen? — years ago certain it would suit me the rest of my days, but dubious prognostications are made at twenty-four, are they not? I find it fairly restful though, between sorties."

Ann was looking out at a garden through the window, a tangle of dull greenery overcome by neglect and frost. The white cotton wraith of the Lascar cook showed briefly in some far corner; what was he at? Picking herbs? Looking for something?

"This land leased to the Gerards at Blackow Hall," she said, as the cook spun round, exultant, a huge tabby cat in his arms. "My uncle drew up the lease fifteen years ago, is that so?"

The Doctor, who had advised Francis Forsie against it at the time, seized the poker and attacked the fire with violence, scattering ash. Once, he remembered, he would have enjoyed wrapping it round Forsie's ears.

"No rent has been paid for four years. Why? It is a twenty-one year lease, Dr French. Should I not expect rent for the next six then?"

Miss Pennyquick seemed to wake up suddenly, stirring in the corner where she had retired to be out of the way of the mongoose. "Miss Mathick knows that her uncle had a ..." She cast about desperately, a flush in her thin cheeks. "He was in love with Caroline Gerard." Her eye caught the Doctor's, found it sympathetic; perhaps they both wished Francis Forsie had been less excitable, less precipitate, less unlucky in love. After all, they had both seen him drink himself silly over that capricious woman.

"This Caroline Gerard was the present Sir Harry's mother, I understand." Ann had returned to her chair and under it, unexpectedly, she found the mongoose.

"His mother indeed, and I doubt his paternity is in much dispute though later events might shake one's faith in it. She married very young, was barely eighteen when your defaulting Harry was born, a child herself still. Her husband was a good deal older, sympathetic, honourable, but ... How to put it kindly? Scarcely a romantic figure perhaps. Caroline found Blackow did not suit her, strayed hither and thither in search of consolation, gained quite a reputation. Oh, yes, quite a reputation. But old Sir Harry was apparently unaware of any shortcomings in her behaviour, adored her wholeheartedly, and trusted her word. He was a generous man. He was generous enough to take all the Thorn land on the Blackow Hall side of the Gorse at a considerable rent – quite unjustified – simply to help Forsie out of a financial difficulty. They were not even friends. Forsie had no friends to speak of, though he was good company and had his own sense of honour, whimsical though that was. It was simply that Harry Gerard had money, his estate was in good heart, and he was the sort to reach out a hand to those in trouble. And his family and the Forsies had lived alongside each other for centuries. It grieved him to see Francis in debt, gambling heavily, half dead with drink, but it would have grieved him more to see strangers at Thorn; it was bound to happen sooner or later. So he made his offer: a twenty-one-year lease, an exorbitant rent – three guineas an acre, Miss Mathick, for what was then indifferent hilly land worth no more than a few shillings – and first refusal if the property should come up for sale."

There was a pause during which Miss Pennyquick examined the backs of her bony hands and the mongoose got up on the table and eyed the snake in the glass case with his bright little eyes.

"I told Francis not to go ahead with it," the Doctor continued, with a sudden lunge forwards as the mongoose put its inquisitive nose over the top of the glass. "The whole village knew by then he was meeting Caroline Gerard in secret. I felt it dishonourable of him to take money from the cuckolded husband and I told him so. No, sugar, no, not the grass snake, she does no harm to anyone. Go out to Lal and he will give you some milk," and the door shut on the mongoose. "Would he listen?" asked the Doctor, picking up the coffee pot and peering hopefully inside. "Not Francis Forsie. His debts were pressing and he was always half drunk in those days. That woman ... That woman befuddled him as much as the brandy."

There were only dregs, lukewarm and bitter. A shout brought the Lascar at a run, and a fresh brew was demanded. It duly appeared, together with another plate of pastries.

"The rent has not been paid since old Sir Harry died," said Ann quietly, as a surprising shaft of sunlight pierced the gloom and lit up the abandoned tortoise shell, the grass snake, and the crumbs all over the violently-coloured carpet.

"He never found out, you see." The Doctor was presenting her with another cup of coffee, pressing her to take a pastry. "Though how that was possible ... And he may have been over-generous to a fault but he was no fool. Who can say? But after Caroline tired of Francis and the other fawning rogues she ran off to London and that was the last we heard of her until she died – killed herself, laudanum or some such, and everything hushed away, every squalid detail suppressed. Old Harry Gerard died a year later; young Harry swore it was from a broken heart. Certainly the man had no more wish to live, which may amount to the same thing. Young Harry rode to Thorn, told Francis to his face he refused to pay the rent on the Thorn land and would not do so until the lease ran out. He said it had already been paid in full, in cash and in kind. Yes, I thought you would see his meaning. He is a sad rake and a proper fool at times, that boy, but he never lacked courage on the occasion."

"And Francis made no fuss?"

A look between the Doctor and Miss Pennyquick. The sun went in again and they were left in dusty silence and considerable depression.

"He was disintegrating, Miss Mathick, organs too abused to cope, brain failing too. He was not far from his own deathbed and knew it. What did a few hundred guineas mean to him by then? And however much he swore and raved he could still applaud the boy's gesture."

A clock ticked. The fire spat and settled. Far away there was a calamitous clatter of dropped pans and a female voice raised in shrieking denial.

"So I am to turn a blind eye, Dr French, and allow things to continue as they are? There are more than fifty acres there – improved now, well cultivated, high ground that drains well. My uncle's sins are nothing to me, Thorn is everything. I would like that land."

"Then you must consult a lawyer."

"I thought it might be more neighbourly to approach Sir Harry in person. Miss Pennyquick looks darkly when I suggest it but will not explain why. Why, Dr French? Is Sir Harry an ogre?"

"Far from it. The truth is he spends most of his time in London leading an expensive life; the estate suffers for it. Of course his father had a great deal of money and there must always be hope. If he could be persuaded to settle, to marry to advantage and take some interest in his farms … Who knows? But I fear you may whistle for your rent, and for your acres. At twenty-six he acted out of temper and grief; at thirty he might find it convenient to be awkward for other reasons. And you will find him a difficult man to move."

Ann's smile, he felt, did not indicate any softening of her resolve. She would drive Hollin's pony to the door of Blackow Hall at once if nothing was done to restrain her. "Sir Harry is not there," he said. "There is only the housekeeper, and she rarely knows when he will visit."

A whiff of spice came under the badly-fitting door. The snake began to slide out of the glass case, and the Doctor picked it up gently and put it back. Gravely Ann and Miss Pennyquick took their leave, and gravely the Doctor saw them to the street.

"I will drive by," he said, bowing sketchily, "I will call on you."

From within came fearful shrieks, the crash of breaking china, a yell to raise the dead. The mongoose dashed out, something between its jaws, and fled between the legs of Hollin's pony.

"He is eating something," said Ann, bending to see.

"Only an egg, I trust. My dear Miss Mathick, farewell. You and the mongoose are firm friends already, it seems. Is that pony really safe? The brute will upset the trap."

At the last minute Ann leaned from her seat, whip poised, the pony already in motion. "What is the name of the mongoose?"

The Doctor blinked, grinned.

"Why, Bombay Jack," he said.

Blackow Gorse was half a mile wide in places, barren and treeless; on one side of it Thorn at the foot of the lane that led to the river, the wide, high-running river with its mill and slippery ford; on the other a gentler slope, an expanse of ill-kept parkland, and a square mansion, scarcely a hundred years old and still looking bleak and unfinished.

"It looks shut up," Ann remarked, parting the brambles, "and there are weeds in the drive."

"It is nearly always shut up, gone to ruin since old Sir Harry died. Half the land was left fallow this year and all the cattle sold at Michaelmas."

"And what is young Sir Harry like?" Ann was picking thorns from her skirt.

"The last time I saw him, up here on the Gorse, he looked uncommon well. But then any man looks to advantage on a good horse. And he always had," and here she smiled tightly as if at some memory, "a sort of charm about him."

"Like his mother, I suppose," Ann remarked drily, jerking the pony from a gorse bush and climbing back into the trap.

"No, not like her at all, more like his father but with half the sense and scarcely any manners."

In a while they reached the disputed acres now farmed by Blackow. Ann stood up precariously.

"I can see it all." It was a brave sweep of land, as good in reality as on paper. It was hers and it was not hers, an irritating state of affairs.

"Is it worth arguing over?" Miss Pennyquick demanded. She was puce with cold, rigid in her seat.

"It is Thorn land."

Thorn had become her passion, she who had never been allowed passions, only duties. It had been her duty to marry, she remembered, Miss Millington had told her so.

A little later, turning in at the yard gate, she said thoughtfully: "We need seed corn, horses, better stock, tiles for the barn. And above all men, help for Hollin, and help in the house."

Miss Pennyquick's silence suggested pessimism, a score of understandable doubts; and the fact that she was as stiff and chill as an ice-pudding, quite unable to move.

Hollin had his own ideas about Harry Gerard. He made several incoherent remarks into his beer mug at supper the next evening.

"What did you say?" asked Ann sweetly, dispensing cold pie with a generosity that was making Miss Pennyquick's eyebrows dance.

"A giddy boy, up one minute, down the next; smiles and frowns, sweet or sulky as the mood takes him. Every girl in the district setting her cap and all for nothing, unless she was willing …"

"That is quite enough." Miss Pennyquick thrust his plate at him and heaved across the jug of cream. She had been surprised in the brewhouse once by a young Harry Gerard tipsy from some village celebration and had been kissed soundly and memorably. The sight of the cider press and the vinegar smell of it never failed to resurrect the moment. To him she had simply been an old woman, an eccentric old woman ripe for some teasing. But she had not been old and once, not so long ago, had been as eager, rounded, and shy as any girl. Harry Gerard had seen her through a mist of strong ale and claret injudiciously mixed, and afterwards had begged her to forgive him with a smile.

Successive rumblings from the chimney corner during the next few days gave Ann only a sketchy and contradictory impression of her neighbour at Blackow Hall; Hollin was seldom coherent with a jug of beer to hand. He had also taken to guarding his former privileges jealously: his chair, his drink, his extended mealtimes, his frequent, unexplained comings and goings. He seemed always underfoot, always complaining. Shaken so rudely from his routine of apathy and self-indulgence he was as petulant and annoying as a small child.

Ann, in the face of such truculence, had to hire four more men to work on the farm without advice, except the rather irrelevant details supplied by Miss Pennyquick about their family circumstances, their proclivity to debt, or their tendency to drink too much and in bad company. A dozen applicants — some merely curious about the Thorn heiress — were reduced to six and then, after much deep thought with no very clear results, to the four who eventually turned up, one cold and foggy morning, to start their first day in Miss Mathick's employment. A similar harrowing process yielded a plump, cheerful girl called Maggie West to help in the house, and a formidable cook of heroic proportions known only as Mrs McGinly. Mrs McGinly ruled the kitchen absolutely from the first, and Hollin was forced to abandon his seat in the hearth and take to the yard where his underlings congregated expectantly every morning. Miss Pennyquick, ousted just as thoroughly, assumed her proper place as housekeeper and grew wonderfully dignified and undeniably more efficient.

No news came, by Pashman or any other source, to indicate that Harry Gerard had returned to Blackow. Life at Thorn was thoroughly, unrelievedly domestic; the advisability of green for the new parlour curtains occupied Miss Pennyquick's energies for a whole week. Ann, bored with the house, inspected her barns, her few new cattle, her first dozen Leicesters, and her diffident and tongue-tied workforce. The vexed problem of horses and their equipment loomed at once; Hollin was no judge of horseflesh, that was clear, and there was an endless dispute about the efficacy of the latest machinery, how it was no good, too complicated, needlessly expensive.

Local farmers did not drill their seed, they broadcast it, and they were deeply in love with their turnips, a crop Ann did not think would prosper on Thorn clay. Dissension, discord — and

29

what about the water meadows, Hollin demanded, and the further side of Warren Hill with its steep slopes and miserable copses? What would she suggest growing there? And while they were about it, what was that about improving the Gorse? How could such pasture be improved? It was abominable, always had been, always would be. Norfolk sheep did well enough on it. What else did she want?

Late January was damp and mild, but by now only Pashman's cart reminded them that any world existed outside their own narrow and unharmonious one at the foot of the lane. There was no time for visiting, Ann found, and no carriages braved the narrow, boggy track to Thorn. And at last one miserable day, depressed and disillusioned, she flung on cloak and scarves and walked purposefully away towards the river, leaving a mutinous and argumentative household to its own devices. Hollin was most of the problem − but how to remove Hollin deftly and kindly and without bitterness? She walked quickly, flapping her arms to keep warm, and soon the slate-coloured water and the weatherboarded mill appeared. By the time she turned for home she had walked her temper out, walked out disappointment and despair and blinding frustration and every other emotion except this abiding, unbidden love for Thorn. She climbed the lane to its gate in a fury of decision: Hollin must leave, Jim Knight must take his place. And there she paused, gloved hand on the gate bars, seeing the Doctor's yellow-wheeled gig at her door, a smart brown cob tied on behind.

Miss Pennyquick had ushered the two men into the drawing room. As Ann threw off her cloak in the hall she declared in a hoarse whisper that the Doctor was "in a rare mood, like a boy" and that he had a new wig and was wearing it straight, a phenomenon indeed. And who was his companion? Miss Pennyquick did not know, but a young man, and prosperous, and no fool.

"I trust we find you well?" was the greeting as Ann opened the door. "Miss Mathick, may I present Mr William Claverden who is, or so I believe on good authority, one of the best legal minds in Norwich. I took the liberty of consulting him about your lease. I thought perhaps, were you to discuss the matter with Sir Harry, the presence of an attorney might help his concentration."

William Claverden appeared likeable, even distinguished, though not inclined to smile much, not easily impressed. He was some age between thirty and forty and his clothes, though well cut, were worn carelessly, coat and waistcoat unbuttoned.

"Your servant," he said briskly, with the merest nod. He had very dark eyes, narrow and gleaming, which gave an impression of subdued ferocity. He would make an enemy of distinction, was the thought that came to Ann as she returned his nod.

"I must say at the outset that to recover the unpaid rent might be a costly business, not worth pursuing," he said.

"I wish only to take the land in hand again. May I not do so? It is almost the best land on the farm for the purpose I have in mind."

"It would not do to fall out with near neighbours, Miss Mathick. It may be more sensible to leave things as they are."

"I have no intention of falling out with Sir Harry Gerard but why should I compromise? They are my acres. And Thorn is all I have; I must be allowed to fight for it as hard as I please."

The Doctor had warned William appearances might be deceptive, and so they were. At first sight he had thought Ann Mathick a thin, ill-dressed little thing, hair and breathing anyhow — had she been running to get such pink cheeks, such a windblown look? Now, her head up and her great eyes burning, she looked as if she could fell half a dozen Harry Gerards at a blow. And yet for what? A wasteland of thistle and dead grass, a sprawl of dilapidated buildings, a few sheep and lean, unproductive cattle. What could she hope to achieve, a parson's daughter in a farmyard? Very likely she had no idea, had never heard of rotation, could not tell one end of a tup from the other.

"Dr French has suggested I accompany you to Blackow Hall this afternoon," William said deferentially, though he was not a shy man nor one who took much notice of other people's feelings. "It seems Sir Harry has returned for a breath of country air."

31

"By the look of his house he will get more of that than he intended." Ann's face was transformed by laughter.

The Doctor poked at his wig, indubitably new, meticulously curled, as full-bottomed as befitted his profession; he poked it assiduously until it slipped a little, and then he tugged at it experimentally until it made him look tipsy.

"He has been back two days. He may well have taken a chill by now. And his visits are always brief. He is likely to be on the point of fleeing to Bath or Brighton to take a cure. And I did not think you ought ..."

"To visit him by myself since ladies do not call on bachelors? You do have a low opinion of me, and after I admired your tortoise shell!"

The yellow winter sunlight broke in and showed up all the imperfections Ann's belligerent housekeeping had failed to correct: the worn and stained Turkey rug, the scratched and ill-used furniture, the frayed upholstery. William cleared his throat. He had come reluctantly in the wake of the Doctor, intrigued but only faintly so. On any other day Thorn itself, the venerable, decaying house with its rolling acres of neglected scrub, might have caught his interest; any other day Ann Mathick herself might have done so. But today he was suffering the effects of a late night in the company of a deranged old man intent on bequeathing property he did not own to half a dozen imaginary relations; no supper, one small glass of inferior port, a shortage of candles, and a cataleptic fit compounded William's memories of the evening. He had gone to bed at three, been up at six, had eaten an indifferent breakfast, had found four or five pressing matters in his post and on his doorstep. By ten o'clock he had been glowering, monosyllabic, thoughts turning longingly and hopelessly to beefsteak and veal pie. And then the Doctor had blown in on an icy draught and without any proper introductions, and had made himself free with William's books and tobacco, and had produced this tale of unpaid rent and passion and revenge. William had listened with an entirely involuntary fascination, rescuing his books as they were discarded, alarmed to find the Doctor shedding his wig on to a

32

clutch of sealed documents and his coat on to the floor as if that was where he generally left it. The upshot of it all was the Doctor sublimely at ease in the best chair in a positive fug of pipe smoke and William with indigestion.

"You are in a hurry, Mr Claverden," said Ann, making for the door; could she endure that fierce stare a moment longer? "Of course you are. Forgive me. I will only keep you a moment."

A soft cry of "Barbara!" brought Miss Pennyquick at the gallop. In a moment, it seemed, the gentlemen were being entertained to a prodigious quantity of Francis Forsie's smuggled brandy and a mountain of succulent little fruit pies, a McGinly speciality. Ann had vanished up the wide front stairs to change her dress. Miss Pennyquick, relishing her position, made no attempt to leave the room.

"How do you like your new mistress?" the Doctor asked cheerfully, discarding the new wig altogether and with it a good measure of his seriousness, reverting at once to his more characteristic self, half pirate perhaps, half satyr.

"I think she will do very well, sir," Miss Pennyquick said staunchly, her look daring him to press her further.

The young lawyer, examining the brandy bottle, raised his eyebrows. "No wonder the farm is a ruin. He must have paid a fortune for wine of this quality. There are barrels of it in the cellar, I suppose?" A wry look, a half smile. The Doctor grinned, lodging his wig carefully on the brass finial of the sonorous longcase clock.

"In some things his taste was faultless. In some very few things. Hmm. Come, Miss Pennyquick, you have eaten nothing ..."

But Ann was at the door, dressed impeccably in soft blue, her wayward hair pinned into a discreet mass of curl under a grey bonnet with a curving white feather. She was so much shorter than William, the top of her head scarcely on a level with the crisp folds of his neckcloth, and she was undeniably plain; yet there was a restrained grace about her, and an unusual quality of resolution.

"Miss Pennyquick," said the Doctor with a sidelong glance at William's surprise, "hide this brandy until I come again. If I may sometimes roast my knees at Miss Mathick's fireside, and smoke a pipe and drink a glass of this, then I shall indeed be blessed."

He spun round, gave Ann his arm, swept her to the door and away. William, glaring, retrieved the abandoned wig from its lordly peg and, more hesitantly, the Doctor's large cloth bag with the drawstring neck in which something unidentified squirmed silently.

"Let us hope it is not the snake," said Miss Pennyquick encouragingly as he passed.

Hollin stumped across the half-frozen mud, swearing under his breath.

"Where've they gone then?" he demanded, staring after the departing gig and its outrider.

"Blackow Hall."

Hollin gave Miss Pennyquick a long stare and then a humourless guffaw. "They'll come home tail atween their legs then."

Miss Pennyquick slid the brandy bottle behind her back before his dim eyes chanced to see it, and shook her grey head with its demure, snowy cap.

"You always were the most cheerful man I knew."

3

BLACKOW HALL, imposing from the park gates, gave the rather different impression of deserted decay from the foot of its stone steps. It stood uncompromisingly foursquare, doors and windows exactly aligned, nothing exaggerated, nothing alarming, and everything shabby. Below a stone-flagged terrace and another, gravelled one, rough lawns sloped down to an artificial lake old Sir Hrry's father had employed several hundred men to dig; the lake was choked with rushes and seemed, even from a distance, slimy and unpicturesque.

The Doctor and his companions were admitted by a spare, round-headed little man who might have been a jockey masquerading as a butler. He did not look pleased to see them, neither did he send them away. The air of dusty neglect was overpowering. Ann, peering up at an acre of dismal portraiture on the faded walls, caught the Doctor's despairing eye and gave a small smile. He had restored his wig and with it, she realised, the status quo; certainly without it they might have been refused entry. It was extraordinary and a little disturbing that a simple piece of headgear, admittedly voluptuous, could change a man's appearance so completely.

The butler-jockey showed them into a large room in which a tiny fire smouldered in a cavernous, over-ornate fireplace and any number of red velvet chairs stood about looking stiffly uninviting. The elegant shuttered windows gave a fine view of the stagnant lake and the bleak, ruined gardens.

The Doctor, an optimist, poked at the sulky flames. William joined Ann in her contemplation of the rampaging weeds.

"That is the Gorse, I suppose," he said, "beyond those trees. How high it rises. A wretched tract of land, thorn and bog, and yet they still graze sheep there in the summer, the Doctor tells me. What can they find to eat? Or do they relish brambles and green slime? I always understood they lived on grass."

Beside them was a large blue vase on a pedestal. Ann was staring at it in horror. 'Bonaparte and his generals could hold a council of war inside," she observed. "Did you say sheep? I do beg your pardon, I was not paying proper attention. Sheep, Mr Claverden, chiefly eat grass, just as you thought."

"But there is none on the Gorse."

"I have it on good authority there is a trifle, enough to support the local breed at any rate; but then, Norfolk sheep are wild, cunning creatures, irritatingly independent. I daresay they have learnt to scratch a living on the little available and that is why the farmers love them so."

The Doctor approached, carrying the poker. "You have some Leicesters, I hear. Are you going to give a ram to your Norfolk ewes?"

"No. I only have Leicesters because I was offered them at a reasonable price. What I want is a flock of South Downs, fat, profitable South Downs, and I want to run them over that land," and she swept a hand towards the leased acres, barely visible beyond the great beeches of the park.

"And the Gorse?" asked the Doctor, dropping the poker on a silk footstool.

"The Gorse should be drained and reseeded. It would be the work of a lifetime." An eloquent shrug of despair.

Behind them the door opened and a man stepped into the room. Ann turned, still sheltered beside William's substantial person, and saw Sir Harry Gerard for the first time.

"Miss Mathick from Thorn, I believe," was his cool greeting.

He was not tall but his slenderness and the way he held himself suggested that he was; he was not handsome but a straight nose and high cheekbones lent character to an undistinguished face; he was no longer a boy and yet a boy's reckless spirit and mocking humour shone in his eyes. No wonder, Ann thought, Miss Pennyquick blushed at the mention of him; he only had to move to charm.

He did indeed. He had a quick, unconscious grace, of all his attributes perhaps the only one not calculated, not overstated. The Doctor gave him a deep bow, too deferential to be true, more an expression of dislike. Introductions were brief: William's rude and intelligent stare was the kiss of death to amiable exchanges. Ann, who felt she had not made a favourable first impression – though to be sure she had done nothing more than stand and be scrutinised – tried to make up for it by speaking warmly and boldly of her enormous satisfaction at finding her nearest neighbour home at last. At this the Doctor made several disagreeable noises and retired to an armchair, taking an opportunity of assuring himself the inhabitant of his bag was still in good temper and disposed to sleep.

"Your rent, Miss Mathick? Has the Doctor not explained? I consider the rent on those acres paid off long ago."

"But they are still my acres." Ann had retreated to the window and, unexpectedly, removed her bonnet, dislodging several curls while doing so. In a disarray both physical and mental she turned hopefully to William, but he was retrieving the poker from its resting place on the pink silk and was innocently or deliberately taking no notice. He went to the fire, restored the poker to its proper home, and then sat down on a chair like an episcopal throne, crossed his long legs, and studied the toes of his muddy boots. "I cannot weep for the feelings of your dead father or the moral shortcomings of my dead uncle. It is my land and you pay me no rent. You do not even use it, it is abandoned, shut up." Ann swung round on Harry Gerard with a little spurt of impatience.

"No doubt the lawyer has the right and wrong of it as clear as day," he replied genially. "I have a lease, Miss Mathick, which is good until 1805. You may sue me for arrears but I assure you I have no intention of paying a shilling. What should we come to then? The tipstaffs?"

Ann put her head on one side. "Surely you and I have no

quarrel, Sir Harry? The injuries were in the past." But she saw at once he was completely unmoved, his face hardening if anything.

"How can a woman farm Thorn?" he demanded abruptly.

"With difficulty if all my neighbours are as hospitable, as candid, as eager to please as you are."

There was a silence fraught with emotion, most of it Harry's and subdued with difficulty. The Doctor smiled; William dug his hands into his coat pockets and allowed himself a wide, outrageous grin. My God, he thought, this child will get the better of him yet!

The child, standing straight and slender in the spot she had chosen for herself, was apparently unaware of causing a sensation. But her very stillness was a challenge.

"Tell me, Miss Mathick, is Miss Pennyquick still at the farm?" This was Harry in retreat, anxious to please, to appease, to melt hearts.

Ann nodded. How difficult it was to remain unaffected by that slow, charming smile.

"Poor Miss Pennyquick! I confess I kissed her once behind the pans in the dairy or somewhere. I was three parts drunk and she ... Can you imagine Miss Pennyquick in lace ruffles? Perhaps your uncle had bought a gown for her. I swear I kissed her thinking she was someone else."

Ann inadvertently crushed the brim of her bonnet, dislocating the feather. "You are cruel then as well as charming," she said.

"A harsh judgement! I kissed her without malice, I swear it. She forgave me, I assure you. Ask her whether she remembers."

"I was not referring to your actions, Sir Harry, but in your making them public in such a light-hearted manner."

A spasm of temper in Harry's face, gone in a moment. But William had seen it and saw fit to intervene, leaning forward with a brisk: "I do not see any point in continuing this conversation; if Sir Harry refuses to let you take the land in hand again and continues to withold rent then ..."

"Then you are set fair to earning yourself some fat fees, are you not? Miss Mathick will beg you to write letters to me and I will feel obliged to instruct my own man to write Miss Mathick suitable replies; this may continue until either Miss Mathick becomes bored with the business, or one of us is dead, or the lease runs out and the matter is solved instantly and finally without any legal interference whatsoever. You, Mr Claverden, and my own adviser Liveman, will be richer men because of us and we shall simply be poorer and no wiser."

William's narrow brown eyes studied a gloomy picture on a far wall. His anger was intense but his quiet voice gave no hint of it. "The land is neglected and unproductive, Sir Harry; you withhold it out of spite. Would it not be reasonable to let Miss Mathick put her sheep on it and have no more argument?"

"Sheep?"

"Sheep. Have you an objection?" Ann cried. "Would buffaloes be more acceptable?"

"You are laughing at me, Miss Mathick. And I see your opinion of me is very low, very low indeed."

There were no deer in the park, Ann was thinking, and the house smelled of damp, mice, and soot. She wondered what it had been like in the days when Caroline Gerard had run across the grass under the great trees on her way to Thorn – and had her young son watched her go? Yes, he withheld the land out of spite, he would never give an inch where Thorn was concerned.

It was nearly dark; it would be a devilish ride back across the Gorse even though it was no distance at all.

"You may keep your acres, Sir Harry. I wish you joy of them. You will be welcome in my house whenever you care to call. Mr Claverden, Dr French – it is very late. Good day to you." This last to Harry who was attempting to waylay her on her determined course for the door.

"You are right," he said, "we have no quarrel, you and I. But you must allow me the Thorn acres; I loved my father very much. Call it a whim, a flight of madness, but understand it and forgive me. If you are at Thorn I will come back more often. I may even entertain again here at Blackow. How would that be? In my father's day there would have been a ball in your honour. He was ... He was hospitable and candid and eager to please."

She blushed only slightly and retracted nothing. She appeared

39

unmoved by his low, urgent appeal, his contrite smile. She said quietly: "Your estate is in ruins and your house like a vault. You do not care for it in the least. And you will return to it just as infrequently as you ever did."

The Doctor stepped up to grasp Harry's limp hand. "She means to make a success of the venture; she means to save Thorn, to reap good barley, to grow fat sheep. And who knows she may do so, Sir Harry. She may do so indeed."

"Thorn is entirely hers?"

"Entirely."

"She is no Forsie, thank God," Harry said fervently, watching her step across his draughty hall. "She does not resemble them in the least particular, the very least. Why, she is almost dowdy."

The Doctor tucked his squirming bag under his arm. "I advise caution on that score. She does not wish to come to blows with you but she is tenacious, resilient; you must not discount her lightly. And whatever you think she still has Forsie blood in her; remember what devils they were at getting their own way."

Out in the drive he found William handing Ann into the high gig. There were snowflakes in the wind and the darkness was closing in.

"What *is* in the bag?" Ann demanded as they sprang wildly for the gates, the Doctor's horse eager for its supper and the Doctor an indifferent whip.

"The bag?" It was deposited in her lap, under the rug, and gave several convulsive heaves. "Only the mongoose, dear girl, only Bombay Jack. And he does so hate the cold. I promised Lady Barsham I would take him to Upgate for the amusement of her grandchildren."

"Tonight?" The wind was strengthening, the darkness likely to be absolute, such a mass of cloud was even now gathering over the straining oaks. Ann had no faith in the Doctor's powers as a horseman, rather dreaded to see him in charge of any beast, the beasts invariably knowing, the Doctor innocent and vague.

"Tonight. I am expected to dinner."

"But you have not changed."

"Do you think I should do so? It did not occur to me. but the delay ... I would have to cross half the district running back and forth between High Common and Upgate. No, no, surely I am acceptable. At least, I have never yet been turned from the table."

Ann laughed. The mongoose thrust this way and that. The restive horse made a series of bounds and the Doctor cried "Whoa! Behave!" ineffectually and pulled one rein and not the other.

"You will be in the ditch shortly," said a voice of doom behind, and William rode alongside, cloaked and concealed like a highwayman, snow in the brim of his hat.

The Doctor was heard to remark he did not give a damn for ditches, that he and his horse had long ago come to a working understanding, that the mongoose would catch its death, and that Sir Harry Gerard was a fop and worse, a foolish one.

"But I must try to live in amity with him," Ann remonstrated, clinging to her seat as they took the lane down to Thorn at a racking canter, the breech strap hard up against the horse's quarters. "His land lies next to mine."

William plunged forward to the horse's head and reached out blindly in the dark for its bridle. "You will live in sweetest concord for evermore, dear Miss Mathick — if you lend him a few hundred guineas and never ask him to honour his bill."

The cold eased in February and sunshine gilded the wet and sagging roofs of Thorn's dilapidated buildings. Hollin, up a ladder pegging tiles, refused to come in for meals but ate his portion perched on the ridge, swearing between mouthfuls.

"What have you said to him?" Ann asked Miss Pennyquick.

Miss Pennyquick hotly denied this latest bout of ill-humour could be ascribed to anything she had said and threw the blame entirely on Mrs McGinly, who had taken to ordering Hollin to leave his boots outside, her scrubbed floors more important than his sensibilities.

"But you and he were quarrelling yesterday," Ann persisted, "I heard you. The tinkers on the Gorse must have heard you."

"I called him a silly old fool, and so he is. Have you seen that

41

cottage of his? A hovel, not fit for a human. And his bedclothes like …"

Ann jumped up, scattering threads and thimble, tossing down the cushion cover she had been stitching so unenthusiastically. "But of course! I meant to see him about it. I walked that way the day before yesterday and was struck by the peculiar smell. I would have called on him but never had a chance, Mrs Palmer driving up as the Doctor drove away, and then the last geese to kill, and seeing Mrs Tofts up Wash Lane."

Mrs Palmer, who was sister to the gracious Lady Barsham at Upgate Place, but who had herself – she made embarrassingly plain – married beneath her, had called unexpectedly, having taken advantage of the improving roads to remember her social obligations. She had arrived fully prepared to meet a loud, buxom woman, depressingly unfeminine – gossip had reported Miss Mathick variously since the district had seen so little of her, but it was known for a fact Jim Knight had been in Norwich buying cattle and that the Reverend Goodber had struck a bargain with her over a score of his Leicesters. In the event poor Mrs Palmer was confounded, discovering Miss Mathick neither loud nor in any way buxom – rather the reverse – and carrying away an impression of good manners and strong opinions unfortunately mixed. There was also a dim suspicion that the girl had been poking fun, most unforgivably, at her visitor; at any rate her eyes had sparkled strangely once or twice.

Mrs Tofts, on the other hand, had found Ann brisk and cheerful, had been exceedingly grateful for the gift of two beef and kidney pies, some fruit, and a cloth full of sticky buns. Ann paid her the three months money owed to her son Jimmy, Hollin's unfortunate farm boy, and a little extra as she was dispensing with his services; in her estimation no decently run enterprise should need the inconsiderable and disgracefully cheap labour of a boy of twelve. She advised Mrs Tofts to put him to some trade and heard, not for the first time since coming to Thorn, a diatribe against local conditions, the contrariness of skilled men, difficulties of getting apprenticeships and no money to pay for them, and the superabundance of twelve-year-old boys in every cranny and corner of the county, all equally hard-working, intelligent and ambitious.

Certainly Mrs Palmer and Mrs Tofts combined to make Ann forget the whiff of corruption she had caught from Hollin's cottage. Now, much to Miss Pennyquick's consternation, she was remembering it with a vengeance, slopping through the mud to the long byre and around it and through the empty stackyard and into Home Field. She was half-way across before Miss Pennyquick caught her up, panting and with her puritan face on, her skirts held indecently high to show skinny legs in mud-splashed white stockings.

"If he knew ..." she began.

"It is my cottage," Ann replied without slackening pace, "and I won't have anyone at Thorn living in squalor."

They reached the wooden bridge over the beck, a minor though inconvenient tributary of the main river. Just beyond, crouched beside a hazel copse, was the cottage Hollin had inhabited since the first summer he had been at Thorn.

Ann pushed open the door. The smell was overpowering. Miss Pennyquick found flint and candle and revealed, with some reluctance, the single stinking room. The fire was out, the floor unswept, a cooking pot on the hob half full of something going bad. An underlying reek of stale alcohol – gin? – suggested that on Sundays when Hollin never put in an appearance he possibly drank himself silly and stayed in bed. Ann gazed in silence, trying not to breathe.

"How can he live like this?" and then, on a wave of fury, "Why, Babs, why?"

Miss Pennyquick, uncertain whether to resent the use of that long-forgotten diminutive, started but said nothing. The candle shook and then steadied, the flame tall and true.

"Your uncle never paid his wages half the time; either he had no money or was too drunk to remember what he had."

"So why did Hollin stay?"

The answer being complicated and not, in truth, fully understood by Miss Pennyquick – nor even perhaps by Hollin himself – there was another long pause. Then: "He cares for this place. After his wife and child died there was only Thorn."

Ann sank on to a stool and clasped her hands between her knees like a child. A scraping noise from a dark corner and yet another odour identifiable among the many suggested mice at least, possibly worse.

"How many times did he go without pay?"

"Who knows? How many trees in Greatwood?"

For a moment the two women stared at each other in the candlelight; it was a white wax candle, Ann saw, one of the best from the house. Miss Pennyquick's unthinking retort from her distant High Common childhood had, of course, said everything.

There was a commotion and Hollin stood in the doorway, eyes bright as a ferret's. "This is my cottage."

"I think not," Ann rose, noting as she did so the greasy plates on the table, the charred rushlight, the dark stains of damp on the walls; and what could anyone expect, for the place sat with its toes in the beck and all around the damnable holding clay.

"Tomorrow you and Maggie will clean this place until a decent man could step across the threshold without fear of being sick. You," and she ignored Hollin's choke of indignation, "will make it fit to live in. Is that understood? Water costs nothing, soap and scrubbing brushes we have in plenty up at the house."

"And who are you to poke your nose where it's not wanted, Miss precious Ann Mathick? You don't impress me! It will take money and a strong arm and an iron will to get this land back to what it was before your old fox of an uncle drank it to poverty."

She had been going to dismiss him, settle him in the village if he would go with a generous pension and whatever else he wanted within reason. She saw now it would be cruelty. She put up her chin and met his furious eyes.

"I have money and you still have a strong enough arm. Or do you? Are you going to fight every change, damn every improvement out of hand?"

His grudging respect, nurtured in secret many weeks, was still a frail plant, liable to be torn asunder by adverse winds. He stood mute, unable to defy her and wishing that he might.

"I want to see the whole farm tomorrow, every field, every

copse, every hedgerow." She was in a damn-you-all mood now. "We will start after breakfast. Whatever else you have to do, leave it."

What Hollin said to her departing back was mercifully blown away on the rising wind.

In the morning however he appeared in gloomy and inconspicuous brown, his Sunday clothes, and with his balding head covered by an old but decent hat. He had taken the trouble to brush a quantity of dust, mud and brambles from the pony, a remarkable improvement, although nothing in the world at this late date would help sweeten the pony's evil disposition.

"I suppose," said Ann as they set off towards the Gorse, "you are going to tell me yet again there are no fences whatsoever and nothing growing but weeds."

"Something of the sort."

But he did not need to tell her anything, she could see very plainly for herself, and after a while even *her* optimism sagged and she ordered him to pull up and spent some time in silent meditation, her eyes on the little hills rolling north to Norwich. The well-thumbed maps had tumbled disregarded at her feet, her bonnet too. The desire to achieve something, even the smallest something, with the resources at her command, had died away; the warm glow, the inner certainty of success – however distant – had diminished. She felt cold, miserable, unsure. She felt, for a brief and terrible moment, completely alone and completely overwhelmed.

"Drive on," she said to Hollin. "Go right here. Go down by those oaks."

But it was all the same, unfolding on either side, every view depressingly familiar. Warren Hill, Long Meadow, Carr Meadow and Pigg's Piece were ragged and rank, choked with the remains of nettles, couch, dock, ragwort, thistles; Ten Acre was scrubland. There were dying trees and decaying copses and blocked drains; there were stagnant ponds, rotted gates, a great noise of rooks, and everywhere disconsolate gulls ranged along the overgrown headlands. The watery sun was fitful, the wind still strong. Ann could hear the sigh of it in the elms and old oaks, in the brave beeches along the Blackow boundary. There was a smell of dead leaves and damp earth and winter.

She had looked at it before, many and many a time, but had never tramped yard by painful yard round every desolate enclosure.

"How long has it been like this?" she cried at last, struggling back from a close inspection of Hogs Bit.

Hollin still sat in the trap, as sober as his respectable gear. He did not look at Ann. When he had looked at her he had read in her expression exactly his own feelings the day Francis Forsie had told him there was no money for more seed, shut up the damn fields, what did they matter? He had seen anguish and anger inextricably mixed, and had seen despair too, that cursed emotion he knew only too well.

"How long? Ten years, give or take."

Ann stood rigid, her cloak blown about her, tendrils of wild brown hair escaped about her high forehead.

"How long will it take to clear it?"

Hollin shrugged; he had never believed in miracles.

"That depends how many men and beasts there are to do the job. With the five of us ..." Another shrug, as expressive as a Frenchman's, as mocking, as hopeless.

They drove down to the mill, nominally Thorn property but obviously functioning by some different laws from those understood by honest Mr Savill. It paid no rent, indeed it ground hardly any corn; Ann had been hard put to it to discover what it did do, other than shelter the miller, his voluble, blowsy wife and his various offspring. Passing Thorn the pony jibbed and Hollin swore, laid about it with his whip. Ann looked at the range of red roofs, the banner of smoke from the great kitchen chimney torn away by the wind. I love this place, she thought, and a fierce delight, sudden and breathtaking as a starburst, broke inside her. Hollin, setting the pony straight at last, saw her face light up, saw her chin lift again, her eyes burn.

"Terrible hard work," he said slyly. "Not for anyone without the right stomach for it."

"I was never afraid of hard work. I tell you, we will have the best crop of barley in the county on Warren Hill within three years and Sir Harry Gerard will grow pale with jealousy at sight of it."

Hollin shouted at the pony and got the flicker of an ear in response. "All you may get from Sir Harry Gerard," he said sourly, "are promises and a broken heart."

Afterwards he remembered this statement, somewhat dimly, and judged himself a prophet.

An unexpected visit from Dr French had enlivened Miss Pennyquick's dull morning restuffing pillows from an ancient feather mattress. The last of the smuggled brandy made an appearance together with Mrs McGinly in person bearing a tray of eggs and bacon 'for what she heard the Doctor say he had not had breakfast, being out to a fever'. This welcome and unexpected feast he ate seated by Ann's drawing-room fire, reprehensible conduct that made Miss Pennyquick grind her teeth, though she did not draw too near to remonstrate, possibly due to a strong respect for the fever he had lately been visiting. After a while, seeing he was engrossed with buttered toast and one of Ann's books, she returned to the dusty feathers and left him to it.

The Doctor devoured every morsel of food, brushed the crumbs from his lapels, and stuck his feet on the fender. A clock ticked. A little ginger cat looked in and went away again. Outside in an elderly apple tree a blackbird sang. The room was draughty and the fire smoked periodically. The Doctor stood up, browsed along a shelf, and sat down with a battered Congreve in which Francis Forsie had scribbled some accounts. He changed the Congreve for a *Pilgrim's Progress* and wished he had sound morals and inextinguishable hope. Then, lest he grow morbid, he opened the staircase door and shouted up to Miss Pennyquick, choking in one of the bedrooms, that she must tell Ann he wished to see her as soon as possible, do remember all speed and urgency, delay might cause untold difficulty. Miss Pennyquick, coughing her way to the drawing room, found him gone and Mrs McGinly looking in to gloat over the empty dishes; she had taken the Doctor to her heart entirely.

The afternoon brought a lessening of the wind at last, though ragged storm clouds still massed over the Gorse. Ann, having returned from her expedition with Hollin to a late meal of greasy duck, interrupted by Miss Pennyquick's sneezes and Mrs McGinly's colourful assertion that the Doctor had eaten quite half a pig and a dozen eggs, found she was obliged to pay a visit to High Common. Miss Pennyquick, loath to be left behind, remonstrated in vain, and was left a score of instructions ranging from cooking up the apple jelly to overseeing the pig slops. This, Ann reasoned, would keep her too busy to make mischief with Hollin or Mrs McGinly.

Maggie laid out her best blue dress, one of the few to survive the ruthless cull in the north, but time was pressing and allowed her to do little more than pile her hair up anyhow and hide it under a hat.

"You cannot be back before dark," said Miss Pennyquick, "you should not go alone. If the matter is urgent the Doctor will call again – though perhaps not, he is a little eccentric in his notions."

So he was, Ann conceded, if he could consume half a pig and a dozen eggs at a sitting. Miss Pennyquick glared, refused to smile, and fled away to rouse Hollin into harnessing the objectionable pony once again. Hollin, distracted from his tile-hanging, volunteered his services as guard and coachman; Ann simply laughed. But at the gate she turned back to thank him, raising the whip in salute, and he nodded and suddenly grinned, and went back to his ladder whistling.

The drive to High Common, Ann found, was not without hazards. The pony shied and sidled, and there were tinkers on the Gorse with sharp, skinny dogs and scrambling, yelling children. In the deep shadows under the trees he saw inexpressible horrors and not even the whip would move him until he chose to do so. Ann, growing hotter and losing patience, had just called him one of Hollin's choicest epithets when Harry Gerard appeared before her on a dashing grey.

"Miss Mathick! But are you in difficulties? That is not Hollin's pony, the notorious Abraham? Why, he must be thirty-five and toothless! I rode him when I was a child in the nursery."

Ann could not help but be reminded of Miss Pennyquick's

assertion that all men look well on a horse. Harry Gerard was in his one true element in the saddle of a high-spirited horse, one which slobbered its bit into quantities of foam and rolled its wicked eyes and edged sideways with its tail up.

"I cannot tie this brute to the trap or I would drive you myself," he said, "but something may be done. Pray, slack your reins and brace yourself."

He brought the grey up against Hollin's pony, catching the bridle just above the bit and forcing him forwards willy-nilly. The distant shrieks of the tinker children were borne to them on the wind. "Should you be alone?" asked Harry. "It will soon be dark."

"I am only going to High Common to see the Doctor."

"But what if it rains? And what if this disgrace to horseflesh puts you in a bog?"

"I am quite used to driving alone. And I do not find the pony impossible, only tiresome."

She saw his grin, saw too that he appreciated spirit and a direct answer. Perhaps he found both rare in a woman. She felt his eyes taking in every detail: serviceable cloak, drab dress, flat bodice, hair a mass of wild curl. Damn the pony! He was pulling sideways now and the grey was snorting and windmilling his elegantly pulled tail.

And: "For God's sake get out!" exclaimed Harry Gerard in a moment. "We can do nothing with him like this. He is only fit to be fed to the hounds. Here," a crushing grip to haul her down, and a bright, amused stare of those very blue eyes. "Can you ride? Could you sit this brute as far as the village? If not there is nothing for it but to walk."

Ann had no wish to impress him; she knew if she sat on the grey she would do so. He would be astounded, and he would admire her profoundly. She tried to look politely shocked while the devil within her clamoured for the chance to take up the lathered reins. Harry's eye was speculative; he was waiting for an answer. And it was almost as if he guessed her indecision.

"I cannot ride astride in this skirt, Sir Harry," she said the next moment with the flicker of a rueful smile.

"Do you think you could hold him then, while I teach this monster his manners?"

The grey was hers, clashing his bit in her ear; Harry was in the trap and picking up the whip. Ann saw the pony's ears lie flat instantly as if he was well aware what was coming.

"I will be a moment," cried Harry, "only a moment."

But left alone in the gathering dark Ann wondered if she would ever see him again. Stifled shouts floated back to her from among the trees, the drum of hooves, a distant crash; and then silence. The grey, restless and nervous, pawed at the ground and trampled in circles, treading on her feet. Five minutes was an eternity. The gloom was deepening, a pheasant called warningly, a cold wind made her shiver. Then all at once there was the sound of wheels and hooves again and the trap burst towards her, going full tilt.

"I think we have come to an agreement," Harry said, pulling up. Certainly he had got the better of it. He had lost his hat and had a bramble scratch on his face but his eyes were laughing, and yes, the pony was subdued, sweating but steady, a pained brown eye turned to Ann where she stood playing the grey like a salmon.

"You should buy yourself something more suitable. Surely you cannot mean to go visiting in this?" A disparaging glance at the whole equipage: pony, harness, trap.

"I can and do. But you are right, of course."

"I cannot recommend anything," Harry told her, taking charge of the grey while she climbed to the driver's seat. "None of my horses is suitable for a lady's hack. But no doubt such a paragon is to be found in the district. Ask the parson. Ask Barsham, all his are quiet as cows."

She laughed then. And he laughed too, one foot already in the stirrup, the grey revolving maddeningly, ears back.

"That devil has no manners at all," Ann said, asking the pony to walk on and finding him instantly obedient.

"Very few. But do you ride, Miss Mathick? I have one a little more sober than this if you would dare."

She felt it was a challenge, a deliberate challenge. A sudden inexplicable elation made her want to take it up. "It would not be lack of courage, Sir Harry, but lack of time that forced me to decline."

"An excuse! A nonsensical excuse!"

A jay flew out of the shadowy woods. The grey horse gave a tremendous leap sideways. Harry got him straight again, sent him on without the least exertion, a grin from ear to ear. "Would it be considered improper if you and I were to ride our boundaries, to discuss legal matters, to settle ... to settle our dispute?"

She told the pony to trot, her eyes resolutely to the front.

"There is no dispute," and then: "What do you do in London, Sir Harry?"

He plunged alongside. "I enjoy myself."

"Your land is in worse heart than mine."

"I do not care for land."

"But it will hardly pay you to let it go to ruin. What becomes of your income then?"

"Farming is a chancy business; there are investments with quicker, more reliable returns."

"Such as?"

They were approaching High Common, a light or two winking distantly through the darkness. Harry Gerard was silent. Then: "Perhaps not more reliable," he conceded after a moment, "but certainly quicker to return substantial interest."

"But in what do you recommend me to invest in order to share in this substantial interest? After all, the price of corn has never ..."

"Do not tell me it has never been so high. No doubt. But it is the labour of getting it to the barn and converting it to cash that I do not care for, the constant watching of the weather and bickering over the thatching of the ricks, who is to do this and who that, and how many feet to leave between ... My God, a wearisome process! I have a manager, Sendall, who could not manage a herd of swine; I sometimes think he knows as much about good corn as I do, or should I say as little? But how to find an honest man who will not take advantage of my long absences?"

The grey was half frantic to be away. He pulled and plunged.

Harry sat still and quiet and unperturbed. Ann gave a sideways glance, brief and horrified. "Too much corn," she said drily, then: "Perhaps you should not be away so much. Alternatively you might sell your estate since its wellbeing bores you so sadly and make the most of these mysterious investments, live like an emperor on your substantial interest."

His smile – what she could see of it – was genuine, unaffected, delighted. "But then I should only feel compelled to buy another estate. What is an emperor without land? There must be a park for the deer and the peacocks, if nothing else."

"Then maybe you should go to India and live entirely surrounded by gardens. You could have tigers instead of a mastiff for your guard and as many peacocks as you wished."

"You are mocking me, Miss Mathick."

She smiled. She put up a hand to push her hat on more securely; the wind howled energetically across this high plateau, this vast expanse of open land.

"There is the village," drawing up. "Thank you for your chivalrous assistance. You will be welcome at Thorn if you care to ride that way. I promise never to bore you with the price of corn."

His horse fretted and fumed, churning up the ground. He brought it up beside the trap, reached over to hold out his hand.

"Good night, Miss Mathick. I shall certainly call at Thorn. And I shall bring a horse for you to ride. Or to buy. That would be neighbourly, would it not?"

She shook his hand solemnly, finding it thin and strong. The darkness hid his face entirely now but she knew that he was laughing. Then he was gone, and she made for the lights of High Common, the pony still amenable, the wind coming at her in gusts. It was cold but she felt warm, glowing; she felt alive. Here was a man who did not care what he said to her, who would applaud her directness, who would hate her to pretend a prudery or patience she did not possess. Here was a man she could laugh with, could treat upon equal terms. He appealed to her sense of the ridiculous, her sense of adventure; to all that was worst in her, Miss Millington might have said.

The Doctor did not like him, that much had been made clear; William Claverden had been blunt in his opinion also. But a blighted childhood might account for much. It seemed to Ann as she pulled up outside the Doctor's door that she could quite understand why Sir Harry Gerard might hesitate to live at Blackow, why he might never hope to cross the threshold at Thorn.

But he would cross it, she thought. And she hoped – a furious, consuming hope – that he had the audacity to bring the promised horse.

The Doctor was skirting the problem delicately.

"I cannot say the boy is like him," he announced firmly and wondered at once if it was a lie. He had not really noticed what the boy looked like.

"But he claims to be Francis Forsie's son?" Ann threw down hat and gloves and went to stare into the fire.

"He does, and he may be the first of many. Now it is generally known Thorn is in new hands other equally desperate mothers might choose to test your charity."

"How old is he?"

"He looks sixteen but he could be more, several years more. His mother went to Newcastle, the stepfather a miner. The boy is half starved and has been at work since he could walk. Pashman dropped him off at daybreak like a package, said he was asking for Thorn."

"So why did Pashman bring him to you?"

"He said he smoked a trick – his very phrase – and in any case, Thorn is not on his round this week."

"Is the boy not capable of making his own way? How many his age would travel half England to beg charity from a stranger?"

The Doctor rang the bell. The little maid came and went away again at his bidding and a quiet descended, in which the Doctor and Miss Mathick looked hard at each other and divined a tenth of each other's thoughts on the matter.

"He loves his mother, she commanded him to come. The

stepfather did not want him, did not like him, and then the mother refused to let him go down the mines. Wait till you see him. He has 'Make something of me' writ large all over him. I did not have the heart to send him away but nor could I wish him on your doorstep before breakfast; it could all be lies, of course."

All the time he was speaking the Doctor was pulling at his wig. With his last word he snatched it off and tossed it, with a low growl, on to the nearest chair. Behind him the door opened abruptly, someone large loomed into the light, a deep voice said boldly: "I am come, sir. Thomas Lark," as if he might not be recognised.

"Tom Lark, come in, come in, please meet Miss Mathick. Miss Mathick is Mr Forsie's niece and may or may not be your cousin."

But the Doctor had been mistaken, Ann was thinking, her back to the cheerful blaze and her eyes taking in every detail: this boy was the Francis Forsie of her mother's miniature, the square jaw, the waving hair, the bright blue eyes. He was tall, would grow taller, and there was a promise of breadth and depth; he towered over her, over the Doctor.

"What did your mother ask you to say to me?" she asked.

"That she would be obliged if you could find me honest work and a roof over my head."

"That was all?"

"That was all."

A Forsie after all, the Doctor was deciding, taken aback, a God-damned Forsie from his dirty fair hair to his ill-shod feet; how Francis himself had stood like that in this very room, head up, shoulders squared, defying censure! He glanced across at Ann apologetically, aware he had misled her, but she was smiling, moving to sit gracefully on the shabby chair where he had cast his wig.

"Is your mother a good woman, Tom Lark?"

"Let no one say otherwise," was the retort, and the boy turned a fiery red and appealed to the Doctor: "You knew her, sir."

"Oh, yes, I knew her. Hannah Lark, a little red-haired thing, very merry. It is a shame she was not proof against Francis's enticements."

"He gave her money to keep me," Tom declared defensively, as if to prove to them he thought no ill of his dead father.

A hush, a moment of meditation. Ann met the Doctor's eye and saw it was darkened, distressed.

"I wonder there was no provision in his will," she said softly.

"He stopped all money when my mother married."

"Ah, that was like him," the Doctor exclaimed, rooting under the table and producing the mongoose, sleepy and benign. "He would not have blinked at keeping another man's child while the mother of that child was his mistress – he would have considered it a quibble, a meanness, to do so. But it was foolish of him to expect another man to feel as generous towards his own bastard."

Tom Lark was scarlet, fists clenched.

"You must come back with me to Thorn," said Ann, reaching for her hat. "If you wish you can work for me, sleep and eat in the house. After all, the place is large enough. If it is not to your liking there might be work to be had on a farm elsewhere, or employment in Norwich …"

The Doctor wondered whether to point out the pitfalls of taking in the illegitimate children of disreputable relatives, but a glance at her face showed him she could guess most of them and was amused, if anything, and undaunted; that lift of her chin, that bright stare, told him what she thought of gossips. Nevertheless he felt obliged to glower, the mongoose tucked under one arm and chewing the loose end of his neckcloth.

Ann crossed to his side. "Go on then, warn me I shall be cast out of polite society! No, dear Doctor, I will not consider and be sensible. If Francis was indeed his father – and who could doubt it? – then Thorn is his home. And if he was not, what have I lost?"

"Your reputation in the neighbourhood?"

She petted the mongoose, detached the neckcloth from between its sharp teeth, smiled up into the Doctor's face. "And how much do you think I care for that?"

"I do not believe you care enough about yourself at all," and then: "Dear Ann, you are on dangerous ground."

It was the first time he had used her name and it seemed, as he said it, a celebration of their growing friendship.

Tom cleared his throat, shuffled uneasily. "I can go elsewhere. I have done my duty. It will be no trouble to find work in Norwich, or maybe Yarmouth ..."

Ann, her hand on the Doctor's arm, turned in a second. "There is a place at Thorn if you want it. It does not matter to me whose son you are, nor should it matter to anyone else."

They made their way to the trap. The Doctor, taking advantage of the moment, kissed Ann on both cheeks and then handed her into her seat with: "Can that pony be got to behave? It thinks only of mischief. Do be very careful up on the Gorse, the tinkers may be poaching. Your lamps are filthy and far too feeble."

"Tom will keep me from the tinkers. As for the lights, they are all I have. And it has been known, so I am told, for a certain medical man to cavort about the country after dark without any at all."

Half an hour later the trap was safe at Thorn, the kitchen door thrown wide, and Hollin was grumbling on the threshold, blunderbuss in hand. He had expected to find her dead, he said, robbed, murdered; at best overturned in a pond. Miss Pennyquick had prevailed on him to fetch the gun, to go and look. He peered at Tom on his way past to stable the pony and gave a croak of surprise and a terrible wheeze of laughter. "By God!" he said. "By God!"

Mrs McGinly had pies and cold meat on the table, a poker ready for the ale. She was the only one of them who could almost look Tom in the eye. Miss Pennyquick, who remembered Hannah Lark indistinctly, said nothing but looked darkly, very darkly indeed.

"His feet are raw with blisters," was her comment to Ann in the interval of indecision over which of the many empty bedrooms could be properly assigned to a Forsie bastard. "Quite raw."

"So the Doctor told me," replied Ann mildly.

"Has he walked far?"

"Perhaps two hundred miles. He rode part of the way with some gipsies, I know, and a carter with a waggon full of smoked herring. I think there were some travelling showmen too, and dancing bears and jugglers. But yes, two hundred miles on foot, and sleeping where he could. Do you find it disagreeable that he should stay?"

Miss Pennyquick gave a cackle, eyes flashing. "I thought ... seeing him in the doorway ... it was Francis come home."

And it might have been, for by this time Tom was snug by the kitchen hearth uncomfortably swollen by his huge supper and already drifting off to sleep, his long person dwarfing Hollin's old chair and his hair ruddy in the firelight. He opened his eyes though, dreamily, when Ann came in, and gave her a slow, shy smile.

"You are very good," he said indistinctly in his pleasant voice with its Newcastle undertones. Strangely, nothing of the accent of his Norfolk childhood remained.

"I am very practical. This farm needs labour."

"And you will let me sleep in the house?"

"There is nowhere else. All the cottages except Hollin's are let or sold or have fallen down. And why sleep in a hayloft when I have seven bedrooms empty upstairs?"

And as she passed him, making for the dairy to discover Mrs McGinly and discuss the pig's head, the boiled fowl, and the tarts for the next day's dinner, Tom caught her small hand in both of his. Unclouded blue eyes in a strong merry face, albeit a dirty one, gazed up at her. He said nothing and in a moment let her go.

"What was that animal at the Doctor's?" he asked, leaning back again, eyes narrowed.

"Oh, the mongoose. A mongoose from India. He is called Bombay Jack."

"I should like one," said Tom cheerfully. "I should like one indeed. Could the Doctor find another, d'you think? Or should we have to go to India?"

4

THE MORNING brought Mrs Palmer with her two daughters and consequently all the local gossip and a great deal of barefaced curiosity.

"This house could be so charming," she began, shown into the drawing room to find Miss Pennyquick sewing and Ann in the middle of some long-neglected correspondence, "but my dear, I do so like the way you have arranged the curtains, and they are new; such fine stuff, from London I daresay."

From Norwich, chosen by the shopkeeper in accordance with my ignorant description, Ann might have replied, but she set down her pen and rose smiling with a sweet: "I am so glad you like them."

Mrs Palmer's daughters, seventeen and eighteen, smiled politely back from the sofa where they had been signalled to sit. Their mother had drifted to the mantelshelf where a fine old clock had caught her eye and beside it an oval portrait in oils of a fair young woman – the late Ann Forsie perhaps?

In the course of the next ten minutes Ann and Miss Pennyquick learned all there was to know about Lord Barsham's recurring stomach upsets, his shortage of partridges, his inability to get a good keeper, and every minor catastrophe of the last week in his large household; after this it was the inadvisability of going out in the cold without a head covering, the extraordinary lateness of the vicarage baby – why, they seemed to have been waiting weeks and not a hint of it wishing to make an entry into the world – and the inexpressible hardships of having to travel to London for dresses, no Norwich dressmaker being in the least competent. And then, turning from the window where she had been watching Hollin drive the bullocks back into the yard through the broken-down wall, she announced: "We are to have a ball at the end of the month and you must come, Miss Mathick; I insist that you do. And of course Miss Pennyquick. Of course."

Miss Pennyquick resumed her sewing without appearing the least surprised or overcome by being included, after so many bitter years, in High Common society. She was dressed in dark grey, her cap severe, firmly anchored; she had made the transition from housekeeper to lady's companion in a moment. Her self-confident smile in response to Mrs Palmer's generosity made Mrs Palmer retreat a little and pluck irritably at the admired new curtains.

"We are usually so quiet about here, only two or three balls a year at best, some card parties, musical evenings. There is always Norwich, of course, the theatre and the Assembly Rooms, St Andrew's Hall, but what a journey, what a grinding and jolting for an hour or more …"

There was a murmur of disaffection from the sofa. "You are too lazy, Mama, that is the truth of it. Why, if we had attended half the dances we had invitations for Julia would be married by now!"

"Sophia!"

There was an embarrassed silence during which Mrs Palmer cast reproachful looks all round, Sophia looked mutely defiant, and Julia blushed crimson and stared fixedly into the fire. She was a perfectly pleasant, passably pretty girl with soft brown hair and a shy smile, but was undeniably put in the shade by the younger Sophia, vivacious, charming, and impertinent.

"I am afraid I know so few people in High Common," Ann began quietly, while Miss Pennyquick went in search of Maggie and the obligatory tea tray, so inexplicably slow in putting in an appearance.

"But how could you? The weather has been so dreadful since

you arrived. You have met our parson, no doubt – his father was Lord ... How vexing, I have quite forgot who his father was, but a Lord for certain. And his wife, poor lamb, when will she be delivered? And you have met our doctor, our medical genius; he is on intimate terms with Lord Barsham. Yes, I know, it seems so unlikely, but they have been friends for years, most exceptional friends I assure you."

At this moment the tea tray put in an appearance at last but its impact was momentary; in three minutes Mrs Palmer was away again. "The Doctor is a trifle strange sometimes, of course, a little foreign in his ways. He has been abroad, America, Canada, India. He is excellent in a crisis but at all other times I could wish him a little less abrupt, a little more sympathetic. And oh, have you met Sir Harry Gerard? He is home at last, has been these past weeks. He was always charming, quite irresistible. I shall send him an invitation but no doubt he will have returned to London, and in any case such a country affair will seem so tame to him, do you not think so?"

"I think it would be ill-bred of him to give that impression," said Ann.

Miss Pennyquick coughed. For the first time in years she had an overwhelming desire to laugh.

"There are no balls at Blackow now," Mrs Palmer continued, acutely aware suddenly of Miss Mathick's darkly mocking eye. "Old Sir Harry was very generous to us all; his house was thrown open at least four times a year. They were great occasions. The ballroom at Blackow is splendid, oh, a dream. But now we rely almost entirely on Lord Barsham at Upgate."

At last, at last, she took her leave. Ann escorted her to the carriage, standing grandly in the mud with a cold and discontented coachman rigid on the box. She felt that in Mrs Palmer's eyes she might soon, along with the Doctor, be labelled strange and a little foreign in her ways; she suspected she was only invited to the ball because Mrs Palmer wished to have the dubious honour of introducing her properly into High Common and because she was too old and too plain to pose any kind of threat to the Miss Palmers in the marriage market.

Back in the drawing room she found Tom straddling the Turkey rug, arms akimbo. Maggie had been going through old trunks of clothes in the attics – thus explaining her slackness over the tea – and had found him an outfit in which he looked handsome enough, if a little old-fashioned: snuff-brown breeches, brown stockings, good buckled shoes, all fitting well and flattering enough, for he had a good figure for all its immaturity; a decent white shirt, a plain stock – drunkenly tied – and a dark green frock coat finished him off. Ann clasped her hands together and gave a little cry of laughter, for he looked so sober, so manly, so inordinately proud.

"All I can say," said Miss Pennyquick, "is that something ought to be done about the lice before he starts parading like Paris in his father's clothes."

Tom grinned. His answer to all adversity, great or small, Ann was to find, was to show all his good straight teeth cheerfully and then plunge forward to overcome it.

"Who is Paris?" he demanded when Miss Pennyquick left the room.

"I have forgotten, but quite obviously you must ask Babs. Now, kneel down here and let me tie that neckcloth; you have wound it round and round like a bandage."

So Harry found her busy at this task, having walked in unannounced through the kitchen. She was leaning forward over Tom's wild hair saying: "If you are infested we must raid the stillroom for a cure, or consult the Doctor," and then: "Hold still, do, and let me finish this knot."

When she looked up she saw Harry's questioning glance, and started, the linen falling into a muddle at once. "Why, Sir Harry! Have you come to pay my rent?"

It was a bold stroke. He looked mulish, but it was a look that passed. "Perhaps I have. Would that surprise you?"

"Astound me." She was in control again, fastening the neckcloth deftly. "May I present my cousin, Tom Forsie."

That too was a bold stroke. Tom seemed happy enough about it though, and held out a large rough hand to Harry with the merest nod in place of anything more respectful.

"I did not know," Harry said carefully, "there were any Forsies left."

"Did you not?" and she led him to the sofa, bade him sit down, rang for Maggie. "But have you really come about the rent?"

Would he have the nerve to deny it? She saw his fair brows draw together. "I could give you five hundred pounds," he said abruptly, sounding astonished at himself for such a capitulation.

"Are you aware you owe me something in the region of a thousand?"

"How unlike you not to have the exact figure to hand! Let us say I have a great many creditors at the moment and all clamouring for their money."

"Then I must be content with the five hundred. I would so much rather simply have the land. If you released the land I would cease to be one of your clamouring creditors; I would not look for a penny."

Miss Pennyquick entered with a letter. Harry stared at her and then, remembering the dairy — had it been the dairy? — scowled and looked away. It seemed hardly possible this was the same Miss Pennyquick but that bright, haughty glance betrayed her.

No more was said about the lease. Tom excused himself and went to try on the half dozen hats discovered in crumbling boxes behind the trunks. Miss Pennyquick took up her needle again. The conversation flagged and faltered, Ann feeling exhausted by Mrs Palmer and suddenly, ridiculously tongue-tied, and Harry stunned by her calm acceptance of five hundred pounds he had not got and her even calmer presentation of that gawky boy as a Forsie when any kind of a legitimate Forsie he could not be.

"Mrs Palmer is the loquacious lady with two spindly daughters, I recall," he said to some mention of the projected ball.

"You must look again, Sir Harry. The youngest is uncommonly pretty."

Sprawled on the sofa, booted legs crossed, his hands in his pockets, Harry considered her. "Whoever marries you will have Thorn," he said.

Ann gave a startled laugh. She conjured a mental picture of a nameless, faceless husband tackling the orchard with a billhook the way she might have to herself in the near future if Hollin continued to prevaricate. Who would want Thorn?

"I have not considered marriage, not for a long time. But I have a fancy to make this place fine again."

"It will take you years, and be ridiculously hard work. And your temper and your brave spirit will go to ruin and you will never have any money. You deserve something better, Miss Mathick."

He had come to stand in front of her and with one of his large, irrefutable gestures he swept forward to take her hand in both of his: "This place can only break your heart," he said, "I could not bear to see it."

Miss Pennyquick sucked in her breath, put aside her embroidery. But Harry gave her his widest, most mischievous grin, and dropped a kiss on Ann's knuckles. "Come outside. Come outside and see what I have brought you."

What he had brought her was as she had expected: elegant, restless, lean. A little like its master, Ann thought madly, too much energy suppressed or misdirected.

"Take no notice," Harry said, as the horse started at the sight of the two women. "He is full of courage, that is all."

And oats and beans, Ann thought. She knew Miss Pennyquick's bleak stare concealed a snake-pit of emotions, heaving and seething, but in the event the expected remonstrance was fairly mild: "That beast is not for you to ride? Dear Lord, your neck will be broken in five minutes! How could you think of such a thing?"

But Ann had thought of it often and was determined upon it. She was gone to change in a moment, laughing.

And the brown horse was full of courage, there was no disputing it, and certainly had an unassuagable desire to gallop; it was invigorating if nothing else.

"Your hat is unpinned," was Harry's comment as they reached the far side of the Gorse after fifteen tumultuous minutes. "But you sit uncommon well. I never thought you would hold him."

"You mean you hoped he would run away with me? How chivalrous! How neighbourly!"

"I hoped nothing of the kind, only that you were competent enough to keep your seat. He is used to go on, he cannot abide being checked."

"That much is obvious," through gritted teeth. "What are the chances of making him stand still a moment?"

They were under the trees now, breasting tangles of brush and bramble stems. Ahead was the Blackow boundary.

"There used to be cattle," Harry said with a blank stare at the neglected grassland.

"The place is a wilderness." Ann pulled up the horse and dismounted, led him to the fence. "Look there – overrun with rabbits. And half a dozen of those trees need felling. Why will you not do it?"

He twisted in the saddle, staring down to the distant roofs and chimneys of the house. "I do not care for this place. I daresay I never shall."

And then he swung himself down beside her, leaned back against the dilapidated rails, and the horses snatched great mouthfuls of sour grass and slobbered green froth everywhere. "Ann, there is a place ... yes, a place ... oh, you would like it, you surely would. It is so beautiful. You have no idea of the freedom, the excitement."

He was so close his sleeve was brushing hers, and she was acutely aware of his extraordinary vitality, his warmth, even his heartbeat. But she was also aware he did not see her, he smiled upon some inner vision, some remembered perfection.

"And do you own this paradise?" She took a step away.

"I own it." He was as delighted as a child.

"But where is it and what is its name?"

"Where? Oh yes, where. Somewhere ... somewhere off the coast of Africa, I believe."

"Are you not sure?"

"I am sure it lies in that direction but I cannot swear latitude or longitude; I am no navigator. But it exists and I have been there," and he reached for her hand, held it, his eyes still alight with the vision. "It is called Sable Island."

Should she pull her hand away or let it lie, acquiescent, between his dry palms? "You do not mean to take me there, Sir Harry?"

Her hand was free. He was pulling her horse round, preparing to help her mount. "Would you come?" A speculative flash of the blue eyes. "Would you? I believe you would. You are wasted here. Damn the place! What is it but scrub and thistle? Why should you care about it so?"

She made the effort to search for an honest answer, but he tossed her up into the saddle as if her silence made him impatient.

"Perhaps because I have nothing else," she said at last, taking up the reins, "and perhaps because I cannot bear to see good things go to waste."

"But are there no lovers? No young men a-wooing?"

"None."

"Which only goes to show how dull-witted they all are hereabouts."

She laughed. The horse shied. Ramming her hat on, all the reins in one hand, she said: "Why do you not feed your horses fewer oats?" and vanished into the undergrowth with a crash and the drum of furious hooves.

Up on the windy level she took a pull and the horse slowed.

"I believe I shall accept Mrs Palmer's invitation," said Harry from behind.

"Why not? You would be the centre of attraction. You have been away so long, they tell me, you are almost a stranger."

He was alongside now, watching her frown of concentration, the way she bit her bottom lip, as she tried to bring the brown horse to order. "Perhaps I shall stay at Blackow longer than usual. After all, there is a great deal to be done."

She was aware it was disgraceful to ride a cross saddle in a habit; a yard of petticoat hung down, spattered with mud. And was half her hair adrift? A mass of curl was tangled in her collar. "I do not think you will ever do all that needs to be done," she said. "Your heart is not in it. Your heart is lost to ... to this island of yours."

They came down to Thorn across the lower slopes of Warren

Hill, across her bleak, sad fields where the rooks lifted on the wind and the raucous gulls were ranged on the freshly-turned furrow. They had made a start here at least, Ann thought. And ahead was Thorn itself, the thready smoke rising, everywhere the bleat of the miserable, confined Leicesters.

"How on earth did you come by an island?" she asked suddenly. "Did you buy it?" It could not be a simple matter, she was thinking, to buy an island off the coast of Africa. Were they not usually hotly disputed? Were they not always vital to trade, defence, prestige?

Harry gave a shout of encouragement as the grey flew the pile of broken-down gates and fence posts at the bottom of the field. "Oh that," a look over his shoulder, a grin, "I won it. I took it in lieu of a debt."

Her arms nearly pulled out, her hair down, Ann still followed, crossing the Home Field flat out, the wet turf flying. She had lost all sense of dignity; who cared a fig for dignity? It was exhilarating; her face was scarlet, but who cared for that either?

And in the stockyard she found Harry standing quietly, looking at the Leicesters. "Yes," he said, as if continuing some genteel conversation, "I took it in lieu of a debt. It was the best thing I ever did in my life."

The gulls rode the wind; the great trees bent this way and that; across Blackow Gorse, bleak and heathery, the carriage made ponderous progress. Inside, conscious of crushing their finery, Miss Pennyquick and Ann played cards companionably and with extreme difficulty in the light of the little swinging lantern.

"It is no good," Ann said after a while, "I cannot concentrate in the least."

"Mind your skirt! Ann, Ann, you have dropped half the pack in the straw."

"They will have to stay there then. We cannot grovel for them. Mrs Palmer would think we had come direct from the farmyard." Miss Pennyquick was in brown, unrelieved, discreet, matronly brown; she did not look as if she had been near a farmyard in her life. She looked correct, even severe. And it was as well perhaps. It was unlikely they would all accept her without qualms, she who was reputed Francis Forsie's loose woman: As the Palmer house came in sight, gloriously ablaze with candles, she shrank back a little. "I cannot imagine why you insisted I come."

"Because I wanted you to come. And in any case Mrs Palmer invited you and I am wicked enough to enjoy the prospect of that overbearing woman strangling in her own good manners. Apart from that she sent her carriage for us, and I had no wish to rattle around in it alone like a pea in a drum."

The carriage in question slowed, swayed; above them the long windows were brilliant with light and the sound of music was already issuing, tinnily, on the frosty air. Twenty vehicles had already done their worst with the immaculate gravel by the time Mrs Palmer's own disorged its passengers at the foot of the grand steps and rolled away round the back to the stables.

"Courage," insisted Ann, propelling Miss Pennyquick upwards, "they are only human beings, not wild beasts."

"We make an odd pair."

"Do you think so? I cannot see why. You know, we have come here to enjoy ourselves, not to be cast down by other people's moral indignation and shameless hypocrisy."

"But they all thought I was your uncle's …"

"Did they? Then you see what poor fools they all really are. Good. Look at the footmen, there must be a score and all in greasy yellow coats. Here is Mrs Palmer all smiles. Babs, quickly, do look a little agreeable. And remind me to mention the playing cards."

The ball was a success. Mrs Palmer was assured of that half an hour after it started. The whole of the county was present, as she joyfully pointed out to her unresponsive husband over the next day's breakfast. The whole of the county, of course, included a great many people she knew very slightly, and some she felt she knew too well, and others, like Miss Mathick of Thorn, whom she wondered whether she ought to know at all.

The girl was commonplace, insignificant. Or was she? After a shaky start she had apparently acquired dancing partners for the entire evening within fifteen minutes; even the dotty old Admiral who could never stop talking about Lord Howe and the Glorious First of June had cornered her for the cotillion. And there the girl was absolutely blooming and lifting that square little chin and putting them all in confusion with her decided opinions. And there was Sir Harry Gerard, a nonpareil in a splendid blue coat, bending over her hand and making her blush. And there was Dr French, irritating and extreme physician, weaving his way among the young people to talk to her, touching her elbow in a most proprietary way and steering her off towards the supper room laughing and waving his hands.

Mrs Palmer, taking the opportunity to thrust Julia under Sir Harry's nose, was pained to find him looking wistfully after the disappearing Miss Mathick.

"Do you think she is out to catch a husband?" This with a confidential smile.

"Miss Mathick? Why, how should I know? It will not take her long to find one, I daresay."

"Do you find her personable, Sir Harry? I thought her entirely eclipsed by the younger, prettier women, but there you are, I do not look with masculine eyes; it has often seemed to me men are attracted to the most unfortunate ladies, quite indifferent looks and no character."

"Are you implying Miss Mathick is such a one?"

His tone warned her she was on the edge of a chasm. She pushed the blushing Julia forwards a little with an arch smile.

"I meant no unkindness, only a mother must be permitted to think her own daughters the most lovely, the most charming. Do you not remember Julia, Sir Harry? For certain you played together as children here and at Upgate."

"It seems unlikely, Madam. I suspect there is a great disparity in our ages."

"Oh no," exclaimed Julia suddenly with even deeper blushes. "For I clearly recall you driving the governess's donkey all over the lawns. But it is true you were quite grown-up and I was only five or six."

Harry did not wish to be reminded of childhood; his had been lonely and miserable, blighted by his mother's promiscuous excursions, his father's bitterness, his own lack of companions. As he had told Ann, he did not care for Blackow, but that was simply because he had once cared for it deeply.

He offered his arm to Julia. "I was about to suggest I fetch you refreshment, Miss Palmer, but would it not be more pleasant to go in search of some together?"

And Mrs Palmer fell back with a look of extreme satisfaction. Harry Gerard was handsome and engaging and if he abandoned the business of his estate for more light-hearted pursuits, well so did many young men; his father had owned a noble fortune, a great deal of property in Norfolk and beyond. It would take a lifetime to squander such wealth. And these disturbing rumours of drunkenness, dishonesty, debt — what were they? Rumours, insubstantial as a mist. How could a man of Harry Gerard's standing be in debt? It was not a word known to the genteel wives who gathered in Mrs Palmer's company several times a week; debt was for the royal family, great lords, and the abject poor.

Sir Harry Gerard would do very well indeed for Julia, very well indeed. Why, did not everyone know a good, industrious wife was the making of any man?

At the entrance to the supper room among other duennas and stray relations of the dancers too staid, too old, or too shy to join the general body of merrymakers, Miss Pennyquick sat in some state. Those who did not know her — and there were many — were cordial and incurious; those who did ignored her. It was scarcely as bad as she had expected and she found the courage to bestow an ingenuous smile on Mrs Palmer's illustrious sister Lady Barsham, who not only knew of her and of all the gossip of nearly thirty years, but had met her several times at Thorn in the long-distant days before Francis Forsie had shut himself off from the world.

"You are holding court. What splendour!" The Doctor was before her, benign and humorous.

"I never thought I would own to enjoying it, but there is something to be said for being confined in the matron's corner."

"An exalted view?"

"Exactly. That girl of General Black's, how she dances! And have you seen the youngest Miss Palmer flirting with every man in the room. Those eyes!"

"I cannot say I have noticed. In any case, I treated her for the measles and familiarity so sadly breeds contempt. You are radiant, Miss Pennyquick. Ann will be so glad for you."

"Where is she? I thought I saw her with you. Do you like her dress? So simple, so suitable."

"I admit I detached her somewhat unkindly from young Gerard. I do not like him. He is perfectly pleasant, and witty, and he cannot be faulted in his choice of tailor, but something is lacking, something anatomical perhaps – heart? He smiles and charms but he does not know how to love people. Or am I just a cynical old man?"

Miss Pennyquick plied her fan. "She is not a fool," she remarked.

"But she is young and alone and tired. We have all ached to lean on someone else for a moment at such times, to be flattered and pursued, to be made to laugh."

"Does he pursue her?"

"I cannot be sure, but he pays her an inordinate amount of attention and every word honey, every smile for her alone. By the way, Lawyer Claverden is here, soused in the best wine by all those cunning rich who do not care to pay his bills but trust he will ever be their friend."

And he was, though by this time he had escaped the cunning rich and was dancing with Lord Barsham's second daughter Charlotte, whose auburn curls were spectacular, entrancing, and whose huge eyes challenged him to struggle on gravely with the failing conversation. She was so lithe, so light, so very, very young; he felt remote and ancient, dry as the contents of his legal boxes, avuncular and appalled at it. He was thirty-three and she looked at him as she might at an old man. The fact that he was impeccably dressed for once and that he was undeniably attractive in a piratical way – his hair being so short and his face so oddly scarred across the cheekbone – was nothing to her. She flitted into his grasp and away again, whirled hither and thither by another three gentlemen at least before being returned, breathless and sparkling, into his own orbit again. And then out of the corner of his eye he saw a flash of rose pink and the movement of a brown, imperious head and felt the impact, though now he could not see her at all, of those fine dark eyes.

"Mama wishes us all to marry dukes," Charlotte was saying, "though Frances disappointed by becoming a parson's wife, even if he is to be a bishop – which I heartily hope for everyone's sake he is not. Of course Mama is not ambitious for us in quite the way Aunt Lizzie is ambitious for Julia and Sophia. Julia dotes on Harry Gerard and I can quite see why, but he is not to be mentioned in our house any more, Papa calls him a scoundrel ..."

The words poured over William without effect; he emerged dry from the deluge, having heard nothing. His smile was kind and he exerted himself with regard to manners but Charlotte, more sensitive than he realised, was fully aware of his cordial disinterest. She was bold enough to take an exceptionally hard look at him as he relinquished her to a young cavalry officer, a local boy, swaggering in his uniform. She was rewarded with a distracted smile; he was already turning away, searching for someone. She would like to meet him again, she thought, but in a moment she forgot him, the uniform claimed her, and Mr Claverden had vanished in the crush.

He had gone in search of the elusive rose pink, and he found it by a huge display of greenery at the very back of the supper room, a wintry display but undeniably effective. It seemed Ann Mathick had just this minute retired from dancing to admire it in the company of a tall young Scot who was training to be a surgeon, one of Dr French's protégées and son of a prosperous local farmer. Her hair was a little disarranged, her eyes brilliant. Was the fellow so amusing then? William arrived before her, serious, commanding, and she looked up, half startled.

"I think the next dance is mine," he said stiffly.

Ann choked a laugh and looked up, wide-eyed. "Is it? I am not at all certain. Mr Cummings, do excuse me."

She took William's arm graciously but with the confidence of a sister. "Have you something to tell me? What a barefaced lie just now! To say we were engaged to dance when you knew we were not. Shame, Mr Claverden! But I did mean to write to you before this; Sir Harry has paid me five hundred pounds."

William cleared a way through the press by putting his broad shoulder to it, much like an Indiaman breasting a heavy swell. He could feel – for some reason was intensely aware of – Ann's hand clutching indecorously at his sleeve as he forged ahead regardless.

"Five hundred? He swore he would not pay a shilling. What has moved him to this fit of generosity?"

"I could not say. But do you suggest I refuse it?"

"Oh, take it, take it! I wager you will see no more than the five hundred. I have heard some disquieting tales of his financial ruin – likely, imminent, or already upon him depending on the source."

"You mean he has no money at all?"

"I am not in a position to judge. Do you want me to make enquiries?"

"No, no! But could a man with no money dress as he does and keep such horses and spend such a time at Newmarket? Mrs Palmer, who thinks of him as her son-in-law elect, has already confided to me that he visits Newmarket frequently and with a roll of her eye that tells all. She does not approve of betting money and yet cannot find it in herself to censure Harry Gerard, he has charmed her so."

William snorted. "He has charmed you too. No doubt she thinks to frighten you off with a little exaggeration. A cautious mother takes no chances. She has seen him kissing your hand – an old-fashioned courtesy but how effective – and there is your money, such a temptation to any man, even one already wealthy."

"He thinks me plain and treats me like a sister."

"It is not the impression I receive." Rather sour.

"That is simply his manner then, a sort of affectation. He means nothing by it. He flirts with all women because he cannot help it."

"And how they like him for it! So strange! He seems so damnably false to me."

Ann was laughing. She had let go of his sleeve to fall into step beside him as he slowed beside the buffet table and cast a despairing eye over thirty kinds of cold meats and their accompanying side dishes.

"You have dragged me round the entire room for nothing," said Ann. "We are back where we started."

"But without Mr Cummings. Is anyone taking you to supper?"

"No. But look, there is the Admiral waving. Stop! I will not allow you to gallop me off again. He may be a little mad but he is perfectly harmless and he dances very well indeed."

William found himself rapidly outmanoeuvred. The Admiral bore down in front and behind Harry Gerard came quietly to take Ann's elbow with a brotherly solicitude.

"Miss Mathick, you promised me this dance, I think."

His blue eyes gazed briefly into William's. Blue of speedwells, blue of the southern ocean, blue like sweet Charlotte's, William thought. Of the two pairs he infinitely preferred Charlotte's, smiling between their curving lashes and guileless as a baby's.

"You remember Mr Claverden, my lawyer," Ann said, refusing to be carried off.

Harry had hoped perhaps to be allowed to forget him; the sacrifice of the five hundred pounds still rankled. He took a moment to smile. But the Admiral had William by the sleeve and was about to embark on a monologue the subject of which, it was clear, would bore anyone but a naval man to suicide. Harry bowed politely and steered Ann away; the musicians were striking up one of the last measures of the evening.

"He does not like me, your Mr Claverden," he remarked as they took their places. "He is stiff with disapproval."

He was not the only one: the Admiral too was looking thoughtful. "Gerard did you say? Gerard of Blackow? I knew the old man. This puppy has an insolent stare, God dammit, and a deuced high opinion of himself. But Miss Mathick is a grand girl, no airs, no silliness; my sister Mrs Warden was saying so earlier: a grand girl and no fool."

William was tempted to retort that all women were fools but it was, after all, sheer nonsense, and only reflected his gloomy state of mind. That he had been deeply in love with Mary

73

Chiswick and that they had shared an understanding of the future disposition of themselves and their worldly goods had been unassailable facts; Mary's sudden marriage to George Bolton and her subsequent inability to look William in the face were also facts. But three years was surely too long to continue remembering with such pain? It was true he now regarded his younger self, so simple, so ardent, with a sort of sour amusement, that of the mature man for the green boy. But he had truly loved her and he had not loved any other woman enough since to wish to make her his wife. He had grown wary, shy even. For if Mary Chiswick had repudiated his passion for mercenary and parental whims, how much more cruel might be frivolous and light-hearted females?

It was as well cynicism did not entirely suit him. William's humour was dark and dry but could not be annihilated. A sense of proportion and of the ridiculous must rise at last. He could meet Mary now and smile and make a leg and ask cordially after her health and her husband, her baby or her mother or anything else of hers without betraying any feeling whatsoever. His was a face that usually did so; his complete absence of expression when confronting Mary was a sobering indication of how deep the wound had gone and what rigid self-control had been needed to survive its healing. Only Mary, of course, knew whether she still wept at the thought of her own betrayal and of his dead, polite gaze when he looked at her.

The Admiral had reached a point in Howe's battle where the great old *Defence*, crippled and unable to steer, was taken in tow by the *Niger*.

"The *Caesar*," William said automatically, his mind still on the more recent past. "Or if you wish to be accurate to the last degree the *Phaeton* first and then the *Caesar*. The *Niger* did not take the tow until a week later."

The Admiral stared. "You speak with a deal of assurance, sir. Have you relatives at sea? Did you know someone in the action?"

It would not do, William saw, to make a confession: he would not shake off the Admiral then until the carriages were called. He said gravely: "Yes, indeed, someone I know very well was an officer in the frigate *India*."

Luckily Mrs Palmer chose this moment to intervene, panting with the news that Kilthorpe Manor was let at last and to a gentleman from Essex. William, who had no idea where Kilthorpe Manor was nor why its letting should be a matter of importance, listened with half an ear and watched the crowd ebb and flow in the doorway of the ballroom. He knew no one apart from his few clients: Thurston, Benington, amiable Barsham; but he saw the Doctor's shabby green coat bobbing in a corner, and suddenly the merest flash of rose pink. She was still with Harry Gerard then. Curse the man, what was he up to? The music was rising to squeaky heights, but then William had no ear for music, danced infernally, and was never at his best in large social gatherings. He returned his attention to Mrs Palmer for a moment and found her speculating on the Essex gentleman's culinary preferences should she invite him to dinner. The Admiral looked glum, his habitual expression when deprived of the opportunity to discourse on Lord Howe. William was thankful no one in the room except the Doctor had the least idea he had been in the *India*, he would never hear the end of it.

"But Mr Claverden, you look so serious! What can my sister have been saying?" Lady Barsham was at his elbow, large, statuesque; no two sisters could have been so unlike each other.

"Claverden is connected with the Navy," said the Admiral.

"Oh, but I should have guessed it! My servants all jump at his commands."

"I mean he has relations at sea."

William remained dumb, but was given a shrewd glance by Lady Barsham, and looked up only to catch another glimpse of rose pink and that damned blue of Harry Gerard's coat. And why should those two colours close together irritate him so?

"Where is that strange little girl from Thorn?" asked Lady Barsham.

"Ann Mathick?" Mrs Palmer was torn between gratification at the success of her ball and righteous indignation that Julia had been so disgracefully abandoned — after a mere ten minutes — by scapegrace Sir Harry. "Ann Mathick is dancing with Harry Gerard; they have danced together several times and he has carried her ices and fawned about her all evening. I cannot think what he sees in her, she is quite nondescript."

Lady Barsham put a restraining hand on William's arm, seeing his black brows snap together alarmingly. Of course, he was the girl's lawyer too, she remembered. "She seems pleasant, open, unaffected; eccentric perhaps, yes. And not quite the elegant young heiress hoped for by High Common. As to what Harry Gerard sees in her, why, he sees Thorn and a fortune, my dear."

"She intends to spend the fortune on the farm, they say," Mrs Palmer was trying hard to bring herself to dislike Ann, but was finding she could not do it; and she was sometimes foolish but seldom unjust. "It will take some courage to set the place to rights."

"Well, it is time someone spent something on it," was her sister's dry comment.

"She should sell up, buy a house in Norwich," said the Admiral. Women on a farm, he was thinking, must be as terrible as women at sea.

The Doctor appeared, urgent, disorderly. "Excuse me, ladies, but I must bear Mr Claverden away on an errand of mercy."

Both women stared, and the Admiral made a growling noise and fished for his snuff box, but the Doctor, who could be as inscrutable as he chose, merely smiled a wide sweet smile and bore the tall dark man away through the throng.

"I believe I have had enough for one evening," William said as they gained the hall and so the front door, cluttered with departing guests and the officious footmen.

"I thought so. Did you ride over? Of course. It is a foul night, you know," and they bent to look out, rain blowing furiously into their faces. "This started over an hour ago. So why not stay with me until tomorrow? It would save you a long wet journey to Norwich. Ah, is that Mrs Palmer's carriage — that one, that disgrace in yellow and maroon? I have to find Ann before she leaves. I winkled you out on purpose to lend me moral support."

"I am surprised you need it."

"Oh, I do indeed. I have the strongest feeling this is neither the time nor place to say what I am about to say and Ann Mathick is no shy maid to blush prettily and hang her head when chastised out of hand by a sour old army surgeon. She will either laugh or spit fire, I am sure of it."

William nodded to a slight acquaintance. "Chastise her?" And then he felt a hand on his arm, found Charlotte's bright eyes, that preferred blue, smiling up into his.

"Mr Claverden, I had no notion you knew the Doctor! The Doctor has looked after me since I was a baby. Are you very good friends?"

Taken aback, William assented hesitantly. Charlotte had reached out, ingenuous as a child, to take the Doctor's hand and then, in a rush of pale silk, kissed his stubborn chin. "Best of men," she declared in a low voice, "your frown is tremendous. Have you not enjoyed your evening?"

She was enchanting and had no idea of it. William saw the candlelight kindle her russet head. He wished suddenly that he and not the Doctor was the object of her affection; he was touched by her innocence more than by her loveliness. But then a slight figure in rose appeared, the Doctor's arm jerked and his look became hawkish; Charlotte was swallowed up behind the greasy footmen, the voluble guests.

"My dear Ann, let me help you to the carriage."

"That would be ridiculous," she said at once, but with a startled, sideways look at the Doctor and the truculent William, "you would be soaked. If you truly wish to do me a kindness you could find Miss Pennyquick. I mislaid her somewhere between the palms and the musicians."

The Doctor signalled William. "Secure Miss P. if you can," and he wrested an umbrella from one of the footmen, taking Ann's arm.

By the time William returned with Miss Pennyquick Ann was already installed in the Palmer carriage and the Doctor craning in at the door.

"I know you mean well," Ann was saying, "but you must allow me to choose my own friends. Because he is frivolous and unreliable must I make him my enemy?"

The Doctor sighed, stepped back to allow Miss Pennyquick inside. He took his leave cordially but with a scrupulous politeness uncharacteristic of him, and then he stood back and watched the carriage drive away. "Her objection is natural; I have no right to interfere."

"Harry Gerard?"

They ducked in out of the rain. "Harry Gerard." The Doctor made a sketchy bow to someone far in the distance, someone beckoning him, but he deliberately turned away. "He is in pursuit of her, that much is plain enough. But why, William? To amuse himself during a dull winter? He has stayed much longer than usual at Blackow already. Why? To pay court to Ann or to avoid the tipstaffs? He has given her five hundred pounds, did she tell you? I cannot believe he would do so out of disinterested charity."

"Then he has his eye on her fortune."

Charlotte was leaving. Framed in a fur-lined hood her face turned, radiant, to smile at that boy in uniform. William gritted his teeth.

Lord Barsham emerged, wrung the Doctor's hand. "How is Bombay Jack?"

"Tolerable. I shall dine with you on the fifteenth."

"Sixteenth. Charlotte, bid the Doctor good night."

She did so; another hush of silk, another kiss, another innocent, smiling look at William. The Doctor chewed his lip thoughtfully and watched her go, and then pulled at his wig a little. William wondered if he would throw decorum to the winds and take the wretched thing off.

"Is the mongoose ill?" he asked.

"Miserably. He mopes, he pines, he whimpers for India, dust, heat and snakes."

"Do you?"

A fair eyebrow rose, the ghost of a smile flickered. "Do I? I pine for many places, for the sight of old friends, old shipmates, but I will not die of melancholy, dear William, like poor Jack."

Riding to High Common behind the Doctor's hooded gig, obstinately refusing to tie his horse on the back and ride in the dry, William breathed in rain and fierce wind. Ann Mathick, Ann Mathick, said his horse's hooves. But why should he care about Ann Mathick? At the place on Blackow Gorse where he knew the land dipped away to Thorn he gave a despairing glance into the dark as if he might see her somewhere beneath the writhing trees. But if he thought coherently at all it was simply to wonder why anyone should choose to live in such a remote and blasted place and to yearn, abruptly and inexplicably, to be back on his long-relinquished ship.

5

HARRY GERARD called at Thorn; he called exclusively at Thorn. High Common was prostrate with amazement – and also with chagrin, for there were respectable unmarried daughters all over and not enough suitors. It was quite obvious, of course, that it was Miss Mathick's fortune which drew him across the Gorse and down that steep lane to the farm, for it could not be her face, and what else was there?

What else indeed?

The first time he called after the ball he dared to ride round to the long-unused front door, his horse leaving deep imprints in the weedy flowerbeds, and he knocked thunderously on the blistered oak until they all came running. Ann had remonstrated, half furious, half laughing: "You leave your manners behind when you come here then, Sir Harry. Does it not strike you that is a kind of contempt?"

But he would not have it, and it was not true in any case.

"It is because I know you set no store by outward show. Would you really want me to sit in your drawing room discussing the weather, or the war, or ... or the price of corn?" he demanded.

She could not think of anything more dull, she said, and pray, trample the borders some more, weeds and flowers were all one to her.

The second time he came the day was fine, cold and dry. He

walked over, his greyhound at his heels, and he found Ann in the yard making an inventory. He looked over her shoulder: flails, sieves, bleeding knives etc. etc. His eyes met hers.

"Must it be done?"

"It must."

"Could not young Tom do it?"

"Young Tom is away with Hollin in pursuit of a mad dog."

"I called to see if you would care to walk to the river?"

She would care, but what about the inventory? He said damn the inventory, the day would be over before she had finished it. And it would be: already there were rags of purple cloud over the Gorse, a perceptible deepening of the grey light. She bent to stir the rusty contents of a box, frowning. "I am not at all convinced of the necessity of bleeding the animals spring and autumn. Does it really do any good? I shall have to ask the Doctor."

"They have always done it," Harry said flatly.

"Yes, but why?"

"Someone must have found it efficacious."

Ann shut her box. "Or swore he did for fear of looking foolish. But I will go into it; the Doctor must explain the science. I will not do things simply because they are the custom."

"They will not love you for that attitude."

"They? Who are they? And how much do you care for the world's opinion, Sir Harry?" Not a great deal, she supposed. She suspected he was incorrigibly self-indulgent; no, she was sure of it!

They walked down to the river, deeply engaged on the question of the world's opinion, and at last, breathless and laughing, she leaned on the rail of the footbridge and watched the angry water swirl away beneath.

"How sad you cannot stay at Blackow," she said, "you would so cheer up the neighbourhood."

"I have no intention of becoming an asset to High Common."

"But how you will disappoint all those desperate mamas on the lookout for a perfect son-in-law!"

"How can you say such a thing? Am I not so very far from perfect? I neglect the estate, I gamble, I am extravagant."

"Ah, but you look the part."

She was on the far side now, stepping from the path to tread a soggy patch of water plants and stand on the very edge. The day was failing, the river darker already, the spreading shadows under the little bridge dank and cold.

"We must go back," Harry was holding out a hand. She found his grin untrustworthy and irresistible together. His grasp was impersonal and brief, hauling her easily from the sodden greenery.

"How much longer will you stay?" she asked as they started up the hill. It was night beneath the trees, mysterious, silent. Behind them the river was a dull gleam, a mist, a distant hushing between the trembling willows.

"I cannot say."

Ann, drawing her cloak more tightly about her, felt a stab of anguish and of irritation, the one following the other instantly — for she did not wish to be moved by Harry Gerard to anything but laughter: there had been too little of that in her life these last four years.

But perhaps it was too late already; perhaps it had been too late since the moment he had appeared before her on the Gorse, sitting the grey horse as if he grew out of him.

"I will be sorry to say goodbye, Sir Harry," she said.

He looked at her. After all it seemed his admiration was genuine. He could not help himself, he must applaud her spirit. And the ghostly dusk lent her a strange enchantment, her pale face indistinct, her great eyes compelling.

"I have never met anyone like you," he said.

The beginning of April brought a further hundred pounds and a note: "I cannot resist your entreaties. I shall pay in full."

"You see," said Ann to the Doctor as they took tea in a companionable way before her crackling fire, "he is not such a bad neighbour after all."

"You are both playing a game." The Doctor was painfully aware how often Harry Gerard called at Thorn; the village was busy with the news, eager for the first real hint of scandal. "It is the land you want, not the money, and he only pays it to flatter you and so that you think him the model of excellence; he cannot bear to be disliked, although he behaves outrageously and pretends to rejoice when he is shunned."

"I have not noticed he is shunned."

"But he is not unreservedly welcome." The Doctor bent to give a quick poke to the fire, which did not need one. He could not face her steady and sensitive eyes. He knew instinctively that from now on she would always spring to Harry Gerard's defence, and that there was nothing he could do about it.

"Hollin and two of the men will start work on Warren Hill as soon as the weather clears," she said, turning to look out at the rain streaming down on the cold wind, "and after that there is Long Meadow to sow. They are out unblocking the last of the ditches today but no doubt they will give up and come back," and then a brief smile, a sudden change of mood: "I have made a most exciting purchase. You cannot imagine how life will be improved by it."

It was resting, its shafts on blocks, in the empty corn barn. The Doctor, hustled out under an umbrella, was compelled to say anxiously: "But it looks too dashing, too bold. Are you sure it is quite the thing for social calls, for jogging about the lanes?"

"I thought you would approve. I depended on it.'

He did, of course. His sudden delighted grin betrayed him. He touched one of the high green wheels. The gig was crazily-sprung, but elegant, elegant. "And what paragon takes the place of Hollin's pony?"

The paragon was tall, rangy, nervous, and rolling his eye. The Doctor stood at a sensible distance, gazing in awe.

"I was once warned never to buy a white-legged horse," he said, "and surely that wild look betokens mischief? But he is fine enough otherwise – if you can hold him."

"I bought him very cheaply."

"I assumed as much. Your eye for a bargain will be your undoing."

"I gave only twenty guineas for him."

"Good God! Such nobility does not come at twenty guineas – you might have paid more for a farm horse! So he has wicked habits, is vicious, runs away, kicks. But there, I suppose these are trifles compared with the bottomless pit of depravity that is Hollin's pony."

Inside again they fell to talking about Francis Forsie over the buttered muffins.

"Tom looks so like him," Ann said, "and he loves Thorn already, is always about the fields even when his work is done. I think he has even spurred Hollin to greater efforts by such enthusiasm."

Francis Forsie had loved Thorn too, the Doctor remembered, in the days before Caroline Gerard jumped her little grey mare over the orchard gate into his life. The Doctor could recall that incident quite well, having been privileged to witness it from the step of his gig as he prepared to drive away, and he allowed that as an effective entrance he had seen none better.

"Your buildings look watertight at last," he remarked, hoping that perhaps other things were too, that Harry Gerard's storm-force assault might be in vain, that Ann could ride out the worst unscathed. He dismembered a muffin with some venom. "I saw William Claverden this week," a safer topic, he thought, than either the Forsies or the Gerards. "He is a frequent visitor at Lord Barsham's. He is sorting out some legal quibble over rents and paying compliments to young Charlotte all at once, it seems."

"Is he not much too old for her?"

"Thirty-three for eighteen? It could not be more satisfactory. And he would make a good husband – a little inattentive perhaps but no one any the worse for it. However, Lady Barsham would not approve of a match, he is still making his way in his profession, and for all that he looks set fair to make a fortune by it he yearns for the sea most terribly; besides which he cares little for convention. *That* would discourage any mama."

"Mrs Palmer does not seem discouraged. She called yesterday and spoke of him glowingly. Or does she hope to catch him for Sophia as he reels from Lady Barsham's fury?"

"I like him. He calls spades spades and wrestles manfully with the law, which is a knavish box of tricks. He keeps a neat lodging in the city, very neat – that is the sailor in him. And he knows a good wine and he collects miniatures."

There were no more muffins. The Doctor brushed helplessly at a dribble of butter down his coat. Ann handed him his tea, smiling. No, he thought, she would never be beautiful, never, but her face, angled and stamped with such decisiveness, would grow only more distinguished with time; and could such large, brave eyes ever be less than arresting? The girl had style, he had always known it; and courage too.

"Mr Claverden a seagoing man? Does that explain his bearing, his brisk manner? I have thought once or twice he has the most terrible stare of any man I ever met."

"He was sent to sea at fourteen by his father, another nautical gentleman, but the father died and the guardian, an uncle of strong opinions I believe, cut him out forthwith and put him to the law. He qualified, came of age, bid farewell to the uncle and ran headlong back to the Navy. In due course he was promoted captain to a sloop, an insignificant warship used mostly for reconnaissance work, but he did very well in her, gained a reputation for fairness and efficiency. I am not sure why he gave it all up: an unlucky love affair perhaps, there was one, or the mutinies of ninety-seven – that business touched him deeply, I know – or maybe the unlikelihood of being made post-captain, so few ships available, no influence in the Admiralty, his years away from the service. Who can say? At any rate he cut off his pigtail – I am entirely unconvinced he ever had one – and returned to the law."

"And is unhappy?"

"He desires the sea as Bombay Jack desires his native dust and heat. He will not admit it, but it is so."

This led to a digression on the plight of the mongoose, recovered but morose. The Doctor felt it would be a kindness to send him home on one of the Company's ships. "A fine East Indiaman," he said with a certain wistfulness, "and what a pleasant change from a frigate crammed with sick soldiers! How Jack would enjoy it!"

Returning to William they speculated a while on his sloop.

The Doctor, to whom sea voyages were anathema, was nonetheless quite able to describe a three-masted ship-rigged sloop, could even discourse knowledgeably on the difference between a cannon and a carronade, demonstrating with the help of a rolled-up piece of paper, the butter knife, and a lump of coal.

"I have asked for Mr Claverden's bill," Ann said at last, down on the floor retrieving the sooty cannon-ball. "I have sent several notes, none acknowledged, and I have visited his office twice without success. He wrote me a terse message after my second visit saying he must insist I make an appointment – as if I would not if I could! His clerk or servant or whoever that sinister little man is who lurks in the outer office – such an impassive stare he looks stuffed, at any rate unreal – was unable to suggest any convenient time and made me feel quite immoral for even daring to cross the threshold."

"Clipsby," said the Doctor by way of explanation, "his name is Clipsby and he used to be a gunner – on the sloop one supposes. He lost his leg, quit the Navy. He has a rare gift for figures, an instinct for business, and a devotion to William little short of miraculous. I should not take his attitude to heart; sailors have superstitious minds and strange ideas about women."

"So too have lawyers! Do you think your William will call, or shall I be forced to fly in the face of convention and disturb him at his breakfast as the only hope of settling my account?"

"Your account must be trivial. Perhaps he does not wish for payment."

"He has spent some time looking into the lease, has written several letters – to me, and elsewhere in the hope of further information. It has not been my experience that lawyer's letters come any more cheaply than noble horses." A gleam of a smile, "Oh, shall I call Maggie to sponge that lapel? And you have coal dust all over your breeches!"

But at that moment Miss Pennyquick entered on a wave of indignation. The room crackled too with the licking flames of Hollin's bad humour issuing from the kitchen beyond.

"They are all back," was the brief statement, "dripping bog all over the floor and wanting hot ale and pies. And the Warren is waterlogged and cannot be ploughed till June and there is not a stock-proof hedge this side of the Gorse. All the usual. And Hollin wants to quit."

"Does he mean it?" Ann could imagine the spitting, hit and run battle that must have taken place in the kitchen, as many pyrotechnics as a firework party and Miss Pennyquick, Hollin, Mrs McGinly and Jim Knight hurling insults like grenades.

"He says so."

"Then he can say so to me."

The Doctor stirred. "It is the rain, dear Miss P., the rain and the cold and the frustration of not being able to do the job he set himself. Tomorrow he will feel differently, will view the gappy hedges more philosophically."

But the following morning, though the wind had shifted to the west and was tearing at the newly-instated tiles on the barns Hollin was holding fast to his decision.

"You cannot leave now," Ann declared, reduced at last to a cry of anguish, an hour of placid argument having failed to shift him. "We have made a start and a good one. And I depend on your advice."

It was not entirely true, for he had been disobliging and recalcitrant more often than not, had fallen out with the men, had countermanded her orders. But lately he had seemed more settled, even mildly optimistic, had been known to smile, to crack a sour joke.

"I've had enough," he said, "I've had enough of this place, hogweed, thistles and damn clay."

"It is the same place it was the day before yesterday and you seemed content enough."

Hollin stood, tall and shambling, in a shaft of watery sunlight. The men were out in the yard waiting to start for the Warren, picks and spades and billhooks to hand. Rough voices and half-hearted laughter reverberated in the distance, punctuated by the occasional outraged shriek from Mrs McGinly at the kitchen door.

"It's the talk," said Hollin.

"What talk?"

"Talk of you and Gerard." A rascally pause. "I've no mind to work for a Gerard."

"A Gerard! But you work for me!" She found herself blushing though, shamefully crimson; his meaning was clear enough. And of course it was true there was gossip, how could it be avoided?

"For how long?" Hollin asked with a foxy look, eyes bright with triumph.

She ought to call him impertinent, she thought, ought to turn him out. But how could she? She had once wished him anywhere but at Thorn and she was ashamed at the memory. He loved this place, as she did.

"If that is how you feel there is nothing more to say."

He shuffled a little. She looked crushed and vulnerable, and young. And he suddenly had the wit to recall the day he had taken her round the farm, the way her face then had looked as it did now, as if the spirit had been quenched, as if the light had been blown out. His grudging admiration caught him up, overcame him. It was true, they had made a good start, and they still had seed to get in.

"I could stay until … until such time," he said.

She did not ask until what time; they understood each other perfectly well. She assented gravely, wondering why he had withstood siege for an hour only to capitulate so abruptly and inexplicably. One thing was certain, only with his cooperation would she achieve anything at Thorn but weeds: he knew every foot of the land, every drain, every pond, every bank of shade and exposed corner and band of sticky clay.

"I cannot see him leave us," she said to Tom later as they played draughts to the wail of the strengthening wind, "I may once have wished him to the devil, he was so cantankerous and contrary, but even the wreck of this place meant more to him than the wealth of all India."

"Poetic, but it might be true. He thinks you will marry Gerard." Tom always referred to Harry as Gerard and looked embarrassed and disagreeable as he did so.

"Does everyone think so?" A small voice, and hesitant.

"Would it surprise you if they did? Has he asked you?"

She dropped three draughts and was compelled to grovel on the hearthrug for them, straightening with a sigh, cheeks flushed. "No. No, of course he has not asked. Nor will he. I am ... I am a novelty to him. In a week or two his interest will turn elsewhere."

She believed it. She had no illusions about his attention, was quite convinced that to Harry Gerard she represented no more than Thorn — and thirty thousand pounds. Yes, he liked her boldness, her independence; he liked as much in his horses. But the gossips were right, it was the money he strove for, not her heart. So she told herself, over and over, in the long quiet reaches of every night and in the weary, crowded days, organising and planning. So she told herself every minute, it seemed; and then his brief touch stirred all her suppressed longing, her half-buried hopes of finding more to love in this life than an old house and the exacting land. She ached for him to kiss her. It was terrible, but it was true.

"I wish you would be careful," said Tom gently.

"Careful not to make myself the object of talk in the village? Or careful not to become the latest conquest of darling Sir Harry?"

He hated her to be bitter. He scooped up all the draughts in his large hands with a croak of annoyance and glared at her across the board. "It is not your feelings he cares for but your fortune," he declared. He had intended to be mild, to be comforting, but it was out now and he must bear the consequences.

She did not seem angry. For a moment he thought she had not heard him, deep in some study of her own. But then she looked up and smiled, a tight, thin smile that did not cheer him in the least, and said calmly: "I am sure you are right. I am certain of it. By the way, you never told me what happened to your mad dog. Did you find him? Was he shot?"

It took Tom a moment to gather his wits. "Oh, the dog. Yes. We found him way beyond Priddy's Barns and Turner did for the poor brute. Whether he was mad or not is another matter. He looked wild, I admit."

In the end, Ann was thinking, I will go mad for love of Harry Gerard, or for lack of him.

"No point in mourning for a dead dog," Tom told her, misinterpreting her sober look. "If he was really mad he could poison the whole district."

And he began to set out the draughts again, click, click, click, concentration wrinkling his brow and his tongue thrust between his teeth. "I will beat you this time," he said, and then, a little less confidently: "Well, at any rate, I shall try."

The next day brought domestic crises of the usual kind: Mrs McGinly with a cut finger and blood in the pastry, Tom confessing to the midnight consumption of a whole pork pie and a jar of strawberry jam, the kitchen chimney smoking them all out into the yard and garden, and Hollin's pony trampling down another ten yards of fence. Ann retreated to her bedroom, monastic in its simplicity, and sat in the blessed quiet writing yet another entreaty to William Claverden. Occasionally the screech of voices from below told of continuing drama; Ann put her hands over her ears and re-read her stilted phrases. He would send no answer, he had sent none to her other requests. She frowned. A crash from the yard and a raucous tirade of unimaginative swearing indicated a reluctance on the part of the pony to return to his stable while the fence was mended. Ann seized another sheet of paper and wrote furiously, spattering ink: 'Come at once. Most urgent. Do not fail me. Ann.'

"Pashman will take it," Miss Pennyquick said on seeing the slender letter. "He should call this afternoon."

"Will he deliver it direct?"

"If you pay him." Pashman delivered as direct as he could, Miss Pennyquick might have said, which was not always as direct as people liked. He was a carrier, as he frequently reminded his desperate customers, not a mail coach. All the same a shilling had been known to work miracles.

The letter was duly despatched and jogged its circuitous route to William's outer office and the brown hand of Clipsby. Pashman received something for his pains there too but possibly less than he had hoped for. Clipsby for his part shovelled the thing under William's nose with half a dozen others and made some disparaging remark about too much correspondence and too few settled accounts.

"Anyone would think you were entirely mercenary," said William, turning over the letters without much interest.

"Which we all knows you are not," was the rejoinder, "and which is why you needs to be looked after by someone who cares about the cash."

"Hmm. This case of Spencer's ..." William began, and then slid a fingertip into the papers before him and extracted one letter, the address on which appeared to have been written by someone in a passion.

Clipsby remained silent, waiting for orders. William forgot him, unfolding the single sheet, reading the sprawling summons.

"Miss Mathick becomes imperious," he said, more to himself than to the patient Clipsby, "though to tell the truth I have contrived to neglect her business. There is no help for it, Nat, I shall have to go."

Clipsby remembered Miss Mathick, he did indeed: a small, whip-thin, managing person who had looked as if she wanted to slap his face. He also recalled why it was William was neglecting everybody's business but Lord Barsham's and all the wrinkles on his much-wrinkled brow deepened considerably. He did hope the Captain was not falling in love again.

"Today, sir?" was his only enquiry.

William tossed the letter down. It was late already. By the time he reached Thorn it would be the hour of their evening meal and by the time he got home again ... Damn the girl! Why did she have to write now? And what had happened to send her into a rage, or such a fright — there were two blots, a drizzle of ink spots, a frantic, dashing signature — and make her so commanding?

At least the rain had cleared. William rode as fast as he cared to, which was sometimes very fast and sometimes less so, depending on whether his involuntary anxiety for Ann had got the better of his irritation or not. The country was bleak, the trees dripped. His horse's hooves gouged great holes in the mud and threw up sticky clods of turf when they galloped. The wind was still wintry, persistent and penetrating. By the time he reached Blackow Gorse and turned to drop down to Thorn William was in a strange frame of mind, half anger, half uneasiness. He did not like being summoned as if he were a straying dog, especially by a young woman who had stirred his interest and tickled his admiration. He slowed the horse to a trot in the slippery lane and turned in at the buildings. The place looked handsomer already, he saw: the roofs were sound and the gates had been mended, and he could see sheep in the wide pasture behind the house. How much of her money would be left in twelve months, he wondered, if she was really determined to see this project through? He dismounted stiffly and cast about for Hollin.

Nobody appeared at his shout. Seeing there was no help for it he put the horse in the first empty stall he could find and splashed crossly to the back door. He entered on his knock, still charged with conflicting emotions, and so discovered Miss Pennyquick in the act of throwing a fistful of uncooked pastry at a very small cat.

"Lord!" was her frightened exclamation as he burst in, "but you should have come in the front!" For a moment she did not recognise him but looked as startled as if he were a robber, her eyes round marbles in a dead-white face.

"I did not think the front was ever used. Is Miss Mathick at home?" He removed hat and cloak.

"Yes, sir." An ungracious, ungraceful bob of a curtsey and a hard stare of something bordering on dislike, "She is going through Mr Forsie's bedroom. If you would step into the parlour I …"

William dropped the cloak and hat on the settle and made a quick appraisal of her floury hands and the wreck of her pastry-making over the great elm table. The cat, presumably caught in the act of thieving the contents of the pies, was keeping out of range in the chair Hollin usually occupied by the fire. It was a little ginger cat, busy with its paws, washing scrupulously.

between each toe. There was certainly no evidence a formal evening meal was about to be eaten, and there was the resinous smell of the oven firing. William felt his stomach contract and cursed himself for an optimistic fool.

"I have very little time, Miss Pennyquick. May I not go up?" And before she could protest he had opened the staircase door by the side of the fireplace and had vanished upwards, his boots clattering on the worn oak. Miss Pennyquick, decorating a pie with dexterity but no imagination, wished him joy of his encounter and did not bother to call after him that he had used the wrong stairs.

On the back landing William blundered into three empty rooms before he found the door to the front part of the house. A distant banging followed by a smothered exclamation of annoyance drew him to a doorway opposite the main stairway and he entered with something of the ferocity of a man in command of a boarding party, coat-tails flying.

The room was big and square, and in chaos: drawers opened, papers everywhere, books in toppling piles, a spilled vase of dry flowers in the grate along with a pile of cold ashes, a quantity of furniture anonymous under dustsheets, and a blaze of candles over everything, candles stuck on shelves, on a table, on a pile of … what? Wig-stands?

In the middle of the floor Ann sat cross-legged in a dowdy blue dress reading a letter. Her hair was loose, tumbled to her shoulders in a mass of curls, and her feet were bare. The Ann Mathick of Mrs Palmer's ball, of the beguiling rose pink and undeniable, surprising grace, might never have existed. But her look as William crossed the threshold with such violence was almost reproachful and not at all as startled as he had hoped.

"You sent for me." He stood there with an air of rather insolent arrogance, as if he were defying her to treat him again like a servant. He was punctiliously clean, correct, and conservative, and only his dark eyes, narrow and shining, suggested the devil lurking within. The light glittered on his cropped head and showed up, to his advantage, the strong lines of his face. "Well?"

93

Any other young woman, found shoeless and with her hair down in a welter of dust, junk, and antique correspondence, would have blushed at least, he thought. Ann Mathick gave a warm smile and stood up slowly, scattering letters like leaves.

"I did not think you would be so prompt," she said amiably, stooping to thrust a clutch of papers into an old leather satchel. "Have you galloped all the way?"

Was she laughing at him then? He subdued his rising temper only with an effort. "I really am very busy. I can spare you half an hour, no more."

She blew out all the candles except two in candle-holders, and handing one to William led the way with the other down the main staircase.

"I will keep you no longer than five minutes. Did you come in through the kitchen? We have become much grander since your last visit and try to receive callers by the front door. I expect you terrified poor Babs. She has taken over from Mrs McGinly owing to Mrs McGinly's retiring to bed with a cut finger and a headache — I fear Tom caused the headache — and it was baking day, of all days, everything to do, the oven contrary, and Hollin a veritable Jeremiah."

By this time they were in the drawing room. Ann had achieved wonders with half a dozen hairpins but curls still escaped the knot and sprang across her slender neck. William watched her bend to the fire and then, remembering his manners and his better nature at the same time, strode across to take the poker from her cold and dusty fingers. "Let me. But what is it you wished to see me about? What is so urgent I must break my neck for it?"

She was looking for something behind a chair. Her voice was indistinct. "I did not ask you to break your neck, Mr Claverden. I am sorry if the note was terse and ... misleading, but I had been reduced to desperate measures. I do not like to owe money. I have been trying to settle my account with you for some weeks and since you cannot find a moment in which to send me a bill I have made a wild guess at the sum involved and have ..." — she emerged breathless, clutching two dusty bottles; laying them on

the cushions she reached down again and produced two more —
"... decided to pay you in kind."

Two brandy, two claret; they promised well. Ann did not deny they might turn out to be vinegar, she had no idea how long they had lain in the secret recesses of Francis Forsie's cellar.

"Are they acceptable?" She mistook his turmoil of emotions for just one: speechless surprise. She brushed away one of the curls and left a smudge of dirt on her cheek.

"They are quite acceptable," was all he could say, burning with anger, shock, bewilderment, and a flat sense of anticlimax. So what *had* he hoped from her?

"The Doctor told me you appreciated a good wine. I am truly sorry for the note — it was my last resort; but then I did not imagine you would act on it so furiously."

He wondered now why he had done so. Then she crossed to him, took the poker gently.

"Please put it down. You look so fierce. Was it so very disgraceful, commanding you to come?"

"I thought there had been an accident, some upset with Gerard at least," he said stiffly, looking bleakly down at her neck and the straying brown hair as she lodged the poker in its place.

"Then you must forgive me. And as to Sir Harry Gerard ..." Her hands plucked suddenly at her shabby blue skirt, and she stopped, and lifted troubled eyes to William's face.

Was it an appeal? If so, how dare she! The Doctor had said she was losing her reason over Harry Gerard, that she had gone riding with him, walking, that the fellow was always at Thorn. Well, she would hear no praise, no congratulation from William Claverden.

"I cannot like him, or trust him," he exclaimed. "It will surprise me greatly if he intends to pay off all his debt. Indeed, I seriously doubt he has the means."

"Perhaps it no longer matters whether he has the means or not. We will come to some agreement. And in spite of everything I like him, Mr Claverden. He is good company. How many people do you know who are unfailingly cheerful?"

"None. And I have a suspicion Harry Gerard is not unfailingly anything either, except perhaps unreliable. He lays siege to Thorn, the Doctor tells me. Have you asked yourself why?"

She met his penetrating look. "He is after my fortune," she said with a smile, "is that not what they all say?"

He suspected it was, though his sole source of information was the Doctor and the Doctor was no gossip. He gathered his gloves, the wine. "I am glad to see you have no romantic illusions."

"Of course not. Why should I?" A look like a tigress, a lift of that chin. "Any I had were dispelled long ago by a clerical gentleman who briefly – oh, so briefly – wished to become my husband." She had started for the door. "It is dark already. I did not realise it was so late. You must stay to dinner. I know Babs spoke of a chicken to roast. Or would it be considered yet another scandal if you ate here with two unmarried ladies and Francis Forsie's natural son?"

This was no way to treat William Claverden; his scowl deepened. He could not wait for dinner, he said, expressing perfunctory regrets that fooled no one; there had been no chicken in evidence, he remembered.

No one answered Ann's call. They stepped into the kitchen where Miss Pennyquick was choking on ashes as she swept out the oven ready for the bread, and for the pies, tarts, biscuits, small cakes, and buns ranged over the table waiting their moment. William took up his hat and cloak.

"Such a late bread-making," he remarked innocently.

"We have been attended by disaster and delay all day," Ann said. "The oven has been fired twice already."

A hostile stare from Miss Pennyquick said all the rest. William gave a wry smile. "The wine," he said abruptly, feeling a sudden obscure need to mend this awkward relationship, "may I leave it with you? Perhaps you will allow me to call for them," and he stood the bottles on the table by the pies, "on a day when I am not riding the cob. The saddlebags are hardly big enough."

In spite of his protests Ann carried a lantern to the stable for him; Hollin had retired to his cottage long ago after a row with Miss Pennyquick, she told him. In the stall where he had left his horse she held it up, swaying a little.

"Mr Claverden, have you ever heard of Sable Island?"

He was busy with the girth. "Sable Island? I recall it lies south-east of Halifax. A devil of a place for wrecks, they say. But I have never sailed in those waters."

The lantern dipped and steadied. "There is not another of that name somewhere ... somewhere off the coast of Africa?"

He gave a shout of laughter. "Africa! No, indeed! Unless, of course, I have missed it on my charts."

Ever afterwards he would remember her face in the glow of the lantern, the draught easing more curls from their precarious knot, her eyes like pools of peat water, deep and dark.

"Harry Gerard talks of it, he often talks of it. I wondered ... You have been at sea a great deal, I know. I was sure you would be able to tell me where it was."

William had been going to bow and stick a foot in the stirrup. His feelings were still on the boil. Furious with himself for running at her call, furious at being tricked, taken aback by her motive, her present of the wine, moved by her when he had no wish to be: all this and more made him want to leave without ceremony, ride out his bad temper on the road back to Norwich. But her face in the soft light was white, intensely serious. Why was he not able to resist this steady, direct appeal? And what *was* all this about Sable Island?

William forgot his hurry to go, his curt goodbye, and reached out to take her free hand in his large warm one. "To the best of my knowledge the only Sable Island in the world lies off Nova Scotia, but if you wish, if it is important, I will make enquiries."

She smiled, withdrew her hand. "Do not trouble yourself about it," she told him, "it is of no importance at all."

For she could not bring herself to tell him that so far she had only discovered two things in the world to stir true passion in Harry Gerard, so true she did not doubt him when he spoke of them, nor mistake the shining in his eyes, nor his open boyish delight: one was his horse, the fretful grey, on whose back he was a god; the other was Sable Island, that most mysterious paradise.

A quick perusal of the larder revealed only cheesecakes, a cold boiled tongue, suspect mutton, and a derisory amount of souchong tea. Ann, with a reproachful look, added another six items to her comprehensive list and then stood on her toes to peer out into the yard. Tom had just returned from Scole with the new draught oxen, great mild beasts, tired and bewildered.

Lists. Life had been reduced to lists: of things needed, things to be done, of crops previously grown and in what fields, of crops growing, of crops to be grown, of fodder, of beasts, of implements. And every day the wind blew and the trees bent double and it was cold.

She left lists and larder, left the cutting of the loaf sugar, left the pile of accounts on her little desk. She pulled on a cloak, stout boots, gloves, and let herself out of the front door, crossing the Home Field and then the Hayfield at the foot of Warren Hill, making her way steadily up and up, until she gained the top and the trees – and freedom. Now she struck off across the Gorse, hugging the cloak to her, stung by wind and dipping branches. Up here the wilderness, which seemed to her natural and ancient, did not fill her with the same misgivings as the poor, sallow, condemned fields. No one had struggled long years to wrest this place into profitability or order, its rankness was nothing new, nothing that could be laid at Francis Forsie's door. But the fields, her fields, what was to be done with them? Already she had spent more money than she cared to think about and once or twice had bought dearly too: bad corn, a bad horse, an unreliable labourer. Some days she believed she would win the fight, was determined to win; other days despair drove her to this rank grass, to these tangled copses and useless ponds.

She had come to Thorn resolute, charged with purpose: the farm would prosper. There would be fat cattle on Carr Meadow and corn, corn to astonish, down the stony slopes of Pigg's Piece. But in terrifying moments of honesty, rising at dawn to open the shutters and look down on her decrepit yards, her weedy garden, she doubted she could ever succeed. When these black moods struck she could do nothing but hang on and endure, walk herself silly on the Gorse or by the river. She had no one with whom to share the misery: Hollin was still sceptical, still apt to take refuge in monosyllabic resistance; Tom was too inexperienced, still finding his place; Miss Pennyquick, though her loyalty was now unshakable, clearly thought her a fool to have such grand schemes; and the Doctor ... The Doctor was never there when she needed him.

There was a shout from behind, the sound of hooves. She turned to find Harry pulling up two yards away, sweeping off his hat.

"Dear Ann, you look lost and wild. Are you not cold up here?"

"I have grown used to it."

He dismounted, fell into step. His concern touched her. For he was concerned, she was sure of it. His moods were mercurial though: he might laugh in a moment, and mount and be away.

"A sad view," he said as they paused to take a long look at the distant water meadows, the swollen river. Ann was silent. He looked into her face and appeared to read it carefully: the shadowed eyes, the tiny frown. Then he took her arms, a hard, determined grip. "I will not tolerate such a down-hearted Ann Mathick. I told you it would be a thankless task and so it is, but you must not let it break your spirit."

She looked up a little shyly into his thin, eager face. "You warned me it would do so a long time ago. Perhaps it has."

"No! No!" For if he loved anything it must be her stubborn optimism, her strength, her fortitude. "Tomorrow things will look better. You are never cast down for long."

She was not prepared for his kiss, so swift and sweet, not prepared for the warm life of his lean body against hers, not at all prepared for the rush of longing. He let her go the moment after and turned his face towards the water meadows again.

"I remember telling you I had never met anyone like you. That is the truth. And we are not indifferent to each other; I am glad of that."

She thought that perhaps he was not as glad as he could be, that he was drawn to her reluctantly, that he was undecided whether to resist. But who knew what went on in that head of his? For who knew at what minute he would play the fashionable squire and what minute the undisciplined child?

"I must go home," she said, shaken.

The grey horse trampled all round them, rolling his eye. Harry swore. He gave Ann a quick, desperate look as if he wanted something of her but was afraid to ask, or maybe did not even know what it was. Then he said dully: "I wish I had met you years ago. I do. I do indeed," and he mounted, gathered up the horse, replaced his hat.

And then he was gone, leaving her staring at the bold imprint of impatient hooves in the mud.

6

MAY. The dust covers were being removed at Blackow Hall. Harry was home again after some weeks in London and rode daily on the Gorse, watching Ann's ox team wrestling with the elements. The wind, the eternal wind, was strong and cold. At last, skidding down to Thorn, he dismounted on the kitchen doorstep and gave himself up to Miss Pennyquick's dubious hospitality; Ann was in High Common with the Doctor and was not expected back for an hour.

He waited. Sprawled in Hollin's chair he cradled a mug of ale and stared into the flames and waited. Mrs McGinly let it be known she was affronted; Miss Pennyquick, ablaze with memories of the dairy, was taciturn to the point of rudeness and made no move to offer anything to eat or even a second mug of ale. When Ann blew in, hat aslant on her springing curls and skirts hemmed with mud, she found them sunk into a gloom of antipathy; the atmosphere was thunderous.

"Have you been waiting long?" she asked, divining Miss Pennyquick's thoughts if not Harry's.

"All morning."

"But you should have let me know you might call. I had an appointment in the village and then had to call on Mrs Palmer who is planning picnics of all things and wants some 'young people' to make merry at them. I might have been there hours but we were interrupted, thank Heaven."

They were in the drawing room now. There was no fire and the window was open to the playful wind. Harry stood at ease on the Turkey rug and dug his hands into his pockets, the sun striking in to light his brown head. He was dressed well. But when, Ann wondered, had she ever seen him other than well dressed? And he was smiling at her as if she were the woman above all others he would choose to be with.

"I have been in London," he announced, "winding up my affairs. I have decided to live at Blackow."

Retrenchment, was her first thought. He was wearing a ruby pin in his neckcloth, almost lost in the folds of starched white. Not retrenchment then. Perhaps a desire for temporary anonymity? William had sent her some slight and tangled information about Harry's private life that had not surprised either of them: women, gambling, the usual overindulgence of a man with money and fluctuating sense. It was possible he was being pressed by creditors, gently, insistently pressed; a month or two in the country might seem expedient, even pleasant. On the other hand, Ann had seen the windows of the Hall shining with a new brilliance as she had swept over the Gorse in the high-wheeled gig: clean windows suggested servants, servants suggested a prolonged stay.

"I wished to see you most particularly," Harry was saying.

"About my rent?" It was a joke between them now, but her swift, happy smile met no response.

"No, not about the rent." An unusual hesitancy, a sliding away of his eyes put her on her guard. "Surely we have forgotten that business?"

Ann sat on her favourite chair by the empty hearth and gazed beyond him to the desk where she struggled with her accounts and wrote biting notes to William Claverden about the lease, about Harry's parlous finances, about Sable Ísland – and where she read his biting replies. She remembered almost every phrase he had written; he was as economical with words as if he expected every one to be translated into a naval signal. And the one memorable time he had called at Thorn since her presentation of the brandy and claret he had simply said: "You will find it easier to get snow to fall in June than to get any more money from that fly boy." It was not the money, Ann had protested again, it was the land she wanted, that precious sweep of well-drained land for her South Downs. Would not Sir Harry let her use it anyway now? Was she not on intimate terms with Sir Harry? Had she not already said she and Sir Harry would reach some perfectly satisfactory agreement?

"Are you listening?" Harry asked.

She nodded, her eyes returning to his face, only he swerved away to the window as if, after all, he found it embarrassing to face her. He took his hands out of his pockets and braced them against the frame, staring out at the garden where she had made some slight impression on the luxuriant neglect.

"Would you consider marrying me?"

At first she thought she had misheard. In the silence she could hear the deep tick of the longcase clock, the muffled, unmelodious wail that was McGinly singing over the supper pans.

"Marry you?" Her voice was scarcely audible.

"Marry me." He rounded on her, appealing, eyes lit with laughter and enthusiasm. "What a match it would be! All the land from High Common to the river, from Hackthorpe to Upgate, would be ours – and you, dear Ann, would send imperious invitations to Lady Barsham she dare not refuse and would have the largest flock of Leicesters in the county!"

"South Downs." Ann sat improbably still. For a moment she felt she had stopped breathing but that was foolish. Her cheeks were cherry pink, she pressed her palms to them.

"Forgive me, I was expecting a business proposition." Her smile was strained, her eyes cool and dark.

"Do you not care for me?"

She was silent. Then: "Ann, do you not care for me? Should I go on my knees? I have never found myself in this position before, proposing to a lady who doubts my sincerity."

"You mean all the ladies to whom you have proposed thought you were serious? Good Heavens!" She had recovered, was ready for anything.

"Ann, you do care for me. Say you do. Say you will marry me. What's the matter? Has that devilish lawyer been putting out stories about me? A harsh, unsympathetic man, a puritan."

Ann, in a storm of emotion, could only say stupidly: "Oh, get up, do not play the fool like this! You will ruin your breeches grovelling on the floor and Babs will bring the tea in a moment and think you have lost your senses. I could not possibly marry you! How on earth could I marry you!"

"Easily. So easily."

"You want my money," and she saw his slight movement, the almost imperceptible shying away; she had stung him then, had hit the mark. "There is not so much as there was."

"I care very little for your money." Her look warned him not to deny he had any interest at all. "I have enough of my own. You have not seen Blackow recently. You would be amazed. It is being cleaned attics to cellar, fires lit, furniture moved; new curtains, new everything. My father would have approved, would he not? I am giving up London entirely. And how could I hope to run the estate with no money – no money of my own?"

And then it was as if his energy could no longer be contained, he could not bear to stay still another moment – or perhaps he was afraid she would think too deeply about his question and come to some intelligent answer. He reached for her hands, pulled her up. "Oh, come out of this place! Come out! I cannot abide it here! No, you do not need a cloak, the wind is slackening."

But up on the Gorse the wind was keen and devilish. Harry strained her against him, and kissed her, and kissed her. "You see," he cried, "how easy it is. We love each other!"

Was this love then? This and this? Could he bring her to a shivering wreck so quickly: no strength, no self-control, no will? He made her mad for him: a farm girl in a ditch, every minute stolen, could not have been more ardent. And if she surprised herself she surprised Harry. Who could have expected this wanton? He was almost afraid for a moment of what he had wakened, but the moment passed, for her back was against one of the oaks now and he could do with her as he liked. He could have taken her there and then but the sound of carriage wheels and the shrill yapping of small dogs did something to restore them to their senses.

"Marry me! Marry me and be damned to the gossips!"

"Give me time ..."

Her mouth looked bruised, her chin certainly was. What time did she need? What was there to consider?

"Until tomorrow," he said, and released her.

They walked a few yards side by side but not touching. "You will never be happy here," she told him suddenly.

"I was once. I do not remember how long ago. I swear to you, the only place I shall ever abandon Blackow for is Sable Island. You would adore Sable Island, I know it."

"Would I?"

"I shall take you there."

"When?"

"When ... When it is possible. You must go alone from here. They will be watching out for you. I shall walk back across the Gorse."

She still did not seem able to breathe properly, nor to grapple with the mundane. "Your horse," she said wildly, "what about your horse?"

"I will fetch him tomorrow," and he had left her, striding away towards Blackow as if he could not bear her company a moment longer.

"That man means no good," Miss Pennyquick announced, finding Ann in her chair in the drawing room several hours later.

"Harry Gerard?" The name was like a sigh.

"Who else? I saw him coming down the hill looking about him as if he owned the farm. Then he sits in the kitchen with an ale pot. What gentleman would do that?"

"The Doctor would."

"The Doctor lives by his own laws, could sit in the gutter up Ber Street and still be respectable."

"All right, my uncle then."

Miss Pennyquick made a queer noise, half derision, half anger. "Your uncle ... The Gerards never brought him any good. He loved Caroline Gerard, perhaps she was the only woman he ever loved. And she led him a dance from Upgate to Blackow and back again, made him look a fool, an old fool and a blackguard. Well, he was neither of those. He was rough and shrewd and hard, not cruel, not vicious, not dishonest. Then she turned him on his head, had him running out like a silly boy to meet her in the woods, rode in here laughing and made fun of him where the servants could hear. He had always liked his bottle – the Forsies did – but she sent him blind roaring drunk. After she left him, left Blackow, he cared for nothing. He wallowed in wine and self-pity till he died."

Ann said: "Yes. Yes, I see," and then, even more distracted, "I have a letter to write. And tell Mrs McGinly I will not want any supper."

She sat at her desk to write it, pushing aside the painstaking accounts, the lists, the bills. She felt as if she was drowning in shame, and yet she knew that if he appeared at her window she would go out to him, would not care if anyone saw her. She put her face in her hands, tried to think of the future, of the farm, of marriage. You will not be happy, said an inner voice, this is lust, lust, lust. She took up her pen. What could she write? I want him, I should not want him, please help me? How impossible. How could she even confess to such a frenzy of longing? Her pen spluttered, stopped. With an effort she forced herself to add another line, to sign properly and boldly underneath. He would never recognise what it was, never guess it cried out for his help, for him to come to her as his most austere, analytical self, biting, bracing. Even his name was a shout: 'Doctor Alexander French', but he would not know it, would only think her ink had been mixed a little too strong.

It was dark already, she could scarcely see. She walked slowly to draw the curtains, to light the candles, and saw, high over Warren Hill, the bright cold crescent of the new moon.

Dr French was out all night with a fever case and away half the next day delivering a baby and sewing up a leg wound he privately felt had only a slender chance of coming right. Even then he did not open his correspondence, though Heaven knew there was enough of it, until he arrived in Norwich for a medical dinner attended by a great many eminent and some few very frivolous people but all of them out to eat and drink as much as possible. Between mouthfuls of a sort of blancmange that struck him as a dish fit only for invalids, he contrived to look at Ann's letter and cast a hopeful eye over the scrawled lines.

He choked on the pudding and was heartily thumped between the shoulder blades by his neighbour, an ebullient young surgeon from Suffolk. "Bad news? I hope not."

"No, no. This appalling concoction! If you like it, pray eat mine."

The young doctor did so. In the background a scrape of violins announced an after-dinner entertainment of lugubrious and respectable boredom. Dr French jumped up, made scanty apologies – heard all over the hall and sounding like a pack of lies – and ran for his coat and gloves.

"What is it?" William said, opening the door to him as several church clocks struck eleven.

"I have received this. Read it! That outrageous Gerard has proposed marriage!"

William hauled off the Doctor's coat and urged him to the fire. It was a chilly night. He barely read Ann's brief letter before reaching across the paper-strewn desk for one of his own.

"I was handed this an hour ago. Clipsby had it from that fellow Pashman. It must have been in every taproom in Norwich."

Dear Mr Claverden,
    Yesterday I received a proposal of marriage from Sir Harry Gerard. Today I have accepted him. In the circumstances it would be dishonourable of me to ask you to enquire further into his financial affairs.
                    Yours very sincerely
                    Ann Mathick

"My God!" said the Doctor, and then: "Young Tom delivered mine last night, in the dark, Lal said. William, I have failed her."

"What are you talking about? All she says is that he has asked her to marry him, that she does not know what to do, that she needs the advice of a friend. Two lines. If you had given your advice she would not have taken it. And did she expect you to ride out to Thorn at midnight, hang your business, your comfort, you health?"

"She did," said the Doctor, "and I should have gone."

The rain was nothing more than a drizzle now but it blew dispiritingly across the water meadows; all the far woods were lost in mist. Ann, leaning on the gate of Pigg's Piece and watching a heron coming in to land along the river bank, blew on her cold hands and shivered.

The sun had deserted them for almost a week. Tom, Jim Knight and Hollin had been out every day to the straggle of copses between Warren Hill and the Gorse, hacking, chopping, clearing the debris of years. The oxen, finished with their patient trudge of the sodden earth, took to hauling logs with remarkable docility, but then, as Jim pointed out when Ann had walked up to view progress, they would do anything for young Tom. She could see them now, six harnessed two-by-two to the dead oak felled only yesterday, waiting for the signal to start back to Thorn; and there were the men, bent forward as they walked, sacks over their shoulders to keep off the wet, gathering up the last ash rods and hazel thinnings. In a sweep to their left the long incline of Warren Hill, a haze of young green, and below and below, beyond where she herself was standing, the flat meadows fringed by osiers and willows, dotted with her poor collection of cattle.

The middle of May, the hedges a cloud of blossom, half of it dripping and ruined. A cursed week and not only for the unseasonable weather. The Doctor had almost lived in the wing chair by her fire, persuaded to move only when the clamour of the bell heralded some distraught patient. Between times he had been everything from cajoling to rampantly furious, and his much-abused wig was more often on the floor than on his head, his surgical instruments scattered on the writing desk, his neckcloth awry. Who was he, Ann demanded, to take up residence in her house and give her gratuitous advice? He should have come before, said her look, it was too late now.

It was not, to be strictly truthful, advice that he gave her: he told her plainly not to marry the man. He swallowed what Mrs McGinly put in front of him – and Mrs McGinly, who thought him a great character and worthy of cherishing, did him proud with lamb, trout, soused herrings, no mutton or hash all week – and he fixed Ann with a glinting eye and told her she was a fool, that she would pay for her folly the rest of her life, that she would be left at Blackow penniless with six children while Harry died of drink or the pox in some London gambling den; that the only friends she would have after six months would be spongers and charlatans, thieves, tapsters, nagsmen, cockfighters; and at one point, inflamed by her intransigence, he had taken leave of all civility and the whole of his unreliable temper and vowed it would be better if she let Harry Gerard bed her here and now rather than marry him simply for the sake of respectability.

The flood of wine as she had knocked over her glass had been scarcely redder than her cheeks. "How can you say so?" she whispered.

"It is not a crime to want a man, dear Ann. Have him by all means if you must. But do not marry him, do not give him control of your affairs. In the long run you will lose no more in the eyes of the world than if the Archbishop of Canterbury had blessed the union."

There was a silence during which he realised he had hit upon some truth, that quite probably if she could square such behaviour with her upbringing and her own ideas of moral conduct she would indeed allow Harry Gerard to do as he pleased; perhaps if marriage was not in question she would do so anyway, unable to withstand him. But marriage was in question – and it offered her the chance to salvage her self-respect.

"Do you love him?"

"I do not know."

"And I do not believe," the Doctor said, "you know what love is."

After this he removed himself to High Common, wrote a note by way of apology "for such presumption", hoped she would always count him her friend. He could not know it but she almost cried over this and even, now he had gone, missed his insufferable company, his wig on the coffee pot, his pipes in the knife box.

The one person she had hoped, a little absurdly, might call in person to give her his congratulations or otherwise, simply sent his latest bill instead – improbably small, which angered her – and a stilted line expressing his obviously false good wishes. It seemed she had seen the last of Mr Claverden. And as her world turned and faces came and went, opinions expressed freely all over the neighbourhood, gossip thick as treacle at every social gathering, it also seemed that she had mortally offended Babs Pennyquick, who became brusque and evasive, and took to spending more and more time in the kitchen with Mrs McGinly and Maggie. Whenever Ann pursued her there a tacky silence fell, an air of reproof, of holy indignation. And the pans glittered, the food was always on time and always excellent, the great table was scrubbed daily and was as impeccable as the holystoned deck of a man-of-war; the fire was a furnace. Ann came to dread crossing the threshold, so much did this show of excellence act as a reproach – though why it should be so she could not explain. She appreciated this was quite possibly her household's way of coping with a crisis but its extraordinary effectiveness startled her; why did she find herself so moved by half a dozen sparkling plates and dishcloths white as her petticoats?

Tom, taking a lead from Hollin, turned mulish and would hardly speak.

"Do you really think I would turn you out of Thorn?" Ann demanded on the Thursday of that sunless week, helping him plant vegetable seed in the patch of garden he had won, unaided, from the nettles at the back of the house. "I have settled that Jim and his family will move in when I leave; I want to take Mrs McGinly with me to Blackow but that is for her to choose; Maggie is staying on. You have no reason to be anxious."

He had grown, she noticed, even taller and broader. His open face, very fair and freckled, usually so cheerful, was now hard and reproachful. He had acquired a new maturity in his months at Thorn, in his work with the men on the land, on the backbreaking ploughing and seeding; he was nineteen as far as they could tell, a great deal older than anyone had supposed.

"Blackow is only a mile away across the Gorse," she said gently, since he was clearly not going to admit he was afraid for his own future.

"Could be China for all I shall see of you there," was his reply, in his worst, gruffest, most countrified voice, the one she knew he kept for just such occasions.

"Would you like to go to China?" She was grasping at the frivolous to avoid the need for conflict, private or public. She drew a neat drill with the hoe and watched him stoop to shake seed from his roughened hand. They were nice hands, she saw, large but long-fingered.

"Perhaps. Is that what you have in mind? Embark me on an Indiaman and send me as far away as possible? Or should I join the Navy?"

His stare was furious. Her innocent question had exploded in her face. "Do you truly believe I would do such a thing? I was simply asking ..."

But nothing was simple any more. Since that sleepless night she had spent by the cold ashes of the drawing room fire, the candle spluttering to nothing in the early hours and her bare feet blue with cold, and since that luminous, wet, fragrant morning Harry had returned for her answer and she had given it him, life had become complicated and unbearable. But she would not give up her plans, for Thorn, for Tom.

Tom was scowling. "That row is finished. When is the wedding to be? The Doctor said ..."

"Has he been talking to you about me? That was cruel."

"He looks worn to the bone and half as old again. I met him up on the Gorse yesterday, his pony had run him off the road and he had lost some papers and packets into a bog. I helped him fish them out."

111

His stare this time was doubly accusing. It was her fault then that a middle-aged man, undoubtedly eccentric, forgot to eat on account of her impending marriage to Harry Gerard. She gave a little cry of fury and anguish and suddenly sat, clutching the hoe, on the soft, tilled earth.

"Why is everyone against it? What does it matter to anyone but Harry and me?"

"You don't deny he is ..." a bleakly defiant face, rather scarlet. "well, a shifty cove."

"And what do you know of him, Tom Forsie?" He had become a Forsie quite naturally, as perhaps was only proper in the circumstances. "What does anyone know about him? He has not lived at Blackow since he was a boy."

The breeze lifted her soft curls under the straw garden hat she wore, and she seemed entirely unconscious of her clean skirts spread across the tidy rows of seed. She looked shy and distracted and yet her eyes flashed, her chin was up; she reminded Tom of the young deer in the woods at Upgate Place, half inclined to fly but held by some thread of courage, some imprudent curiosity.

"Babs says you have lost your senses." He felt he needed to goad her, needed to make sure she was sure, that she had thought out every implication.

"Perhaps she is right. I certainly feel that I have," was the honest answer he might, by now, have come to expect, "but I have the right to do so, have I not?"

"She says she cannot leave Thorn, that you may dismiss her but she cannot abide the thought of Blackow." He knew that would hurt her, almost hated himself for saying it, even knowing she must, oh, surely, surely, be quite aware of it already.

"I have no intention of dismissing her as well she knows. She is welcome to stay at Thorn. Connie Knight is praying she does, so Jim tells me."

There was a false brightness in her tone; she was not yet entirely resigned to quitting the house, now that it had become home, now that she had probed every dim and dusty recess, marked every slipping tile, battled like a lunatic with the fearsome kitchen chimney, unreliable in anything but a strong westerly.

"She don't like Gerard and I'll wager he don't like her," Tom said gloomily, eyeing his seedbed where Ann's skirts had swept across. "But she ought to go with you," and to her questioning glance: "Someone of your own."

If the vast Atlantic had separated Thorn from Blackow they could not have been further apart than they were in Tom's mind; that bare mile was an infinity of uncharted wilderness which she, in her stubborn idiocy, was going to cross in order to live among alien people. She sighed, took off the straw hat — what was the point of it, there was no sun — and looked up into Tom's pleasant, ruddy face.

"How we wish for so many things we cannot or should not have! And most of them selfish, if not all, and some positively wicked. I wish I did not have to leave Thorn, but I wish to marry Harry so I must; I wish to be free to make my own choice and yet I would be sorry if the Doctor, or Babs, or you, did not try to influence me because then I would know you cared nothing for me. You see the contrariness of things, the complexities and inconsistencies of human nature."

Tom, who had not been listening but who had been thinking irrelevantly how fragile and helpless she looked, crouched on the earth at his feet, bent down to raise her up and as he did so dropped a shy kiss on her curls and turned away immediately, groping for his seeds.

Later she sent him, with misgivings, in the gig to Norwich in order to deliver William Claverden's account by hand. She might have gone herself but instinct, whispering and clutching at the back of her distraught brain, told her that if anyone could snatch her from this marriage now William could. It was mysterious but there it was. Her earlier desire to see him, her hope that he might ride by to collect or even drink from one of his bottles, was quite dead. And in any case Tom was eager to go, he managed the white-legged chesnut better than she did herself, and he deserved a holiday from the unremitting drudgery of the farm. She gave him half-serious warnings about ale-houses — he probably knew more about such places than she did — and importunate ladies — even Norwich had more than enough of those – and how not to address Mr Clipsby in the outer office, a man no doubt used to taking a hand to powder monkeys and the like or even flogging men at the mast or whatever they did in the Navy; and then she gave him enough money to buy himself a new coat, seeing he could not live in his father's cast-offs for ever, and felt ashamed to watch his face turn scarlet with suppressed joy.

He returned late at night having walked from Trowse which was where the horse had disobligingly cast a shoe and not a smith at work or even to be found, and by the time he turned in at the yard everyone but Ann had gone to bed, or been sent there, and the kitchen fire was a smoulder of hot ash and red embers. He put up the horse and came in with a storm of energy, face aglow. He had not minded the walk, had even rejoiced in it; the night was cold for May but the stars were bright and clear, it was an inspiration to look up. The horse, sore-footed and subdued for once, had been companionable; the thought of Thorn, his assured welcome, his own clean bed, enormously comforting. He sat down at the table to demolish a cold pie and half a pound of cheese and most of the jug of ale, describing between mouthfuls the perfection of his new coat. Ann, with a sudden laugh, recognised a long line of Forsies, never without money to pay a tailor or a smuggler of good brandy, in every expansive gesture and dwelt-on particular. When she questioned him about his reception at the lawyer's offices he said he had done exactly as instructed, even down to his humble approach to the terrifying Clipsby, and that he had seen William himself 'all dressed up something wonderful to go to dinner with the Lord Mayor' – could that be possible? – and that William had been in one of his cross-me-and-I-shall-give-you-fifty-lashes tempers, black brows drawn together and stare like a basilisk. His hair was even shorter, Tom said with awe, if that were possible.

"But what did he say?" Ann demanded.

"He said he supposed you were too frightened to come yourself," said Tom with ingenuous honesty, "and the brown wrinkled cove with the pigtail said ha, he would not be at all surprised."

"Clipsby! What right has he to express any opinion on my conduct? But what about the letter, did Mr Claverden say anything to the letter?"

It had been a very short message asking William to call when he was in the neighbourhood and not to forget his wine, kept separate and closely guarded by Mrs McGinly in the cellar.

"He read it." Tom paused to wipe his mouth, looked wistfully at what remained of the cheese and decided against it with an effort. "I saw him."

"But he did not say anything at all?" Ann persisted.

"Oh, no." Another pause to cut a wedge of bread and wash it down with more ale. "Oh no, he tossed it on the fire."

Carr Meadow, Pigg's Piece, and half of Warren Hill were to be Tom's, on that score Ann was adamant. Miss Pennyquick's astonishment, Tom's bewildered exultation, the Doctor's amazement and gratification, washed and flowed about her like flood water round the drowned willows by the mill leat. She had sat up all night with the account books and a pile of musty deeds and receipts and bills of sale, with crackling old maps and mouse-nibbled volumes on the law of property. There were fifty acres sheltered in the bend of the river under the long climb of the Hill, two big fields, the woods, a rise of patchy heathland beyond. A man could build a house there within a toss of the road and farm as he liked.

It was almost June, the land emerald under the sun, the poor, straggling roses coming into fat green bud. Ann's face was delicately coloured, by the warm wind, by anticipation. Harry had not yet returned from London and his letters were not as frequent as she might have wished: 'So many accounts to settle ... am going to sell my government stock ... have sold the grey and the Town carriage, have bought a fine beast fit to carry emperors and a new curricle ...' Nevertheless Ann waited with excitement stirring, with longing rekindling at every fruitless post, every further delay, until only a vigorous walk over Warren Hill and the Gorse could cure her restlessness and once, to everyone's consternation, a wild ride on the white-legged horse, who took her from Thorn to High Common faster than she had believed possible and delivered her breathless at the Doctor's door. He was out so she was forced to ride back, her arms dragged from their sockets, her skirts rucked up. On the Gorse she met the Doctor's gig, bowling along at its usual rate, the horse in a mad state of excitement and the driver singing a bawdy sea ballad out of tune. He was miserable she had called when he was from home, he had been required at Upgate, Miss Charlotte with a temperature, a bright and fevered eye – nothing more serious, in his opinion, than a touch of William Claverden; she fancied herself in love. Ann smiled, persuaded him to Thorn to share her tea, and tried to charm him into his old easiness of manner, that happy state of burgeoning friendship. But what might have been with Ann Mathick of Thorn should not, or could not, be with Ann Gerard of Blackow. He was cheerful but somehow reserved, somehow wary, as if he feared to say too much at the least excuse, as if he could not bring himself to wish her well.

And then the day after she received a cursory letter from Harry, only adequately affectionate and almost tipsy in its confused dashings and underlinings: 'Do not fear, I shall be with you as fast as the mail can bring me ... I have lent the horse, best of horses, to a friend for a week ... Let us marry at once. What do we care for those carping fools? They are jealous, simply jealous. I can arrange a special licence. Let us marry the day after I come home."

It was not what she wanted but she thought it might be for the best. The plain old church where she sat every Sunday between Miss Pennyquick, in old-fashioned stays, and Tom, in Francis Forsie's full-skirted coat, was the place she had fondly imagined echoing her promises to Harry Gerard. It smelled of damp and beeswax and the fragile clerestory windows sprayed light across the regimented pews and worm-eaten pulpit.

And: "Is it proper to give me part of Thorn?" Tom asked that last Sunday, wrestling with the churchyard gate while Miss Pennyquick, out of earshot, talked jugged hare and prunes to Lady Barsham's housekeeper.

"Your father was a Forsie." Witness how well you look in his coat, Ann might have added.

"You do not know that." It was a challenge. His eyes met hers. Across the gate she gave him back his stare, trying to remember herself at nineteen. And then she did remember and started at the memory: her brief engagement, such stormy scenes before and after. How lucky the Reverend Fiddler had found another girl in time, a girl whose father could promote him to a substantial living and who could, presumably, stomach his pompous sermons on crushing the devil. Strong will in a woman was anathema, he had once told Ann, vanity a bestiality and carnal desire ... unthinkable, unmentionable. Her mother being a Forsie and therefore having strong opinions on most things including carnal desire, Ann begged to differ, having been brought up to challenge unqualified statements. Oh, the courage of nineteen and ignorance! Surely a wife and husband, she had suggested daringly that June evening in her father's garden, could desire and not sin? The Reverend Fiddler had been appalled, had read her a lecture on self-restraint, on purity, on the banishment of lewdness and a variety along those lines. Very soon after – after Ann's own tempestuous withdrawal – he had married Miss Brunswick.

"You do not know Francis Forsie was my father," Tom repeated, swinging on the gate with a boyish impatience. "Are you listening? He could have been anyone."

Ann shook her head, smiling. Her Forsie forbears were staring at her with irritation from his tanned face. Pray God he did not turn to drink or gambling, she thought, and end up as they all had, debauched and cheapened and in debt.

"Do you not want the land?" she asked as they walked to where the gig waited, the sun glinting on its splendid springs.

"Of course I do. But how will I manage?"

Miss Pennyquick was panting up behind them, almost blown asunder by the playful wind but saved by tight lacing and hatpins like meat skewers.

"Until you are of age the land will be in trust, the Doctor and Mr Claverden are the trustees. They are understanding and honest and they will not quibble at advancing you enough from the fund I have set up to enable you to buy seed and equipment."

He choked, brick red with embarrassment and happiness. He held the chesnut until Ann and Miss Pennyquick were seated and then let him go with a yell. The horse leaped away, so did a dozen others tethered by the wall. There were shouts and a din of exclamation, some smothered cursing and a shriek or two from the women. Tom, quite unmoved by the pandemonium he had caused, set off at a run after Ann and the gig, his face split by a huge grin, his hat snatched off and waving.

Back at Thorn Ann found Hollin astride the ridge of the cow byre pegging the last of the tiles. He looked his usual disagreeable self when she commanded him to come down for ale and cakes. He swayed precariously, dropping a hammer. He was too old for such antics, she thought, and his head for heights was suspect to say the least. She told him he was a fool and to come down at once.

"No more fool than you are," was the retort, "marrying a man with no money, no sense, and no Christian thoughts in his head."

"What does it matter to you? And why are you pegging tiles on a Sunday?" Was it, she wondered, Hollin's equivalent of Mrs McGinly's shining pans?

"You know what that rogue'll do with this place? He don't care for the land. He'd sell it soon as step through the front door and then you, not a brain in your head as far as a man can tell, will be out in the streets in your shift begging your bread." He pursed his lips, self-righteously, abrasively angry.

"Harry would not sell Thorn," she protested, but she felt a sudden chill about her heart.

Hollin bent forward. He was enjoying his superior position on the roof and meant to make the most of it, and he had never been a man to worry overmuch about the deference due to his employer.

"Don't his eyes size up every pennyworth when he lords it down the hill on his flash nags?"

Ann turned away. "What about the fifty acres going to Tom? I suppose that cannot please you either."

A grunt; the clatter of a dropped tile. "He looks like the old man. But he don't know nothing about the land yet."

118

"He can learn. Better Tom than Harry Gerard surely?" She wheeled to face him, furious, but the question was not quite as sarcastic as she would have liked.

"Both bastards," was Hollin's dry comment. "Of the two I would put my money on Tom; got it in him to be a gentleman."

She could not let it go. Whether she was angry at Hollin's audacity or the smothered suspicion he was half right she did not know, but anger overwhelmed her, and all the weeks of frustration and waiting and hoping, ignoring the Doctor's strictures and Tom's low looks and Miss Pennyquick's dark glances, burst into a positive fire and fury.

"You have no money!" she cried, and quite idiotically, for he had enough tucked away under his bed, Babs said, to pay for a dozen new suits and ten pounds of the choicest tea and had been seen to gamble prodigiously years ago on the only horse race ever to have been held in High Common.

Hollin gave a wheeze of laughter. "And when you are married to pretty Sir Harry you won't have nothing," he said.

7

BIGOTED OPINIONS apart – though there were plenty of those – the marriage was viewed with less scepticism than might have been expected. Under ordinary circumstances it would have been called a sensible match, but neither Blackow nor Thorn could be relied on to provide the archetypal hero and heroine. Apart from this there was a certain flavour of irony about the mixture – there had been twenty-five years of sour relations between the two families and such things, in remote communities, become legendary.

Among the congratulatory notes Ann discovered something more sobering.

Dear Miss Mathick,

The documents relating to the trust are now drawn up and require your signature. If you would care to call at my office at your earliest convenience the business could be completed in a few minutes – perhaps you could arrange with the Doctor some mutually convenient time.

Your humble servant
William Claverden.

The sly humour of the signature pierced her: William was no man's humble servant, nor any woman's she doubted, not even the lovely Charlotte's. Independent and self-reliant she had always found him; now she recognised a hardy intractability to match her own. He did not approve of her marriage and he was not going to great lengths to conceal the fact; on the other hand he would make no futile attempt to dissuade her as had the Doctor. It was a great mystery and childishly irritating that his attitude should cause her any heartache, but it did, and she was too honest not to admit it to herself at those moments when honesty triumphed over illusion. If he had thundered to her door and forbidden her, with one of his remarkable frowns, to commit the folly of marrying a Gerard, if he had laid bare her hopes, her shameless, ignorant desires, and all the frustrations and stifled ambitions of the last five years, in that hard, low voice now so familiar, well ... what might not have happened? She dreaded meeting him, having to speak. She shrank from his disapproval and despised herself for shrinking. She tried to dislike him or to be indifferent and could do neither.

She sent him a terse message saying simply: 'Wednesday at noon. The Doctor is agreeable. Ann Mathick.' and afterwards spent an hour grubbing out weeds with astonishing fury, plunging energetically into the far reaches of the garden until the whole place looked like a battlefield. Away from Harry she wondered at the nature of her love, and the little doubts that had always worried her in saner moments crowded in. When Wednesday came she was still in this strange mood and took two hours to dress instead of her usual fifteen minutes, scowling through her wardrobe but finding nothing suitable to give her the courage to even cross William's threshold, choosing, discarding, putting on and taking off. In the end she wore brown, a colour like Thorn mud and not flattering in the least, one of her old dresses from the north. It made her look sallow, and her plainest bonnet, the same dismal hue, made her look dull and undistinguished. Nevertheless she sailed downstairs on a tidal wave of determination: it had to be done, she would get it over as quickly as she could.

They took the trap, the gig only seating two, Tom and Miss Pennyquick both in uncertain tempers, though why was a mystery, especially after a breakfast fit for kings: smoked herring, bacon, at least two dozen eggs, toast, marmalade, a dish of chops and kidneys. Ann had eaten nothing, coming down to find Tom bloated among the debris, Miss Pennyquick silent but reproachful, staring in wonder at his broadening chest, his large hands, his straining waistcoat.

Hollin's pony took umbrage at being asked to trot into High Common and stopped dead at the first house; Tom soiled his best coat, his new one, lately delivered by the tailor, in getting him to think better of his obstinacy. At the Doctor's door they were met with the intelligence that the Doctor had already left for Norwich in his own gig, that he had been in a tearing hurry as he had to make a diversion at Fritton to sew up a finger, that he had gone out in his oldest coat and with no hat and would Miss Mathick oblige by taking his best of both and making sure they and their owner were somewhere united.

In Norwich, after a painfully uncomfortable and over-long journey, they confronted Clipsby with bold stares. Ann saw him start with astonishment at the bag she carried, large, shabby brown, clinking gently. With what seemed like a delicate dislike he ushered her into the quiet room where William stood waiting.

He looked his most striking – this was Ann's first thought – his exceedingly short hair allowing all attention to be on his face with its well-defined scar, its dark jaw and those shrewd eyes. He had an air of impatience, of controlled temper, as if he wished this interview well over and his quiet room rid of such irritating guests. He bowed over Ann's hand with the minimum of fuss and no warmth and exchanged brief remarks on the weather and the state of the roads with Miss Pennyquick, who kept discreetly to the rear, and then, with a white grin, asked Tom how he would like being a farmer.

Tom thought he would like it very much; he stood awkwardly, a fiery colour. He was scarcely an inch shorter than William and promised to be a good deal broader.

"The Doctor is late," William said with resignation, for he was well acquainted with the Doctor's imperfect time-keeping. "It would be unfortunate if the appointment had slipped his mind."

"He was called to Fritton to a butchered finger," Ann told him, heaving her bag on to the table and untying the string. "If he can persuade the horse to face in the right direction he should be here shortly."

The brandy and claret were revealed; there was an awkward little pause. William tried to smile but it did not reach his eyes. His glance was level and considering, as it always was.

"I did not mean to neglect your invitation."

"I am quite sure you did not." Oh, you did, you did, she thought. And why should I care? Why should I? "Is that the Doctor? We have had instructions how to make him presentable, have brought his best coat and hat."

A noise of greeting, explanation, the sudden bursting open of the door, and there he was, Clipsby pulling anguished faces behind him, left in possession of a glass jar containing something pickled.

"William! Am I late? No, on the hour!" The wrong hour but they did not have the heart to point it out. "Would you mind telling Clipsby to be especially careful with my finger; he vows he will not have it near him."

Words were exchanged at the door, murmurings of dissent and disgust from the other side. Tom was moved to ask whether the Doctor preserved all the limbs he amputated and the Doctor said no, most sorrowfully, he had not the room and in any case very few had any value for research. Miss Pennyquick, feeling queasy, stopped Tom's next query – on the value for research of such a small specimen as an ordinary finger – by rushing in with: "Your coat, Doctor, and your hat, sent up with us by your cook," and grovelling for them in the depths of the capacious bag in which they had been packed.

The Doctor raised one mobile brow and gave a disconcerting grin. He was sorry, he said, if he offended anyone by appearing in his working clothes. Nevertheless he stripped off his vile bottle green and shrugged himself into neat black superfine, allowing Ann to settle the crumpled lapels.

William returned, rather cross, rather steely about the eye. They turned their attention to business. An hour passed. The nature of the trust was explained, its documents spread on the table beside the venerable brandy. Clipsby marched in, marched out, glared at the Doctor, brought glasses on a shining tray. The claret was opened, opinions expressed as to its nature, its origins, its temperature.

"To Ann," Tom said self-consciously, lifting his glass of the stuff. "I hope I make as good a farmer as she predicts."

William cocked a straight black brow. "Miss Mathick is that rare being, the complete optimist," he said drily, and they all knew it was not Tom's coming struggle with his overgrown acres to which he alluded.

"I was not aware optimism was a fault," Ann said.

"This claret is a prize," the Doctor intervened, "have you more or are these two bottles the very last?" Why was she all in brown, he wondered, and such a lifeless brown? She seemed nervous too, and that was unlike her.

"I am so glad it is irreproachable. If it had been bad Mr Claverden would have thought I'd brought it out of mischief," and then quietly: "There are a few more. But I shall only open one if Mr Claverden condescends to call at Thorn."

William came to fill her glass. "You will be mistress of Blackow when I next come visiting. Perhaps you might give a bottle to the good Doctor and he and I will share it to celebrate your future happiness."

He was fully aware Harry did not like him, she saw that. She saw also that he would never come to her at Blackow, however urgent her summons. He would have no more to do with her once she was married to Harry Gerard.

Harry Gerard. Harry Gerard. Did she love Harry Gerard? The Doctor had told her she did not know what love was. Let him tumble you in the straw like a kitchen slut, he had said, and then see if you still want to marry him, if you still love him. Even at the memory her cheeks flamed. She looked up, found them all staring at her curiously.

Clipsby entered with the look of a man hard pressed. "Major Laidlaw is in the office, sir. I cannot fob him off, he's insisting … I told him you were engaged but he's in a fit of grief and don't take no notice."

William said: "Tell him I shall be out directly."

Clipsby withdrew to console the Major. William gathered his documents. He made no formal leave-taking. He was a man, Ann decided, who abandoned most of the formalities within the sanctuary of his own house. She was glad. Instinct clamoured for her to leave, to avoid his all-seeing eye.

"You may rest easy," was all he said to her. "Tom's acres are quite safe now," and then, without any noticeable feeling: "I wish you well."

He raised her hand as he spoke and dropped a kiss on the knuckles. But his dark eyes mocked and his kiss seemed clownish. He did not wish her well at all, she thought, and what was more, he no longer cared to conceal it. And then: he has a complicated nature like the Doctor's, deep, deep; and then: he will make a formidable husband, as disarming as he is arrogant.

But: "Thank you," she said.

And William was astonished at how shadowy and hurt her eyes were, how unhappy her soft mouth, and he was wondering what he had said to displease her. For surely she loved this fellow Gerard and was determined to be happy?

It was the first week in June and the weather was perfect, every morning more beautiful than the last. Harry, pursued willy-nilly by bailiffs, galloped to Blackow like a madman and arrived in a luminous dawn, dishevelled and laughing. They had been expecting him for at least a fortnight and had sunk into an apathy of waiting, so that he found the house cold, dusty and ill-provisioned. But someone with sense and imagination produced a breakfast fit for Bonaparte himself: kidneys and eggs and new-baked bread, a tarnished silver jug of fresh coffee, a pint of cream too thick to pour. Afterwards he slept an hour, tumbled in a narrow old bed in a back room like a boy, brown head cradled in his arms. Then he washed, shaved, drank a pint of strong ale, and mounted his horse as if for combat.

The Gorse was a green wilderness dotted with browsing cattle. The great oaks were in full leaf. He rode at speed and the speed went to his head as it always did, so that he turned off the road and flew over the fence into the woods at the top of Warren Hill, galloping headlong across Tom's precious acres.

Ann, alone in the garden, saw him coming. And she saw, as he came close enough, his young, exultant face, his wide grin of pure joy. As he reined in beside the shoulder-high hedge at the bottom of the lawn she knew he had not even noticed her, that he was concentrated on the horse, on himself, on the exhilaration of his mad ride.

Her heart, so unreliable now, quietened, the trembling stopped. And then he had flung himself from the saddle and was making for the wicket gate. "Ann! Ann!"

He was a yard away, face all smiles. Then he was a touch away and had lifted her tight against him, his mouth on hers.

"Lovely Ann! How I have missed you! All that courage and good sense. D'you think you can make anything of me? D'you think we'll survive together?"

She could not answer because he kissed her again, and anyway there was no sensible answer. Then a yell behind them made him set her down, head up, eyes light and angry.

"That young fool!" he said.

It was Tom, she saw, coming round the corner of the house. His freckled face was sweatily pink, broadly amused, and then, seeing who it was, affronted, furious, resigned, all in quick succession. His bow was sketchy, his eyes hostile.

"I swear he is a yard taller," Harry said easily, holding out the reins of the cavorting black horse. "Here, you can take this lovely fellow and put him somewhere cool. Rub him down if you like. He is a deal too excitable."

"Over-galloped you mean," said Tom sullenly, staring at the reins without making any move to take them.

"Please do it," said Ann abruptly, touching his arm, "or take him and ask Hollin to see to it."

The moment was past, the reins changed hands. Harry put a confident arm about Ann's shoulders and steered her towards the front door. "Did old Forsie leave any wine in the cellar other than the suspect claret?"

"It is no longer suspect. Mr Claverden and the Doctor have

tried it and it has occasioned eulogies."

"Claverden? Why should Claverden plague you now? And why waste good wine on such a sober fellow?"

To turn him from William she said with a smile: "You sent no letter to tell me you were coming home. And I expected you on the mail." It was not a complaint, merely a statement. Her face was lifted to his with the questioning innocence of a small girl's.

"Did you? Of course. Yes, of course the mail. But the horse was returned, the fool could not ride him, was run away with and jumped off and half trampled to death. But the beast is only full of courage, likes to go, needs a firm hand and a gentle one. It don't do to lend horses, Annie, mark my words. It don't do." He gave an affectionate glance in the direction of the yard, whither Tom and the black horse had vanished. "I could not wait another day. I no sooner had him back than I was in the saddle and on the road. Are you not pleased? The mail is abominably slow, lurches like a ship, and they will never let a stranger take the ribbons, even for a monstrous bribe."

She wished she could believe he had fled London out of impatience to be with her. At the door she turned, still in the shelter of his arm. "Do you still mean us to marry at once?"

His whole face lit up. "I do! Dear girl, I do."

He had released her, was plunging past calling for Maggie and Mrs McGinly, calling for bread and cold meat and wine, and then bestowing kisses to shrieks of indignation, laughing like a boy.

It was a warm day but Ann shivered, though whether it was some kind of queer relief to have him home again or the first breath of the cold wind of the future she did not stop to ask.

The wedding was delayed: Blackow was not ready to receive her. Harry seemed ill at ease, inordinately quick to lose his temper – and this in a man who hated discord, who fled from quarrels. More often than not he ranged far over the countryside on the black horse, returning late, so late they had given him up, and then slept only fitfully, up at dawn and into the saddle and away. The servants he had engaged polished and painted and arranged the furniture and he would come home and immediately order things redone or undone. He received a great deal of post, from London, from Dover; the greater part of it he fed every night to the kitchen fire. He ate little – his butler Praed carried him egg-nogs and cold pie at strange hours – and he had several falls from the wily black which left him bruised and shaken. And all the time at Thorn Ann tended the garden and taught Tom to read and write and supervised the baking, and the brewing, and the jam-making, and waited, waited.

And then he was gone. Praed sent over on a pony to tell her he had left for London on the mail, he would write, would be back. But he did not write and three days passed, and four, and Ann rode the white-legged chesnut to Blackow and made shaming enquiries at the front steps, only saving whatever dignity she had left by remaining firmly in the saddle while Praed shuffled in the gravel below. But she fooled no one: she was desolate and they knew it. She began to think he would never come back.

It could not be, of course. On the fifth night he was throwing stones at her window, laughing at her surprise; surprise and relief. Oh, the vast incalculable relief!

"Hush," was her instinctive warning, with a glance round at the darkened house.

"Come down," he begged, but she would not, it was unthinkable. Besides, she still had some rags of pride. And then: what might she not do if she went down? For she was overwhelmed with joy to see him there, with simple, crazy joy …

"Where have you been?"

"London."

"So half the neighbourhood has told me. But why?"

"Nothing that would concern you."

"I thought you would never come back."

"How little you trust me."

"I was so afraid."

"Of what?"

"Of losing you." Their fingertips touched. She was leaning perilously from the old casement, he was stretching to meet her.

"Come down," more sweetly. She shook her head. The cloud of her loose hair hid her longing.

He loved her, she thought; he must surely love her. For whatever he had been doing in London he had come back, had come to her at once, flinging his bag into the hazels on the Gorse, skimming down the side of the Hayfield.

And he was happy, on fire with emotion, with energy. He almost danced in the flowerbed below, sometimes caught up in a tangle of rose shoots, sometimes stepping back to crush the spindly lavender bushes. The smell of herbs rose strongly all around them: lavender, thyme, rosemary. And from far off, borne on the little night wind, came the faint, faint, indefinable fragrance of the acres of seeding grasses, the ripening hay.

"Ann, let me in."

"No." How she ached to do so, how, the house to herself, she would run to the door to draw the bolts. But there was Babs, there was Mrs McGinly, and there was Tom – though Heaven knew he slept deeply, would sleep through anything short of cannon fire. She was answerable to no one, should have had no other considerations but her own, and yet ... And yet the thought of those sleepers troubled her, held her at the window, kept her from temptation.

"Tell me where you have been," she said as Harry leaned suddenly against the wall beneath, smiling, one hand lifted, flat against the old bricks, as if certain her own would reach and grasp it in due course.

"Everywhere. Nowhere. London. It was a tedious business, nothing you would care about. Do you love me, Ann Mathick?"

"I love you."

His grin was pure delight. For the first time she wondered whether he was a little drunk. He had such shining eyes, such a look ... How eagerly he stared up, and how wildly. He was in a mood to pull her bodily from the window if only he could have gripped her hands.

"We will be married," he cried softly; had there been any doubt then? "Everything will be done properly. And no one will part us. I have done with the old life. Done with it."

He did not seem to expect an answer, or any comment. She made none. But a little worm of doubt moved slightly, slightly; a dozen questions hung unasked between them. She withdrew a little into the shadow. It seemed to her – though only dimly – that there was some particular of his old life he did not wish her to know about. But then he had spun away, taking great strides over the greenery, calling back: "I will come tomorrow," and was gone, walking quickly and with the barely-contained energy of his oat-crazed horse, up, up, along the Hayfield again, brushing both hands across the waving grasses.

She watched until he was out of sight. Slowly her body cooled, her mind grew rational again. He was a foolish, adventuring boy, unstable ... untrustworthy? No. No. She closed the casement, bent her forehead momentarily against the cold glass. No.

He came again late the following morning, exquisitely dressed as if he was calling on royalty and with a bouquet of rosebuds, creamy white, from a very old, very precious bush.

"I have resolved to be virtuous for the rest of my life," he said, elbowing the drawing room door shut behind them and turning to tip up her chin so that she was forced to look at him. "Do you think I shall succeed?"

"It would be so trying to live with an entirely virtuous man. Could you simply promise, perhaps, to indulge in less expensive activities?"

"What activities?" He did not move and yet for a brief moment he changed before her eyes; he was instantly harder, older, less appealing. But then, relaxing, he was a lover again, stroking her flushed cheek with his finger.

"Mrs Palmer has been here," she told him, "with scandalous stories of gambling, at Newmarket, at Crockford's; I did not know you were a member. And gossip speaks of women too, many women."

"And what do you know of Crockford's?" He kissed her small frown. Was he trying to divert her from the women?

"Nothing. Only that fortunes can be made and lost there."

"But you know Mrs Palmer is only piqued because you have deprived her of a son-in-law."

"You do not need to gamble for a fortune, you have one already."

"You cannot mean the fields of my ancestral estate? You know I cannot farm, I am no farmer."

"Between us we could do so much."

"No, between us we should come to ruin. *You* manage the estate. *You* direct the men, pay the wages, balance the books. You are good at it, enjoy it. I shall preside over your parties and balls and sometimes, but not often, your policy meetings."

The roses were crushed between them, pale, fragile, headily fragrant. He bent to kiss her, a long, breathless, stormy business.

The door opened.

"Miss Pennyquick told me to come straight in," declared the Doctor with a wild glance.

"But of course! And you must wish us well. We will be married at the end of the week."

The Doctor murmured something too low to catch. He bowed stiffly to Harry, stooped to bow to Ann. She could not meet his eye yet, that was something; he felt wickedly pleased by it for tangled reasons of his own. And he had never seen her so charming, so charmed. As she spoke her look was on Harry, and was brilliant. She was in love. The Doctor snarled.

"I wish you well with all my heart," he said, and then tried some innocuous conversation with Harry about the weather and the land. Harry put himself out to be civil – he was in a rare mood – but since it was obvious he did so there was soon a painful silence and glum looks.

"Blackow is being cleaned, sprinkled with rose water and crammed with flowers," Harry remarked eventually, seeing his hint about wine was to be ignored and that his bride had regained control of her breathing but lost something of her good humour. "Every window is open to the sun, and dust, dirt, and ten cartloads of antiquities have been banished for ever. How could my father have lived with such furnishings?"

"You are not going to buy new?" Ann was half horrified, half incredulous. "What do furnishings matter? You see, this is the very extravagance I warned you against!"

The sun invaded, turned Harry's hair to amber. "You must allow me to indulge my whims and fancies when making a home for my wife."

Oh, he would say something so obvious, so crude, thought the Doctor, but then saw Ann's blush and her downward glance. How damnable then that such schoolboy wooing could have any influence at all, as if she was seventeen still, knew nothing of the world.

"The end of the week then," he mused aloud, his other thoughts well hidden by an expression of genial inscrutability. "Friday perhaps." Harry paced to the window and stood, glorified, in a burst of sunshine.

"So soon?" Had she no misgivings? Yes, of course she haad. When she was not looking at Harry her face was pensive, secret, stunned: the face of a sleepwalker. The Doctor remembered telling her to bed with the man, not wed him; dear God, would he give his own daughter the same advice? But he held to it. He foresaw a quagmire of dissent ahead for her, a veritable ooze of accusation, denial, counter-accusation, shame, anguish, loss of dignity. But nothing he could say would move her, nothing at all.

Their eyes met. Ann smiled. How honestly he wished they might be happy and how steadfastly he refused to believe in such an outcome.

"I came to bring you these," he said, recalling William's strictures with a start. "I hope they are not marked." He drew a sheaf of documents tied with red ribbon and sealed most emphatically with red seals from his deep, old-fashioned pocket, a pocket until recently overflowing with titbits for the mongoose.

Ann was clearly uneasy. She took the papers with a trembling hand and stowed them immediately in her little desk. She locked it quickly and firmly, turning back with a smile. "I had forgotten the wretched things. How tedious legal business is. Will you stay and eat with us, Doctor?"

"Legal business?" Harry was all ears, stepping back from his pool of sunshine to stare across at them both as if they were conspirators. "Surely not more dealings with that man Claverden?"

"Oh, just a small matter I wished cleared up before ... before we marry." Her voice shook slightly. Was it the small matter or the marriage that made her unable to meet Harry's eye?

"What exactly?" he demanded, pleasant but imperious.

But Miss Pennyquick, mistress of inopportune entrances, had never made a more welcome one. She stepped in without a knock, bristling with irritation.

"That boy lobbed a tile at the cat and it took all my fresh linen off the lavender bushes." The tile or the cat, they wondered. "If I catch him ..."

"He means no harm," said Ann. "He ..."

"Harm! I wish you would tell him to start behaving like a gentleman if a gentleman's what you mean to make of him."

Harry's darkening face was threatening. The Doctor stepped forward. "Dear Miss P., may I claim a minute of your time? You know there was once borage at the bottom of the orchard here, and what was it? Feverfew? Tansy? I just wondered ..." and he propelled her, rigid but acquiescent, out of the room.

"You intend that child of Forsie's to go on living here?" asked Harry as the door closed.

"Why should you resent him so? He is nothing to you."

He was silent, immobile; all his good humour was quenched. She started towards him. "Harry, he is hardly a man. He is trusting and open, a great, cheerful, affectionate lad. I will not have him become a savage. And he must visit us at Blackow as often as he can. Could you not teach him how to dress well?"

"You expect me to tutor him in the social graces? Annie, are you mad? And besides, he dislikes me. And in case you have any ideas about Miss Pennyquick, I have no intention of having that long miserable face in my house."

"But she would make you an excellent housekeeper, which you need, as Mrs Peck's leaving ... And I would like her to come."

"To Blackow? Never! That sack of bones? Your uncle must

133

have been a desperate man to take her between his sheets."

"I am certain he never did. Harry, do you have to talk like this?"

"Did she tell you she lived here innocently with him twenty years? My dear Ann, how could you believe her? She ..."

Ann sank into a chair. "Stop! Please stop! What does it matter? What does it matter whether they were lovers, whether Tom is his child or not? I like them. And we should look to the future, not the past."

"I hate you when you moralise," he said.

But then he relented, seeing her so crushed; he was a creature of change, wild opinions, wilder enthusiasms, his intentions ebbing and flowing by the moment. He knelt at her feet, contrite, taking her cold hands in his.

"Dear Annie, we shall be married the day after tomorrow. I don't give a Turk's monkey for anyone but you and I want you to myself at Blackow ... Ann?"

His head, the soft clean hair all ruffled, was bent into her lap. She had an overwhelming desire to put her hand on the nape of his neck. She did nothing; her hands stayed quiet prisoners between his own.

"Why must it be Friday?" she heard a voice say, her voice distant and unfamiliar. "Why not tomorrow?"

He lifted his head and his eyes burned with laughter, with decision.

"Why not indeed?" he said.

Miss Pennyquick and a solicitor's clerk, pressed into service while delivering affidavits, were the witnesses. The church was huge, light, full of the sound of feet advancing and retreating, of nosy children, of whispering old women. The street noises penetrated too: the shouts of some scuffle in the Haymarket, the rumble of drays and coaches. The sun came out fitfully and between times it drizzled and leaden clouds blew up temporarily against the clerestory windows and blew away again. The service was brief, the ritual brisk, the clergyman was gloomy and Miss Pennyquick sullen, the solicitor's clerk anxious and distracted: he could not be prevailed on to give the bride away and shrank back into a pew, biting his lip terribly. There was an aura of illegality over the whole affair, no banns called, a sour flavour of undue haste; there was also a hint of intrigue, such a well-dressed, respectable couple being married by special licence.

When Ann looked up and met Harry's eyes she found a blankness there that frightened her. He mumbled – most unlike him – and forgot to put the ring on her finger until the priest guided his hand with a sigh of impatience. When it was over he bent to kiss her and then hesitated, as if he had remembered something unpleasant perhaps or even painful. He brushed his lips against her forehead, took her arm tightly, and steered her away down the aisle between the staring women.

Outside in the fresh, stinging breeze he looked down again into her face and now he was smiling. He was in his best blue coat, almost too fashionable for Norwich, a buff waistcoat, white breeches, boots as glossy as his beloved black horse. There was a flower seller on the corner of the Haymarket who blushed at him when he bought a bunch of pink roses to go with those Ann already carried.

"Are you happy?" he asked, handing them to her.

"Yes. Of course." They were pretty but almost scentless, unlike the buds from Blackow he had given her that morning.

Miss Pennyquick was tying her bonnet more firmly after a glance at the unsettled sky. It was noon. The solicitor's clerk hurried away, the richer by several gold coins but much distressed in spirit. The parson came out to wish them joy and Ann, with a sudden lifting of her unwarranted depression, donated all her roses for the altar.

"Now for the wedding breakfast," said Harry, and laughed at her surprise. "It is all arranged. I arranged it last night. You must not mind if elegance doesn't prevail, that is all. Mrs McGinly is doing her best with whatever comes to hand. And I sent commanding invitations to your adored Doctor and anyone he cared to bring, and to Mrs Palmer, and to Upgate Place."

"Not Lady Barsham? Harry, how could you be so improper?"

"You do not think she will step in to lend her countenance?"

The laughter welled inside her. "Oh, how could you do such a thing?"

Her hand was in his, the city through which they passed only a dream. She had no regrets; in that one moment of magic she had no regrets at all. It was perhaps the last time she would ever think so.

"I do not give a rood, perch or pole for Lady Barsham's countenance," said Harry loudly. "We will do very well without her, without them all."

So they drove back to Thorn in high spirits in the dashing green gig, Miss Pennyquick behind in the trap with a taciturn Hollin, who had refused to take any part in the ceremony but had bothered, Ann noticed with a flood of gratitude, to plait silver ribbons into the horses' manes for the occasion. At Thorn were two of the Blackow maids, agog, an irritable Praed, Mrs McGinly and Maggie in flounced cotton and absurdly starched aprons, Tom with a glowing face under disorderly hair, Mrs Palmer and Sophia in state on the sofa, and the Doctor in his best coat, his neckcloth in great swathes.

"It is supposed to be the latest fashion," he said to Ann as she greeted him, "but it is not quite right. It needs the touch of an experienced hand: your Harry's, for instance."

"You look unbelievably handsome and I am so glad, so very glad you came." And he did look uncommonly striking, she thought with surprise, grave and distinguished.

He kissed her cheek lightly, a most paternal gesture. "I could not let you go without a word on your wedding day. It was lucky I received the invitation for I was out until dawn and Jack had chewed it to ribbons by the time I returned; it took all of an hour to piece it together. But here," and he fished in his pocket, "I have a gift for you."

It was a little ivory box, intricately carved and lined with silver. It was something he had found in India, he said at her exclamation, he hoped it would serve as an ornament if she could find no other use for it.

Harry peered over her shoulder. "A trinket box," he said. "You

136

may have it for your dressing table," and he bowed to the Doctor with undisguised dislike and passed on to sample the cold chicken.

The Doctor was thinking how slight Ann looked in her cream and pink sprigged muslin, how hurt — for the merest second — and how cheerfully, if the opportunity ever presented itself, he would dismember Harry Gerard and use him for an anatomy lesson.

"If I had had a thousand guineas, my dear, I would have given you those," he said, and meant it.

"Only you would have told me to spend them before I became his wife," she said softly.

She touched his hand briefly and then went to stand beside Harry, asking some trivial questions about the splendid table of food Mrs McGinly appeared to have conjured from the empty air. The Doctor watched her and he was smiling, but his smile was undeniably ferocious. Then Tom loomed at his side, a little the worse for the wine cup and, the Doctor suspected, a morning's indulgence in strong ale.

"Is she happy?" Tom demanded, gazing over all the intervening heads to Ann on Harry's arm.

"Do you not think so?"

"I know she will not be this time next year, maybe this time next week. I cannot like him. I cannot believe he will be good to her."

The Doctor led him to the window, open to the sun and the smell of roses. "You may be wrong."

"I hope so."

The Doctor, whose own misery was as deep, though no longer so acute, sought to divert him by mention of the East, of the mongoose — still in dismal spirits and not yet despatched on the promised Indiaman — and of foreign food: French, Spanish, American; and then of the flora and fauna of anywhere and everywhere. When he chose he could be entertaining and informative; Tom revived a little, sucking in the summer air, listening to the low voice telling its amusing tales. But at last, only a little more sober and a little more resigned, he said coldly:

"I would not go to the church. Was that so unkind?"

"Prodigiously unkind. She would have liked you there. But that is past now and she is not a girl to blame you for following the dictates of instinct."

Mrs Palmer was before them, asparagus between her fingers. "Is it not the most cheerful party? Why, Dr French, are you not eating? Pray do introduce me properly to this young gentleman; we have met only in passing."

The Doctor made introductions. Mrs Palmer gave Tom a thorough scrutiny and found him enormously tall, almost overpowering, with a ruddy face and angelic yellow hair. She perceived at once an unfortunate resemblance to the dead Francis, that disreputable goat of the neighbourhood, and if she was surprised to find his offspring polite, tolerably well-spoken, and handsomely dressed she gave no sign of it. She said: "How lovely Miss Mathick ... Oh, but I should say Lady Gerard, should I not? How lovely she looks. It is quite remarkable."

She did not mean it unkindly, but did not suppose it had escaped their notice that Ann Mathick had no claim to beauty whatsoever. They all gazed in silence for a moment, hearing Ann's quiet voice and Harry's laugh and a distinctly unladylike squeal of amusement from Sophia.

"You do not look too well, Doctor," Mrs Palmer told him some time later, dimly aware of some distress in his face or his manner, she could not tell which. "You were not out all night again? How can you drive so many miles in the dark on strange roads and in such deep country and come safely home again? But tell me, is dear Charlotte entirely recovered? My sister swears the poor girl is herself again but I find her sadly wasted."

"She is like my mongoose," the Doctor said absently. "She needs sunshine and occupation and a great deal of attention."

"It was a dreadful fever."

"It was the very slightest. A dance would restore her, Mrs Palmer, a ball or a picnic or some other frivolous diversion. Can you not arrange something?"

He was still looking at Ann, she found, and he seemed distracted, strange.

"We must wish them happiness," she said, following his eyes. It was not true after all that his misery was less acute than it had been all these past weeks. A feeling of foreboding, almost of dread, was still with him. The Doctor turned to look out at the grass, the wide blue sky still trailing the rags of storm clouds over Warren Hill, the few old roses struggling into bloom.

"Eat and be merry while we can, eh?" said Hollin's rough voice in his ear. He was chewing on a pork pie and looking most lugubrious. By the door, almost strangled in his Sunday best, Jim Knight was giving Ann his congratulations.

"Yes," said the Doctor bleakly, "while we can."

The fourposter had obviously been built for a megalomaniac, its tester somewhere up near the ceiling, several hundred yards of brittle silk lashed in each corner. At least the linen was new and sweet, thought Ann, but she blew out every candle but one anyway so that she could hardly see any of it. And then she stood, barefoot, brushing and brushing her hair, and thinking of the mad ride from Thorn, the horse practically bolting, Harry's arm around her and his shout triumphant across the Gorse. Because of Harry's genuine joy, because of the wine she had drunk, Blackow had seemed less like a mausoleum, and there was a deep, unconquerable satisfaction in leaving everyone but Mrs McGinly and one maid at Thorn for the night. But where was Harry? She had come up here hours ago, it seemed, and sat by the window waiting, trying to calm her over-stretched nerves. There had been no sound from below, no sound at all in the whole of this echoing, uninhabited pile. She had undressed, something she had dimly hoped he might help her with, and had put on the virginal cotton nightgown with its tucks and ribbons and two score little buttons from neck to waist.

The door opened, closed. When she had control of her breathing she turned to face him and promptly lost it again.

"What have you got on?" he asked. "It looks like a sheet. And why are you almost in the dark?"

He walked across the room, throwing his coat into a chair, his neckcloth with it. He was close enough now to see the badly-disguised fright in her huge dark eyes. She stood at the end of the bed, her hairbrush dangling from limp fingers.

"Where have you been?" she asked, but as he moved she caught a whiff of the stables and knew before he answered her.

"To see if the horses were comfortable. To lock up. No, come here. You look so different with your hair down."

His kiss dissolved her. After that where was there to go but backwards on to the bed? His hands sought her breasts but found only pleat upon pleat of lawn and the tiny, infuriating buttons.

"Damn these things!" he said. "I can't wait."

Nor did he.

8

It was hot, a dry, oppressive heat; they had forgotten what rain was. The hay was stacked but the corn harvest was in doubt. It would be too hot, the men said, to shear the wheat, too hot for anything.

In the opulent bedroom at Blackow Ann threw back the sheet. Light dazzled through the high windows, wide open to let in the night air – and even that stifling – curtains and blinds undrawn. She went across to close them, to prepare for another day of siege, and she leaned for a moment looking out to where the cattle stood nose to tail beneath the massive oaks in the park, switching miserably at the flies. The air was windless, lifeless; it was hot, hot, and only eight in the morning.

And where was Harry? Where indeed. This was the second time he had ridden off without warning, and not to a race, or a fight, or a meeting with any dubious friends. The last time, two weeks ago, he had been gone three days, had arrived back exhausted, elated, his clothes filthy; word had reached Ann, by Hollin, by Pashman, by one nagsman or another, that the black horse had spent two days and a night at Scole up to the ears in oats, that Sir Harry Gerard had caught the London mail. She had been torn between hurt, exasperation, and anger. On his return she had kept temper and curiosity in check just long enough – he had obviously been expecting a fuss but his look dared her to make one. But his abrupt disappearance had frightened her, and the fright still lingered and now and then rekindled her indignation, so in the end she begged him, here in their high, wide bed, to tell her where he had been.

He would say nothing, looked secretly triumphant and amused. She must not mind it, he told her, if he vanished from time to time on business of his own, she must be patient and discreet and as incurious as was humanly possible. And to stop any further argument he had pushed the sheet from her small breasts and watched her eyes go wide and dark at his touch.

She remembered all this as she turned to the dressing table and found the note propped against the Doctor's little ivory box: 'Business in London. Back Friday. H.' She picked it up, stared at it as if the very shape of the letters would give her some clue to his whereabouts. The writing was dashing, a sort of breathless attack on the page, bold but chaotic; much like his lovemaking, though that, of course, she was forced to accept uncritically, since she had no experience of any other.

'Back Friday.' But would he be? She had never expected him to be content at Blackow. Perhaps once, had it remained the cherished and well-run estate of his childhood, one where there was no neglect to reproach him, no disconsolate workforce, no lack of servants, no lack of fat rents and full barns – but not now. He did not love the land, in that he had not misled her; he did not care for life in the country apart from the sport it afforded him; and when it became clear that half the local society was going to take a leaf out of Lady Barsham's book and ignore him, and that those who did call generally came to see Ann and not himself, he grew restless and peevish. No, she had never hoped he would settle down to be the country squire, but she had never imagined he would escape so abruptly and mysteriously.

Was it to do with the letters? She dressed herself slowly, and in the half-dark of the curtained room found her own face in the mirror only a pale blur, as if sleeplessness and anxiety were destroying it, as if soon nothing but her eyes would remain, huge, deep-set, underscored by the tired blue-grey lines. Outside, she knew, it was already as hot and silent as noon, the very earth scorching. As she pinned up her hair she was aware of her damp neck, the beads of sweat on her forehead. So was it the letters? Harry had a considerable post and he never spoke to her about any of it, unless there was a rare invitation to them both, or some unforeseen bill. Perhaps it was money. He could not be bothered with accounts, he said, would leave it all to her, but she had no idea how much he spent or even how much he had to spend. She knew the outgoings of the house and the farms, at times felt horrified by them even though she allowed no extravagance; she knew to a penny the price of the seed they had bought, the day-labour they had hired, the horseshoes put on or removed, the new ox harness, the sheep hurdles; but she knew nothing about Harry's outgoings, only that they were erratic and variable, suggesting that he was still gambling — and losing, for he had drawn on her money several times recently, large sums.

And then last night he must have got up, dressed, saddled the black horse, and simply ridden away.

She would get nothing out of Praed, she thought, that silent, self-effacing and strange little man. He had made it clear from the start he was Harry's servant, preferred to be valet rather than butler, cared nothing for the daily routine of the house. He and Miss Pennyquick never spoke, communicated by venomous looks or not at all, though this was nothing to the animosity between him and Mrs McGinly, who had been seen to drive him from the kitchens with a war cry that might have encouraged the Goths and a pair of carving knives. Ann only knew he would no longer pass through the servants' door but went outside and right round the house when he wanted to get to the butler's pantry.

This morning she found that Miss Pennyquick — a newly severe Miss Pennyquick who had taken up residence in a spacious but forgotten room on the first floor and spent a great deal of time there — had already breakfasted and was away to the kitchen garden. A roll, a cup of coffee, was all she needed. She felt ... She felt as if she wanted to walk and walk, to walk away the little, clinging fears and the doubts and suspicions. She put on a straw hat, went out into the heat.

On her way across the gravel she hesitated, assailed by a vision of Babs bent over the sunburnt lettuces, the ancient gardener full of gloom beside her. No, she could not bear to see anyone. She must walk, walk. She made for the park fence across the lawns, climbed it – and that was the end of her stockings, three great holes appearing – and then swung away uphill, keeping to the shade.

Even under the trees the grass was bruised and parched; there would be no grazing at all soon, Hollin had told her, echoing Sendall's cheerless prognostications, and they would have to feed the new hay to the beasts. By the time she reached the edge of the Gorse – another fence, more damage – her dress was clinging moistly to her skin, her neck was wet, trickles of perspiration starting from under the straw hat. And here was no shelter, a vast expanse of bare waste to cross, even the thistles withered. She crossed steadily, as a traveller might cross a desert in dogged pursuit of a fabulous, forgotten city. By the broken gate into Ten Acre she paused to rest, leaning against the unsteady post, drawing in deep breaths of dry, unreviving air. The furrows of Ten Acre – it had been bare-fallowed on her own instructions – were baked so hard a man with a pickaxe might have toiled at them in vain, for this was poor land, the poorest of all Thorn's land, the land they said would never grow corn, never make good pasture. Her hopes might be muted now, a little crushed, but they were still there; and the weeds were to die, at least.

Even the water meadows were yellow brown. From the edge of the trees of Warren Hill she gazed down at them, at the shrunken river. And then there were the roofs of Thorn, and she could hear the plaintive bleating of the sheep, the barking of Tom's new dog, shrill and furious.

There was no one about. The kitchen fire had been let out: it was unheard of, a scandal, but they could not stand the heat. Without abrasive Mrs McGinly the place was ever so slightly greasy, dull, shabby. The dairy was cool, not as cool as usual but cool enough, though no one had put up the shutters and some of the milk had already started to turn. Ann helped herself to ale out of the jug, and it was warm and disagreeable. There were baskets put ready, lunch for the reapers; they would be harvesting the wheat on Long Meadow, a meadow no longer and her first truly reclaimed field. She wandered through the hall to the drawing room. Her chair was still by the fire and the clock still ticked, but her little desk was at Blackow, and the portrait of her mother, and the other odds and ends that had made it home. The room looked almost as she had first seen it, that inauspicious December evening. Cleaner, she thought, it was cleaner. She felt a sudden anguish and did not know why.

On Long Meadow the reapers were in a line and the rhythm of the scythes rose and fell; they could not keep it up for long, they had to stand back and wipe the sweat from their eyes. They were all there – Tom, Jim Knight, Ben Storr the shepherd, three others. Hollin was organising the women and children to stook the sheaves.

Perhaps they saw her by the gate but only one of the smallest children, one of the shepherd's six, gave her any kind of salute. They were far too busy to stop: by ten the sun would be too hot to work and they would have to lie under the hedge or go back to the farm, only starting to scythe again in the late afternoon. She could see Tom, stripped to the waist, yellow head aflame, but he was bent to his task, only straightened a moment, shifted his grip, went on. These were her fields, she thought then, their contours so familiar – how many times had she walked them in the cold and windy spring, deciding their future? She was on intimate terms with them all: the degree of neglect, the patterns of soil, that poor, weedy soil, robbed of its fertility. Moving to Blackow had not altered her affection for Thorn, had perhaps increased it. Now she stood in the burning heat and looked and looked, until the wheatfield and its reapers became a golden haze under the intense and staring blue of the sky. She turned at last and walked away, back towards the Gorse. Only for a moment did she glance through the limp leaves of the oaks to the gleam of Warren Hill's further slope, where all the barley stooks were bleaching in the sun.

Over there Harry had kissed her, had asked her to marry him; she could feel again the hardness of the tree at her back, of his mouth on hers. And the Doctor's voice was in her ear: 'It is not a crime to want a man ... Have him by all means if you must. But do not marry him ...' She swung away, stumbled over the cracked, baked earth by the boggy drinking places, scattered half a dozen scrawny ewes from under a gorse clump, the only shade for miles. She was so hot, wet through; by the Blackow fence she stopped to take off her shoes and stockings, watched by the suffering cattle. And all the way down the hill, the ruined grass crackling under her bare feet, the Doctor's voice returned to her over and over: '... I do not believe you know that love is.'

The afternoon brought Mrs Palmer, glowing but undefeated. Her horses were foaming but the carriage smelled only of rose water. She declined refreshment, declined to step down. She was on her way home from Norwich, she told Ann, from some enervating meeting to raise money for the hospital, a roomful of charitably inclined ladies gasping for air and ideas together. She spoke of her sister at Upgate: 'so fatigued by the heat'; of Charlotte: 'no doubt but Mr Claverden is not serious in his attentions, he is so restrained, so circumspect'; of the dusty roads, the poor harvest: 'and no grass anywhere, no grass at all'. Her round little face poked out: "Dear Ann, are you not afraid you will suffer heat stroke? Does not Sir Harry insist you stay indoors until evening?"

Sir Harry insisted nothing, except she did not ask where he went. Ann smiled, replied mildly, reiterated a hope Mrs Palmer might come in for iced tea. Mrs Palmer declined again, prepared to leave and then thought of something else.

"The Doctor. Have you seen the Doctor?"

"Once. On the Gorse."

"He does not mind the sun."

"I believe not. He and the mongoose are restored by it."

"Does he not visit you often? You were such friends."

The paint on the carriage door looked fit to blister. The gravel burned through Ann's shoes. "He has been very busy." She would pay in self-loathing for that diplomatic lie. "I believe he has been operating under Rigby. At least, there has been a great deal of to-ing and fro-ing between High Common and Norwich, they say, and medical students here, there and everywhere revelling till dawn."

Mrs Palmer sighed, and unstoppered the rose water. "I have not heard of it. But he is an unpredictable man at all times. You will give Sir Harry my regards and explain the unfortunate circumstances? It would be unfeeling of me to receive him when my sister does not."

Lady Barsham did not receive him partly because Lord Barsham would not — some long-standing quarrel, intricate, obscure — and also because Harry, meeting her in Norwich as she had left the Assembly House to enter her carriage, had been drunk enough to kiss her hand and call her, in front of several delighted onlookers, the most delightful old hag in the county. This was the night Ann had told him about the land in trust for Tom, the poor weedy acres; Harry had signed all the legal documents thrust at him after their marriage with scarcely a glance, had certainly spent no time studying maps. He had not noticed the absence of the fifty acres, she had had to explain it to him. And it had nearly been the cause of a hellfire drama, he had been furious, shocked, and, she suspected, more than a little jealous. No wonder the gentry refused to visit, he had said, if it was generally known she had set herself up as a charity for Francis Forsie's illegitimate children.

The carriage rolled away in a dust cloud. Ann sought the kitchen and Mrs McGinly, a Mrs McGinly practically immobilised by a white apron starched like a board, her face purple.

"There is no need to send up any dinner. I will have apricots and a glass of wine."

"You have not eaten all day."

It was not perhaps entirely respectful, but then they had never stood on ceremony. Mrs McGinly had come to Blackow only for Ann's sake, at Ann's entreaty. It had not, in her opinion, been any change for the better. The kitchens were vast, dank, subterranean; there were far fewer servants than they had been designed for and in any case they had not been designed by anyone who had ever set foot in a working kitchen: the water had to be carried along two passages and down fifteen steps. There was none of the homeliness of Thorn, and none of its dramas; if the truth were told she might have confessed to missing even Hollin and his infernal muddy boots, his sour tobacco, his awful cheerlessness.

"You look ill," said Miss Pennyquick to Ann much later, thus confirming the impression she seemed to be giving at the moment. Miss Pennyquick had just returned from an unsatisfactory dinner at the parsonage where she had talked Isaiah and pickled walnuts the entire evening to the parson, the parson's wife, and the parson's brother — lo and behold, another parson.

"I do not. It is simply this odd light." They had not lit the candles, though it was ten o'clock, and the light was storm-light, phosphorescent, unreal. The storm was passing some miles to the south and it was only the weird glow they received at Blackow, and a few drops of warm rain.

"How could he leave you so, without warning, without a word?"

"I am going to bed. I hope your evening was not as dull as it sounds."

Miss Pennyquick looked out at the silvery haze in the distance that was terrible rain falling on some part of Suffolk, and thought. "They were very kind," she said at last.

"I know the parson wishes Harry would pay towards the renewing of the pulpit, it rocks when he declaims in anything louder than a whisper. It must be rebuilt. But I am afraid Harry will donate nothing except possibly a diatribe against sermons."

"It wasn't mentioned. They asked me if I would care to help at the dame school."

It was a capital idea, and a heartening solution: Miss Pennyquick and Harry Gerard were not easy under the same roof. A certain competence with small children was one of Babs Pennyquick's underrated attributes, and one Ann hoped might help her when she herself had babies. But the silence was too long, a whole minute too long.

"And?" Ann saw a thin smile somewhere in the mysterious shadow.

"I accepted, of course. But oh, how condescending that man

148

is! And in ten years he never set foot inside Thorn, thinking the old man a reprobate, thinking I was no better. It was always clear what he thought about lost sheep."

"And now you are respectable you are invited to dinner."

Miss Pennyquick snorted. Her eyes flashed. "I could," she said tartly, "have thrown the soup at him."

Even hours later, walking in the peculiar half dark, in the warm mist, Ann could not smile. The thought of Babs hurling the soup, only prevented from dissolving in a froth of resentment by tight lacing and whalebone stays, could not move her. She ached with the loss of Harry and felt, obscurely and confusedly, that she had lost him to a more distant place than any depicted on a map. In ten minutes she was too hot to walk any more, and sank to the hard ground under a sweet chestnut, seeing the ghostly shapes of cattle far away beneath other trees. It was abominably quiet, no owls hunting, no bats, no rustle of leaves; a profound silence, a waiting for the next unbearable heat.

And then a voice, a hand reaching down. "Annie, what possessed you? You look like a wraith. You nearly killed the horse with shock." But the horse looked as usual, irritable and devilish, perhaps rather too sweaty.

"I expected you Friday." She felt his kiss on her hair.

"I have come from Scole at the gallop. I could not bear to say away a minute longer."

Whether she believed him or not she could not say; certainly he had ridden the poor horse hard. But his motive? Ah, that was imponderable. His face gave no sign he had enjoyed himself wherever he had been, nor that he had returned as strangely elated as last time, as deeply satisfied.

"I wish you would tell me what this is all about," she said.

"One day." He had his arm round her, was guiding back to the fence. "I promise that one day you shall know everything."

He put up the black horse, was more careless than she had ever known him over its bed, its food; he did not even bother to rub the sweat off its heaving sides. He was depressed, profoundly and violently depressed; she had seen it once or twice before. In such a mood he would take to the saddle or the bottle, whichever was most convenient. His face reflected the last of the storm; and was it her imagination or did he look much thinner, his cheekbones prominent, his eyes sunken?

The sleeping house was cool. In the bedroom Harry stared from the open window and then abruptly pulled down the blind. He turned to find her standing just behind him and noticed, for the first time, that she had been out walking in her shift, her hair loose, her feet bare. She looked like a gipsy. No, she did not. She looked fey, slender, her small breasts clearly visible through the thin lawn.

"You look so tired," she said.

He was; and his kiss was sweet and brotherly. "You must not wander outside without clothes on," he admonished, flinging off his own. "What if someone were to see you like this?"

"But who would see me in my own garden at three in the morning?"

"Anyone. The Doctor is often out at night."

She laughed into the pillow, half in, half out of bed. "He would need a spyglass to see anything at all from up on the Gorse and of all the people to think of ... The Doctor must have studied more female bodies than the most notorious libertine that ever lived."

Harry reached over and plucked at the little ribbons at the neck of her shift, but when they parted he did not touch her, he simply put his head into the curved hollow of her shoulder and closed his eyes.

"You were right," he said, "I am so very tired."

And in two minutes he was asleep, hot and damp and heavy against her, and the dawn already drizzling gold under the blind and across the floor.

It was going to be another hot day.

There was some dispute about dredging the lake.

"We cannot afford it," said Ann as calmly as she could, "it is a nonsensical idea. Like the ball."

"We always had a Christmas ball at Blackow when I was a boy." Harry sounded petulant and his frown was deepening. He was seated astride the arm of a chair, swinging one booted leg and swiping idly at his spurs with his riding whip. He had been for an early morning ride through the dripping woods and up on to the Gorse, scattering sheep and the camping gipsies with equal abandon, exhilarated as always by speed and a sense of freedom. He had returned to find Ann at her weekly business of squaring the accounts – until lately a monthly affair – and the sight had made all his tender good humour evaporate. He had ranged the room like a tiger until he had finally alighted on the chair arm, disconsolate, deflated, and sulky.

"We could manage a small party, some dancing perhaps. Harry, can you imagine what it would cost if we did all you suggested? And what for? To cut a dash? To show Lady Barsham that even if she will not call we can thumb our noses at her in the grand manner? Oh, Harry, when will you ever grow up?"

He got up. He was a litle drunk already, she thought, and it was only nine o'clock. He was looking at the wall where the sombre face of a long-dead Gerard stared and scowled into eternity.

"The lake used to look so fine," he said miserably.

"And if the land was in good order and making a profit there would be money to spare to make it fine again."

"A slow business. Better to invest in …"

"Racehorses? Or poor demented cocks? Or faro tables? Harry, can you not see how I am trying to help?"

He could see, but it made no difference. "I am no farmer," he repeated. He walked to the wall and deliberately turned the offending portrait back to front.

"You said I should run the estate. Well, how can I do so if you gamble away every penny we have?"

"I have not done anything of the kind."

"But you are always at races, or cockfights, or worse. You come home drunk and without a coin in your pocket. And I have no idea what money is left in the bank."

"Ask them, they will tell you."

"Why will you not tell me?"

But he strode across the room, snapped shut her account book and plucked the pen from her inky fingers. Then he bent to drop a kiss, half affectionate, half exasperated, on her smooth head.

"You have tamed all those curls," he said softly, digging into the fine swirl for the pins. "I liked your wild hair. I did so like it."

She pushed his hand away. Her eyes, level and grave and tired, met his. "We must talk about Blackow, about Thorn."

"I am not interested in Blackow or Thorn."

She stood up, the slim, hard account book between them, clutched to her as if it were that piece of wreckage a drowning man clings to when he is almost exhausted. She looked plain, plain and defeated.

"Will you forget this mad idea about the lake?"

"Only if you will concede my mad idea for a ball."

There was a silence. The wind sighed round the long windows. The disputed lake was whipped to a grey flurry and the lawns were covered in leaves. It was the end of November, sour, brutal weather, the roads like lakes of mud.

"We have no money," Ann said. His eyes were laughing, she saw, his eyes and his fine mouth and all his narrow, mobile face.

"But we shall have, we shall. Sable Island is in business again. Any day now I shall receive the first part of a fortune, a veritable fortune. And we may have a ball a week if we wish and expense go hang."

She did not wish, she found, for a ball a year. For some private reason her heart ached for the daily round at Thorn, for the great smoky kitchen and the quiet drawing room that had been her own, for the worn Turkey rug and the old clock, and upstairs the solid oak bed where she had slept alone and at peace.

"Sable Island?" She had forgotten Sable Island, she had not heard the name in months.

"There will be money coming in from Sable Island, I promise you."

"What ..." The words stuck in her throat suddenly, she had to take a breath and start again. "What does the company trade in?"

"Company?" Harry had strolled away to the window, was looking out at the view, though whether he was admiring or deploring it was unclear.

"I assumed there was a company in which you had invested your money."

He started. "Oh, that. Spices. Annie, for Heaven's sake, leave the wages for once! Come and ride with me. We could go down past the mill."

"If you like. But Babs must do the wages." He would be quite prepared to leave them to another day, to let the men go home empty-handed; he rarely thought of all the consequences of his actions.

And: "What spices?" she asked as they cantered side by side up the drive to the Gorse. Already they could hear the yap of the gispy dogs, smell the woodsmoke and something acrid cooking.

"Damn you, get on!" This to his horse as a rabbit got up under its hooves and it swerved. His head flared gold in the weak grey light and then was extinguished in the shadows under the trees, and he was lost to view in a thicket. Had he quickened his pace on purpose?

Ann slowed. He always rode too fast. Had he wanted her to come up here to take her mind off something? What? The wages? The ball? Sable Island?

Sable Island. William Claverden, whom she had seen once during the last five months and then painfully and briefly at Mrs Palmer's, to whose house she had been invited without Harry, had told her that to the best of his knowledge the Sable Island off Halifax was the only Sable Island there was. And spices? The market in spices could not be so buoyant, not now and not … Her mare snorted, shied, stumbled in a soft place and ducked forward again. Ann held her up, catching a glimpse of a grinning face framed in a tangle of brambles and wild rose thorns.

"Tom? Tom Forsie, come out!"

He emerged, scratched, hilarious, his face muddy.

"You've lost him. He went down Warren Hill lickety spit and never looked back. I saw you dawdling in the copse."

"I am not dawdling. And you look like a tinker! Why do you refuse to come down to the house any more? I sent a note with Rose when she went to Thorn for the butter. You have a trunkful of decent clothes and no excuse not to appear presentable in company."

"I shall come when he leaves again."

The silence between them was heavy. Tom saw he had hurt her and cast about for some means to make it up, but there were none. The facts were plain, after all. Harry spent more and more time in Norwich drinking and gambling, or riding half the county away to cockfights, or the races, or God knew where. Sometimes he was away from Blackow for days on end, several times he had been to London on the mail. But why? Ann said nothing or she said he was 'on business'. Already half the neighbourhood was busy with the talk of how he was often too drunk to ride, how he only got off the coach at Scole to drink himself silly at the inn; it was not true, or it was only partially true. But why?

"Things will get better," Ann said. She said it often and it became harder to say.

Tom put a brown hand on her rein. His nails were cared for, she noticed. Jim Knight's cheerful, shrewish little wife was keeping him up to standard then.

"For you, I hope." He was in earnest, his face puckered with anxiety.

"You do not have to be uneasy on my account."

"The Doctor says you are unhappy." The Doctor was kindly continuing his education, Ann having so little time to spare for it these days.

"The Doctor is an old fool." Not true and lamentably impolite anyway. "Does he not see the improvements?" And her arm swept out towards the dark acres the plough teams had left only recently. Yes, there were certainly improvements. Land untouched for years swept down towards Thorn or Blackow in glorious, satisfying swathes of brown.

"He says the cost is too high."

"He says too damn much." That the cost, for instance, might not only be reckoned in money and man-hours. "He has no business discussing such things with you."

If Tom was startled by her language, her loss of temper, he did not show it. He said stolidly: "He cares for you."

It was true, she knew it; he was not an affectionate man but with her he had sometimes come close to being one. And she thought of the ivory box, who knows how precious to him, carried home in the bowels of a heaving ship after being mishandled on battlefields, after travelling by elephant and contrary army mule.

Tom thrust up his hand: it held a piece of crumpled paper.

"I did this. It slopes a little too much, I think." He hovered for her approval, fist balled on the neck of the little mare. Ann bunched her reins, smoothed out the sheet. There were several lines of flowing writing like waves breaking on a beach: 'Dear sir I remain your humble servant, I remain your most obedient humble servant, I am very sincerely your own Thomas Francis Forsie.'

It might not have been sense but she could not help admiring it. "Oh, Tom, such an improvement!"

A distant shout indicated Harry's impatience. He must have been as far as the river already and come back for her. Ann thrust the paper in her pocket.

"Come to the house tomorrow," she said. "We are to have a ball at Christmas and you must learn how to dance."

And she left him snorting with laughter, skirting the gipsy camp with its fires and ragged children and sharp dogs, and trotting downhill to her fractious husband.

"Where have you been?" he demanded.

"I met Tom."

He turned the black horse and rode beside her. After a bit he said gloomily: "I hate to see Blackow run on a pittance, half the rooms shut up."

"What can you expect? You have spent all the money, yours and mine."

"Not all of it."

"What is there left?" Everywhere she was extending their credit; her careful accounts tottered.

She had tried to shut her eyes to the truth, something she rarely did, and it had been difficult, like putting on a blindfold when swimming near a weir. But two things had happened: firstly the Gerard lawyer had arrived in a post-chaise, having galloped all the way from London to pant up to Blackow just as breakfast was being cleared. He found Ann supervising an inventory of house contents and Harry away in Swaffham 'on business'. He had served the Gerards all his life; he was respectable, stout, brimful of righteous indignation like a kettle threatening to boil over, and he was so upset he stuttered most horribly. Restored by food, tea laced with brandy, and Ann's singular calmness, he blurted out that he must see Harry at once. Ann said that it was impossible Harry should be home before midnight. Liveman hurtled from his chair and had a bout of hysteria on the hearthrug. It was a matter of reckless overspending, the bank refusing to advancing anything further, and there were debts; there were debts and certain people were pressing for payment. Lady Gerard could have no idea, of course, but there were predictable and unfortunate consequences of such pressure; if it were generally known Sir Harry was under siege lesser creditors would join in the general clamour, and there would be a decidedly nasty set-to ending quite probably in court, in prison, in flight.

The second thing had been the polite, ominous note from the Norwich bank asking if Sir Harry might call at his earliest convenience; only it had been addressed to Ann. Obviously Harry had received summonses of such a kind before and had ignored them. Ann, weighing all the possibilities, had thrown the letter in the fire and had gone herself, sailing into that holy place of business in her most outrageous hat, her eyes dark as coals. She had learnt nothing, needless to say, except that there was no money.

Now she and Harry jogged down past Thorn to the river. He was still beside her, he who always rode ahead, and as they started into the racing ford he pulled up, leant over for her hand.

"Ann." It was an absurd place to hold a conversation and he knew it; the water was up to the horses' knees. "Ann, say you have no regrets."

Who knows what regrets she might have? She put up her chin.

"I love you."

His blue eyes smiled. He raised her gloved hand, kissing it. Then her horse plunged, eager for the bank, a spray of cold water soaking her skirts, and their hands were parted.

9

IT COULD not be said that Lady Barsham disliked Ann Gerard, although she did nothing to quash the rumour that asserted she did; she had, after all, met her so seldom. She was not a stupid woman, nor was she vindictive, and now that it was made clear to her that Harry Gerard was further beyond the pale than she had supposed, she was only glad she had never had any serious ideas of letting one of her girls try him in matrimony. Blackow was mortgaged to the rafters, everyone said so; the pity of it was that such flagrant gossip should be so believable. And though the story of little Ann Mathick's ill-judged marriage might have been the latest news for all of thirty-six hours her struggle in the unequal battle – against debt and Harry's drinking – was definitely of more lasting interest. Thus Lady Barsham, enjoying an afternoon with friends, found herself fencing with Mrs Carleton on the subject of the Blackow estate, modern agriculture, and 'Lady Ann'.

"I am sure I know nothing about these things," she protested wearily, but terrified lest the conversation swerve to turnips or horse beans.

"I hear the Gerards are in debt to the eyebrows," remarked another voice beyond the tea dishes. "How the poor girl can hope to survive with a husband so addicted to gambling I should not care to imagine. Why, Jack was at Newmarket for the last meeting and said he saw Harry Gerard laying monstrous bets while the talk was all how he scarcely had a penny to his name. Jack had it on authority the man lost at least four thousand pounds."

There was a general hush during which six idle and expensive women wondered at such scandal and frivolity, and at how even likeable rogues could grow tiresome and unattractive. No-one, however, saw fit to venture an opinion aloud: Lady Barsham was well known for her scathing treatment of the ill-informed and the priggish. Therefore the silence lengthened while a fresh topic of conversation was hastily sought, and into this silence was shown a louring Dr French, speechless with vexation at finding a roomful of women when he had called about a poisoned hand, bunions, and the mysterious affliction that had laid low the smallest, meekest, most irreproachable housemaid. Lady Barsham, also vexed, but mainly that he should call at a time when he might guess she would be receiving, asked him with cool politeness to wait in the library, she would be with him directly, and stared exceedingly hard at the shrinking maid who had let him in.

"Such an odd little man," Miss Petersfield said as the door closed, "and so fierce! When Maria had the fever he marched in and said she was shamming! Mama nearly died he was so rude. And Maria fainting and being sick and crying out so piteously! He banged out of the house laughing – laughing! Mama said were it not for his reputation as a brilliant man she would not have him in it again, not if life depended on it."

Lady Barsham, who admired the Doctor, and whose life had depended on him more than once, turned at the door. "And did Maria recover after such shabby treatment?"

Cissie Petersfield stared. "Well, she was better next day but Mama insisted, of course, that she stay in bed a week."

In the library Lady Barsham so far forgot herself to exclaim: "So Maria Petersfield was shamming! But how odious of you to tell her so, how unprofessional, how foolish; think what guineas might not have poured into your lap from a half dozen sympathetic visits, a quantity of violent green medicine, boxes of little blue pills. Will you never learn how to conduct yourself in polite society?"

The Doctor's glance was humorous. "You are making a sorry attempt at teasing. Are you upset? Is the hour inconvenient? Young Maria had been at the port, or the claret. She was as sick as could be and with the devil's own sore head and she was doing her best, helped a little by nature, to convince them all she was dying of some dreadful plague. I can trust you to be discreet, dear lady, can I not?"

Lady Barsham gave a girlish grin. "How I have always liked Maria! More spit and vigour than the rest of the family together and most definitely a sense of humour. I daresay I should not admire her for trying the port – I would be sorry to discover a daughter of mine doing so – but really the girl has nerve, and great powers of invention."

They turned to mundane matters, domestic, exceedingly dull. The cook's poisoned hand, the bunions – Lord Barsham's or anyone else's – the Doctor could deal with in his usual pepper and vinegar manner without disturbing her ladyship at her tea party; the housemaid's condition was another matter entirely. It was quite certain she was with child: even Lady Barsham had been forced to that conclusion without the benefit of medical science. And there was all this talk of drowning or otherwise doing away with herself, unceasing tears, no appetite, fainting fits, general despair – though at no time had she actually admitted the truth of her condition, even denied it vehemently. Lady Barsham, who ran a well-ordered house, and who was concerned with the spiritual and moral welfare of her servants, felt sorely tried by all this; like a captain in charge of a tight ship she was doubly struck by any irregularities or gross misdemeanors. And the worst of it was she suspected the butler.

"Is it of any consequence who has fathered the infant?" the Doctor demanded at the end of her lucid summary, her short catalogue of requests.

"Who else is to support it, poor child?"

"You, no doubt, as you have done before and shall again."

"Oh, that! But that was long ago when I was young and sentimental and abysmally foolish. And besides, times have changed, people are more moral nowadays, less broadminded about such things."

"I had not noticed." The Doctor was departing kitchenwards,

reflecting on the dim past when moral rectitude had been less in evidence and on the present, moral hypocrisy abounding. Brisk, professional and wholly terrifying, he ran the trembling cook to earth and did what was necessary for her hand; he drank off a great deal of scrub, devoured some beef pasties, and went in pursuit of bunions with vigour. Then he climbed to the top of the house and did his best with the little maid, as tender and charming as he could make himself and as nobody except possibly the mongoose ever saw him.

"You may dismiss your unworthy thoughts about the butler," he said to Lady Barsham an hour later in the drawing room, only lately emptied of its gaggle of perfumed tea drinkers. "It seems she has a sister in service at Blackow and has made the acquaintance of another, less admirable butler than your own."

"That greasy little black man, that ..."

"Quite so. You have seen him then? He has the appearance of a race rider though he has never been one, I understand. It seems he did not promise marriage, a point more in his favour than not in my opinion, and made sure she understood his intentions were wholly dishonourable; she is merely distraught she will lose her place and not find another."

He gave a bow, brief and stiff, as if he had now done with the problem, it was Lady Barsham's own. And then, about to depart, he said: "You know, it was cruel of you to turn your face against Blackow. Ann Gerard has done you no injury."

"I know you are her particular friend. Of course I have nothing against the girl. But I know too much about her husband and I refuse to have him in my house – Oliver has long been against him in any case. And then recently I heard some ... some chance remark that decided me beyond any doubt. I had begun to wonder if I should try an acquaintance, but now ..."

The Doctor walked back to a chair and leant on it, picking destructively at its cover. He looked pale today, and slightly dusty; and he was wearing black, which was unusual, and which always made him look distinguished but gloomy.

"Now?"

"Alex, I do not break confidences."

161

His look was peculiarly bleak. "But you have heard something significant and to Harry Gerard's disadvantage?"

"Anybody who listens may do that. The boy was always fly-by-night, headlong after excitement just like his mother."

The Doctor prowled round the furniture. "But this is something out of the ordinary. You have no real reason, except perhaps spite – and you are not a spiteful person – to bar him from your house. Many men drink and gamble and have unfortunate lapses in public."

"Oh, that! He insulted me most charmingly – I am not at all surprised Ann Mathick found no obstacle to marrying him. I know of few women in her place who would not have done so."

"So what have you heard that is so terrible?"

Lady Barsham walked to a window and looked out at the pleasant view across some acres of lawns coloured by fallen leaves. From her intense expression and the long silence she might have been making mental calculations on the height of the tallest oak and its distance from the broad terrace; the Doctor, watching her closely, was aware of a great inner struggle. It was not, however, to do with mathematics.

"Charlotte and I were in Town, shopping, paying calls. We did not have a London season this year as you know; I took the opportunity a few weeks ago of visiting those friends we have been forced to neglect. Oliver was at Oxford with a man named Clifdon, a bull of a man, very given to roaring at nothing; the eldest son is part of the racing crowd, the sporting set. The talk at dinner turned to luck, chance, the wheel of fortune. Young Clifdon said he had known someone put a hundred pounds on a horse not to win – a very private bet, you understand, and not to win. The horse was pulled up. Of course there were suspicious circumstances. There was the rumour of an enquiry, a great deal of dirty linen was likely to be washed in public. In the end the incident was ignored. The man who had laid the bet was Harry Gerard and he won two thousand pounds by it."

"Is that all?" demanded the Doctor, who feared it was not. "He has never, to my knowledge, represented himself as a saint."

"Clifdon said, either then or later, that he knew for certain

Harry Gerard had been engaged to be married to some girl in Kent, and not so long ago, not long before Ann Mathick came to Thorn."

"Perhaps it was called off. Engagements come and go, dear Louise, it is the way of things."

Lady Barsham, having come so far, was afraid to go further. A melodramatic feeling that she was currently redirecting the cold hand of destiny seized her. Usually forthright, she was not insensitive, nor did she underestimate the tragedy that might follow if what silly, frivolous Jeremy Clifdon, always given to exaggeration, had said was true. She stared helplessly at the Doctor and then stepped forward, perplexed, uncertain, deeply troubled.

"Clifdon was very sure that he had married her," she said.

"How in God's name do you think he could keep two wives at once?" asked William that evening over the debris of their dinner together in his quiet rooms in Norwich. "How could such a thing be possible?"

He and the Doctor often dined. They had discovered how often their tastes coincided and perhaps their aspirations also. They were both honest men, though the Doctor could be secretive and William devious; they both owned to bad tempers, occasionally and hopefully in some good cause; they both tried to be temperate in all things and only partially succeeded.

"More wine? No doubt there is no substance to the story," the Doctor searched for an unemptied bottle, "and it would be like Harry Gerard to boast in his cups about some pretty girl in Kent."

"Why Kent I wonder?" William pushed his glass out; the wine was red, pungent, indisputably of the full-blooded south. It was just the accompaniment for game pie, especially the richest, most exquisite, most indigestible game pie he had ever tasted, cooked by the Lascar and brought by the Doctor in a hamper containing several other such culinary miracles.

"On the other hand, if it were true," and the Doctor scratched his bristling head – his wig was lodged on a spare candlestick down the table, "why, then, it would be bigamy."

"It would throw a jaundiced light over Lady Gerard's situation certainly." William was inclined to dryness, even acidity where Ann was concerned. "And over Gerard's business arrangements. He has mortgaged Thorn, Templeton is party to the deal; it will be common knowledge shortly. And yet I met Mrs Palmer – oh, so loquacious a lady! – at the house of a client the other day and she informed me that Sir Harry is toying with the idea of draining the lake at Blackow and restocking its refreshed waters with the finest ... something. Carp? Who dare guess? It struck me then that such high flying is bound to end in a painful way, possibly a fast ship to America – and that could be an exceedingly painful way to see the world."

"I knew nothing of mortgages. I understood they had no money. Ann would not say so, of course, but I read her face. I called the other day and found her hard at the accounts; she joked about doing them weekly now, to 'keep up with the bills' as she put it."

"You knew before she married it would be like this."

"I should have tried harder to stop it."

"She entered the affair with her eyes open. You did all you could."

"Perhaps more than was proper. Well, she has made great strides at Thorn. The house is in good repair, the buildings sound. And now all to waste again, I suppose."

William was thinking of France and a brief but splendid episode in his not-too-misspent youth; he had been at sea too much for any serious dissipation. The taste of the wine brought back some rosy memories.

"All to waste. Everything to waste when feckless Sir Harry gallops across the country on his damn uncontrollable horse. There is always Tom ... He loves those acres."

"And if feckless Sir Harry were married before?"

Possibilities crackled about them. William sighed. He had done his best these six months to push the thought of Ann Mathick far back in his crowded mind; an obscure sense of disappointment – in himself, in her, in something that might have been but most definitely was not – lingered on. But it was only that, a smoky lingering trace. He had been disappointed too often – who in the Navy had not? – over prizes, promotion, the sailing qualities of certain of his ships, and certainly over women, who loved the uniform but dare not contemplate the inadequate pay and the long separations necessary to a sailor's wife – and probably in that order. Disappointment was almost an old friend. But the thought of Ann still made him irritated, and he reached for the wine bottle.

"Two marriages? Would he be so rash? Would he dare so much? No!"

There was a moment's quiet. The fire spat and a log fell from the andiron in a shower of sparks. The game pie sat uneasily. The Doctor looked suddenly distraught.

"You have drunk too much," he said slowly and clearly, as if he himself had not.

"Never! But I will tell you this, Alex dear friend, sweet Miss Ann chose a hard narrow bed and must lie in it. At the moment – and only at the moment, I say – it contains Harry Gerard, Norfolk's most charming liar, cheat and whore."

There had been that girl in Provence, rounded, golden, and there had been olives, all those damn olives and sardines. Sardines? Yes, sardines; he remembered most distinctly she had tasted of sardines. And not at all like Ann Mathick. Ann Mathick was too little, too thin – my God, he could circle her waist with his hands! And no breasts, and no charm, and no ... She had put up her chin at him though, eyes brilliant, compelling.

William heard the Doctor's voice from far away.

"I want you to find out if there is any truth in this story. Go to London. Go to Kent even."

He heard his own voice answering automatically: "It will be expensive."

"I can afford to pay."

The wine tasted like iron suddenly, heavy and dull. William slammed down his glass. "Damn Ann Mathick!"

The Doctor raised an eyebrow, gave a half smile, but he was resolute. "And while you are in Kent," he said mildly, "you might deliver Bombay Jack to a certain Captain Thrussel and see him safely stowed on the Indiaman *Tagus*. It would hardly be out of your way if this woman of Harry Gerard's is still in Canterbury. I hate to see him go but he must have his sun and I ..."

"You must meddle in what is none of your business."

"I have to know the truth."

And so do I, thought William gloomily, though God knows I do not care for her in the least.

It was strange that their only serious quarrel should not be about money.

"That damn inquisitive Doctor!" Harry cried, his boots leaving a muddy trail over the black and white marble of the hall floor as he followed her into the library. "Why does he come to see you so often? You are not ill."

Ann was groping for a pile of bills at the back of the desk. "You know he is my friend; and he does not call often at all. Four times in six months. Is that often?"

"But he is always about, in the village, in the lanes, driving like a madman over the Gorse and scaring the cattle. And now today, emptying his bag all over the table in here, letting that wretched animal chew the curtains, asking personal questions."

"What questions?" She was scarcely listening. The fact that bailiffs had called the day before looking for Harry and she had had to send Tom, burning with understandable indignation, to waylay and warn him on his way home from Norwich, was still fresh in her mind.

"About my London clubs. What is it to him what my clubs are?"

"Perhaps he was simply trying to be polite, to make conversation."

"Well damn him! He should keep away from my house! Never ask him here again, Annie. Never!"

These last two weeks he had deteriorated, she thought, straightening from her search and leaning with her back against the desk. Every day he seemed worse, more wild, more querulous, less able to grasp the immediate, always and always inclined to brood on a rosy future. He was growing untidy too and his eyes were restless and dimmed; he looked thin and dissipated and ill. Yes, ill. Her heart seemed to contract. How could she help him if he would not let her? She touched the smooth wood of the desk for a moment as if to reassure herself of the unchanging, then she said quietly: "Harry, we must talk."

"About money, I suppose?" He was petulant again, his flicker of temper out, done, forgotten; his blue stare slid past her to the windows, to the view of the terrace with its tangle of old roses, almost leafless, whipping back and forth in the wind. It was a cold day; up on the Gorse there had been half a gale, vigorous and chilling.

"You have never been open with me," she held a slim packet of letters in her hand, "and now you have mortgaged Thorn and told me nothing. Oh no, spare excuses; spare everything, even explanations. The thing is done. But could you not have told me yourself instead of letting me learn from backstairs gossip and Mrs Palmer, and a nasty little message from the bank?"

Oddly, her calmness reassured him. He was in a fragile mood, caught between self-pity and bravado. He despised himself for drinking heavily and in more sober moments still tried, to no effect, to think seriously for a solution to his predicament; but then hopelessness would close in and the bottle was to hand again.

"I was afraid to." He would be honest then, if she desired it.

"Harry," she said on a sort of sigh.

If she had wept and implored and howled, if she had tried to kill him with the poker, she could not have moved him more. The one word said everything. If he had been William Claverden he might have pondered the subtle inflections of the English language, but he was not William. He said: "Annie, it will come right. It will all come right," and then, fired by the dramatic, "I promise! Any day now there will be news ..."

"From Sable Island? I was not aware you ever received letters from abroad." Only from Dover recently, always Dover.

"You have not opened any of my letters?"

"You know I have not, I would not, except those you hand me. And you need have no fears on that score – Praed intercepts the post most conscientiously."

167

Harry swore softly and stalked to the window. "I did not want you troubled with my debts."

"But I am! How could I fail to be? How can I pay the men? How do we eat? And there is the ball, the silly ball; the invitations are sent out already."

"There is no question of cancelling the ball." He swung to face her, digging his hands into his pockets, throwing up his head. "Sable Island will pay for the ball, will pay everything. But we must be patient, must manage a while longer ..."

He saw her stare of bewildered disbelief, her thin pale face with the eyes smudged and lined by anxiety. But she was as erect and self-contained as ever, the letters – bills, bills, bills he supposed – still held loosely in her hand.

"How long must we manage?" she asked.

"A month, maybe a little more. I told you ..."

"You told me once Sable Island would make our fortunes. Harry, there is only one Sable Island, a ... a devil of a place for wrecks," – how she remembered that dismissive, disdainful voice – "and it is nowhere near Africa. It is the other side of the world."

He saw the tears in her eyes and came to take her cold hands, to detach the letters and drop them carelessly on the floor. "You have every right to call me a rogue, to mistrust me in all things but two – I care for you, and Sable Island will bring us luck and a fortune."

She did not ask again where it was. She said gently: "It may be difficult to hold out until the new year. How much do you owe? How much do you really owe?"

"Too much," he said lightly. She was in the circle of his arms but was rigid, withdrawn.

"How much?"

The silence lengthened. She waited, head up. It was difficult to see she was breathing. Was it his imagination or was she really so much thinner? Perhaps, after all, that damn doctor had been paying a professional visit. Not a child, he hoped: oh God, not a child! There had been no sign of one yet and just lately he had slept alone and in drunken stupors; until things were better he must continue to keep away from her.

"Ten thousand," he said when he could not decently keep quiet any longer.

Perhaps her eyes widened a little, it was difficult to tell. But suddenly she leaned back on his arm and laughed, and all her old sparkle came back. "Ten thousand! A trifle! But there is no hope unless we are drastic, unless we retrench."

Retrench was not a word Harry understood.

"How can you bear to go on?" he asked, amazed.

"You smell of drink. Can you not go and bathe? Oh, don't mistake me for a model of virtue! What you lose I lose. And I tell you this, Harry Gerard, I have no intention of quitting this place in my petticoat and tramping through Norfolk begging my bread."

William went by stage to London, circumstances conspiring to confound his expectations of either riding, going post, or driving himself. It was many years since he had last sat inside a common coach – no outside seats were available – and he had ample time to reflect there on his singularly unattractive role in this tedious domestic drama. He had given his opinion, salty and scathing, to the Doctor before setting out.

"This is a ridiculous business! By the time I return he may well have been arrested for debt."

"Debt and bigamy are different crimes," the Doctor had replied patiently.

Such a journey, William decided, should only be undertaken for a crime as serious as murder. On his brisk walk across the city to the Maid's Head he saw the mail leaving the Rampant Horse with all the usual commotion and wondered whether, seeing he had not been able to get a seat on it, he ought to have delayed this crazy expedition to Kent until he could. The stage was almost as fast but had untold eccentricities: a swashbuckling off-leader and what looked like a blind wheeler being two of them. They were six inside and elbow room was scanty owing to everyone being muffled to the ears against the coldest day of the winter. After an hour the air was stale and sour.

William, unctuously polite, begged to be allowed to lower the sash. Hostile eyes regarded him all round.

"Fresh air never did harm," announced the large woman on his left, shifting her wicker basket fractionally so that she had a better view of the striking man about to let too much of the stuff into their foetid enclosure. William reached across her with difficulty. The rush of blessed air was undeniably freezing and caused an outcry; the sash was raised at once.

The coach slowed with a great deal of jerking and whoaing and the rattling of chains and poles. The flat levels of the Waveney were all round. They were in Suffolk then.

"Late," remarked a plump little man in an old-fashioned tricorne, consulting his watch. "He will make up for it after the next change and have us in the ditch."

There were several shrieks at this and general consternation. The wicker basket jumped up and down with its owner's emotion. William wondered what would happen if he confessed to a mongoose in the box at his feet – he had been loath to trust Bombay Jack with the rest of the luggage in the boot – and he gave a mild, private grin. For a while after that he amused himself trying to guess the occupations of his fellow travellers, then he stared through the smeared window at the grey and frosted countryside which all appeared, in this particular place, slovenly and unkempt. Then he tried to sleep, but that proved impossible, although he had, in his rather adventurous life, slept in far worse places than an English stage coach. There was a deal too much picking up and putting down: in thirty miles his companions inside changed entirely twice over; and there were altercations over geese, travelling alive or dead, the case was unclear; over a young girl with a lapdog which was continually sick; over the absolute resolution on the part of the coach proprietors that no fish should be carried in their vehicles, not even paying double fare. Lunch, which William had hoped might be a leisurely meal, was eaten at the run, and besides which was almost unbelievably indigestible and overpriced.

The afternoon found him trying to sleep again, in vain. For a while he ranged among memories, and he recalled with a momentary pang his years in the Navy. Even now he could not truthfully say why he had left the service, although the hope of promotion was so very slight now that his only influence in the Admiralty was dead and his exemplary record had to stand alone; the chances of making post-captain were infinitely remote. He had been trained in the law, he had some aptitude for it and a mild affection, even a sort of inner amusement. It appealed to him when in eccentric humour, and in a fit of just such humour he had thrown up the sea and bought himself, with his share of prize money, into the office of a London man, a devil for the very worst criminal cases. A year of this was enough for William. Used to the repetitive depravities of the lower deck, to the summary justice of a ship at sea and at war, he found an unrelieved diet of misery and crime depressing in the extreme, the interminable quibbles of the courts infuriating. He missed the sea beyond measure but refused to admit it; was offered command – command, and most handsomely paid, oh most handsomely – of an Indiaman by an old friend in the Company, but passed it up with impressive nonchalance as if Indiamen were to be had two a penny. Instead he travelled north to his mother's county and those quiet rooms in Norwich where he could hear the cathedral bells and see the masts crowded along the wharves.

It was not entirely satisfactory. He was accustomed to few possessions, had often been penniless apart from his pay in the early days, though there had been money in trust for him from his father's estate; he was acquainted with nearly all the weaknesses of the human character. He should have been content with a modest income, a few friends, and sufficient business to keep him occupied – but he was not, and he was irritable and unhappy. He had been a respected, conscientious officer, a little unorthodox perhaps, a little too ready to question superiors; but he was imperturbable under fire, could get the best out of any man, and lived for his ship. He had served under flogging captains, hearty captains, brave, indifferent or drunken captains, and he had learned from them all: and besides he was a natural seaman. He had won command of the *Siren* wholly on merit, having been sent with twenty men in a cutter to surprise and take

171

a privateer brig hidden away in a small cove; along with the twenty men he had had two unreliable and ancient nine-pounders, a quantity of small arms, and a great deal of swagger, foolhardy courage, and native ingenuity. Was this penchant of the British, he had wondered, for sending handfuls of men against far superior forces in the expectation of remarkable victories really just a lack of foresight? But the brig was surprised and taken for the loss of two lives and the mast of the cutter. A week later William was given the sloop-of-war found damaged and drifting after an encounter with a Frenchman.

"It is less than you deserve," his captain had said with a savage look at the small vessel wallowing in the swell as her crew rigged jury masts and rudder, "but the *Siren* was a happy ship. Now Pritchard is killed they should have another as honest and able."

It was the only commendation he received, but the appointment was confirmed: he had the sloop and the promotion, was master and commander. His luck had turned, perhaps was to keep turning, was to bring him action, prizes, recognition. At this point, he recalled, he had written a dozen letters home to Mary Chiswick charged with excitement, ambition, hope, and passion. Some of it had been quite flagrant, a little too passionate for its reader perhaps. Or had her parents read the letters as well and taken the first steps to sever their impressionable girl from such an outrageous and unprincipled young man?

One thing had been sure, if he was to advance higher he would have to fight his way there. Only he and the *Siren* were sent hither and thither with despatches, ran back and forth between the worn-out ships on blockade duty, saw French men-of-war and privateers on the horizon and had to leave them there; then ninety-seven and the mutinies at Spithead and the Nore, a great deal of grievance, dark talk, discontent. William too was discontented; the damped-down fires of ambition sprang up and roasted him thoroughly. The first man to fight on behalf of sailors' conditions, captain of a cheerful, loyal, efficient crew, nevertheless the events at Spithead only made him more aware of himself, his own condition.

Then Mary Chiswick had married Bolton.

So to London, so to Norwich. He might have had an aptitude for the law but he had none for social life; years of dealing with tough seamen, and stupid seamen, and seamen pressed or volunteered but either way criminal, made him impatient with the vagaries of those who had led less difficult and more sheltered lives. Sometimes he was not sure, after all, if he could survive without the Navy; he did not seem fitted for life on land.

His practice grew in spite of all this. His acquaintance with some of the old county families, either through connections of his mother's or some small legal business here and there, served to circulate his name and augment his reputation; and he was personable and educated, if a little forbidding. Soon he could afford to move to a better house, a more fashionable quarter – but he preferred to stay in his bare bachelor's rooms over the office. He did not care for fashion, did not care for prestige; it never crossed his mind he might try to cut a dash, he would have laughed at it. Money meant nothing to him now beyond a means to eat and to sleep dry and to purchase his wines and his precious miniatures – and he could do without those tomorrow if he chose.

He deplored his own weakness in giving way to the Doctor's whims; for that was surely what this was, a whim. Of course Harry Gerard had not been married already when he married Ann Mathick, and no enquiries in the many tap-rooms of Kent would reveal any lady who had been loved, jilted, or remotely connected with him.

William admitted a slight interest in Ann, the very slightest. He thought of her with exasperation and his respect was unwilling, to say the least, but he did think of her and he did respect her. He also wondered whether she truly loved Harry Gerard or whether, as the Doctor asserted, she had merely needed someone to satisfy her starved senses. Damn the girl! And she was not even pretty!

At some time towards dusk he let down the window again and several flakes of snow blew in. All the insides were male by now and were only silently indignant. The countryside looked even greyer, colder and more disreputable. William wished fervently he was back at sea; the sea was the very devil but it never looked shabby. He sat for some minutes with the freezing blast hitting him in the face. If there had been any chance of promotion, any faint hope of a frigate, he would have stayed …

By the time the coach reached London he was sharing the much-breathed air with five different companions and had a wretched headache and imperfect control of his temper. But with the impeccable politeness of which he was occasionally capable he held the door while two women passengers descended. One was a middle-aged countrywoman, the other young and pert and gaudily dressed: her cloak parted to reveal a stupefying décolletage, a bodice that would have been considered unacceptable at a debauch. William, who had not bothered to notice her until that moment, gave a disconcerting shout of laughter. Was this, he thought, what Harry Gerard's 'wife' would be like?

The girl snatched the cloak together, affronted. Her eyes were bold, though, demanding his attention. They did not get it. He looked at her as if she were a troublesome child, an irritation.

In truth, he did not see her at all, not after that one moment of revelation. He was intent on his nagging inner voices. Well, what if Gerard had another wife? It did not matter to William Claverden if the man had ten wives living. Why should it? He strode away, in a dark and dangerous mood, his fashionable hat square on his shorn black curls – a bad sign – and Bombay Jack under his arm.

10

MEANWHILE THE Doctor was at Thorn pursuing Education.

He had driven over for his weekly visit to find Tom and Miss Pennyquick in sole residence, all the furniture in disarray, and everywhere the signs of disorganised departure. Jim Knight had found a very good position as a manager over New Buckenham way and had gone there along with, as Tom put it, 'all the little knights and dear Mrs K. in her best Norwich shawl'.

And Maggie?

"To Lynn," Tom said, looking downcast at the thought of a return to Miss Pennyquick's puritan cookery. "Poor Maggie! She howled all night, swore she would not go. At the finish she declared she would only leave if Ann wrote to her, if she could return after Christmas to see ... to see how things were settled."

Things had obviously been settled so far with resolution and ferocity: for once even Tom had been taken aback by Ann's majestic mood. Blackow was to be shut up, there was to be a general retreat to Thorn. And he had found himself strangely touched by the nature of her sweeping economies: apart from Jim Knight the rest of the men were staying. Miss Pennyquick must manage the house as she could, the farm was not to suffer more than was necessary.

"And Mrs McGinly?" The Doctor himself would baulk at removing Mrs McGinly if she had no desire to go.

"Ann has found her a place in Norwich, cook to one of Lady

Barsham's cousins, I think. Anyway it is a huge house, an enormous responsibility, and a positive step up in the world. But you can tell how pleased she is by the fact that no one dare go in the kitchen at Blackow, she has a carving knife to hand and a whole battery of dishes and bowls. The place has resounded to the crash of breaking china and the howls of the poor unfortunates who dare cross her for at least three days now."

The Doctor considered. "You will be the only one to come out of this well, you with your fifty acres."

Tom swung from the fire impatiently. "You mean she will lose Thorn? Why?" And then, with a sort of childish anguish: "Oh, why did she have to marry him! Why, why, why?"

"She was in love with him."

"And he has made her look old and thin."

This was not strictly true but the Doctor was too honest to pretend he did not take the point. "So all this is what she calls retrenchment," he said, looking about.

It was. The Doctor had a sinking feeling it might be all too late, that Ann's bold advance on Francis Forsie's neglect would turn into more than ignominious and hasty retreat, that all the signs were there it was only a matter of time before she was driven out, annihilated. He found Tom looking at him hopefully – did the boy expect him to conjure a miracle to save them? What could save them, except a miracle?

It was time to work. A clean neck and knee breeches did not make a gentleman, as Miss Pennyquick pointed out several times a week. Tom wrestled a while with basic mathematics and then passed on to the mysteries of grammar. At Ann's own desk – brought from Blackow on a farm cart – he wrote his first letter to her at the Doctor's dictation, a letter so excruciatingly polite it was a masterpiece of formality, a letter expressing great interest in the weather and the health and spirits of 'your ladyship's household'. The phrasing seemed ill-chosen: the spirits of her ladyship's household had never been lower. Tom and the Doctor noticed nothing untoward however, and Tom signed it with a flourish, scarlet with achievement.

The Doctor then fell to discussing ancient salves, bee-stings, and cheeses with Miss Pennyquick, who brought in the last of the London tea – 'so special, so frighteningly expensive, ordered simply because Sir Harry,' and here she curled her lip, 'would drink no other.'

"What about the ball?" Tom's opinion of the ball was as plain as Miss Pennyquick's of Sir Harry. "Lord, I can't take this stuff, it tastes like hair oil. It don't seem right to charge so much for shrivelled leaves and a pinch of orange."

"The ball is still on?" The Doctor was astounded.

"It is. Though how it will be paid for is a mystery," said Miss Pennyquick coldly, "and scarcely an invitation turned down!"

It would be quite like Harry Gerard to have asked two hundred couples, thought the Doctor, and damn the cost. He shuddered. Tom too was silent, remembering his dash to warn Harry of the bailiffs; he could only have done it to save Ann's distress. Even now he felt ashamed of himself, knowing he could cheerfully have seen Harry taken up for debt and borne away to unsavoury captivity, he disliked him so intensely.

"I have just the cure for this depression." The Doctor was studying the troubled face under the rampant fair hair. "It was intended for another patient but he will not grudge us a glass," and he pulled a bottle of rum from under his coat.

They had hardly drawn the cork when they were interrupted by a crash without, the sound of boots hurrying, of hooves, of muffled curses. A maniacal Pashman stuck in his head.

"Sent to find you," he was wheezing for breath. "Her horse has come home by itself. Everyone going in circles at the house and only that b——— of a chestnut for anyone to use to have a look."

The Doctor stepped forward. "Lady Gerard was out riding?"

"Took His Eminence's horse, that black bastard like the devil incarnate. Bold she was, seeing His E's to London or the like. Said she was going a-visiting, no one knows where. You should see them all! Damn old women running in cackles like a lot of silly hens!"

Miss Pennyquick felt this was poetic licence: only Praed and Mrs McGinly, a housemaid and the groom were left at Blackow.

She said: "May I beg a ride in your gig?" to the Doctor, already on her way for bonnet and cape. "I walked over. I would like to get back as soon as I can."

Tom had burst away to the kitchen for whip and gloves. "I'll take Hollin's pony." And he was gone, the door banging, a tremendous yell at the field gate a moment after.

"He only has a bridle," Miss Pennyquick said somewhat irrelevantly, "he should take care for his silly young neck."

She and the Doctor repaired to the yard. The wind was cruel and Pashman's sweating horse looked understandably depressed with life. The Doctor helped Miss Pennyquick into the gig.

"Buy a jug of beer," he said, bending to press something in Pashman's grubby palm, "and something for the horse."

Pashman stared, decided it must be a joke and began to grin. The Doctor's face dissuaded him. He closed his hand on the money and spat. "Don't fret about Her Ladyship," and here a delighted sneer, "I saw her leave. Rode that brute like a jockey and out of sight before you could blink."

But the Doctor and Miss Pennyquick, steering an erratic course for Blackow, did not feel reassured in the least.

"She was in a wild mood," Miss Pennyquick admitted as they hurtled down under the bare, straining trees to the huge square pile that was Blackow. "This is the third time in a month Sir Harry has run off."

"Run off? Oh surely not!" The Doctor had one hand to his sliding wig and hat, the other trying weakly to take a pull at his bolting horse.

"He left her a letter," was the sober reply. "Of course I do not know what it said." Then she gave a shriek as they shot past the steps and fled towards the stables, to draw up with a slither by the sullen groom and the white-faced chestnut.

"Good, good," cried the Doctor, "mount and be off!"

What the groom said in answer to this was luckily drowned in the clatter of hooves. He vanished at the gallop, on the saddle if not in it, and the Doctor, his mind turning to broken bones, cast about under his seat to make sure he had his instrument bag.

At Thorn Tom was also encountering the nastier side of the

equine character. Hollin emerged from the byre to see what the shouting was about.

"Can you catch him?" Tom demanded, burning with frustration as the shaggy grey pony circled just out of reach with the maddening cunning of his kind.

Hollin dug into his pocket. A mouldy collection of unidentifiable objects came forth. The pony stopped circling and looked interested. Hollin made a soft noise of encouragement and then turned on his heel and walked back to the gate; the pony followed. There he received the rotten titbits and put his head meekly into the trap bridle; in place of the driving reins Tom had knotted a frail piece of rope. Hollin looked at it with derision.

"Not had a leg across him for years," he said.

"That can't be helped. Oh, stand still! Stand!" This as the pony did a neat pirouette worthy of a cavalry charger and came down solidly on Tom's toe. Hollin grabbed the grey forelock.

"Get up," he ordered unsympathetically. "Miss Ann'll be dead afore you reach the top of the Gorse."

In the saddle Tom looked insecure, but he had no fear of the pony, only a fear of parting company with it and losing his means of finding Ann. Hollin let go. The pony exploded into a canter. Tom faced him at the hill and gave him his head; they were out of sight in a minute, still together, but less cohesively.

Hollin grunted and made his way back to his cottage. It was creditably clean these days and the pot over the fire smelled of good gamey fare, excellently seasoned. He put on his good brown coat and his old, rusty hat, and picked up a stout walking stick. Then he made his way slowly to the river bank and began looking, seriously and methodically, among the osiers and the tangle of root and branch beside the water. He too had seen Ann that morning, and going hell for leather with half her hair down and the horse pulling like a mad thing. She had been down on the water meadows, apparently making for the ford by the mill.

But that black beast of Harry Gerard's had been crazed enough to try to swim instead.

All this time Ann had been sitting in Lady Barsham's blue

drawing room sipping a most exquisite tea, the name of which was so peculiar she dare only ask for it to be repeated twice in case they all thought her impossibly stupid. She supposed Harry's wretched horse was home by now or perhaps, empty-headed brute as it was, it had carried on blindly for Suffolk.

"My dear, we must send word to Blackow," said Lady Barsham, pouring more tea and casting an anxious eye over her unexpected guest. Ann was dressed in a cast-off gown of Charlotte's, which fitted her very badly and did queer things to her pale complexion.

"That would be kind." Ann privately thought it would also be unnecessary. Babs was at Thorn for the day and no one else at Blackow cared a fig where she was, except possibly Mrs McGinly. But it would not do to appear ungracious, especially since her precipitous entrance across the manicured lawns, now scarred dramatically with hoofmarks.

"Charlotte, will you see to it? Send Mount with a message and tell him to use the cob; there is no need to harness the pair. Oh, and ask Susan if Lady Gerard's bath is ready. I simply fail to understand how heating hot water for one person can take such a very long time."

Charlotte left the room with a smile. Lady Barsham, eyeing the closing door, said quietly: "We have not been good neighbours, I fear."

Ann concentrated on her tea. "I understood you did not wish to invite my husband to your house after the incident in Norwich. Harry has no sense of timing and no shame."

Their eyes met. Lady Barsham understood a challenge when she was offered one and felt heartened. This girl was better, oh far better, than she had supposed; this girl had courage and a sense of humour. And nerve. To watch her veering across the flowerbeds on that headstrong black, hat gone and hair in loops, skirts muddied to the knee, that had been something! And perhaps if the black had had any kind of feeling left in his mouth after years of rough riding, and had eaten less corn and been given more exercise the girl might have stopped him. As it was they had taken the low box hedge by the stables together and on landing he had smelled horse in an instant and had swerved violently, sliding on the immaculate gravel. Ann had dropped in a tangle of damp skirts at the feet of the speechless head gardener and they had both watched Harry's graceless horse making his escape into the avenue; in ten seconds he was out of sight. There had been a fragrance of wet earth and crushed thyme and leaves; the gardener was apparently struck dumb for ever. Ann had risen slowly, had felt her bruised arms and found them whole, had brushed stones and dirt from her sorry skirts, and had turned to find Lady Barsham hurrying from the house followed by a whole suite of curious servants. Thus the drawing room, the tea, and Charlotte's unbecoming finery.

"The Doctor," said Lady Barsham, "told me we might be friends."

"The Doctor is meddlesome but irresistible." Ann gave a brief smile.

"He has a great regard for you."

"He is very full of sound advice. Sometimes it is too much to bear."

"I understand perfectly. But you must humour him. He is quite the most reliable friend to be found anywhere. Ah, news of the bath perhaps."

Charlotte had returned and hung, almost shy, in the doorway. "It will be ready in a few moments. But oh, Mama, there is a letter just come for you and I am sure ... The hand is certainly Mr Claverden's. So I have brought it in."

Lady Barsham raised her plucked eyebrows. Then she cast a look at Ann and found her politely indifferent. She allowed herself a tight smile. "No doubt he wished to write to you, my dear, and supposed, correctly, that would be improper. I cannot for my life understand why else he should take up his pen to me."

She slit the wafer and read. Her smile faded and a small frown settled. Charlotte began to look a little frightened.

"He is not ill? He is such a difficult person to advise but he does take so little care of himself; he laughed when I told him once he should wear a thick coat in the cold and rain."

Ann tried to imagine herself suggesting to William that he put on or put off anything at all, even his hat, and could not do it. He would fix her with that dark and omnivorous gaze of his and she would not dare open her mouth. And was he really in love with this pretty, generous, but very young lady with the large eyes?

"He was a sailor, you know," the pretty young lady informed her, having had no reply from her mother who was absorbed in re-reading the letter.

"So I understand."

"He told me all about it," a gross exaggeration. "He said 'I was at sea' when I asked him what he was doing in ninety-six because that was the year ... Mama, are you sure nothing is wrong?"

Lady Barsham, who had decided it must be a day for surprises and was trying not to mind, put away her letter most firmly in a deep pocket. "No, of course nothing is wrong. What could be wrong? Mr Claverden is in London for a week or so and is simply polite enough to inform me of it and enquire after our health. He has gone on an errand of mercy for the Doctor's poor mongoose. For a man of his temper he has taken some trouble to give a good impression of himself."

She did him too much justice: he wrote without preamble and no further noticeable formality after the blunt 'Dear Madam' at the top of the page; and he wrote only that her information regarding Harry Gerard was, in the Doctor's eyes at least, worthy of investigation, that he had been – very reluctantly, there could be no doubt – persuaded to investigate. He had not had time before he left Norwich, however, to call on her for further particulars, supposing she had any, of the girl in Kent. So had she? Was she willing to impart them if she had? And would she write to him at Lincoln's Inn under the name of Melburn? Yours etc. Wm Claverden.

The man was exasperating. And then to receive such a letter with Ann Gerard sitting ten feet away talking ships to Charlotte. Ships?

"I am sure you are wrong to say Mr Claverden was a sailor, Lottie," she rebuked gently. "I am certain it would be more correct to describe him as an officer."

"Oh he was! He was. He had his own ship, the *Siren*."

"How singularly inappropriate the names of some vessels are. I was under the impression sirens lured unsuspecting mariners to their doom. Perhaps I am mistaken." Lady Barsham felt the letter crackle in her pocket and shifted delicately on the sofa as if it were a grenade. If she refused to tell William the few facts she had absorbed about Harry Gerard's disreputable affairs, she thought, this slender, resilient creature thrown so theatrically into her kitchen garden might never be touched by scandal and might live in happy ignorance for ever – or for a month; or a week.

A maid knocked to say the bath was ready. Lady Barsham gave complicated instructions and waved Charlotte away to help. Then she went to find her husband to tell him they would have a guest for dinner, and afterwards made for her writing desk with its curlicues of brass inlay and ingenious secret drawers; in one of these she put William's letter. Perhaps she would not answer it. She felt a small stab of anger at the Doctor for busying himself in the matter. In another moment she had forgiven him. He was furiously fond of Ann Gerard and was only acting for her good. Or was he? How amusing, she thought suddenly, if some deeper affection had been engaged; she had known him for years but had never seen him pay any particular attention to a woman.

And then she wondered idly whether William Claverden, being a seafaring man, knew Kent at all well and whether there too, as in Norfolk, he had influential friends. But she comforted herself with the thought that if the girl existed at all she was most probably a tap-room slut, pretty, ambitious, and unhealthy. And there were plenty of those, she supposed, in every county in England.

The bath left Ann pink as a rose. The fire had been gloriously stoked, the water near scalding. Charlotte had perched on a footstool and talked through the whole process without appearing to draw breath, giving an opinion on everything from the boredom of country life to the flash and fire of Harry Gerard's insane horse.

"Too much fire, not enough sense," Ann said, swathed in a robe as voluminous as a cloud, her skin glowing, "but then he has been so badly treated all his life. Harry bought him for his looks, and for his speed — he has won some races in his time, I think. He has a long and shadowy history and was to be had very cheap."

"How could you dare ride him? Does Sir Harry not mind?"

Sir Harry did not know, but there was no need to go into that. Sir Harry had hired a post-chaise for this latest escapade and had left a note explaining nothing, the writing all over the place, an ominously sentimental 'Think of me' at the end, and an afterthought: 'Look after the horse.' Ann studied her damp hair with a wry smile, ramming in hairpins and then plucking them all out again. "Sir Harry will only mind if the poor silly beast has broken its leg or flayed itself in the brambles," she said with a sudden flash of a look at the awed Charlotte, "but since it has already survived so long against the odds I daresay it will get home safely."

Charlotte, seated now on the edge of the lavishly decorated bed, did not quite know what to make of her guest. She was such a little, insignificant thing, and yet … Just now, pushing up her dark hair with both hands and giving that bright stare in the mirror, she had been startling, magical.

There was a scatter of hairpins on the floor.

"I wish there was no ill feeling between Mama and Sir Harry," Charlotte was stooping to retrieve them. "I would so like to come to a ball at Blackow. Is it as fine as they say? Oh, how you will enjoy it!"

In the face of such enthusiasm, genuine and ingenuous, Ann quailed. That wretched ball! If only Charlotte knew how she had fought against it, had longed to call it off, to forget it entirely.

"Blackow is vast and undistinguished," she said quietly, "except perhaps for being the coldest house in England. Someone with taste, and imagination, and money might do wonders with it. We never shall. There. How is that? Better?"

Her hair was swept up loosely, a few stray curls escaping at her temples. Without Miss Pennyquick's rigorous ministrations it had reverted to unmanageable rebellion. The face beneath looked vulnerable, very pale. Charlotte smiled approval and came to offer a last pin.

"You must not mind Papa. He does not ... He does not care for the Gerards. He quarrelled with old Sir Harry before I was born, something very trivial and silly no doubt. It seems strange because they were in the army together, grew up together; they had been such friends."

"I was told that no one ever quarrelled with old Sir Harry."

"Well, Papa did."

"I suppose it takes so little to set men against each other, anything can do it."

"I always thought it was something to do with the estate. Papa once owned some land on the far side of the Blackow lake. But what does it all matter now? Only ... You may wonder why he is so reserved. He swore he would not have a Gerard in the house."

Night had fallen, the shutters were closed, a maid tended the fire and dropped them both a respectful curtsey. This was luxury, thought Ann, and luxury allied to the homely comforts necessarily demanded by a happy and unpretentious family. Charlotte was laying out a dress of cream velvet, lace at the neck and sleeves.

"It was one Frances used to wear before she married," she said with a hint of apology. "It is rather old-fashioned now, but all mine are too big for you and Hester has nothing suitable, she is only fourteen."

It was an inch too broad, that was all, but the fuller skirt and the tight waist were flattering. Ann, who never spent long in front of mirrors, was quietly pleased.

And: "Do you care for Mr Claverden?" was her unexpected question as they put the finishing touches.

Charlotte blushed raspberry. "I think he is a gentleman," she said in a voice that suggested she had begun to distinguish between men and found some so called not gentlemen at all.

"Oh, he is. But ..."

The door burst open. Charlotte's young cousins, twin

daughters of her mother's brother, had escaped the nursery. They gazed in awe at the strange lady in the lovely dress but were reassured when, in bending to inspect their identical dolls with a smile, several dark curls sprang out of place and blew gently across the lady's high forehead.

"You see how it is," said Charlotte mournfully, "I am never left alone a moment. There are always people staying, coming and going, always something to be done. How could I spend a minute in Mr Claverden's company without someone by? It would be impossible. And I would so like to hear his stories about the sea!"

"I have never met a girl like it," Lord Barsham told his wife as she prepared herself for bed.

"Which no doubt accounts for your disgraceful behaviour."

"I made her welcome."

"You stared at her all evening as if she had three heads and scarcely spoke a word. When you did it was to remark unfavourably on women who rode out alone on horses crazed with bad temper and too many oats. You were rude and offhand and perfectly uncivilised and you know it."

He hovered in the doorway watching her nightly ritual. He had discarded his wig and looked balding and florid, a big nose very prominent and his wide-apart blue eyes still giving him the look of a small boy when he glanced up suddenly with that particular surprised innocence.

"Well, the girl was damn uncivil too, sitting there in Fran's dress arguing about beans. Beans! What a subject for the dinner table – horse beans! And bringing up Forsie's name, that disreputable old dog. Did you know she has given some land to his bastard, that upstart young brute with the yellow hair?"

"I am sure the boy with yellow hair is her business, as is the settlement of her land. But did you have to be so chilling?"

"What could I have said to her?"

"How should I know. But you were the one who started the argument about the best way to grow beans. You did it to embarrass her. Well, she has more courage than you credit her with: she turned the tables and played you at the same game — and won. She proved quite conclusively she knows more about land improvement than you do. I can only applaud her."

"She is a Forsie."

"Half a Forsie."

"She is a Forsie and she married a Gerard. What do you expect me to do? I could never applaud her, whatever she may do or say."

There was a silence while Lady Barsham studied her wrinkles and meditated deeply. Then: "You should have seen the way she jumped the box hedge, that great black animal all in a lather. You would have thought he was taking the river the way he flew into the air."

"She has made an impression on you and Charlotte, I see that."

"I think she is a deal too good for Harry Gerard."

"She chose him, my dear Louise. She knew what to expect surely? He will be in the Fleet before long, I daresay. Or fled abroad. He has debts of thousands in London, Chorley told me only the other day."

Lady Barsham opened a little round pot of glaucous stuff that smelled of cucumbers. With infinite care she began to massage it into the offending wrinkles. She thought of William Claverden's letter in the recesses of her desk and of her stern resolve not to send an answer.

Dinner had not been a success but it had shown her something at least: resolve must be stern indeed to withstand certain pressures. The flaring candles down the long table had shown them an ethereal creature in borrowed clothes with uncontrollable hair and huge, fearless eyes; a realist, an optimist, excessively stubborn, and determined too, like Harry Gerard's horse, to survive against the odds. Lady Barsham, sound and sage, had recognised strain and anxiety in that white, challenging face: strain of coping with money — or without it — with Blackow, with a straying husband — talk of long absences who knows where — and of course with Thorn. When she spoke of Thorn her voice had a different quality, like a mother speaking of a favourite child.

"The Fleet? The Fleet or the Marshalsea." She put the lid back on her little round pot, carefully, carefully. "Well, we shall certainly have to save Ann from that."

For it had just occurred to her that if Harry Gerard had been married before something might yet be saved from the wreck, and God willing, if they were in time, that something might be Thorn. She had no knowledge of the law but she was beginning to have a clearer idea of William Claverden; he did not strike her as a man who would leave many stones unturned.

The girl's name had been Stratford, her family had lived in Canterbury; she would write and tell him so in the morning.

The morning came, the letter was borne away, and so was Ann, by Tom in the sporty gig.

He had taken several falls from Hollin's pony the day before, had a huge bruise turning colour on his cheekbone, a cut chin, scratches all over. He had spent hours scouring the countryside only to return to the news that Ann was safe at Upgate Place, had been invited to spend the night there, and had accepted. Relief mingled with indignation. He had felt suddenly ashamed of his excessive concern, his frantic dashing up and down to find her, and at the same time furious to think that while he had been risking his all being run away with and bucked off and trampled on and even bitten, she had been taking her ease in the finest house for miles. But by the morning he was sober, and he took care to dress well and to remember the manners Dr French had taught him – though who was Dr French to teach manners? – and Lord Barsham had given him a glass of claret and regaled him with a saucy story from his army days before he had even realised who he was. Having been obliged to speak his name again, Tom found a pair of eyes extraordinarily like Harry Gerard's looking squarely into his own, and then Lord Barsham coughed and said hoarsely: "How foolish of me not to see the likeness. There is no doubting Francis was your father, no doubting it at all."

Another glass of claret followed. Tom showed an intelligent interest in Lord Barsham's estate. By the time Ann appeared, dressed to go home in her sponged, rejuvenated riding habit, they were lost in a cheerful discussion on the virtues of Longhorns, of Devons, of permanent pasture, of drainage, and of the mysterious blights that attack peach trees.

"A bright, likable young man," Lord Barsham afterwards reported to his wife, "and when you think of his beginnings ... I must swallow all my prejudices, I thought him as promising as he could be. Alex told me as much, I remember, though it had escaped me for the moment."

But Lady Barsham, watching the flash of green wheels down the long, stately drive, did not reply. She was thinking of her letter and the possible consequences, and for the time being all power of rational conversation had left her, and all she could feel was dread, dread and a horrible conviction she had set in motion the wheels of tragedy.

"Mama, Mama!" cried Charlotte, running in with two spaniels and the little cousins at her heels. "Oh Mama, who was the tall young man with fair hair and the dreadfully bruised face? Had he been fighting? I saw him in the hall and he gave me such a bow, and a great flourish of his hat. And the way he drove that terrible horse that pawed great holes in the drive ..."

"That young man is no concern of yours," Lord Barsham said with gruff authority, all his prejudices revived in an instant. He had serious reservations about Claverden, but to see his daughter form any attachment to a Forsie by-blow ...

"Papa," she was hanging on his arm, importunate, sweet-smelling, "Papa, do say we can go to the Blackow ball."

Lord Barsham's groan was resigned.

The green wheels were gone now, his wife realised, the rhythmic beat of the hooves fading; and her letter had gone too, would be already far beyond Diss, rattling at ten miles an hour through deep Suffolk country, out of reach for ever.

⚜

Blackow was being made ready for the ball and was in uproar. Ann removed herself to Thorn and slept in her old bed. She was woken in the night by the scratching of mice and an overwhelming desire to know where Harry had gone and when he was coming back; it was a week since she had been at Upgate and she had had no word from him.

She slid out of bed, shivering as her feet touched the cold boards. In the box on the side table by the candle were all her personal bills and receipts, her painstaking calculations, and all the letters Harry had ever written her. She knocked it over as she groped for the tinder-box and had to kneel on the floor to retrieve the papers, and the tears started as she saw his violent handwriting. Where had he galloped to this time? And why not on the black horse? His leaving the horse behind troubled her. She dealt with the tears, took up the candle, and made her way along the landing.

Miss Pennyquick appeared, a vision in a white nightgown, her hair down her back. "What is it? Are you not well?"

"I could not sleep."

Miss Pennyquick hitched her shawl closer. "It will be warm in the kitchen."

They descended together and found the vast kitchen hearth red hot, smoking gently. Ann put on more wood; Miss Pennyquick fetched sloe gin from the dark corner of the larder where she kept it hidden.

"What will Sir Harry say when he finds out you've sold the horse?" she demanded, filling two glasses to the brim. "And shut up Blackow except for the ballroom?"

"I do not think he will care."

"Strange that black devil should drop you at Upgate. Old Barsham was one of Caroline Gerard's conquests, oh, right back when she first came here. I often wondered ..."

Those light blue eyes, thought Ann, the only handsome feature in his heavy face; of course, of course, they were Harry's eyes.

"Is he Harry's father?"

"Anyone could be Harry's father from Blackow to Priddy's Barns or Norwich to Lynn. If he is he tumbled that girl within six months of her marriage, and it would only be charitable to give him the benefit of the doubt ... But I often thought he must be. There is a certain likeness. Barsham is Harry with his sense of responsibility still intact."

That difficult dinner, Ann recalled, that irritable, awkward man refusing to be anything more than very slightly civil. Did he guess her errant husband might be his son? Did he know? And did he dislike the thought for itself, because he did not like Harry and was disappointed, or because of guilt, or because, with life's exquisite irony, he had lost his only legitimate son at the age of eight?

"I fear Harry is in prison," Ann said after a while, staring into the flames and seeing, most unaccountably, the strong and disapproving face of William Claverden looking back at her. There was a spatter of rain at the window, the fire dipped and flared again, raindrops and soot hissed down the wide chimney, and there was an evil swirl of smoke.

"He has always come back before," Miss Pennyquick offered in the way of comfort.

Ann savoured the gin, looking down at her bare feet in the ashes. If Harry could see her now, she thought, like a kitchenmaid, how he would laugh. She missed his laughter perhaps most of all, his laughter and his energy, the spring of his walk. He was in London, she was sure of it, dodging the law, gambling down back streets, trying to make good what he had lost and only piling up the IOUs. She shifted a little. The gin had gone to her head, she felt a glow of devil-may-care — but wretchedly tired as well. And there was William Claverden, whose respect she valued against all reason, looking at her with a sardonic leer from the flames about the apple wood.

"Babs, I am going to London."

"That's the gin talking. Lord, you can't! The ball. Have you forgot the ball?"

"The ball is Saturday. Tomorrow is Tuesday. There is time and to spare. You and Hollin and Tom — and Praed, I suppose — should be able to manage the last arrangements. There is nothing to do at Blackow after all, only decorate the ballroom."

The old house seemed very still, only shifting a little in the wind with a soft creak, the way old houses do. Then: "You know you will find him in a thieves' hole up to his ears in spirits and with a ..." She finished abruptly, aware of Ann's distress.

"I am quite prepared to find him anywhere and anyhow, only that I find him and persuade him to come home." She took the poker and gave the logs a vicious jab. William's mocking features dissolved temporarily in a shower of sparks.

Then Hollin was dripping on the doorsill, hand to the latch. "I saw the light. Anything wrong?"

Someone else who could not sleep, thought Ann. He was swaddled in sacking, a great flap of it tied under his chin with string. He looked like a disagreeable hobgoblin.

"Has to be done," he said.

"What?"

"Finding out what he gets up to when he gallops off into nowhere."

Ann was still holding the poker. It shook a little as she prodded at the fire, but then it was a heavy poker. "If I dress now I may get a seat on the mail."

But to Tom, an hour later, rousing him from deep, untroubled sleep, she said: "I almost hope there are no places. I almost hope he is coming up over the Gorse this minute."

At which he folded her in a huge hug of spontaneous affection like a brotherly bear, and kissed her cold cheek, saying that of course she could not travel alone, he would go with her, he would drive her himself if necessary. She pointed out the difficulties, the disadvantages. In the end he agreed reluctantly to hold sway over Thorn until her return, to take over supervision of the preparations for the ball.

They took Hollin's pony and the trap, calling at Blackow to leave messages for Praed. In the event he was already awake and about, possibly the worse for gin, and was startled and intractable when he heard Ann's plans. He refused to say where Harry might be, refused to say anything, and scuttled for the dank kitchens and the gin bottle.

It was going to be a cold, cold day; in the darkness little flurries of sleet were racing the dead leaves across the lake and the gravel creaked with frost. It was not the time of year or the time of morning to be out in an open trap. But they were late; it was never advisable to be late for a mail coach. At the Rampant

Horse they found it already in the yard, glowing maroon and black in the light of lamps and torches. And there was a seat, the most extraordinary luck. Tom did not know whether to be sorry or elated.

Miss Pennyquick was stricken. "You cannot go alone to ... You must not!"

The sparks were flying from the cobblestones already, the horses held up for the last second. Miss Pennyquick was instructed to stand back and disobeyed, clinging to the door. "Ann, you may be murdered! And he may be ..."

The guard bent to lever her away with his horn and then, as she was detached, put it to his lips to deafen them all with its howl of triumph. The horses plunged; Miss Pennyquick shrank back into the knot of onlookers, bonnet askew. There she was soundly admonished by an official in a massive greatcoat for causing such inconvenience; did she not know His Majesty's mails were under severe penalties to keep strictly to time, accidents and corpses notwithstanding? A few minutes later Tom rescued her from the attentions of a greasy tout trying to sell her a bottle of 'restorative' guaranteed to revive the body and spirit after ten hours in the fastest stage ever driven by mortal man.

"She should not have gone alone," were her first coherent words.

"She wished to." Tom could understand it; he was afraid for her, but he could understand it.

"She wished, did she? She wished to marry Harry Gerard and see where it's taken her: to misery and debtors' prison."

"They will not put Ann in prison." He was clearing a way through the crowd; two coaches had come in and dawn had broken drearily over the rooftops. The horses breathed clouds, every passenger was invisible in greatcoats and rugs. Flakes of snow drifted here and there.

In a yard round the corner the squat and edgy pony waited, held tightly by a small boy with a stick. Tom gave the child more than was usual for minding a horse, conscious of the perils of squaring up such an equine monster. They clattered away through the dim streets in silence until Miss Pennyquick suddenly said: "Go to High Common. Go to the Doctor's house."

They found him at his breakfast, kidneys steaming on the cloth, ham and eggs and something unidentifiable but fishy on a side table. A threadbare full-bottomed wig was draped over the coffee pot and a lighted pipe lodged by the marmalade jar.

"Come in, come in," he called. "What a foul morning."

"Ann has gone to London," said Miss Pennyquick. "What are we to do?"

The Doctor's smile went awry but he was not to be put off the kidneys.

"She will come to no harm. Has she gone to find him? She will not do so. Rest assured, Miss P., she will not do so. London is a large place, and Harry Gerard one man among a multitude."

He sounded confident but his eyes were as bleak and pale as the morning. He read Tom's face and pushed a dish towards him.

"Help yourself," he said.

11

WILLIAM HAD begun his search with mixed emotions and continued it with growing anger. Lady Barsham's letter found him on the point of giving up, having come by a score of unsavoury facts about Harry Gerard during his few days in London but none at all about his 'wife'. It was with a sinking feeling he read the close, elegant lines of the brief message from Upgate Place; Miss Stratford sounded respectable, in spite of Lady Barsham's hints and hopes otherwise, she sounded as if she might have a family, connections, and a valid marriage certificate. William swallowed his breakfast without tasting it, seized the mongoose, and set out unwillingly for Canterbury.

He had no relish for being a spy. And he had come to realise during this odd business that he infinitely preferred the deck of a ship to anywhere else on earth; it seemed to him he might be wise to return to one forthwith. A chance meeting with a fellow officer, now post-captain, confirmed him in this view. The feel of the wind on his cheek and the taste of salt were suddenly very real. And surely all experienced officers were needed now there was every chance of the war intensifying?

The post-chaise to Canterbury was a dark, reeking box on broken springs. The mongoose was tired of being miserable – or perhaps it was not India but simply excitement it craved – and grew lively and obstreperous; it rattled at its box until William released it and then shot about the carriage like a wild thing, turning somersaults and scraping frantically at the windows. William grew warm: he was not used to the vagaries of mongooses and it bit him twice before he managed to confine it again.

He felt equally warm and irritated about other things too: his present unsatisfactory way of life, for instance. And there was Charlotte. He had not intended to court her seriously – she had other, more eligible suitors – but he had found her pretty and entertaining, for a brief while had been enormously attracted by her innocence, her delightful purity. Only what had he to offer her except an adequate income and the delights of an excellent cellar? And did he want to offer her even these? He was too old for her, too cynical. He had knocked about the world too long to settle easily to the kind of ordered life she would expect, and he knew, without even thinking about it, that she would wish to be within calling distance of her dear mama for the rest of her days.

Canterbury was veiled by a thin layer of snow. It was not a town William knew well and in any case he was working himself up into a vile temper – unbecoming self-pity, a larding of righteous indignation, and the ungenerous behaviour of the mongoose all contributing; therefore he abandoned subterfuge and made vigorous enquiries, was exceptionally liberal with his tips. So it was that he arrived in the middle of the afternoon at a tall house, rather fine, but with an air of distinguished decadence. A maid informed him that indeed Mr Stratford did live there but was from home; no, there was no Mrs Stratford, but Miss Stratford was receiving visitors if he cared to step up.

He stepped up. Faded gentility and dust were everywhere, and the smell of damp and long-eaten meals. William trod as lightly as he could across the worn rugs, conscious of his wet boots and his height; he almost had to duck as he entered the drawing room. The girl at the embroidery frame by the window rose with some surprise – he was never quite what anyone expected – and kept her distance as if afraid he might be dangerous.

"Miss Stratford? My name is Claverden. I have some business with Sir Harry Gerard."

Her pale, long face flushed a little but her eyes, curious light eyes like a cat's, did not waver for an instant.

"Please be seated, Mr Claverden. I am afraid you have come to the wrong house if you expected to find Sir Harry Gerard here. I have no idea where he might be. Who told you he could be found here?"

She was in her late twenties, graceless, angular. Her grey dress only accentuated the oddness of her eyes.

"I have to see Sir Harry on a matter of particular importance – and urgently. On asking after him in Town I was told he might be found in Canterbury with a Miss Stratford. I came at once by chaise and now you tell me he is not to be found at all."

"Not here, Mr Claverden, you will not find him here. I am barely acquainted with the man." She had returned to look at her work, running a thin finger over the stitching. "I shall not ask what you are, I do not wish to know. Gerard is ... My youngest sister Harriet ran off and married him. My father has forbidden us to speak of them."

Damn, damn, damn, he thought; so it was going to be true after all. "How long ago was this?"

"A year. Oh, maybe not quite a year. It scarcely matters. I have had letters, a few. They seem to have spent a great deal of time in a succession of dingy lodgings avoiding the bailiffs. Perhaps by now they have taken ship for the Colonies."

It was a once-gracious room cheaply furnished; Miss Stratford knew all about hard times, but she had no experience of dingy lodging houses nor had she ever fled the bailiffs. She looked William in the eye. "Are you after money? I should forget it. I only met your Gerard twice but I have no hesitation in saying that charming though he was he was not a man to pay his debts promptly, nor even," and she tilted her head and gave a queer, cold little smile, "to know what they were."

William felt acutely miserable. He stood up. "Could you tell me where they were last staying? I must find Sir Harry, it is most urgent. But I assure you he does not owe me anything and I can do no harm to your sister." Could he not?

It was difficult for him to look mild and contrite; by nature he looked stern and pugnacious. He did his best however and after a little she gave another unconvincing smile and went across to a side table. There she wrote swiftly and with a sort of seething impatience, bringing him a piece of paper with words sprawling darkly. It was an address in a low part of Dover. William sighed. He knew Dover very well indeed.

"If you find them ..." the girl began as he took his leave, "if you see Harriet ..."

She had put out a hand and it rested briefly on his arm. Had he a trustworthy face after all then?

"Give her my love," she said stiffly, and turned away.

Ann was with Harry in the back room of a narrow old house off the Strand.

"Annie, why are you here? You ..." He was distressingly drunk, stripped to shirt and stockings, hair anyhow. "How did you find this place?"

"I went to your clubs. I saw a man called Fisher. He told me."

"He had no right to tell you anything!" And how had they let her past the door? "Did he know who you were?"

"He said you had been blackballed from the clubs. Is that true? Of course he knew who I was. He said you would be at this place playing faro. And you have not been sober since leaving Blackow, have you?"

She was in blue, in a little blue hat with a white feather that brushed her cheek as she moved. "How can you afford to gamble? What is there left to gamble with?"

"I borrow."

"And then you lose and borrow more."

A little painted slut had let her in, so undernourished her age was indeterminate. The faintest movement behind the half-open door to a bedroom reminded her. And then her agony, so long held in check, burst out at last.

"I want you to come home. Come home before they arrest you for debt! Harry!"

"Please, Ann. Please." He was swaying towards her, a tousled, supplicatory little boy.

She looked into his face through a storm of tears and tried to find the Harry she had cared for, and that Harry was not there.

His eyes were bloodshot, his mouth slack, his chin bristling; he was unkempt, unclean, unknown. She took a deep racking breath and pressed both her hands to her wet face.

"You must come home."

"No, not this time." He seemed to be sobering; he spoke with the old decision.

The window, she found, gave on to a back alley, a tumble of old roofs and dirt-encrusted chimneys. The sky was leaden, the snow falling gently. The smell of this place would stay with her for ever, she thought, the smell of tallow and snuff and cheap scent, of sweat and stale gravy and soot. "Then what am I to do?"

"I cannot come home," a pause, a long pause, "and there is something else. You will understand if you … if you go to this house. Here, take this too. Tell her it is all there is until … later."

He had a screwed-up piece of paper in his hand and a small bag of money. His smile was tight and artificial but apologetic. Ann, struck by the thought he might try to blow out his brains, took paper and bag with nerveless fingers and then caught at his sleeve as he turned. "Harry, what is it all about?" His mistress, she supposed dully, who had perhaps borne him a child. Anything was possible. She could believe anything now.

"About expectations," and he laughed, a ragged, unconvincing laugh, "and how they did not come to … come to anything at all. But they will, they will. One day you will forgive me, Annie, you will indeed." He took her hand in a grip strong enough to hold in check that infernal horse of his. "You have been a dear girl and tried hard with me. I hoped …"

But a tidal wave of pain drowned her, of pain and shame and a terrible sense of betrayal. She cried: "Did you only marry me for the money? They all told me so but I did not … I refused to believe them."

"No, no! I admired you! It might have been a perfect marriage. And I was not penniless, was I? Was I? Who paid for the repairs to Blackow, the new barns? Your money went …"

"To this woman!" A look, desperate and helpless, at the little bag of money she held so tightly in her hand.

"No, I swear it. Not there. I never spent a penny of your money there. I put your money in ... in Sable Island."

And at last she knew that she was drowned, that she could not bear it any more but must close her eyes and go under.

"There is no such place!" she screamed, and she dropped the money on the floor and turned, groping for the window, leaning her burning face against the filthy glass.

"I cannot tell you anything." His voice, she supposed. "Not even now. But you will forgive me."

She did not feel it would ever be in her to forgive. The memory of him riding on the Gorse came back to her, of a Harry courageous, exultant, proud; she could never forgive him the destruction of that vision. That was the Harry she had loved.

Was that girl listening at the door? But Harry was between her and the door. "You will be well provided in the end, Annie. I promise. It is too late for me. But Sable Island ..."

"Oh, Sable Island! Damn Sable Island! Will you never tell me what it is?"

"I dare not. Not until the debts are paid."

"And the ball ..."

"Ball?" Once so important to him it was now a dim memory; before what he intended to do in the next few hours everything paled to such a memory.

"Saturday. You invited half the county; half the county is coming. And none of the bills paid ... What am I supposed to do?"

"You will survive it." A weak grin, a gleam of the old Harry. "Tom will take my place. You will make a gentleman of him yet, great green boy that he is. He loves the land, you know that; like you. He should have had Blackow, not me, would have cared for every tree, every beast, would have trimmed the hedges with his own hands."

He was like a wayward child, Ann thought, rebellious and lost but still able to smile, to move her. And she wondered, without having any properly coherent thoughts at all, if his mother had been the same, and if after everything Francis Forsie had still thought of her with the pity and affection that is sometimes the distillation of dead passion and foolhardy love.

"Harry, where do you mean to go?"

"Today? Tomorrow? Who knows. I have no intention ... I have no intention of troubling you any more."

Was this what they had come to, and so quickly? Was this the man who had charmed her, made her laugh, brought her roses? She could not speak. Her throat ached; if she spoke she would cry.

He gave her a long last look, a calm look, as if he hoped to remember her just like this, haggard and damp and wrestling with self-control, the audacious feather dipping in the gloom.

"It was sweet while it lasted," he said. "We had fun for a short while, Annie, did we not?"

In the reputable inn at Ludgate, in the musty private parlour they had set aside for her, Ann wept until she was exhausted. An hour later, having done her best with cold water and a glass of brandy, she took a fast stage to Dover.

The dark was intense. It occurred to her it was a risky journey, that she would be left practically penniless in a strange town and a seafaring one at that. Kent was unfamiliar, the voices of its country people sometimes incomprehensible; and why should Harry want her to go to 15 Soper Street with a derisory bag of money and no notion who lived there? What had he been afraid to tell her?

It was still snowing, though randomly, flakes here, there, and everywhere. The roads were icy, the horses slipped up twice. Ann slept, was jolted awake, was encouraged to take a warm brick for her feet, slept again, was cajoled to drink a cup of scalding coffee that tasted of mud, was regaled with stories of other journeys, other mad gallops, accidents, of highwaymen, atrocious roads, ladies giving birth at toll-houses. Then sleep again, and cold, and waking with no feeling in her legs, and more coffee, and a fresh team, and the vast cheerful woman at her side exchanged for a forlorn parson. And at last Dover, and the tang of the sea, and a damper cold, less intense.

And 15 Soper Street, Harry Gerard's wife.

She was tall and supple, had once been pretty. Ann warmed

her hands at the fire and watched them trembling with a vague interest as if they were not her own.

"You have seen Harry? But where is he? Where has he been these last three weeks? And why send you with money?" A momentary suspicion brushed aside. "I mean … Could he not come himself?" She had not looked inside the bag, though judging by her dress, the room, the pitiful fire, she was in need of every penny.

"He is in London. He sent no message. He simply asked …" How difficult it was to breathe. "He asked me to give you that as I … as I had business in Dover."

There was no evidence of a child. The room was bare, neat, very poor. The girl had been sewing, and for someone else to judge by the voluminous folds of material pushed hastily across a chair. She wore a wedding ring. The landlady, squinting suspiciously through the bitter dark, had called her Mrs Gerard: yes, Mrs Gerard was in, though it was mortal late for visiting … Ann, who had simply asked for a young lady, had the presence of mind to change her own Lady Gerard to a murmur which could have been interpreted as Lady Jermyn and so gained admittance under false credentials.

The shock was paralysing. The hands she was holding to the fire had stopped trembling but they did not seem to belong to her at all.

"Are you his wife?" she asked.

"But of course. Surely he told you? We were married a year ago next week at a little church in Canterbury. Have you ever been there? Oh, it was so pretty by the …"

"But why … why did he never bring you to Norfolk?"

"Norfolk? He said he hated Norfolk, windy, cold, all turnips and geese." Yes, that sounded like Harry. "He said country life was tedious. He said …" Her troubled eyes met Ann's. "He said the only way he could reconcile himself to Norfolk was to marry a rich wife so that he could repair his house, fill the stables with horses, have twenty gardeners. He was always full of ideas in those days, all of them quite mad. He married me and I was not rich at all, so for a while we lived in Deal, and then we moved here because it was better for him, he was not known in Dover. He had ... he has debts. But he has been away so much, weeks and weeks. I began to think ..."

You fool, thought Ann, you fool, fool, fool, to have trusted him! The white feather dipped.

Then: "You must have been lonely." How lonely, to say all this to a stranger. "You have no children?" A shake of her head. The room seemed colder suddenly. I cannot tell her, thought Ann, I cannot tell her he married his rich wife after all, not this poor deluded girl with the lovely fair hair all dull and unwashed, with the brave blue eyes, the once-smiling mouth. This girl was respectable and generous and simple.

"It was one of his jokes, of course," Harriet said into the strained silence, "about Norfolk, the rich wife. He had plenty of money. At least, he did at first, and then there was very little, and then in the summer he had a great deal again, but he would not say where it had come from."

"I did not know." Was that strange voice really her own? "I did not know until tonight that he was married. We ... we are neighbours, you see."

Grief, conscience, pain, all in one look, in one flicker of the blue eyes. "Did he never tell anyone? No, that is so like him. He lives for himself, for the moment, and he does not care what others say."

There was another pause, an unfortunate pause during which, as well as finding nothing to say to each other, they found their private thoughts almost too much to bear. And then, striving after normality, if such a thing could ever come again, Ann said: "Did Harry ever speak to you about a place called Sable Island?"

It was obviously a bizarre question, that was quite clear, to the girl gathering up the embroidered silk from the cheap old chair. "Where? No, never. All he ever talked about was ships and the sea, sailing away; I think he felt he would be free on the ocean, free from worry, responsibility, debts. When he was here he used to walk down to the waterside and look at the shipping; he could name every vessel, used to point out how they were rigged, everything. But I do not remember any Sable Island."

"I did not know he cared for the sea." A whisper, a harsh, bewildered whisper.

"And I do not believe he has ever been on it, except in a small boat across the harbour."

"He had hopes of making a fortune from this island."

"No, I do not recall it," and then a sad, wistful smile. "He used to say he would have a ship called Harriet one day. He used to laugh about our names: Harry and Harriet. Oh, must you go? I have tea ..."

But it was so late for tea, it was midnight. Ann made a supreme effort, gave her to understand there was a cab waiting.

"He is well?" was Harriet's last question at the door.

"As he always is."

The night was cold, but not as cold as Ann Mathick, alone in Dover with no money, no husband, no home. What had he meant: "You will be well provided"? Had he supposed that, the marriage being invalid, Thorn would be returned to her with apologies? How could that be? Could it be? Was such a thing even remotely possible?

But Thorn was no longer important. It seemed to her that nothing was important, except maybe simply being alive, and that only because nature decreed it should be so.

The wind was rising. She began to walk seawards.

William had been waylaid by an old shipmate, the surgeon of the *India*. Naval strategy and a score of humorous memories were chewed at length over the supper table along with an indifferent pigeon pie and lamb cutlets. At midnight it occurred to William that he had neglected to discover the secret of 15 Soper Street and that the state of his head and stomach argued an early retirement; he had not drunk so much since his last days aboard *Siren*. Accordingly he took his fond farewell, fonder perhaps than was fitting, much fonder than had he been sober: the surgeon had not been in any way a particular friend. Outside the inn the wind was keen, still carrying snow in icy draughts and irritating eddies. He assessed it with a seaman's eye and nose: it would be worse before morning. Then he began to walk slowly back to his own lodging, his hat a little askew on his black waves, his steps a little irregular. Old times! Ah, they had been some times! A hundred more memories assailed him, none of which involved the surgeon of the *India*. He turned a corner, tripped over a wraith of petticoat and some dark stuff, a slender ankle, and what? There was a hat with a wickedly curling feather, a pair of dark eyes, a martial sort of nose. A face he knew. God damnit, Ann Gerard!

She had a strange, touch-me-not look. He said with a commendable attempt at civility: "Lady Gerard, may I be of any assistance?"

She was about to say no, he was sure of it. He seized her arm in an irresistible, ungentlemanly grip, leading her towards the main thoroughfares.

"You need not be concerned ..." she began. Perhaps the look on his face deterred her from anything further. Certainly he looked fierce, and William Claverden was a man who could look very fierce indeed when he chose; and she had a growing suspicion he was not wholly, unimpeachably sober.

"I *am* concerned. Who would not be? It is past midnight and you are walking about the back-streets of Dover alone. God knows why you are not safe in your bed at Blackow."

"I had business here."

"When did you last eat? Or sleep? When? Did you come by chaise? The mail? And nowhere to stay. Oh, of course, how like you! Did you know that since meeting that wretch Gerard you have been distracted? What will it take to bring you to your senses? A drunken sailor with a knife down a dark by-street?"

They had reached his inn. Light and laughter still issued into the silent street. William propelled her into a small parlour with a dead fire and a branch of sad candles dripping sootily. His look, she found, was as penetrating as ever, and undeniably savage, as if he longed to take her up and shake her. He was in conservative browns, as fashionable as was necessary without being exceptional, but his neckcloth was large and snowy.

"What are you doing here?" He busied himself with the wicks, blackening his fingers.

"I have been to see Harry's wife."

Such a quiet, dead voice, so steady. Shock, then. Her face was a mask. He burnt his fingers, caught unawares, and one of the candles went out in a rush of blue smoke.

"Fifteen Soper Street?"

"How did you know? Are you here to see her too? Did you know everything and tell me nothing?"

"Of course not." He rang for service and then stooped to see if there was anything to resuscitate in the hearth. "Until a week ago I had no idea any such girl existed."

He outlined his involvement, trying to improve the Doctor's case a little out of native generosity. He felt appallingly sober all of a sudden as if he had just been doused in the sea. He also became aware that Ann was not listening. She had taken off her hat and her coat and was sitting in a gaunt old wing chair, bolt upright. A lock of hair fell across her forehead and she stroked it away absently.

"No wonder he drank so," was all she said.

"Harry Gerard? Harry Gerard was crooked head to toe: a cheat, a sot, a bigamist. A fraud. Look at all that business about Sable Island. He never owned an island; there was no such company."

She did not hear him. She had put her face between her hands. He felt an impulse to reach over and touch her hair, put an arm about her shoulders, anything; but his other, more ignoble desire was to say I told you so.

"What is she like?" he asked. Be brutal, urged an inner voice; this silence, this self-control is unnatural.

"Harriet? Tall, fair, pleasant, sounds as if she comes from a good family. They have cast her off, no doubt. She did not speak of them. A sweet girl, very innocent."

"Still? She must be sweet indeed, or very silly. And where is Harry?"

"London. He may ... I think he may kill himself."

William gave a snort of derision. "Not Harry Gerard! He would not know how. He will borrow some money and make off for the Continent."

She was crying now but strangely, without a sound. The tears welled up and spilled over and ran down between her fingers.

He could not stand it. "He has beggared you!" he shouted, striding to give another hearty yank at the bell pull. "He does not deserve your tears."

"Perhaps I am not crying for Harry."

"Then for whom? Not yourself."

She was standing now, groping for a handkerchief. The brighter light from the candles showed up patches of wet on her skirt. She must have been walking hours in the dark and the snow.

"For her. For his wife."

"Don't be melodramatic! Her family will take her back."

"They may not. And she has lost everything. She believed in him, believed his worst fault was that of a headstrong child."

"And what did you believe his worst fault was? You were in love with him too. Is your loss any the less?"

A pasty-faced maid stuck her head round the door. "You called, sir?"

"Coffee. Bring us a pot of coffee and whatever there is to eat."

He discarded his greatcoat, flinging it into a chair. He undid his neckcloth and dragged that off. Then he sat down, leaning back, his hands laced over his stomach.

"What are you going to do?" he asked gravely.

"Go back to London. He must be made to do something for that poor girl."

"How could you even consider it? You have no sense left at all."

The maid had returned and gave them a covert glance as she brought in the tray: a dashing, semi-respectable man — what respectable man would toss his neckcloth on the floor? — and a sprig of a girl damp with tears; she knew what *that* was all about. She set down the tray. There was a plate of bread and butter, the scraggier part of a dismembered hen, some stale buns, and a pot of coffee half as strong as William would have liked it and less than half the temperature.

"Harry means well," was Ann's astonishing remark as the door crashed shut. She had recovered, was dry-eyed, dignified.

"I have seen scant evidence of it. Do you want any of this

remarkable repast? I cannot make out the constitution of the buns. The coffee is tepid."

"How can you expect a decent meal at past midnight?" was all she said, refusing the buns, refusing everything. He ate alone and in silence.

Then: "He married you for your money," he announced, seeing off the last of the ancient hen and chasing sinews round his teeth.

"You are so flattering."

He glared. "I see you are yourself again. It is over, is it, the horror of being so deceived? You are prepared to pass it over? Good Heavens, woman, and did he have the nerve to tell you it was his wife in Soper Street or did he just let you go there and find out?"

"There is no need to shout. You do not have to be indignant on my behalf."

This was not the conversation he had envisaged when he had brought her here. But then, had he honestly expected her to cry gently on his shoulder? She looked terrible, her hair was a mess, her eyes red, but she did not give any sign of wanting to weep on anyone's shoulder; pliant, resilient, she would learn to cope.

"Of course his debts were ten times what you expected," he said bitterly, "but you were warned."

"How strange I should have had so many warnings and yet none that he might be a bigamist."

"I suppose you ought to be pleased. This first marriage ... The situation is quite changed, you see."

"The legal situation."

They looked at each other bleakly. He understood her, felt for her – but he did not wish her to see he did, did not wish her to guess at the slightest emotional involvement on his part.

"What am I, Mr Claverden? Neither a wife nor a maid. What position will be allotted to me now?"

"I was not under the impression you cared overmuch for allotted positions. It always seemed to me you were inclined to flout such niceties. I am sure, if you wish, we can make you out the wretched deceived, a wreck of Harry Gerard's greed and duplicity. Is that not the truth, in any case?"

Was he trying to be cruel – he was succeeding then – or trying to make her laugh?

"I do not wish to be a wreck of any kind. I think I would prefer to retire gracefully to Thorn and take up my old life."

"That may not be possible." The complications were frightening, however decisive the law. "You will take my room for tonight. We leave for Norfolk tomorrow."

She was fortified by his unsympathetic attitude, by his arrogant assumption he must control her affairs. She threw up her head. "I must see Harry first."

"No good can come of it."

She was too weary to argue, although he was not fooled by her silence into thinking her compliant. He poured her some coffee – she had not asked for it – and went back to sit down and crumble one of the buns.

"Are you not holding a ball shortly?"

Her eyes widened. "Ball? Saturday. I shall never be home in time." She did not say it with any regret.

William saw an opportunity and dived for it, as he might, in other days, have crowded on sail to catch the slightest breath of wind. "Then you must go back at once."

"Is a ball more important than that girl in that squalid room? Than Harry?"

"There is no answer to that, as you well know. For my part I consider your most sensible course a speedy return to Blackow and afterwards a sober and civilised meeting with Sir Harry – and somewhere more salubrious than wherever it was I suspect you met him last. If you wish me to act for you I will be happy to do so." He did not sound as if he would. "I shall not take a penny from the Doctor for this business: it sickens me."

"To be sure you have made it abundantly clear your opinion of me is very low, that you find Harry derisory, that you consider the girl in Soper Street only a little less of a fool than myself. It might be better if you disengaged yourself entirely and returned to fawn at Lady Barsham's feet or wherever it is you go to further your advancement."

"This bitterness does not suit you."

"I am only following your lead. You are a hard man and an ambitious one."

The creak and sigh of old timbers seemed exceptionally loud. Footsteps passed in the passage outside. A voice called a protracted, raucous, slightly obscene good night. Doors slammed distantly. William retreated to the coffee pot and shook it furiously as if in the hope it might, magically, produce a hot, fresh brew. He scowled.

"It might surprise you to know where my ambitions lay. Only the Doctor has guessed perhaps. I am certainly giving up the law."

He looked up to find her face gentle. "You would do better out there," and she nodded towards the greasy lattice that, in daylight, might afford them a view of two square feet of sea green, "taking rich prizes and flogging poor pressed men up and down ... whatever you flog them up and down."

"I hope I never had a name for flogging. The man who needs to use the cat ..."

"You see, you are full of good advice about ships and none at all about my situation."

"I am hoping to rejoin the Navy as soon as possible."

She was leaning forward, biting her lip. Her eyes searched his. "Not until you have helped me through this business."

He stared. "I thought you did not wish it."

Another wan smile; she looked down at her thin, cold hands. "Of course, I may not be able to afford your fee."

A persistent scratching sound from an odd wooden box in the shadows drew his attention. He stooped to lift the lid and Bombay Jack burst out at them.

"Poor thing," Ann said, as the mongoose worried her damp petticoat. "Has he been confined since you left Norwich?"

"Unfortunately no. With luck his Indiaman is even now in The Downs and tomorrow I can hand him to her second officer who joins her by cutter. I shall not be sorry to see him go." The candlelight picked out the angles of his face, showed up the thin scars long healed, the long, compressed mouth.

"I am sorry for him then. He is an affectionate creature."

210

"I would as soon have travelled with the snakes."

Ann detached the mongoose firmly and he scampered across to William's chair and took a great interest in the tassels on his Hessian boots.

"Perhaps," said Ann softly, "I could pay your bill a little at a time."

William shook his foot violently. "Dear God! I would never have this rogue on any ship of mine! Bill? What bill? Why are you always so concerned with bills? Who knows, I may not charge you. After all, it will be the first and last case of bigamy I shall ever have."

12

THE POST-CHAISE took the avenue to Blackow Hall at the canter and in a swirl of sleet. Tom watched it come from the top of the steps, flapping his arms and jumping up and down.

"Ann! Ann, I am so glad to see you! You cannot imagine what it has been like. Babs is out of her mind and ..."

"Perhaps you could see to the luggage," William said amiably. He guided Ann up the steps, his backward glance indescribably steely.

But it was true Blackow was in confusion, and no wonder Miss Pennyquick was demented. Subdued but seasonal decorations greeted them, great heaps of holly and accompaniments all over the hall floor; there was a painful clatter of crockery off left, sawdust and shavings and melted snow mingled on the tiles. Ann gazed about in despair, seeing only a small huddle of uniformed strangers whispering behind their hands, and then, as she and William hesitated in the gloom, Miss Pennyquick herself bore down on them, hands red — from what type of scrubbing and where? — hair unruly, skirts powdered with chalk or flour.

"I feared you would be too late, only three hours before the first guests ... And you are exhausted! I knew it would be like this. Come upstairs, come quickly. Maggie is here, turned up at Thorn last night with a bag, refused to leave ... She will put a bath ready." Her bright glance turned to William and became enquiring.

"I am on my way to the Doctor's," he said. "Is there any message?"

Ann turned at the foot of the stairs. "Only that if ever he was my friend he will come early tonight."

Miss Pennyquick walked with him to the steps. The postboy and his horses fretted in the twilight below. She gave them a critical stare and then concentrated on William.

"She found him then. It is written all over her face. Have they quarrelled?"

"Not in the least as far as I can tell. I rather wish they had, it would be more natural. It is beyond quarrelling now though, I assure you. And she will need all your help and support tonight."

"He is not coming."

"He is not indeed."

Miss Pennyquick watched him depart and then returned to the battleground. She gave orders, cajoled, suggested; she coerced by flattery, bribery, or threats. An hour passed; from upstairs came the sound of doors opening and closing, nothing more. Gradually the house took on an orderly, festive air, the hall swept clean, the last holly leaf in place, the buffet set up, the dance floor shining. Another hour and the candles were ready, Praed's substitute making sure they were firm, taper in hand. Hollin came in to say that the kitchen chimney at Thorn was 'on the smoke' but that he could deal with it; he had seen the chaise, Miss Pennyquick surmised, and had come for news of Ann. She had none to give, was far, far too busy for anything. He went away disgruntled, a shambling figure in a huge old greatcoat slung about with the inevitable sacking.

Tom darted in. "May I see her?"

"Not if you value your life. It is time you dressed. Then perhaps you can keep this rabble in order while I see to my own finery. I have never set eyes on so many pairs of grubby silk stockings all at once in my life. Footmen! They look as if they belong on stage!"

Upstairs Ann was still in shift and bare feet, face down on the bed. Miss Pennyquick hesitated. What was worse than a quarrel? What was worse anyway than Harry in London and his wife in Blackow greeting his guests alone?

"You cut it fine," she said bluntly, shaking out the pink dress Maggie had hung ready.

"I had to go to Dover."

"Dover! But how was there time?"

"Mr Claverden brought me back by post. And I feel as if I have been pounded in a stone-breaker for days. My bones ache and my head throbs. Is it time to dress already? Oh Babs, how can I face them?"

"Where is he? Where is precious Harry Gerard? He wanted a ball, he should be here to dance at it."

"He is ... detained."

Miss Pennyquick was pinning up Ann's hair, making throaty noises of annoyance. "Not in prison, God save us! I cannot think why you flew down there to find him, you knew how it would be. And why go to Dover? Why, whatever possessed you? What is in Dover, pray, to take you there at the gallop?"

"His wife."

Miss Pennyquick subsided on to the edge of the bed with a creak of whalebone and her face grey with foreboding.

"I knew there was something. Praed has gone. Perhaps his conscience got the better of him at last, his conscience and fear of being transported. He just disappeared, took all his things and disappeared. Pashman took him up, dropped him at Dunston, and that was the last of him."

In a while they were both ready, though it was a grim process. Miss Pennyquick was stately, Ann frail and chilled in ice pink. Tom appeared, in a brave blue coat that only strained a very little across his wide shoulders.

"We must go down," he offered Ann his arm. "I can hear a carriage."

The candles were ablaze, the ballroom a romance of winter greenery, the great mirrors decked with silver bows and stars and glittering streamers. At the foot of the stairs Tom bent to drop a light kiss on her forehead and then left her, striding away to chivvy the slack servants at the buffet and to exchange witticisms with the members of the orchestra who had already been entertained to a large bowl of punch and seemed very sprightly on it. It should have been Harry, Ann thought, watching his tall figure moving amid the holly garlands and the silver streamers, Harry, Harry, Harry. And then, pulling herself together, she stepped across to welcome the first arrivals, as fragile as a sugar fairy and scarcely more alive.

The twentieth guest to take her cold hand and call her Lady Gerard was nearly her undoing. Chalk white she greeted party after party, apologising woodenly for Harry's absence. She saw speculation, noted the flutter of fans, the smiles, the careful half turns that cut off her view, the sidelong glances. Nevertheless she found the spirit to assure Mrs Palmer, who erupted into the hall and thence into the ballroom like a busy firework, that her dearest Harry was not detained by anything more serious than a debilitating cold, a terrible sore throat. A mythical physician was quoted, an imaginative anecdote told. Mrs Palmer countered with a tale of her mother's gout and how, most unaccountably, it had led to pneumonia, which had been the End, of course.

"I would rather have thought it to be a miracle," said William, giving the briefest bow and staring round at the company. "The Doctor must confirm the impossibility of gout turning to pneumonia."

Compelled to admonish him for speaking loudly enough for Mrs Palmer to hear, Ann found herself smiling properly for the first time. And on that smile in came the Doctor himself, wearing his disgusting bottle-green coat and best wig, old-fashioned lace in a froth almost to his ears.

"It cheers me to find you still have it in you to smile," he said, taking her hand. "William told me he had no idea how you really felt for you showed nothing, but then he has so little imagination and never exerts himself to understand other people's feelings. He is a cynic and disregards sentiment entirely."

He looked at her and in that look, she found, were many things: a medical man's appraisal of her state of health, an obvious anxiety as to the state of her mind, a little of the old mockery and devil-may-care, and something else compounded of anger and longing and reproach. They did not have a chance to speak again however as the orchestra was warming to its task, encouraged by – the now unhappy Tom was convinced – further liberal and secret helpings of the punch. The Doctor cleared a way to the centre of the room, some quivering notes brought about an instant hush; Ann found herself alone, every face turned towards her, expectant and smiling. She swayed, helpless, but the Doctor had faded to one side. And then a hand took her elbow. "If we are to grovel to absurd customs then you must dance at least once and right away, or they will all refuse to do so. Come, I warn you though, I have a facility for reels and nothing else."

"We can hardly open a ball with a reel, Mr Claverden."

He had led her into position, other couples forming up beside them. The musicians were ready, primed, glowing. In the flash of a glance Ann saw it all: the long room, repainted and refurnished with her own money, garlanded, bedizened, lit by several hundred wax candles – dare she compute the cost of those? The great mirrors reflected a thousand flames, five hundred gorgeous dancers. And she saw her own slight figure by the side of that much taller one. There was a scrape of violins, a little flutter of excitement, and they turned to each other and the dance began.

It came to Ann after a while that William's coat was the colour of Harry's eyes.

Her hand met his for a second, then dropped away. She stepped back, stepped forward. His palm was dry and hard against hers.

"That is never young Tom?" he said. "Look at him! You would think he owned this place." As he spoke he fancied the remark was crassly insensitive, but she did not heed it, simply peered round him to see.

It was indeed Tom, burnished hair and immaculate breeches, and he was dancing with Charlotte and was, insofar as he would ever be able to, dancing very gracefully.

"Thank God I gave him those fifty acres," said Ann.

It was not to be hoped that the news of Harry's irregular marriage arrangements would long remain secret but Christmas was over before anything was heard at High Common. It was wet and windy, dispiriting weather altogether; Thorn glistened and smoked at the foot of its hill, and the atmosphere inside was worse than out, glutinous with anxiety and unasked, unanswered questions. Then one Sunday, a cold, white Sunday with a searing wind coming down from the Gorse, Ann could stand it no longer and rode off to Blackow, locked up and unwelcoming.

A little later Hollin and Miss Pennyquick drew up in the trap and carried baskets, bottles and boxes indoors.

"You cannot sulk all day in this Godforsaken pile," was Miss Pennyquick's comment to an astonished Ann, "certainly not without eating. Mr Claverden called half an hour ago to take young Tom to a mutton lunch at the Angel and I thought: If that lad can do himself proud, why not Ann?"

Why not? Pressed meats, pies, rolls, relishes made their appearance. There was coffee and tea, rum. Hollin bent his mind to the lighting of the drawing room fire, achieved the desired result with a great deal of blowing and cursing, and then sneaked away to unearth the rum. It only seemed a moment later that the noise of more wheels heralded more guests, this time Lord Barsham and another man, neither very cheerful. They had been to Thorn, had been sent on by the maid. And? And as local magistrate Barsham had taken it on himself to bring them the disquieting reports from the capital along with this whey-faced officer with the sullen manner and the notebook full of unhappy facts: that Harry Gerard owed ten thousand pounds at the last count, and that a conservative estimate likely to be exceeded by up to half as much again, that he had married Ann Elizabeth Mathick in the county of Norfolk bigamously, having another wife living at the time, and that he had evaded capture by laying a false trail to Brighton and then taking the stage – or so it was now believed – to Deal.

In the icy drawing room Ann stood by the window and watched snow melt into the lake. The Bow Street Runner, positioned prominently by the little smoking fire, coughed suddenly and she swung round as if he had shot at her.

"I cannot help you. I do not know where he is." Her voice was calm, the only voice they had heard from her since the ball:

no tears, no shrieks, nothing but this low, quiet monotone. "I am so sorry, of course you must be frozen. I will send for something hot to drink. Have you travelled from London overnight?"

The Runner admitted he had. It was a journey he wished to forget, a journey from a nightmare; he had grave doubts he would ever have feeling in his toes and fingers again after such cruel exposure. And he found this business distasteful, though mostly because as a thief-taker he objected to having no thief to take. He pulled out a large green handkerchief and blew his nose thoroughly.

"The man Praed is a known pickpocket and petty criminal, something of a cracksman according to my sources. Was that known to you, Ma'am?"

"The idea is preposterous!" Barsham intervened.

"I knew nothing about him except he was born in the Fleet," Ann said in that same chill, lifeless voice. "He was my husband's servant; he did not like me, nor this house, nor the other servants, nor the country, nor the weather … In short, I cannot imagine why he stayed."

"Because he had to," the Runner blew his nose again. "This house was by way of an asylum. He was known in London, was wanted to give evidence about a robbery in Aldgate, and there was a little matter of ringers – the substitution of one horse for another in a race. Perhaps that was how your husband met him."

Lord Barsham, who was feeling more acutely embarrassed than at any time before in his life, gave a grunt. "His name was Bragg they think, my dear, Richard Bragg." His blue eyes, those eyes so like Harry's own, met Ann's cold stare and he gave a wistful smile. "I cannot tell you how sorry I am this has happened."

"You could hardly be sorrier than I am."

"There is nothing we can do," the policeman said gloomily, "not until Sir Harry is found. His wife … er, hum … his wife in Dover refuses to say anything, wishes him well by all accounts, but it seems clear she has not seen him since before Christmas."

"What will happen to her?"

"I believe her sister is already with her, Ma'am. There is some hope her family will take her back. But she is still Sir Harry's wife and the old father is a disagreeable old ... gentleman, much given to laying down the law; the outcome is by no means certain."

There was an awkward pause. Snowflakes blew up against the windows on the wild wind and blew away again as quickly. Ann said: "Please be good enough to ring the bell beside you, Mr Cross. You must have some coffee, rum ... Forgive me, I have no idea what there might be. The house has been shut up."

But it was Lord Barsham who rang, and then stood, shifting uneasily, on the hearthrug. "The bailiffs were here this morning, I understand."

"Indeed they were, and finding no one at home they hammered on the door at Thorn, quite incensed. Blackow is lost, of course. I have been given two weeks to leave."

"Thank God you had left already then. Thank God you still have the farm," Lord Barsham cried. "If you were not wed to the fellow he had no right to any of your property."

"Mr Claverden is at work on the legal tangle at this moment. Thorn itself is safe, I think, but a great deal of the land is lost one way or another, sold to raise cash."

"And you cannot guess where Sir Harry might have fled?" asked Cross.

"Indeed I cannot. But if he is the Harry I married he will be across the sea by now and borrowing guilders from unsuspecting Dutchmen."

"He may yet be caught," Cross told her, but without optimism. He sneezed. And Miss Pennyquick entered like a man-of-war in full sail, bearing steaming coffee on a battered wooden tray.

"The whole house is empty," she said in reply to Lord Barsham's civil enquiry. "I must own I shall be glad to see the last of it. It has never been a home. Even when old Sir Harry was here it was always like a place half finished, cold and gloomy. I wish its new owner joy of it, I do indeed."

"You will take some coffee yourself, Miss Pennyquick?" He was putting himself out to be polite. He knew little of her except that she was reputed to have been Francis Forsie's mistress for twenty years — an impossibility, he felt. He thought of her remarks about Blackow: half finished. Like his love affair with Caroline Gerard: half begun, half finished, wholly mad. She had led him by the nose and laughed at his distress, his moral scruples, his desperate guilt — she had been so young, so newly married. And it was more than probable Harry was his child

"I do not care for coffee," Miss Pennyquick was saying, "and you have business to discuss. I shall bid you good day." And she shook his hand strongly — a most unexpected gesture — and did not bother to curtsey at all.

Lord Barsham turned to watch Ann across the coffee cups, so quiet, so neat, so soberly dressed in a dark blue habit. And yet, when she glanced up and caught him looking in her direction, he had an impression of turmoil, of unaccountable agony, of a score of passions damped down but only temporarily.

"My wife," he said awkwardly, and another flurry of sleet hit the panes and hissed in the chimney, "my wife would be pleased if you found time to visit her. Of course, with this infernal weather ..." She made a fitting mistress for this sad and noble place, he thought. She had a dignity and grace he had not perceived before. He remembered the ill-fated conversation about beans. Yes, a wicked humour, and courage too; she would see her way out of this business.

"Ann, a letter for you." It was Tom, not a whit abashed at bursting in without knocking, only that moment jumped off the Doctor's gig at the top of the avenue. The heartening lunch with William, the unexpected lift home, these had put him in a splendid humour, but he made his greetings swiftly, a disdainful stare at Cross in place of anything more polite.

"I did not expect to receive anything today. Pashman had nothing for us this morning." It was a single sheet of paper, she found, folded, sealed. The hand was unfamiliar.

"Oh, Pashman! I saw him. Looked like a fur trapper. Only his nose was visible and that was blue. No, I have brought it myself from the Post Office."

Ann took the letter to the window. Behind her Lord Barsham

and Tom fell to talking agriculture, a subject which had no appeal for the Runner who rather felt he had seen too much of it already since leaving London; he helped himself to more coffee and stared about him with resignation.

Dear Madam,
    This to inform you Sir H. wished to settle on you his interest (as owner) in the privateer *Sable Island* now at sea under Captain Saufret. It would not be to your advantage to make enquiries after her. Word will be sent. Sir H. in hope she will provide the means to settle all debts, hence need for secrecy, creditors in great number and all anxious to secure every asset.
Yours etc.,
Rchd Praed.
Instructed to write by Sir H. Gerard January 20th 1801 at the Royal Garter, Bottle Street.

"Are you unwell?" Lord Barsham demanded, concerned.

"And I did so hope it would be good news," Tom said, at her side in four long strides.

Ann folded the letter, tucked it into the palm of her hand. "It is nothing, simply a note from a friend in London to say that Harry ... to say that he is nowhere to be found, that it is certain he made for the coast."

"But you look so pale." Tom seized her arm.

"I am quite all right." She could see the Runner's curious and intelligent eyes. "Please see that Lord Barsham and Mr Cross have all they need. Perhaps they would care to lace their coffee with rum if there is any left. If you will excuse me a moment."

In the kitchen Miss Pennyquick and Hollin were caught in the act of stirring a dubious-looking punch in a pudding basin, stooped over their concoction like naughty children.

"A privateer?" Hollin asked, scratching his head, the scarlet flush of guilt receding. "What exactly is a privateer? She carries guns, she has a licence to do so, to prey on enemy merchantmen – and enemy warships if she has the chance and the nerve and the firepower."

"A pirate," said Miss Pennyquick, ladling the punch with a soup spoon and tasting it carefully and without shame.

"No, for she has a letter of marque, I told you, a licence to say who she is and what she may do, and she don't take any ship, only the enemy." Hollin's brother had a son in just such a vessel, though it might more aptly have been called a smuggler than a privateer.

A willow pattern cup of the punch came Ann's way. She tasted it with caution and found it something between ebullient and caustic. She choked.

"Hmm, a pirate." Miss Pennyquick hit her between the shoulder blades. "But what have privateers to do with anything?"

"Oh, they were mentioned, that is all. Have you anything to offer them before they go?" A look at the rifled baskets, the remains of her feast. "Mince pies, biscuits? And where is the last of the rum and the wine?"

In the punch, her scalded throat told her. Hollin gave a defiant stare and then suppressed a grin.

"You should be at Thorn," she told him, "not sitting about Blackow drinking and being idle."

"He should be out after the last of the sheep, and so should Lord Tom Forsie. How can the poor beasts live up on the Gorse in this cold?" Miss Pennyquick was debating whether to try Lord Barsham with the punch.

But Ann was not listening. She had sunk down on to one of the hard chairs, hands cupped about her drink, her eyes staring across at the monumental dresser with its ranks of plates and jugs, bowls, meat dishes, soup tureens; only she did not see the dresser, nor the flagged floor, nor the new and temperamental range, nor the rows of saucepans. She saw Harry's face, that face with its high cheekbones, its wide blue eyes. He had always had a quirky sense of humour, she was thinking. In the disintegration of his fortune, his life, his mind, he had still found time to share a last joke with her, and had found too a sense of justice to save her something from the wreck. He had promised she would be looked after: was this then the only promise he would keep? And so much that had puzzled her for so long was explained: his frequent days away – not all accounted for, she now perceived, by visits to Harriet in Dover; the rare times he had been flush with money, money he had sworn he had won at the tables and certainly lost there shortly afterwards; his secrecy over that distant island and its mysterious spices. He had said *Sable Island* would make their fortune; how he must have prayed for a rich prize, and not only that, a rich prize in time. And he dare not reveal anything to her for fear that under pressure she might tell others, and then the ship, putting into an English port, would be seized for his creditors: only as long as the *Sable Island* was at sea could there still be a chance for him – and for Ann, and Thorn, and Blackow, and poor unhappy Harriet.

Ann fed Praed's letter to the voracious range. Were they together again, those two dissimilar rogues? Harry had not written himself, she realised, for fear his hand was recognised and the contents reveal. And she wondered suddenly if Praed had learned to write in the Fleet from one of the many gentlemen fallen on hard times. Like Harry Gerard.

"I must go back. Babs, the pies, quick! And the punch."

In the drawing room Lord Barsham was preparing to leave, laughing with Tom over some absurdity in one of Coke's latest innovations; the Runner looked, not surprisingly, as doleful as when he had arrived. After the pies, the shocking punch, an exchange of further civilities, they took their leave. Lord Barsham bent over Ann's hand as if, in the absence of anything else, he could comfort her with old-fashioned gallantry.

"You will be most welcome at Upgate."

Harry's eyes, she thought foolishly, and tears started to her own.

"I would be delighted," she said.

Tom closed the door on them and looked about him. "What a tomb this is!" and then, a little roughly, "I wish you would cry. I wish you would scream and rage or throw something."

She came to put his neckcloth straight in the way a mother might. "I have cried all I need; and what is the point of rages? And what is there left in this poor, denuded house to throw?"

"I hope they hang him!"

"You must not speak so! I hope they do not find him."

It was the only hope she had left, all the others being dead. And it was not true she had cried enough, but now she cried alone and unseen up on the Gorse, out after the last half-dead sheep lost in the sleet, dragging in Tom's and Hollin's footsteps, dressed in a boy's clothes. The wind alone was bitter enough to bring tears to the eyes; they could not guess hers were for Harry and herself, for Thorn, which she would surely have to sell, for the humiliation and jealousy and pity, the wave of emotion inside her that threatened to break.

"You will die of cold up there," Miss Pennyquick said, helping her out of the half-dozen layers of clothes necessary for the sheep rescue. "What beasts are still there will have perished long ago."

But they had not; the snow, the deep, killing snow had not yet come. And they were the local breed, tenacious. Ann, enveloped in an old jacket of Tom's, a woollen hat pulled down over her ears, eyes red-rimmed and stinging, hooked them from thickets and the frozen ditches. Hollin grumbled at her ceaselessly, hauling her over the deep places like a child, but he made no serious attempt to stop her going, and nor did Tom, who knew that in her unspoken grief she found a kinship with the wind and the driving sleet, with the wild, writhing trees and the bleak, exposed places.

And he also knew – though his mouth grew straight and grim at the thought of it – that Harry Gerard haunted the Gorse and that when Ann stopped and looked up and smiled that odd, wistful half smile, she was seeing him there, riding that mad horse of his from under the oaks at the gallop, laughing.

In February the Doctor made a perilous journey to Thorn across miles of snowy waste, playing postman.

"I have had a note from William," he said when he was alone with Ann, warming his hands at the smoking fire. "Harry was traced to Deal without doubt but nothing more is known. Too many weeks have passed. It is certain he slipped away by sea."

"I hope …" Her eyes strayed to the window and the white sweep of Warren Hill. "I hope he is well and safe. He cannot survive long alone. He is like a child."

The Doctor stirred uneasily. He was tempted to be disagreeable. "He is not likely to survive in any case. His liver, dear girl, must be almost a pathology specimen by now … Yes, perhaps you are right to rebuke me. You are fond of him still. Of course. I was foolish not to consider it."

He had considered it a great deal and had made himself thoroughly miserable by it. He gave her a furtive glance but found she was deeply engrossed by the other letter he had handed her, the blotched seal no less a mystery than the blotched address.

"It went astray," he told her, "has jogged house to house around the entire district. But it is yours, it must be yours. Is not that smudge 'Gerard'?"

She had slit the seal but was sitting with the paper in her hand; something else had occurred to her.

"If Harry had given me something," she said suddenly, "if he had given me something … precious … I suppose it would not in fact be mine? Everything must go to pay his debts."

"It may depend what it is – surely they will not take the rings from your fingers?" It was a foolish remark, he saw: she wore no rings. "And who is to know? A trinket or two will scarcely be missed."

"But if it is more than a trinket, what then?"

The Doctor, who had hung his wig with his hat in the hall, who had thrown off his coat because the room was warm, and who was wandering up and down with the maddening restlessness of his lost mongoose, stood still a moment, wary.

"What did he have to give you, dear Ann, that was more than a trinket?"

She was silent, smiling but silent. He stalked to the window again, glared at the snow outside, and came back.

"You must ask William," he said, "such legal complexities are beyond me."

She saw his distress but did not understand it. It did not occur to her he might mind – against all his more honourable feelings and childishly, so childishly – that Harry had bestowed anything on her other than his name. She saw only a pair of slate-grey eyes in a long thin face of no particular merit staring across at her with a strange mixture of fury and anguish.

"Now that I am no longer married to Harry will you visit us often?" This small reproof for his neglect – she could not forgive him for keeping his distance from Blackow so doggedly, so pointedly – fell on deaf ears: he simply turned from her to cast about for his abandoned coat.

"The letter," he said a moment later, "you have dropped the letter."

She retrieved it, opened it out.

"Harry," she said softly. "News of Harry."

She was aware gradually that he had grown still and cold, that all his boundless energy, that irritating restlessness, had been instantly and completely contained. There was a silence, brief but charged with emotions – all his, and unidentifiable. Then:

"He failed to escape then. He has written to you."

"No. No, it is some friend who has sent to tell me he is out of the country, no more than we guessed."

Another prickly moment; was the Doctor swearing under his breath? At last he burst out: "He is a rogue. He has defrauded you of your fortune and broken your heart!"

"How romantic you are! Do you really believe – and you a medical man – that hearts can break?"

"It is a manner of speech."

"Such a low, unfriendly growl! Dear, dear Doctor, has yours ever broken then? And can you swear time sews them up again as neat as you would do it?"

Was she laughing at him? No, she was serious, grave eyes lifted to his.

"Come," he said, "stop all this nonsense about broken hearts. Mine is made of steel, sweet girl, and is indestructible."

She still studied him: the curve of brow and jaw, the long nose, the hard mouth. After a little: "I do not believe you," she said.

Then she stooped to feed her letter to the fire, watching it curl and crumble in the flames; the letter from a Mr Shaw of Dover telling her to expect the *Sable Island* some time in the next few months, to expect her secretly, most secretly.

Word had been sent.

13

DARK BUBBLING water, the splash and slop of a small boat shoving off, two or more men hitching themselves in at the last moment; there was a stiff breeze and the sea made a blustering roar along the beach. The other noises, once they had left the land behind, seemed even louder: the low rumble of the tiller man's voice, the scrape of the oars, the slap slap as the bow dropped.

Ann sat amidships, a pale face in an immensity of black cloak, and nothing else. It was too dark a night for details. And not one of the men sent to pluck her from the chilly beach was anything more than a voice and a blurred shape. In front, somewhere over her right shoulder it seemed, the ship waited, heaving silently just within the shelter of the headland, darkened, secretive, mysterious.

They were well out in the bay now and the wind was keener. It was such a small bay she had not expected any great change in conditions, but the deep sea swell was already lifting them and letting them down with an ugly roll, the men at the oars pulling hard, now and again a muffled curse. Then a shout, low but clear, and the standing up, perilously, of the man in the bow, and brisk commands in something that was not English and did not seem to be French either. The rowers rested a moment, the little boat lost way; then a nearer shout, sharp and urgent, the sudden momentary gleam of a lantern in the blackness. A blacker blackness loomed, the rowers stroked to order, one two, one two, rest. The starboard oars moved again, the man at the tiller snorted and gave a low laugh, and all at once they turned, with as much grace as was feasible and an exact and practised competence, and came under the side of the *Sable Island*.

A rope ladder dangled uninvitingly. It was wet, which gave no purchase and less pleasure. Hampered by her skirts and the voluminous, gusting cloak, Ann took a long time to reach the deck. Once there, however, several pairs of hands made haste to assist. It was as well they did: a ship's deck in complete darkness is a hazardous place for the nautically ignorant. Ann saw nothing but shapes, heard nothing but disembodied voices speaking – what? French? Spanish? Or was it some patois, or perhaps Breton? Someone had her elbow, was guiding her to the big cabin aft, opening a door on splendid and unexpected brightness, ushering her in. For a moment she was completely blinded and stood blinking foolishly, and then slowly everything became clear. Directly in front of her was a man of medium height, stocky build, an orderly, punctilious air; a man rather swarthy for English taste and apart from that indescribably ugly, his face pocked and pitted as if a miniature army had been digging itself in about it, and criss-crossed with old scars.

"My lady." This apparition bent over her hand. His smile was amused but it did not reach his one good eye that stared at her with undisguised curiosity.

"Captain Saufret?"

"That is my name, Richard Saufret. Come, you have had a long cold wait and a wetting – your boots are dripping, my dear. May I pour you some wine?"

They were alone; it seemed improper but there it was. It also seemed incredible and very slightly ridiculous. Ann unfastened her sodden cloak and let it drop across a table, one end of which was covered with at least a dozen large charts. Then she sat down, feeling damp and foolish, in the chair Saufret held for her, and watched him pour something red and pungent from an odd-shaped bottle. The cabin was spacious, though there would be insufficient head room for a man of William Claverden's height, but it did not show itself at its best, the stern windows shuttered and curtained so that no light escaped.

"You are indeed a lady of courage," said Saufret, bringing her a glass. "Harry said you were but I ..." He shrugged, and it was a French shrug, expressive from neck to fingertips. "I am not a connoisseur of courage in womena, you understand. I have lived at sea all my life, and women at sea are trouble. There is no doubt of that. There will never be women aboard this ship while I am master. But Harry said the *Island* would be safe in your hands and I think I might come to believe him."

She had come alone, had trusted herself to his startled men – not expecting petticoats or a low, clear and undeniably female voice – and now to him and his dubious charity. If he chose to make sail and leave with her aboard he could.

"What message did you receive?" he asked. "I had one that told me Harry was fleeing for his life. His life, Madame? Why his life? Has he murdered, or robbed on the highway?"

"Say rather for his freedom, Captain. A Mr Shaw wrote to me warning me to expect you, later he confirmed the date – as far as it could be confirmed. Until then I did not even know Harry owned any ship; at least, I am not sure I really believed he did so. It seemed so ... unlikely."

Saufret sprawled in the chair opposite, and he took a great mouthful of the strong red wine. Then he laughed. "He is a dear boy, I forgive him anything! If he could have avoided bad company, come to sea ..." The sea to him was a cure for every known vice. "Who knows? But let us to business, let us dispense with the tedious details of our last voyage and then, dear lady, you must have something to eat." A shout brought a small boy at the run and Ann's cloak was despatched to be hung at the galley fire to dry. "Come, come, sit over here at the table, these are the accounts. You have no fear of accounts, I know. Harry told me."

The scrupulously neat figures seemed to indicate a share of five thousand pounds owing to Harry after the capture of two brigs in the Bay of Biscay. "We were lucky," Saufret said with another shrug, "they thought to take advantage of foul weather to creep down the coast, smart little weatherly ships, and tough seamen. But we are not afraid of storms, can outsail anything, anything, dear lady! The prize money is strictly divided, you understand, a fifth here, so much there, law and custom, custom and law. But five thousand for Harry this time, a lucky, lucky strike; one of the brigs was carrying tea and wine. Will it pay off his debts? That boy, he was always in debt, and always when the sea was empty, no fat sails anywhere. Worst of all, for more than six months last year we were laid up for repairs after a frigate blasted us off Bordeaux; six months lost and money spent refitting, a great deal of money, God knows, and that not the first or last time either. The whole spring wasted, wasted. It is a chancy business, a chancy business altogether."

There was so much she needed to ask, but where to begin? It came to her suddenly that it was her money Harry had spent to refit this ship. And now, with no thought for her feelings on the matter, he assumed she would act with Saufret to clear his debts and allow him to return.

But a charge of bigamy – how could he return? A stray memory of her wedding caught her unawares: Harry's unsteady voice and clouded eyes, and all the old women murmuring as he fumbled with the ring. He had been thinking of Harriet, only Harriet.

Ann listened for a long moment to the sea, to the creak of the hull, to distant voices on deck. She had never been on a ship before. There was a peculiar smell, not very pleasant, of tar and salt and boiled meat.

"The crew." Perhaps she should ask some sensible questions. "How many men?"

"A hundred, mostly West Country men and islanders – from Guernsey, dear lady, my own island – and a few Dutch, a Lascar, a Swede." He waved his square hands expansively. "This is the fastest privateer at sea, and she has eighteen guns and some crack gunners. She can tackle much larger ships, and she has done so – but at some cost. We avoid the larger warships unless they are already crippled. Have some more wine, you are still pale from your journey."

Another glass of that robust southern glory and she would not

231

be able to stand upright. She declined graciously and saw his eye gleam. "You have a fine ship, Lady Gerard, a fine ship."

She bent forward. Was it really her feet in those damp boots side by side on this faded Turkey carpet, so like the Turkey carpet at Thorn she had a crazy desire to laugh? Was it really her voice saying calmly and from a great distance: "I must inform you I am not, in fact, Lady Gerard. Lady Gerard at present lives in Dover and has no notion of the existence of this ship."

The eye snapped at her; his mouth formed an oath and then closed on it. He sat, staring her down, waiting for an explanation.

"Harry married me knowing he had a wife already. He married me for my money of which, alas, there is now none left."

"But he told me you were strong, true, courageous. He told me so."

She blushed. "That does not alter the fact I am not his wife. This, and the debts, finally drove him to quit England. When did you last see him, Captain?"

"Before Christmas, long before. Then a brief letter to say he was leaving the country for fear of his life, that in future I was to put myself in your hands entirely, and that I was to let you know the details of any rendezvous secretly, most secretly. This I did through Mr Shaw in Dover, a great friend of mine, of this ship. It was a great pity we could not have been here sooner but ships are at the mercy of wind and circumstance; we chased a sloop across the Bay and would have had her if she had not vanished in the fog."

A peremptory knock at the door and a young man appeared, a tray of delicacies balanced precariously. Ann, beginning to feel alarmed, saw pickled goose, fresh rolls, and sweet chestnuts. Saufret poured more wine and smiled.

"Mr Brandt, join us. This is our new owner, Lady ... Ah, Lady Ann."

Brandt, who had cleared the charts with a sweep of his arm in order to put down his tray, was now busy rolling them up neatly. He was neat enough himself, in a blue jacket and with a dark, meticulously tied pigtail. He gave a doubtful grin and looked shyly in Ann's direction.

"Mr Brandt is the mate, dear girl. How shall I say? The second in command. Do not be deceived by his name – he is from Devon. Here, will you eat something?" Saufret was already wielding knife and fingers among the edibles.

Ann accepted a roll hesitantly and found it new-baked, excellent; it did not sort well with the chestnuts but there was some sticky preserve, a sort of lemon marmalade. She said between mouthfuls: "I know nothing about ships except they have a front and a back called bow and stern. That is the sum of my knowledge. I cannot see how in the world I am to take Harry's place; you can have no idea what stratagems I had to employ simply to reach that remote beach at nine o'clock. I have travelled across England on a lie, have convinced my friends I am scarcely sane, have been reduced to secretly hiring a nag to carry me ten miles through the dark, and now find ..." She gazed about her, half amused, half bewildered.

"Yes, my lady, what do you find?" Saufret asked with a dazzle of his one eye.

"Forgive me, you will think me very foolish, but this ship ... I think I was expecting something more like a ... oh, I do know what they are! A revenue cutter! Yes, more like a revenue cutter."

"You see," Brandt said gently from the other side of the table where he had been keeping very still, his eyes on her face, "very shortly you will be able to tell them all apart, a sloop from a corvette, a frigate, a brig ... It is so very easy after all."

"But what is the *Sable Island*? She is so large, so ... well-armed. And a hundred men!"

"We need a hundred to fight her, we could sail her with far fewer than that. She is what is known as a hermaphrodite schooner – she has square sails and fore-and-aft sails on both masts. She is a wet ship – oh, dear Lord, how wet! – but she is fast, so fast."

"I have not the least idea what fore-and-aft sails are," Ann said with a smile. "Why are they not all square ones?"

Saufret leaned back, goose fat on his chin, and gave a huge shout of laughter. "But he was right, poor foolish Harry! He was so right! You are indeed a precious find. How did he ever have the sense to marry you? But oh, if he had done so sooner you might have made a hero of him!"

Brandt, aware of Ann's distress, gave a discreet cough. "Perhaps Lady Gerard would care for some coffee?"

"She is not Lady Gerard, she is ..." A significant pause, a sidelong glance from that terrible eye.

"Miss Ann Mathick," Ann said dully.

Brandt was more embarrassed than ever, rose to his feet in a jump and stood, slightly stooped because he was too tall for the place, growing pink.

"Yes," said Soufret, unabashed, "yes, Luke, Lady Ann would like coffee. Call Jakes."

Brandt went to do so. Ann said: "Is there no difficulty dealing with your prizes when it is imperative word must not get about that Harry is the owner?"

"It is simply a question of being cautious, of being circumspect."

The ship groaned as the swell lengthened. Saufret stood up, wiped his black stubble with a crisp white napkin, and went to the door. A shout brought a monkey-faced boy, also commendably neat, who sprinted away on the order to fetch Mr Joshua immediately or else. From somewhere came a stifled guffaw, the rumble of some other order. Saufret returned. "I can smell coffee. It will not be long. But it will be dawn before you are safe in your bed. Shall you not be missed?"

"I must run that risk." Behind her Brandt came back with the coffee. "But this ship ..." She became aware they were both waiting, expectant, and it was, she realised, more now than simple courtesy or simple curiosity. They had accepted that she was to replace Harry in their lives; her opinion was to be considered seriously. The thought horrified her. How was she, tucked away at Thorn, engrossed in the pursuit of agriculture, to pursue also the fortunes of a privateer?

"I would be grateful," she said at last, "if you could explain the exact legal position of Harry Gerard, this ship, and you, Captain Saufret. Is she truly Harry's ship? Are you partners? If she is his, how did he come by her? And are there documents ..."

"There are, there are ... Though I must confess, dear girl, that this ship was won at cards by your rogue Harry many years ago. Amused? I thought you would be. How like Harry, we are both thinking. She was laid down in the year eighty in Boston, but was bought by a Frenchman and converted to a privateer. She was taken by the British in ninety-four and a quirk of fate put her on the market where she was sold to a noble gentleman – better he remain nameless – who played once too often in shady company and lost a very great deal: his sails shot to pieces and no steerage, you might say. He asked Harry to take the ship in lieu of a debt and the mad boy accepted. The *Island* lay rotting in a cove down by Falmouth for a year and then I saw her, saw her neatness, her beauty, all her possibilities ..." And his hands described her, making long sweeping passes, his eye shining all the while.

Ann took refuge in the steaming coffee. The ship had made enough in prize money in the last five years to refurbish Blackow twice over and where had it all gone? On horses, on cards, on specious pleasures – and on two wives. Being Harry, she thought, he had taken no account of squalls, of the vagaries of the wind, of the fire power of the enemy; he had lived up to his income and that income was erratic, at times ceased altogether and for long periods – then he lived on credit and prayed. And how ironic that the *Sable Island* had been laid up for such extensive repairs at just that time she had accosted him for those wretched acres. Oh, he still had money, by any normal standards a great deal, but he was never without unpaid debts – he always preferred to promise rather than to pay – and the expense of putting a privateer of such size to sea, and keeping it there, was unimaginable. A run of bad luck, some impatient creditors, and he would be lost. Little Ann Mathick's fortune would insure him against such calamity; little Ann Mathick's fortune would buy any number of new masts, spars, bowsprits and cannon balls.

"It is a little bitter, I am afraid," Brandt said, seeing her expression and misinterpreting it. "We are very low in coffee, it has become a luxury."

"It seems Harry did little for this ship but own her," Ann said.

"He knew her movements as far as he was able; he sailed in her once — a bad sailor, I fear, sick as a dog and confined to his cot — and he never thought of selling, never. Even when she cost him dear," — another look from that sage eye — "very dear indeed."

The wine bottle went round again. Ann refused it firmly and took more coffee. The ship heaved and settled, heaved and settled. A knock at the door brought the monkey-faced boy with a stooping, middle-aged man in tow, a gentleman in an ancient but perfect frock coat, a glaringly white cravat, an impressive wig. He stood just inside the cabin and looked at them one by one, a slow smile spreading.

"This, Lady Ann, is Mr Joshua Shaw of Dover, my agent. Mr Shaw will send to Norfolk as often as he has news of us."

"I fear I shall be reduced to the most terrible subterfuge," she said. She had no doubt of it, no doubt at all.

"Another voyage, a little luck, a deal of … cunning, cunning and perseverance, and Sir Harry may be afloat again."

There was some restrained laughter. Ann intervened with: "There is still the question of bigamy."

"Then we must make enough to pay a clever lawyer to extricate him from his misfortune," said Saufret cheerfully. It was his nature to be an optimist, she saw.

Joshua Shaw helped himself to a chestnut. He had looked rather bleak at the mention of bigamy, but not astonished: he had long ago ceased to be astonished by Harry Gerard. "I will send you word, Madam, when the ship is home again and my discretion," and he waved a hand largely, "is guaranteed."

"It may be several months," said Saufret.

"Several months at least. Let me accompany Lady Ann to the beach. Time I left you, Richard." Shaw was already calling at the door for his greatcoat and boots.

He and Brandt went out but Saufret and Ann lingered meaningfully in the warmth of the cabin. "A banker's draft," Saufret said, handing it to her, "it will help a little, will it not?"

Her hands were trembling. He noticed. "Of course," his voice was gentle, "he will die in debt. We know that, you and I. But we love him not the less for it, eh, my lady?"

On deck the motion of the ship seemed livelier. The brown dawn was spreading to the horizon. A tangle of rigging, the soaring, raking masts were just visible. Mr Shaw waited by the dread rope ladder, talking to a seaman.

A disciplined, good-natured crew, as smart as might be hoped for – this made itself known even in the darkness. An air of competence, of things well done. A fast ship then, a happy ship, and Harry's salvation perhaps. Something floated to the surface of her mind, something from long ago, something Harry had said: 'I took it in lieu of a debt. It was the best thing I ever did in my life.'

Shaw offered his hand. "I am no sailor myself," he told her, gazing despondently at the small boat abob on the swell below.

Ann did her best with the ladder, feeling the ship rolling away from her so that she dangled in air, a clutch of damp linen and clammy flesh, spray and perspiration mingled. It was Brandt who caught her as she let go and saw water and not boards beneath her feet.

"You will learn to judge the moment," he said, as if she might spend the next twenty years of her life paying midnight visits to the schooner. "For a first attempt you did remarkably well. Mr Shaw is certain to get a ducking though: we have often had him half drowned."

As if to give weight to the remark Shaw succeeded in wetting his feet and frightening them all to death by banging his head with an astounding crack against the ship's side. At last they hauled him in to sit beside Ann, apologetic and white, a little stunned. The *Sable Island* fell astern, the rowers pulling in silence, eyes on Brandt in his cocked hat. For the first time Ann caught a glimpse of what she had come to find, here in this tiny bay in the concealing dark: a two-masted ship, nine gun-ports along the starboard side, moving gently at her anchor but with a look, inexplicable but certain, of being on the point of flight, even with her sails still furled against the brightening sky.

"Saufret is a good man," Shaw said, following her eyes, "bold, intelligent, a true seaman. I have known him all my life. You would not find a better captain anywhere, nor a more trustworthy one. Men flock to sail with him. Of course he has his oddities, so do we all. By and large I would hazard my life at his hands before any other man's I know."

They beached. Brandt was over the bow and knee-deep in icy water offering her his assistance. Ann found herself carried twenty yards up the shingle and then set on her feet.

"If ever you should wish to send a message to the ship Shaw will do his best," he said. "He is a tea dealer, knows every Indiaman at sea, every trading vessel under whatever colours, and every master from here to the Malay Straits. He has a house in Dover, another in London. You will find him reliable, old-fashioned, a man of integrity." He broke off to issue orders; they were bringing Shaw through the shallows like a meal sack, sagging ominously. "I wish you a safe journey," turning back to Ann. "Was it wise to ride so far alone and at night?"

"I had no choice. And I shall be hard pushed to be back by sunrise," she said anxiously, her eyes on the horizon and then on the distant ship, revealed little by little across a steely sea.

"Have you no carriage waiting then?" Shaw demanded, reaching them at last after an undignified scramble. "Come, I forbid you to gallop back to Brighton on a hired nag. You must ride with me in the coach and we shall tether him behind."

It was cold, bleak and grey. Ann was thankful to be inside, bundled in a travelling rug, pressed to take a sip of brandy to stave off a collapse of the lungs – "cold beaches are the very devil for bringing on coughs and inflammation" – and regaled with cheerful stories of the *Sable Island*'s capacities, the fighting spirit of her crew – "not a pressed man among them" – and her gunners' reputation as crack shots. By the time they reached Brighton it was raining, a thin, chilly rain, a reminder of winter.

"I hope we meet again," said Shaw, setting Ann down a short

way from her lodging and promising to return the hired horse himself, "but I will write, have no fear of it."

"If Captain Saufret hears where Harry is, you will …"

Shaw leaned from the carriage and gave her a look of ineffable sadness; in no time his hat was beaded with rain.

"Of course. But I should not hold out too great a hope, dear Lady Ann; no, no hope at all. We have seen the last of Harry Gerard on this earth, if I am not mistaken."

At the tall narrow house in the unfashionable street where she and Miss Pennyquick shared four gloomy rooms, Ann let herself in silently and slipped to bed. In another hour she was up again, dressing, and looking out at the full-grown morning, as sorrowfully grey, as bitter, and as chill as its beginnings had promised. At breakfast, making inroads on ham and toast and coffee, she happened to catch Miss Pennyquick's wondering eye.

"The sea air has done you some good already."

"I hope so," said Ann.

"It was a blowy night. So much rattling and groaning. I thought the chimneys might fall. I woke several times and fancied I heard doors closing, keys turning. It was most strange, most upsetting."

Ann poured another coffee. "I am sorry you slept so badly. Is that a letter for me on the side there?"

The letter was from the Doctor, rather short on verbs and inclined to the staccato, but expressive, compelling. 'We miss you,' he wrote, 'Lady Barsham hopes you are not in decline etc. I think it unlikely. William to sea as soon as possible, in touch with Admiralty, uniform at the ready. Charlotte in tears, or thus reported. Unfortunately William's thoughts turned already to salt beef etc. so no inclination to be comforting beyond the ordinary. Must speak to him severely – Charlotte too good a girl for such distress. Very wet here, becomes tedious, but Tom out in fields every day. He has had me to dine, cooks a decent stew but fails with dumplings. Why? Dumplings very simple, I assert. Nevertheless the boy has no notion. Can you remedy this on your return?'

"It is from the Doctor," Ann told Miss Pennyquick. "Tom has been entertaining him to dinner."

"Heaven save him!"

"And he has been helping Mr Claverden finish up that part of Mr Claverden's wine cellar considered unlikely to stand the rigours of a sea voyage."

"They have been drunk, you mean? And you are light-headed too this morning."

"Not in the least. I simply find the air at Brighton bracing. After breakfast we will take a walk and look at the sea."

Miss Pennyquick stared. Brown eyes more alive, more amused than she had seen them in some months, met hers and then danced back to the Doctor's scrawl.

"The sea is grey, always grey, and it makes a considerable noise." Miss Pennyquick had not seen the sea until she had come to Brighton and she had not been impressed. "I do not care for it."

"And I thought I did not. But now it seems narrow-minded to bear an aversion to something I know so little about. If it does not rain all day we must stroll to the front and consider the ocean more closely."

14

"THE *Garden of Cyrus*, I believe," said the Doctor. "But I was never a hearty reader. You will find books there I have not opened in twenty years."

William was browsing along his shelves, mellowed by a good dinner and an excellent wine. He was relaxed, assured, vigorous this evening, confident his readmission into the Navy would be confirmed any day. He had no hope of a command, not now, maybe not in the future; as far as the Navy was concerned he had blotted his record, gadding off to flirt so boldly with the Law. But he had been exiled from the sea too long; he would have taken a berth on a fishing lugger to feel the heave of a deck beneath his feet again.

"I still cannot understand Ann's furious longing for Brighton. They arrived safely, I presume?"

"I had a letter only this morning. She sounds well and happy. The lodgings are all they hoped for, and a very reasonable price. They have Maggie and a hired girl to clean; every comfort, she says, and every convenience."

"It sounds an extravagance to me, seeing she has scarcely any money and still Thorn to run."

"You are too severe, Will. She needed to go, needed to escape High Common for a while, High Common gossip and High Common sympathy, both overdone and both largely false. Blackow in new hands, Harry fled, nobody quite sure whether to invite her to their social gatherings or to consider her some kind of whore – oh, no, that is not too strong a word! Do not raise those supercilious brows at me, Will Claverden! I have seen her grow paler and thinner and more silent for weeks; I have seen her cope with heavy-handed kindness – Barsham's – and invidious curiosity – Mrs Palmer's – and any number of personal attacks, false complaints, cutting remarks, a whole regiment of cold shoulders. It would be enough to wear down the toughest constitution. Let her have her holiday in Brighton. She will be all the better for it."

"You read Herrick at least, I see," William said, thumbing through a dog-eared copy and noting the indiscriminate underlinings. "It was a very sudden departure, on a whim, you might say. And why Brighton?"

"You mean, why not Yarmouth? If it was only sea air she needed no doubt Yarmouth would have answered admirably; there is plenty there, cold, disagreeable, and abominably blowy too. Hopes of a little excitement, some entertainment perhaps, drew her to Brighton. And why not?"

"In March? It must be quite as cold and disagreeable as Yarmouth and a hundred times more expensive."

"You are determined to find fault. I think it was a commendable choice: even organising the journey seemed to give her back a sense of purpose – and that has been sadly lacking these last months."

William abandoned the Herrick, turned over a battered Livy, an even more battered Catullus, a slim and shabby volume of *The Vanity of Human Wishes*, and a beautiful *Paradise Lost*, the pages still uncut.

"And was Miss Pennyquick a willing companion?" He was musing rather gloomily on the vanity of human wishes as it affected himself.

"I gather she is no friend to the seaside, though she had not been there in her life before. She was once obliged to revive a guest of old Forsie's who had taken the cross-channel packet and has never forgotten it. Nor have I. On such small experiences are most of our prejudices founded, I fear. But both she and Ann are in good spirits, active in the extreme, and not constrained by their lack of funds. They walk every day – miles and miles, by all accounts – and grow quite weathered, Ann says, what with the wind and sea mists and so forth."

"And you still expect them home at the end of the week?"

"I have heard nothing to the contrary."

"I have written to Liveman, Gerard's lawyer," William said after a pause, painfully aware of his inability to progress at all in the affair, even over the fundamental point of obtaining incontrovertible proof there had ever been a marriage to Harriet Stratford. "The man is everlastingly gloomy. His offices must resound to wailing and the gnashing of teeth. He is never hopeful, never comforting, never able to suggest any remedy. I hazard a guess he and Sir Harry came to quarrelling once and he has not forgotten it, or forgiven." He sat down, tugging at his neckcloth and then reaching for his wine with a savage grin. "I wish the whole business was over and done. How will she live at Thorn with no money? It is all she will have left – the house, the hundred acres round it, and the furniture."

"I daresay she will rub along somehow. She is young and capable. There is Tom to help on the land and Miss Pennyquick to keep the house. And she will never shift Hollin now, cantankerous old bird; he has developed the most awful doglike devotion to her. Oh, they will all manage tolerably well. And Ann may marry again." The Doctor's eyes fixed themselves on William's shadowy chin. "But why not? She is pleasant to look at, has some fine qualities, a head for business. Why not?"

William looked sullen, the first time the Doctor had ever seen him so. In truth he felt sullen, and resentful; despite all his efforts he was drawn to Ann. He told himself it was nothing to do with her being a female – rather in fact that she treated him with a masculine directness, appealed to his sense of fair play, to their uncertain, undeveloped friendship. She had made it plain she trusted him, depended on him, that he would he doing her an injustice to leave her before a satisfactory conclusion to this unnerving business. On the other hand there was nothing masculine in that particular tilt of her head, that arch smile when she was amused, that damn-all determination when she had set her heart on something.

"Brighton in March is no place for the weak-spirited, to be sure," he said, giving an unconsciously charming and distracted smile at his host and draining his glass. "But tell me, who is the new tenant of Blackow?"

"Alas, middle-aged, married, and childless." The Doctor's eyes lit up, his grin widened. "Poor Mrs Palmer! She has been crying shame and woe around half the neighbourhood, he is so grossly unsuitable for her purposes."

The interview with Liveman, so much dreaded, was immensely satisfactory. Ann had hardly dared hope it would be anything but stormy; she had had little to do with the man, thought him over-cautious and fussy, knew of the vast gulf between him and Harry. But a banker's draft for five thousand pounds is a powerful argument, its bearer, even when an eccentric young lady, most welcome. He did his best to be helpful, though failed to be charming. Ann forgave him with a wry smile, seeing he was not by nature given to be charming. He was commendably restrained when handed a large sum of money with the barest of details, asked little, looked soberly triumphant. To her surprise he had heard of the *Sable Island*, had been struggling for some time to subdue his troublesome conscience about her.

"I do not advocate any illegalities, you understand, but if we may keep her at sea, or at the very least out of those ports where she is bound to fall victim to the bailiffs, then I think we might depend on her to furnish us with more prize money shortly. Of course this is a capital sum, capital. It cannot be hoped that it will be matched again this year, of course, and if there should be any kind of lasting peace ... But this will certainly pay the most pressing creditors, will ease the burden."

"It is still as bad as that?"

"Indeed it is. A very sorry business. A little less than fifteen thousand owed at the final count, a tremendous sum. And now Blackow is gone, and everything else saleable, and with this five thousand from the ship, well, there are major debts of perhaps four thousand outstanding. We shall win through, Miss Mathick, given time and God's mercy."

Yes, they would need both of those, she thought. "You speak as if you doubt the mercy will be forthcoming."

"Forgive me. But I have no stomach for this case. The boy was always wild, always foolhardy, always ill-advised. His father, God rest him, would have died for very shame if he had known – the drink, the gambling, the ... his unfortunate marriage. It is bad blood, Miss Mathick, bad blood coming out."

"An inherited weakness for pleasure and frivolity? I am not sure I believe it is any such thing. I would prefer to think he was neglected as a child and was thrown too much in the wrong company from the start. That was as much his father's neglect as his mother's."

Liveman was unconvinced, but the five thousand pounds had encouraged him sufficiently to offer her refreshment, to enquire after her health, her unfortunate circumstances, her recent stay in Brighton. No, there had been no further news about the marriage to Harriet Stratford, there was some delay over the registers, some inter-parish squabble among parsons; it was nothing new, nothing unexpected.

Ann refused his offer of tea, mentioned Miss Pennyquick waiting below, and there was the journey back to Norfolk; she dare not stay another moment.

"If it is necessary to correspond I shall not mention the *Sable Island*," Liveman said as she reached the door. "We may yet hold the smaller creditors at bay for the time it takes her to effect our rescue."

"And meanwhile who pays the crew, who buys the sails, the food, the thousand everyday things she needs?"

"They must either wait for a prize, use credit, leave the crew unpaid, or turn to their captain for the means. After all, how would it be to his advantage to lose the ship?"

To Miss Pennyquick a little later Ann said: "Thank God we shall soon be home," with a vehemence so out of character it was startling. Four thousand pounds, she was thinking, such a very large sum after all ...

Inserted tightly into the coach, they prepared for the sixteen-hour purgatory ahead. The weather had deteriorated, the day was foggy, the roads indescribably muddy. Ann closed her eyes and tried to sleep but sleep eluded her. Instead memories came and went, memories of that daring ride from Brighton to the rendezvous with *Sable Island* – how Harry would have approved! – of tying the hired horse to a furze bush – how extraordinarily difficult – of the climb down to the beach, of the cold and the absolute dark, of the little boat grinding on the shingle. And then Saufret with his one all-seeing eye.

After a while the stopping and starting, the tolls, the vociferous vendors of this and that who crowded up at every stage post, the jolting and swaying and lurching over horrible quagmires, brought a pinched, white look to Miss Pennyquick, a look of unbearable suffering. Tom, handing her out at the Angel, kissed her cheeks heartily and found them cold and damp.

"Are you unwell?"

"It was the stuffiness, the stuffiness and the smell," she replied weakly.

"You will soon be right again," unsympathetically, "but we have had a drama at Thorn today – Hollin took it into his head to cure that smoking chimney once for all and set the place alight. I found him choking to death in half a ton of soot and twenty flaming birds' nests."

"Thorn burning?" Ann cried, grasping his arm.

"No, no. It was out in a moment." A gross exaggeration but they were not to know. "Luckily Pashman and old Grandpa Cowley were outside in the yard and we all grabbed buckets and had it doused before Hollin had stopped coughing." That was true but then Hollin had coughed a great deal. "The kitchen is a little singed, and odds and ends ... but nothing to signify."

It seemed he had arranged for them to spend the night with the Doctor rather than return them to a damp and reeking Thorn, no kitchen fire and an unconscionable mess. Ann said nothing but had her own ideas about the possible extent of the mess. Hollin's pony being indisposed – two shoes cast in one morning, sore feet, and serves him right – Tom had borrowed the Doctor's brown cob and crammed him between the shafts of the trap, a change for the better even if the poor animal was a tight fit. He drove them to High Common as fast as he could allowing for the state of the roads and Miss Pennyquick's awful greenness – and the Doctor's horse had exemplary manners when not driven by the Doctor – and delivered them and their baggage to the white house with its aggressive holly bush.

It had been a long, wretched journey. Miss Pennyquick, having suffered stoically – or so she thought – the indignities and terrors of stage-coach travel, found herself faced with spending yet another night in a strange bed. She looked at Ann helplessly but found her smiling, untying her bonnet and pulling it off anyhow, stepping forward to receive the Doctor's kiss.

"My dear girl, how good to see you! Life has been so dull! This week would have been unendurable but for Lady Barsham, who swept down on us demanding to know when you were to return, she is so anxious to have you at Upgate as her guest. She took a turn around my books – I have known her for twenty years and we never discussed books until that moment – and went away with a changed opinion of me, I swear, a revision of my mental capacities! Come in, come in. Would you care for wine, tea, cocoa?"

Miss Pennyquick went damply white. Ann touched her arm. "You must go up to bed, Babs, and sleep it off."

"Is it a physic you need?" asked the Doctor. "To settle the stomach or the nerves?"

Miss Pennyquick confessed herself overcome by sea air, odoriferous coaches, and raw beef. A cheerful pink concoction was made up and swallowed gratefully. "Take refuge in sleep," the Doctor advised soberly, "sleep is a great restorative."

He closed the door behind her with a lift of one brow in Ann's direction.

"The coach was abominable, there is no doubt of it, and the meal was almost, almost inedible," she told him.

"And you? How have you fared? Your letters were exceedingly cheerful, all witty observation and sly humour. Has the sea air harmed your constitution? The coach and the undercooked dinner seem to have had little effect."

She accepted his offer of a dish of tea, a plain biscuit. The Lascar cook was unearthed and beamed on her, bringing her a tray with the speed of a genie.

"I have had an adventure," she said at last to the Doctor.

"I suspected something of the kind. The visit to Brighton was not ... uncalculated?"

She felt she must tell someone, and the impossibility of telling William Claverden she was to be intermediary between Harry's privateer and Harry's creditors made her turn instinctively to the Doctor. She plucked a pin out of her hair and twisted it in her fingers, looking into the fire.

"Harry used to talk about an island, an island so beautiful ... He wanted me to see it, he was sure I would love it. I used to think it was just a dream of his, that there was no such place."

"But there is."

"There is. And I have been there."

The Doctor moved to sit opposite. As always he had mislaid his wig. His hair had grown a little, a bristly mixture of brown and grey, and under it his lined face looked tired and drained of colour.

"It is very late, but tell me all about it, dear girl. For if you do not tell me now I fear you may wake so refreshed and sensible you will think such a confidence ill advised." And then, as she remained silent, "So it is beautiful, this island?"

And she tipped back her head and laughed, the first time she had laughed as far back as he could remember. "Yes, indeed. Doctor, you do not like ships, do you?"

"Ships?" The Doctor feared ships were not his particular love, not, at least, when shared with several hundred unwashed soldiers and all sick as dogs.

"Do you remember once explaining to me the exact working of a carronade?"

The Doctor shook his head.

"*Sable Island*," said Ann, "is a ship, a privateer, and Harry's own."

Perhaps there was something in the way she said the name that jarred those sensibilities he had spent a fortnight rationally subduing. The desires of a complex nature are not easily diverted, certainly not eliminated without a struggle. The Doctor had a heart, not made of steel as he had airily suggested, and it had been attacked, besieged, overrun, and sorely hurt recently, just when he thought age and a hundred deeply entrenched bachelor habits would prove sufficient defences. And besides, he had never liked Harry Gerard, had shied instinctively from something false in him. Now Ann, installed companionably in his own living room, spoke almost gently of the fellow, and with a whimsical smile as if his memory was dear to her. The Doctor felt a great stab of white-hot anger he was too ashamed and self-deluding to admit was jealousy and said tartly: "Another of his wild ventures, no doubt."

Ann hesitated. She did not fully understand his abrupt changes of mood, his sour remarks or prickly reticence, though she knew well enough what he privately thought of Harry.

"This one may well turn out to be an unqualified success," she said carefully, her eyes on his hardened features.

But the Doctor, unknown to her, was struggling momentarily in a sort of Sargasso sea of emotional confusion, unable to progress in any direction satisfactorily and hampered by the weed and debris of honour, deep affection – the only word he would permit himself to use – and his own quite rigid code of morality. Simple lust, he felt, would have been so much easier to control than this slippery tangle of feelings, and he grinned at the thought, his sense of humour reasserting itself. Though he found Ann's gaze disconcerting still, her dark, troubled eyes unwavering in their innocent examination of his expression.

"An unqualified success?" he demanded sharply, repressing that wolfish grin. "Nonsense! Why, if it were it would be the very first that unfortunate young man ever had. The ship will be sunk, you can be sure of that. Dear Ann, how can you still be so optimistic after all that has passed?"

There was, he noticed, the old challenge in the quick lift of her chin.

"It would surely be a sin to despair," she said, "and if you think I bear any grudge you are mistaken."

Norwich on a market day was crammed and malodorous. Tom picked his way with difficulty below the castle and came up against a bewildered scramble of cattle being driven from across the river. Further on he had to duck inside hastily at the cry of "Bull! Bull loose!" and found, on looking down, that his clean breeches were splattered with mud. He also found, some minutes later, that William was out and likely to be so all day. This dashed his hopes of a private and affectionate goodbye.

But: "Surely it is Tom Forsie! Tell me, do, how is dear Ann?"

It was Lady Barsham and Charlotte, a burdened footman toiling behind. Tom made a leg as elegantly as he could, which was just elegantly enough. Charlotte's grave eyes considered him for a moment. She saw a tall, broad, golden-haired youth with very bright blue eyes and slightly flushed cheeks, a rather guilty expression. He spoke well but the country accent was still there; she found it nonsensically attractive.

"Ann is quite well," he said. "Brighton was a great success, did her no end of good."

"And do you not think she is much improved since Sir Harry vanished so completely?" Lady Barsham demanded as they made their way with difficulty towards the Assembly House. "She is undeniably pretty at times, smiling, happy."

"Hmm yes," said Tom, feeling that it was Brighton and not Harry's disappearance that had brought about the change, and that in any case the change was superficial and hid untold anxiety and grief.

"You must be very fond of her," was Charlotte's hesitant contribution as they breasted the hill.

"Hmm yes."

They turned as one to make sure the footman was still with them. The wind played havoc with Charlotte's skirts and Tom had a glimpse of a slender leg in a white stocking and a quantity of expensive lace. When he came to say goodbye he shook her hand in both of his rather warmly — rather too warmly? — rammed on his hat, and marched away, only to glance back several times as if he hoped she would still be staring after him.

He gained the Jolly Waterman, paid for the horse — the

chestnut horse, and in a lather of nervous excitement – attached it with difficulty to the trap, and set off to High Common. He would see the Doctor, if the Doctor was at home. He would borrow that book on ships and rigging and ordnance the Doctor had recently acquired – and rather mysteriously, never having shown any deep interest in such subjects before – hoping he might shortly be able to talk sensibly to William of matters nautical and naval, and even write sensibly to him when he should be sent overseas in one of His Majesty's ships of the line.

He was thundering up over the Gorse – the chestnut, like the Doctor's cob, was far too big for the trap and progress was unsteady – when he spied a man on foot not far ahead. The man was tall and walked with an air of knowing exactly where he was going and intending to be there to the minute. He wore a brown coat and a brown hat and his boots were excessively muddy. Tom took a pull at the chestnut.

"Are you bound for High Common?" he asked, leaning out. The horse slid to an abrupt halt, bunched up like a cat and throwing its head about.

"High Common?" The man turned: grey eyes in a tanned face, dark hair in a pigtail, a large nose. He swept off his hat as a sort of preliminary to politeness but then stood, silent and wary, looking Tom over.

"I could take you as far as the village if you like, I am going there myself. You will save your boots at least."

The man in the brown coat returned his hat to his smooth head. "I would accept with heartfelt thanks but I am bound for a farm hereabouts called Thorn. Perhaps I could trouble you to direct me."

"But I live there!" exclaimed Tom, abandoning his projected visit to the Doctor at once. "It is but a little way from here, down the hill. Step up! We will go there directly."

The stranger stepped up and the chestnut was induced to trot on. Of its own accord it took the lane to Thorn and plunged down the steep slope under the burgeoning trees.

"Is it Miss Mathick you wish to see?" Tom asked, conscious

that his passenger was clinging to the seat, a rather absent look on his face, as of a person petrified with fright.

"It is." Spoken through gritted teeth? "I trust she is at home. I was unable to send any warning, things being what they were. Are you her brother? I must confess I understood she had no close relatives living."

Tom, awash with curiosity and pique inextricably mingled, stiffened slightly. "I am her cousin."

"Ah, yes, I had forgot. Mr Forsie."

"Yes," growled Mr Forsie, pique momentarily the governing force.

He did his best to stop the chestnut taking the gatepost with him as they swung into the yard, and shot out a hand to stop the stranger toppling out as they careered up to the back door where the horse dug in his heels and flung up his head with a snort of triumph. Miss Pennyquick emerged, in a grubby apron, hair wayward, nose smutty.

"That trap was needed this morning, and the gig's too big for Hollin's pony. And there you go without a by-your-leave ..."

"A visitor for Ann," said Tom firmly.

The visitor climbed down with relief and removed his hat again. At that moment an upper casement was flung wide and Ann put her head out in a cloud of dust.

"Spring cleaning," Miss Pennyquick said, "and the kitchen's new-painted. We had a fire, you know. Please mind the paint pots. You had better come to the drawing room. Why that boy could not have driven you round to the front, I don't know."

She knew very well: the front door, though refurbished, was grossly underused. To all intents and purposes the front of the house, the only symmetrical, noble side of Thorn, looking over the garden to Warren Hill on one side and the water meadows on the other, was the back. And it was the custom deep in the country anyway to avoid using a front door for anything but the admission or ejection of wedding parties, new-christened babies, coffins, or the Law.

In a minute Ann had come into the drawing room, her hair up in a duster and in an apron a little more disgusting than Miss

Pennyquick's. Her face was streaked with something white – limewash or chalk – and something not so white – soot? She did not look as if she would relish the prospect of visitors. But at the sight of the tall young man in brown her face lit with pleasure. She struggled to remove her apron and waved genially to Miss Pennyquick. "Can the kitchen fire be persuaded to heat enough water for coffee? Is that Tom? You must drive Babs to High Common at once, she had an appointment with the parson about the dame school half an hour ago."

The silence that greeted this was charged with shock. "I could not leave you here alone," said Miss Pennyquick with meaning, "and besides I am a perfect fright, I had quite given up any idea of getting to High Common today."

"Please go. I have nothing to fear from this gentleman. If you will simply tell Maggie to put on some water as you leave we shall be quite comfortable."

Tom scowled. He said: "If you insist I suppose we had better go at once," and he held open the door for Miss Pennyquick with a backward glance hot with disapproval.

"I do hope your gallant cousin will take good care of the lady," Luke Brandt said with a grin. "The horse is a brute and I fear its driver is now in an uncertain temper."

"It serves him right," Ann said cheerfully. "But you must tell me what you are doing at Thorn. Why did you send no message? It is scarcely a month since I was on the *Sable Island* myself and in that time I have had two letters from Mr Shaw of two lines each telling me precisely nothing except to be of good heart and put my faith in God and Captain Saufret."

"I thought you would rather hear the good news in person," said Luke. "The *Sable Island* is safe in Dover and Captain Saufret expects you to dine on board before we sail again. He has been to Liveman himself – and here is a letter from Liveman to you. I can guess its contents, but no doubt he has written at length, and stilted and fusty length at that. What a dry, pessimistic little man he is! The truth is the debts are cleared – all bar a hundred guineas or so, a trifle, hardly to be considered, even Liveman said so – we had a prize a week after you came to us in the cove, a merchantman, a great, bluff-bowed, ponderous old lady, and loaded with grain. Dear Miss Mathick, it was almost a miracle! She had been left behind a convoy, rigging all shot away in some brush with a British frigate, and they were still scrambling to rig a jury mizzen and sway up the ... Oh, but you could have no interest in such things. Forgive me! But that is my news — the debts are cleared. We have ridden out the storm, Lady Ann, and are come safe to harbour."

15

WILLIAM, reining in his cob at the gate, heard laughter and snatches of a familiar ribald song wafting out from the open drawing room window. He looked about but saw no one, only Maggie away across the Home Field on her way to Hollin's cottage with a covered basket. He dismounted cautiously and picked his way across the yard. The back door was wide, the kitchen deserted. Evidence of a thorough scrubbing met his critical eye, and the chimney breast and adjacent wall were newly whitened. He negotiated upturned stools, paint brushes, discarded rags and half dismantled trestles, and opened the hall door. Three strides brought him to the drawing room threshold, across which the noises of immoderate merrymaking came even louder.

He rapped the door with the head of his whip.

Silence. A snort perhaps, the rustle of a skirt, the clink of a bottle? Then Ann's voice, a little unsteady, called out, "Come in," and he did so, at once.

She was seated on a low ottoman, a patterned scarf like a gipsy's round her wild hair, her face decidedly pink and her eyes like stars. On the hearthrug, making a final adjustment to his neckcloth, stood a well-built, tough-looking individual with brown hair in a pigtail and wide-apart grey eyes glinting with suppressed humour. He was evidently embarrassed but not overmuch. He dug his hands into his pockets and gave William a cool glance.

"Mr Claverden!" Ann was on her feet in an instant, holding out her hand. "But so unexpected!" And unwelcome? "What a day for the unexpected! The Doctor said you were away to Lynn visiting relations."

"I have been back some days. The Doctor can never come to grips with time, hours and minutes come alike to him." She had been dusting or scrubbing, he thought. Her cheekbones were etched in grime. She had also been drinking: the smell of wine was faint but unmistakable. But it was not alcohol, he fancied, that gave her eyes their particular brilliance. He stood stiffly, waiting to be introduced.

"Mr William Claverden, Mr Luke Brandt."

Brandt had a crushing handshake, a hard palm. By his voice and manner he was a gentleman – of sorts – and yet those hard palms were an unlikely acquisition of a gentleman. Unless …

"I have a letter from Liveman," William said in his most pompous voice. "His news is somewhat fantastic. I thought it best to ride over as soon as I could. I would be grateful for a word in private."

If he sounded rude, be damned, he thought. Why was she alone here with this piratical young fellow anyway, listening to bawdy songs – toned down, yes, but essentially bawdy still – and drinking at eleven in the morning? Come to that, where had they hidden the bottle and the glasses? He stared at her but only received a warm, amused look in return, a glint of her large eyes. He had never seen her so alive, so far from plain, so clearly happy.

"I will take a turn about the garden," said Brandt genially, smelling resentment and indignation in quantity, and he gave William a peremptory bow and made his way out to the lawn, where he could be seen pacing about taking deep breaths of air.

"Who is that fellow?" William demanded.

"I very much object to your chasing him off to the garden with such sour looks, Mr Claverden. He is a friend. And if you could find it in you to be polite to him you might find you and he have more things in common than you imagine."

"I sincerely hope not."

"You are unkind. And uncivil. And oh, that wretched kettle! I quite forgot it. And where is Maggie?"

She was past him with a brush of skirts, in a drift of sweet-smelling ... what? Lavender? He followed her to the kitchen where she was tilting the kettle on its hook over a sulky fire. "Would you care for coffee?"

"Or possibly claret?"

"You are being infuriatingly discourteous! This is my house and I entertain whom I please. I really cannot think where Maggie has gone."

"To Hollin's cottage." He rescued the kettle from her grasp and poured where directed. Her hair was escaping the scarf and lay in dark tendrils on her slender neck; one ear, rather pink, showed briefly as she bent beside him over the coffee pot. "I have good news, Ann," he said. "All Harry's debts are settled bar the merest trifles and even those likely to be written off before long. Liveman makes no mention of where the money has come from but he is full of pious phrases. I gather he attributes the whole business to the Lord's personal intervention. I am almost inclined to agree with him. How else but by a miracle could Harry Gerard have come by such money?"

The smell of freshly-made coffee filled the kitchen. Ann put pot and china on a tray and left William to carry it to the drawing room. She knocked gently on the window and they saw Brandt strolling back, smiling broadly.

"Be pleasant or I shall turn you out," Ann threatened as they heard the front door snick. "Did I tell you Mrs McGinly is pressing to return? She does not care for the grand family, though they care very greatly for her cooking. I have three letters a week, all very emotional, great crossings-out. She is a dear and I would love her to come back, but there is no money to pay her."

"Have you understood what I have said?" William was astonished, black brows meeting above his distinguished nose. "Ann, the debts are paid. I could not believe it at first. And I would not believe it but Liveman is straight in every particular and would no more lie than run off to Virginia. You are not in the least surprised, are you? It is stale news to you. Has he written to you also then and not seen fit to inform me of it? Or has Harry written? Do you know where he is after all?"

Ann looked up as Brandt entered. A fragrance of crushed grass, earth, and clean, cool air entered with him. He looked about him and sniffed appreciatively.

"I cannot keep Mr Claverden in suspense any longer," Ann said. "He is a reluctant lawyer, I know, but a very good one, and he deserves better than to be teased over this matter. Mr Brandt, please tell him how Harry's debts came to be paid."

At the end of half an hour William's face was dark and savage, Luke embarrassed and silent. The spirit of joyful celebration had quite died and the room was quiet but full of seething emotion, mostly indignation and smothered anger and regret. Luke felt it wise to leave discreetly, slipping away with a casual word as to his whereabouts in Norwich for the next two days, his likely return to the ship on Friday, his desire to escort her to Dover if she was agreeable. He spoke all this in an undertone at the kitchen door, poised between paint pots, and what he felt most was chagrin, at being deprived of the best claret he had tasted in years, of one of the most singular young women he had ever met, and, quite probably, of the extended hospitality of Thorn.

"I shall get a ride once I reach the main road," he said, studying her gravely for a moment and taking her extended hand, "you need not concern yourself."

"I shall try to see you tomorrow or the next day. I shall probably bring a friend with me, someone who has told me how much he would like to see the ship. Perhaps he too could come to Dover to toast Captain Saufret."

"You must come, you must. You brought us luck."

"Are all sailors superstitious?"

"All I have met. But you must admit it was uncannily lucky – to meet a crippled ship, and of such size! Unable to offer any resistance bar a shot in the rigging and another that fell wide. Why, under normal circumstances even such a slow old tub would have been too much for us to tackle, too big, too many guns, as formidable as an Indiaman. No, no, it was luck, incredible luck, and you brought it to us at Brighton!"

"Perhaps it is Harry's luck that is changing."

He shovelled on his hat. He was unused to a beaver after wearing a cocked hat for so many years. He set it straight a little self-consciously.

"Have you had word from him?"

She shook her head. And they parted with smiles but slightly chastened, as if the thought of Harry reminded them of too many unpleasant things that neither would ever care to put into words.

In the drawing room William had unearthed the claret and the glasses from behind a curtain. "There is some left," he said, "would you care to join me in a glass?"

"If you care for it so much you had better take away the bottle. Oh, how could I know you would be so furious about the ship? I chose not to tell you because I feared you might think it your duty to inform about her."

"So that is how you think of me? A fool and an informer."

"I did not say so! But I have no notion of the law on such a matter, nor how unprofessional, how … reprehensible … it might be for you and Liveman to conceal such a thing."

"And you were afraid to ask me."

She was crimson; it was true, after all. "Yes, I was afraid to ask. But it is only a month since I saw her myself."

"When you were in Brighton."

"Yes. Do you hold it against me that I kept to myself information I was given in confidence?"

Of course he did, though he knew he should not; just the sight of her, small and untidy, made him exceedingly angry. "I suppose you have told the Doctor?" he said.

"Only since I returned from Brighton."

"And you did not see fit to tell your lawyer, the man who has been struggling to make sense of the tangle your damn Harry left behind him, to help you keep this roof over your head and enough to live on! Oh no, you had to run like a silly child to share another of his mad schemes. How he loved secrets! How many more do you think he had?"

There was nothing to be done with him in this mood. She retreated a little, as someone might retire to a respectful distance from a volcano. "You cannot imagine how very much I wished to tell you about the ship."

"Then why did you not do so?"

Because you have a strict sense of honour, she wanted to say, and I could not tell how this matter might touch it. But she was silent, and her silence made him angrier still.

"Is it Gerard's intentions, do you think, to pay you back what he stole from you? Yes, stole. Is his cursed privateer to recapture your lost fortune? Dear Heaven, have you any idea what luck it was for her to take that grain ship? In the ordinary course of events the chances of her clearing enough to pay off Gerard's debts were negligible; why, keeping her at sea must cost a princely sum."

She had taken off the scarf and her hair, disconcertingly he found, fell loose about her shoulders. She twisted it up at once, anchoring it with half the pins necessary for the job.

"But it has happened: I can only be glad."

It was a mistake to make such a mild, inoffensive answer; she had never seen him look so angry. He swung round with a cry of "Ann!" that was all exasperation and pent-up rage, reached her in a second, took her shoulders as if he would like to shake her to death – and pulled her up for his kiss.

The kiss went astray: she had put up her hands to ward him off, frightened of ... not that he would strike her, surely? No, never that. Frightened of any physical contact at all. So his mouth found her cheek, and her chin, her nose, a mass of soft hair, before it found her lips, and even then she bit him and might have done so again but he cupped his hands about her face and kissed her so that she could not.

A yell from far off, the muffled clang of something hitting the floor, told them Maggie had returned. A moment later a knock at the door brought an innocent enquiry about fried herrings and bottled gooseberries. Ann, who had been released by William as abruptly as he had seized her, plummeted into her favourite chair and answered distractedly, without looking up.

Finally the door closed again. "Forgive me," said William at once, though he did not sound eaten up by remorse, "I lost ... I should have ... Forgive me."

From the chair came only silence. He turned from the window where he had stepped the minute the door had opened, and found he could see a few tangled curls – her hair had all come down by now – and a slim shoulder. She had drawn her legs under her, was crouched like a child, staring into the embers. He said: "You must forget it ever happened," and then, still no response, "I leave for Chatham in a week."

"You have your orders then." Her voice was very quiet, otherwise quite normal. "When are you to sail?"

"No date has been fixed, but I am to report to the dockyard. The *Petrel* has been fitting out and is shortly to be commissioned. I am to be her first officer."

"What is she?"

"A sloop-of-war, three-masted, ship-rigged – but still a sloop. Not new either; a French ship captured and converted. I fear I shall get nothing better now unless every other officer in the Navy is killed or crippled, and for every one at sea there are two ashore eating their hearts out for a command. Still, a sloop is better than a brig, a transport, a cutter. As the Doctor says, we must be cheerful in our disappointments."

Her voice was even quieter. "But it is better than you expected."

"Far better. It would simply be arrogant to say it is less than I deserve." His breathing was back to normal at last; he gave a wry smile.

The sun was saffron, patterning the faded Turkey rug. More crashing without was followed by the faint noise of hooves.

"Is that Miss Pennyquick back already?" Ann uncurled herself from the chair. "I wager she and the parson fell out over Scripture and that was that. She is helping at Miss Tutbury's dame school, you know."

"I did not know." She would not look at him, he realised. "I would not care to be one of her pupils. And I feel for the parson."

"Oh, I should save your pity for the children. The parson believes in the terrible wrath of God, in thunderbolts, and the souls of the wicked frying in Hell. It would take a dozen of Babs to shake him, I assure you."

William picked up hat and gloves. "I must go."

"Yes."

He hesitated in the doorway. She had her back to him and was tying up her hair in the scarf.

"Ann, I meant nothing by it. Better to forget I ever came."

"Of course."

"You ... Give my regards to Tom."

She was fiddling with a knot. He could see the curve of her cheek, her neck, that was all.

"He will miss you," she said.

The cat had her kittens in the old box bed at the back of the house. This struck Miss Pennyquick as inconsiderate – were there not barns and haylofts, warm, dark, safe places in plenty outside? She was debating whether to leave them or move them when the Doctor clattered along the passage and discovered her.

"Mice?"

She withdrew from the musty dark. "Cats. Are you looking for Ann? She is out with the shepherd."

He had called on the off-chance, he would not stay. He followed her down to the kitchen. "I saw her out riding yesterday evening," he said. "It was quite late."

It had been grey dusk, damp and chill, the sun long vanished; she had been up on the Gorse alone, and galloping. She had been riding astride, her hair tied back in a string, all the white of her petticoats streaked and stained with mud, and she had pulled up only to give him a bewildered smile as if she hardly recognised him.

"She is not herself," Miss Pennyquick was peering up the huge kitchen chimney, standing at the back of the hearth, her skirts about to singe. "Those birds are building again, drat them. Your Lawyer Claverden must have said something to put her in a mood."

It was quite likely, the Doctor thought, making his way up the hill: William was no man for gallantries. The cob slipped suddenly, its rider lurched. Then he saw them, three small figures far down on the lush water meadows, fat sheep in front and behind, a dog circling, another – Tom's terrier – being kept strictly to heel. The shepherd Storr was pointing with a stick, Tom was beside him, hands on hips, and at a little distance Ann, walking with her head down, an old wide-brimmed country hat on.

The Doctor willed her to look up. She did not. In another minute she was next to Tom, putting her arm through his, and there was a great deal more pointing and some frantic gesticulation and then, blown up on the April wind, Tom's huge laugh, at which all the sheep scattered to a safe distance.

"But of course Ann must marry again," said Mrs Palmer when he called later in the day. "We must do our best, dear Doctor, to find her a husband. Why, there is Allard from Hackthorpe, widowed four years now, a sober, charming man, a fine house, five hundred acres. He is not to be sneezed at. Think how Ann would suit him! I must invite them both to one of my card parties."

The Doctor looked briefly down her throat. "You will live, dear lady, live until you are ninety. I shall charge you for wasting my time." He felt the urge to tease her: "As for Dick Allard, he is eligible enough, but a little old for her, confess it – he has three grown-up daughters of his own. If we are to pick and choose among our acquaintances what about Lawyer Claverden?"

"Mr Claverden! I had not thought of it."

"And there is the advantage that they are already acquainted with each others' faults – our doctors, lawyers and parsons know all, do they not?"

"Perhaps," said Mrs Palmer hopefully, "he has been too long a bachelor. He is not to persevere with Charlotte, I know, and look at the catch she is: pretty, unspoiled, no lack of money."

The Doctor prepared to leave. His face took on an unusually glum expression. "I am not sure," he said, "that we can ever count ourselves immune."

Lady Barsham was not at home when she called with some quince preserve, the chestnut groomed to copper lustre, legs chalked and hooves oiled.

"Miss Charlotte is in the garden," said the maid.

They met on the steps of the rose walk, Ann in rustic brown, Charlotte in azure, elegant and unadorned. It was a windy day again, sun following rain and rain sunshine, sometimes both together. Charlotte carried an umbrella but was using it, surprisingly, to swipe a little angrily at the unoffending plants.

"I knew I would like you," she confessed an hour later as they skirted the wild garden — too wet and far too wild today — and came back along the lime avenue, "the moment you fell off that terrible snorting horse right into the box hedge. I heard you laugh. It made me feel unbelievably dull and very ... very cowardly. I would never dare ride anything so wicked!"

They were near the house. Ann said: "I leave for Dover shortly, I hope, but when I return you must come to Thorn. You will find us rough and ready but you will like it, you will enjoy it immensely. You are not like your sisters, afraid of mud and chickens."

Charlotte smiled, but she was whacking at a low branch of tender young leaves. "Did you say Dover? Oh, how I wish ... Is Chatham anywhere near Dover? Mr Claverden is to go to sea next week."

The distance between Chatham and Dover explained, Charlotte looked doubly gloomy. "I suppose you will tell me I ought not to think of him. Mama does. Frequently."

Ann declared it was no business of hers, that in any case the heart was not usually swayed by well-meaning advice, that love in general was ungovernable, unpredictable and uncomfortable, etc.

Charlotte was blushing vermilion by now and had reduced the leaves to fragments. "I think I shall miss him," she said abruptly.

"So will Tom."

The wind blew the particles of leaves away over the damp grass. "I like Tom Forsie," said Charlotte, "there is nothing reserved about him, nothing false. He looks what he feels, says what he feels too."

Ann smiled. "I daresay he will turn out sufficiently respectable. His heart is in the right place."

Charlotte took her arm. "It is, of course it is. He has a kind face, such merry eyes."

"You know, there is the most terrible clatter. Do you think my horse has broken out?"

"No, it is the Doctor!" cried Charlotte, craning to see through the yew hedges.

The Doctor's gig was outside the door. A moment later he was on the steps to the terrace and Charlotte ran up to him. "Dear Doctor, have you come to see Mama?"

"My dear, I have come to find Ann Mathick. Ah, yes, she is with you." He had slipped an arm about her slender shoulders and was guiding her back down, "Ann, Ann, I must have a word."

"So urgent? You came at the gallop."

"I will leave you," Charlotte said, gathering up her skirts.

"No, perhaps not. Wait." The Doctor had her hand. "Ann, I have some news ... Barsham would have brought it to you on his return from Norwich but I thought it best to come myself. Harry Gerard's marriage to this girl Stratford – it seems it was not so legal after all: no licence, no witnesses, the clergyman an actor – Heaven help us, late of Astley's! The poor girl was duped! There never was a marriage. Ann, my dearest, you are Harry Gerard's wife after all."

16

"HOW IT rains," said the Doctor, looking out, "and I did so hope we would have a fine journey."

William was propping himself up by the chimney shelf, hands in pockets. "She still means to go then?"

"To the ship? I have heard nothing to the contrary. Why, at Upgate her only remark was that now she had a renewed interest in letters of marque. I fear Lady Barsham thought her turned in the wits, she took me aside and asked if I thought anything could be done for such severe shock."

"But she *was* shocked?"

"Without doubt. But she still smiled and was undeniably calm. Charlotte was splendid – I have great hopes of that girl – and organised tea and something unobjectionable to eat and shushed the servants away into the back regions. I did wonder for a moment whether I should have broken the news like that but when I heard Ann was at Upgate it seemed an opportunity not to be missed. Miss Pennyquick was at the dame school, no one at Thorn but Maggie and Hollin in a sulk as usual; Tom was out on Pigg's Piece with mud to the eyebrows. It ocurred to me Upgate would suit the purpose admirably, being full of affectionate women, orderliness and common sense."

William bent to whip away the toasting fork he had lodged on the bars of the fire and held it at arm's length, the bread smouldering. "There is nothing that can be done," he said, "it was a mock wedding from beginning to end."

"And how remarkably easy to accomplish such a thing."

"Yes, remarkably. The church was left unlocked and unattended for long periods, any large book falsified neatly may pass as a register, and any man may dress as a clergyman and intone a few prayers satisfactorily. What is so incomprehensible is Harry Gerard's own part in such a travesty: did he have no affection for the wretched girl, no thought for the pain he might cause? Why did he do it? What possessed him? And to this day the innocent Harriet believed herself his wife. I cannot understand the least part of the business, and to tell the truth I am sick of Harry Gerard and all his misdeeds."

"They have taken an objectionable time to discover the thing was play-acting."

"Distance was ever an excuse for idleness," said William with resignation, as a man who knew only too well, "and there was a certain reluctance to admit such a thing could have happened right under their noses. Now, of course, everyone is hanging fire, boggling at the complications. There is only the girl's word the wedding ever took place in the accepted form – the actor-priest apparently denied there had ever been a serious attempt to deceive her, declared it was universally hailed as an excellent joke. He is lying, of course, but nothing can be proved. You realise it is quite likely Gerard will escape this quagmire unsullied – admonished, fined perhaps – but certainly neither hung nor transported."

"The debts are paid, yes. But how can he know?"

"How indeed? Suppose he has taken passage for India, or America? And what of Ann meanwhile? She must wait years before she is free to remarry."

"If I were Ann," the Doctor removed the charred offering and substituted fresh bread, "I would be in no great hurry."

"Of course not. But it is a point that must be considered."

This time the Doctor toasted the slice himself, concentrating fiercely. "I can see why you prefer the Navy," he remarked some time later. "Past and future are irrelevant at sea, moral dilemmas mercifully few. I envy you."

William, who felt himself in the grip of a monstrous moral dilemma, only grunted. The Doctor looked at him queerly. Then: "Why not come with us to Dover? Ann will not mind, and the chaise is plenty large enough. You would enjoy a glimpse of her privateer and will still be in Chatham on the proper date."

"You are very sure Ann will not mind." He had bruised more than her mouth with that ill-timed kiss, he thought: trust, confidence, friendship had all suffered.

"But why should she? And you will be such an asset on the journey; Miss Pennyquick is struck dumb at the very thought of a coach and will be miserable company."

The toast was perfection. In the absence of jam some marmalade was discovered. Outside the spring evening was grey with rain, the whole of the preceding day had been so; nothing better could be hoped for the morrow.

"Close the shutters, Will," said Alex French suddenly, "I have seen enough of the wet."

William went to the window. "They will be flooded at Thorn; that steep lane is a torrent when it rains."

"They are used to it." The Doctor threw open the door and yelled, but there was no response. "Where is everyone today? We need more butter, and I stake my life there is a fruit cake to be had. Dear William, mud, wet, and discomfort are nothing at Thorn. Surely you have noticed how those who live there are blessed with a rare fortitude? Why, the monsoon would leave them unmoved. They would simply order more buckets, some oilcloth, and quite probably a boat."

But to Ann he said: "You must take care down by the river. You will be swept away. You will drown."

He had called with a book for Tom, a thin excuse. He would not dismount though, would not enter the house, and sat with the rain dripping from his hat brim and the end of his nose.

"Oh, and I forgot," he finished, his face all apology, as bewildered and innocent as could be, "I have asked William to dine aboard the *Sable Island*. I told him you would be glad, would count him your nautical as well as legal adviser. Have I done wrong?"

He had, he had; he saw her struggle not to let him see it, shrugging her oilskins closer.

"Dover is not on the way to Chatham," was her dry comment.

"But if we take him only as far as London we will have done him a good turn. Is there any difficulty? I had supposed there was a spare seat in the chaise, that an extra passenger would inconvenience nobody."

Ann's eyes lifted to his, but he could not tell what she was thinking. That there was some new coolness between her and William he was certain, but as to the cause ...

"Well?" He felt the rain down his neck. "Well?"

"Of course there is no difficulty," said Ann. "I am sure he will be very welcome if he wishes to join us."

He does most vehemently but will fight to deny it, the Doctor might have said. As it was he departed feeling a very low dog indeed and almost, but not quite, thoroughly ashamed of himself.

"Look after Thorn," said Ann, kissing him. "This time no charred ruins if you please."

Tom returned her kiss with two and then stood back to watch her enter the chaise. The Doctor shook his hand vigorously and hoped he would read the half dozen volumes he had left out for him. William, at his grimmest, tipped the water from his cocked hat.

"We shall meet again," he said, holding out his hand, unsmiling and apparently oblivious to the determined downpour.

"I hope so," said Tom, trying to look as if it were a matter of indifference to him, which it certainly was not.

Inside the chaise Miss Pennyquick made some ill-timed remark about the efficacy of hot-water bottles, whether or not it was advisable to fill them some hours in advance of a journey. William's reply was inaudible but obviously regrettable. Ann's trembling rebuke was instant, the Doctor's shout of laughter followed it. Tom stuck his head in, gold curls darkened by rain.

"Last orders?"

"None that I can think of," Ann replied.

Another carriage was drawing up, well decorated with High Common mud. A crest on the door was almost obliterated but the colour was familiar, what colour could be seen. Tom craned round. A hand and then a face appeared, the sash fully down, and a low voice said: "Oh, Mr Forsie, are we in time then? I did so hope we might be. I have a basket of Mama's 'comforts' and a note for ... for Lady Gerard, for dear Ann." It was Charlotte and her curious younger sister, a Charlotte in a very artistic, very flattering bonnet, her eyes abnormally bright. Tom, who received the basket with a bow, handed it with a grin through the window of the chaise.

A muddle of thanks, greetings – William frosty, giving the merest nod – more thanks, farewells. The chaise lurched forward.

"But you are wet through!" exclaimed Charlotte, hazarding her bonnet for a look at Tom Forsie.

"It is nothing." His eyes met hers and he blushed. "I shall get dry at the Doctor's, I have some books to collect there."

She bid him a polite goodbye and the carriage swept round, but he saw her little gloved hand raised to wave as it passed him. Tom watched until it was out of sight and then gazed ruefully down at the mud and more ruefully up at the leaden sky. He was alone, Hollin sour, Maggie pert, Mrs McGinly threatening to arrive any moment on Pashman's cart, and no sign of the weather improving.

He became aware of an old man staring at him from across the street.

"I do know who your father was." A beady stare, not quite malicious. "Why, I thought it was old Francis stood there for a moment."

From behind a wiry brown arm shot out. "Tom, Mr Tom! Come in, come in!" said the Doctor's Lascar cook. "I have made a most excellent curry."

The rain persisted, nothing was dry. Even Lady Barsham's 'comforts' – seed biscuits, spiced cakes, little soft rolls, and tiny pots of preserve — seemed to take their flavour from the weather. The Doctor had brought a more substantial snack in the form of a goose leg, coarse bread, and hot sausage, but even this failed to come up to expectation. By the time they reached the half-way stage conversation had long ceased and thoughts of fires, dry clothes and clean sheets were in all their minds.

They put up at the house of a friend of the Doctor, a large house gloomily surrounded by trees on the edge of Hampstead. The friend was another physician and one who, as Miss Pennyquick succinctly remarked in the privacy of the cavernous room she shared with Ann, "came expensive". The house was over-furnished and under-lit, the food at dinner plain but not, it could be suspected, entirely wholesome. The Doctor ate with his usual hearty appetite, apparently unconcerned. His friend ate little and that hesitantly, as if he guessed the indiscretions of his cook, and his wife ate almost nothing at all. She was a drab and retiring little woman and could find little to say to her guests, especially the handsome and morose naval gentleman with the short black hair and devastating gaze who appeared to curl his lip at his wine glass from time to time. But they were kind people even if shy of visitors, especially glad of the Doctor, who fell to talking about enlarged spleens and resurrectors and several other equally unappealing subjects without a moment's hesitation. Miss Pennyquick, having cast around in vain all through the meal for some more suitable topics, excused herself as soon as she was able. William made a less adroit escape but this was only to the terrace, where Ann was walking alone, wrapped up in a sort of tarpaulin.

"You will be soaked. Come in, woman. Surely you cannot mean to take a chill and die before we reach this incomparable ship of yours?"

She pulled the waterproof closer. This was the first time he had spoken to her since leaving High Common. "The rain is easing. And in any case there is a pergola."

"A what? You mean this botched mess of old wood with a naked vine scrambling over it?" William took her elbow with a cruel firmness. "Poor Mrs Larkins has no one to talk to and would be wounded beyond measure to think you preferred to walk in the wet rather than stay in her company."

"Then why are you out here?"

"I came out expressly to find you."

"And if you do not return indoors at once you will spoil your uniform."

He looked well in it, she thought, but that was to be expected, a man as tall, as agreeable. She found his hand crushing, drawing her back to the house.

"You must come in. No good will be served by your being ill in Dover – or anywhere else for that matter."

In the dimness of the study, from whose doors she had illicitly gained the terrace, she discarded the oiled tablecloth which was her improvised cloak. She saw William's energetic eyebrows dance, and then the familiar stern look come over his face. He had been unnecessarily cheerless, she thought, all the way from Norfolk. Had he been manoeuvred into coming as she had been manoeuvred into accepting him? Or was he broken-hearted over leaving Charlotte? Was that it? Did he wish he could support her on his Navy pay? Had he already asked her, secretly, to marry him?

But William Claverden was not the sort of man, she knew, to make promises or extract them behind the rose bushes in Lady Barsham's garden.

How she wished it had been anyone but William who had found her carousing with Luke Brandt – though all she had been doing was sitting on the ottoman listening to a slightly rude ballad and watching Luke down several glasses of that infernal claret. And surely a woman married, unmarried, beggared and deserted, should be entitled to a little pleasure of her own, however extraordinary, however discreditable?

And that kiss – would she ever forget it? True, she had hit at him, bitten him, and it had been a savage business, but ...

William said: "Your hands are cold. Ann, you do not look at all well."

"I hate men who fuss." She withdrew her hands; what was he doing with them anyway? "Perhaps Saufret has some means of communicating with Harry," she said as they left the study. "He is intelligent, broad-minded. You will like him."

"You will not live as his wife again if Harry should return?" William demanded, drawing her to a halt.

"But he is my husband," she said.

She did not think she had ever seen him so angry, he who had no claim on her, no right to give her anything but legal advice, certainly no right to advise her on emotions.

"He is a rogue, a fool, and a fraud," – this in a bitter undertone – "he never cared for you. He has not even sent a message, the merest word, to say he is safe and well, which any man who had your comfort at heart must surely do."

"Then perhaps he is not safe and well."

"You still love him then?"

This seemed to be overstepping the bounds of even a well-established friendship, for he asked so fiercely, so furiously, and looked the picture of murderous intent. She thought, somewhat irrelevantly, that he would have the midshipmen quailing within five minutes once he was aboard the *Petrel*. She lifted her chin a little, tried to meet his hot eyes.

"I cannot forget that I once did, and that something of a fondness refuses to die. He is not a bad man, William, only thoughtless and foolish – and I am quite as foolish as he is."

It was the first time she had used his name. His anger ebbed, then returned with twice the force.

"Indeed you are!" he said.

She moved a step away so as not, perhaps, to singe her toes on the lava flow. He burned in the dim hall; in a second there would be a sensational eruption.

But: "I think," she said calmly, "Harry was too much ignored and overlooked; now he finds affection irresistible. And he had so little experience of it as a boy that he cannot distinguish between love and adulation or …"

"Lust and covetousness!" The outbreak was quite as bad as she had expected. "He has no scruples, no morals. How can you defend him?"

"Who stopped to give him any? Who ever cared a toss for him?"

A trembling Mrs Larkins stepped from the shadows. They both started, begged her pardon, were excruciatingly polite. Ann made a pretty excuse and fled upwards, escaping to her bed, leaving William to make gritty small talk for an hour to a background chorus of medical jokes, medical exposition, and medical anecdotes of a generally gruesome nature.

In the huge bedroom Ann undressed as quickly as she could, rather careless with her one good travelling habit, even more careless with her hair. In the high, lumpy bed she turned restlessly, the musty dark pressing in on her. Miss Pennyquick's snores came faintly from far off. At last, at last, hot and weary, she slid out, groped across the boards to the heavily-curtained window; there was a window seat, as lumpy as the bed but cool. She drew her legs up, let the curtains fall behind her, and leaned her hot brow on the rain-spattered glass.

The pain she had felt at Harry's departure had gone long ago and a strange numbness had taken its place, a strange disregard for the future, for herself, for almost everything. Of course she still cared for Thorn, for Babs, for Tom, but the passion had gone from her caring; a fatalistic mood had enmeshed her. When the Doctor had brought her the news of Harry's cruel deception of Harriet Stratford she had felt nothing at all, only a lamentable desire to laugh. It had seemed a fitting climax to a year of folly. She had not been able to explain this to the Doctor, and had seen a grey anxiety in his face as he had relinquished her to Charlotte's loving attention. She had not been able to explain it to anyone, and she knew she was giving them all a false impression of her true state, the sparkle and humour and determination she had recovered in Brighton always uppermost. Underneath, deep, deep where all her most private hopes and joys and desires lay hidden, there was no life, no movement. Or was there? Was there not yet a warm flicker of real emotion left? Yes, yes, she would be dishonest to deny it. But she suppressed it, ignored it, refused to believe in it. There had been two occasions when the flicker had proved a lusty, living thing, in spite of her frantic efforts, her desperate attempts at murder: the moment she had looked back and seen the *Sable Island* crowding on sail to catch the morning wind; the moment William had kissed her.

How unlike Harry's kisses, Harry's belligerent passion that had left her scarcely wakened – and she too ignorant to tell him. And what now? She thought of herself at Thorn in a long, unsatisfactory spinsterhood, a wife and yet no wife. It was not that she wished to marry again, she never considered it, but how many years could she exist in such a limbo of responsibility without pleasure? And if Harry returned? The debts were cleared, the Canterbury wedding could be explained away. Her calm and decisive reply to William had been a thing of the moment, a piece of involuntary bravado because her instinct refused to submit again to pain, shock, dread and betrayal. She had not lied when she had said she was still fond of Harry, for a peculiar, amused and pitying feeling still came over her when she thought of him – but to live as his wife again? And at Thorn, where she had struggled to preserve her privacy, her sanity? A wave of revulsion made tears come to her eyes. No, no, she could never be his wife again! All the old desire was dead; born of grief, loneliness, defiance, novelty, it had died as they had died.

Another thought: she *was* Harry's wife. Duty and the dregs of her uneasy affection must be considered. She supposed too he had some rights, in law if not in justice. If he returned to Thorn and claimed her now must she refuse?

By the time she slept, there on the narrow window seat, dawn was already breaking at the start of another day of solid rain. She came down to breakfast late and looked wretched, and both the Doctor and William cast anxious and bewildered glances down the table more than once. She ate nothing and drank only one cup of coffee, very hot and strong. Miss Pennyquick, who dispensed it, looked unsympathetic, though equally perplexed.

They found Dover drowning in rain and salt spray, but Saufret's welcome was lavish and cheerful: nothing could cast him down short of a typhoon. Why, this could hardly be called rain, and there was no kind of sea running at all. Did William not agree? All this while escorting them aft to his great cabin. Miss Pennyquick, who had swallowed an unfortunate cry of horror when she had seen his face, began to feel seasick immediately, although the *Sable Island* was moving, if at all, only with the almost imperceptible push of the tide. The Doctor, inquisitive and eager, was mislaid somewhere between the gangway and the cabin and was brought in later by a bemused master gunner, who had found him "looking into the wadding and poking 'is fingers in the powder, sir."

"He is like a small child," Luke Brandt remarked to Ann, having just apologised for the complete absence of tea in the ship, for the Captain did not drink it and had no time for it. Remembering the pickled goose, chestnuts, and hearty red wine, Ann found this quite unsurprising. Luke offered coffee instead, or chocolate, though the chocolate was of an unknown vintage to be sure, he added, having come from the French grain ship and being an uncertain colour into the bargain. Ann, with a glance at Miss Pennyquick's suffering face, said that coffee would suit very well, and the order was given.

"You do not look very well," said Luke in an undertone and sounding genuinely concerned. In the glow of his gentle and sincere admiration Ann began to thaw, to feel herself alive again, a little, a very little alive.

"What is all this?" Saufret demanded suddenly, turning from William. "You are Harry's wife after all? I assure you it is good news. He will find his salvation in your company, dear lady. You must be in agreement, Doctor? She is the perfect wife for him, so sensible, so courageous."

The Doctor looked dark and was silent. Then: "I would be surprised if Lady Gerard views the matter so cheerfully," and then again: "But is this his ship, so shipshape, so regular, so clean? And so large, so well armed."

"I did describe her to you," Ann reminded him.

"You said a schooner — that conjures up memories: I saw plenty of schooners in the West Indies. But none like this, no, not one."

"She is rigged for speed," Saufret said, "and the men are volunteers, Islanders, Devon men ... We take no one unwilling, no sulkers, no slackers, no thieves. Nearly all have sailed with me in other ships. And I have good officers, only the best. You will meet them when we dine."

The coffee had arrived and was exotic, if not exactly fresh. It looked as if it might have been boiled a long while on some galley stove, its taste augmented by the addition of bits and pieces; acorns perhaps, or biscuit, or potato. It might have been some strange form of soup. Over the rim of her cup Ann's eyes met William's and they exchanged dark, sympathetic glances; they could almost have been old friends again. But it was an illusion, she thought, for he had scarcely spoken to her since leaving Norfolk and not at all since leaving Hampstead. The smile he gave her did not touch his eyes, and he was at his most intractable, his most withdrawn.

At the appropriate hour they passed to the table, laid in the open space where the cramped officers' cabins had lately been dismantled; the *Sable Island*, like any ship of war, could clear her decks for action from stem to stern. Usually all the officers ate in the great cabin, Saufret with them. The ship had changed owners and trades several times, her sleeping quarters had been changed with them, now economy, now luxury a consideration. Since Saufret was not a man to care for status, outward show, or the keeping up of any godlike superiority, he cared nothing for the present ill-conceived accommodation arrangements. After all, in a fight, as he was fond of remarking, the carpenter ran up and knocked the whole lot down.

"Ah, the surgeon comes," he cried now as a self-conscious group of men in blue jackets stepped forward together. "The surgeon is not really qualified, dear Doctor, but who is to know? Who is to care? He has the most delicate touch with a knife, cannot be faulted."

The Doctor found a short, spare, hairy man, middle-aged. They fell at once to talking about the treatment of wounds, of the sorts of wounds most commonly sustained in action, of the effects of a poor diet, of sea water, of certain diseases, on recovery. Miss Pennyquick found herself beside a very young man, all bluster and good-humoured impatience. He was Sanders, he told her, and in charge of the guns.

"Medical men think that as they are strong-stomached we must all be so," he said.

"Indeed."

"Are you interested in ships, Ma'am? Have you been to sea?"

Miss Pennyquick shuddered and stated her strengthening conviction that the land, the blessed land, was unsurpassed for beauty, stability and good health. Why, at sea, she said shyly as soup was brought in, one is struck down by the most terrible afflictions simply for the want of eating a lemon. Or was it a lime?

The hot peppery soup was followed by roast pork, rather fat. The officers fell on it with enthusiasm. There was a great deal of brisk chatter and cheerful banter and the exchange of information as diverse as the making of anchovy toast and the science of crop rotation. The Doctor expressed a desire to go below again to finish his curtailed inspection of the ship: Sanders volunteered to take him. Saufret gave a huge bellow and the sweet came in, and cheese. William was discussing boarding parties with a big man named Villacque who was second mate, and had become unusually animated, as relaxed and humorous as Ann had ever seen him. She turned to Saufret and smiled.

"You have been very kind."

"But you are Harry's wife." His stare was inimical, as penetrating as ever. "He gave you this ship. And I like you. Why should I not be kind?"

The Doctor had taken her hand. "Come, we must drink a toast to Captain Saufret, to *Sable Island*."

Ann saw William reach for his glass. "Perhaps," she said, "we should also drink to another ship. Mr Claverden is to sail shortly. His sloop is the *Petrel*. We must wish him a good voyage and a prosperous one."

William's eyes narrowed, flashed across the table. What did he see, she wondered? She remembered the very first day he had come to Thorn, taciturn, unenthusiastic. She suspected he still wished he had never met her, never become involved with Harry Gerard, with that particular piece of rolling country that lay between her own high, unkempt hedges. She could not begin to interpret the motive for his kiss. She had vaguely supposed that since he could not decently hit her he had kissed her to the same effect.

So what did he see? A small dark girl in cream, hair piled into a knot of Grecian curls; a quiet girl, plain, not really succeeding in looking demure in her lace cap, only uncomfortable.

What William actually saw was everything that had ever attracted him to her: her stubbornness, her desire to tackle problems head on, her sudden, unexpected sparkle, her intelligence, intuition, sensitivity. And there was that latent recklessness, that air of passions subdued, restrained. He saw too, of course, her soft, wide mouth and thought how very much he would like to kiss it again, a little less violently.

Ann, in innocence, thought it was her toast that made his brows draw together so – perhaps she should not have mentioned it was a sloop, quite likely a ship somewhat smaller than this one, for all its three masts – for how was she to know how he desired her? But with a sudden chilling certainty she knew that he intended to take his final leave of them on the quayside after this dinner, that he had chosen it as an impersonal place, neutral ground, and dark; in the light of a swinging lantern much would be concealed and the rain would deter lingering.

And it was so. Promptly at the foot of the gangway he turned to shake the Doctor's hand, though the Doctor forestalled this by embracing him. Miss Pennyquick saluted him gravely, wished him a happy voyage, and retired to the waiting carriage.

"Alex will write to me," he said to Ann. "Let him have all your news. I would like to know Tom has gathered in his first real harvest, however small."

He did not ask her to write in person. In fact he said nothing at all after this, only gave her a strained, queer look, touched her cold hand lightly, impersonally, and backed away and was gone.

The rain still fell, though it was less intense now and the suspicion of a breeze was cooling her wet cheeks.

17

THE HOT buttered toast was more excellent in fragrance than taste. Ann, crouched by the sullen fire, apologised between mouthfuls but Charlotte, seated not at all demurely in the old wing chair, only gave a mumbled and dismissive reply.

"The Doctor has received a letter from William at last," she said more distinctly some time later. "He is sailing about very near the shore, it seems. Was it the Channel? At any rate, he is practically within shouting distance of land and is quite furious about it. *And* after missing the action off Copenhagen – that was the week you went to Dover, was it not? Or the week before? Anyway, it is almost more than flesh can bear apparently. Why is it men are always so desperate to grapple with each other, so bloodthirsty?"

"Well, I am sorry he missed Copenhagen for his only chance of promotion lies in just such a battle. Though if I remember correctly sloops do not fight, simply toss in the background and leave all to the ships of the line." Ann was busy with knife, loaf, toasting fork and butter.

"You mean he can only hope for advancement by nearly being killed? He has no influence at all?"

"None whatsoever, or so he says."

Charlotte was silent a moment. "John Everidge, who was to be Frances's husband, was killed at the Nile in some 'ship of the line'." A heavy emphasis here and an uncharacteristic curl of lip.

"And so she married odious and pompous Clanbridge who does nothing but ask you to admire his figure and his manner and his facility for sermonising. He is quite determined to become a bishop and so he might, having an excellent living already and that kind of smile. If John had come home things would have been so very different, and though Papa says he is sure to have died a hero how do we know what pain he suffered? And why, in all conscience, should he have died at all?"

Ann, still musing on the type of smile a future bishop might habitually wear, heard herself murmuring something about duty, choice.

"Oh, it is true John was not compelled to go to sea, but it is one thing to admire the Admiral and quite another to die at his command. And I am sure I should not enjoy having arms and legs hacked off for this Nelson's sake. Should you?"

"You are becoming illogical," Ann said, "and emotional. You fear William may join John Everidge as a dead hero, that is all – and is perfectly natural. Had the Doctor any other news?"

"I am surprised he has not called on you himself."

"He did so yesterday but I was in Norwich with Tom, fitting him for a coat good enough to wear to dinner at your house. He has grown so tall and broad he defeats the tailors: they said accusingly he was 'an unusual shape', which can't be true, for he looks perfectly normal. But of course he would not stand still a moment and I think that upset them; he was like a two-year-old, twisting and turning and poking in the mirror."

Charlotte laughed. "Dear Tom! How I wish I could have seen him! I suppose he is working today?" And she glanced at the May sunshine flooding the garden.

"And every day. No, to be truthful, he has ridden over with Hollin – a very gloomy, reluctant, and exceedingly prejudiced Hollin – to examine a new seed drill of Mr Blakey's at Tivetshall. There was no other news in William's letter then?"

"Oh, a great deal of ship talk, I remember: something about answering the helm perfectly and the French knowing how to build, no bad French ships at all – no patriotic comments, rather a eulogy for French shipbuilders. But he did say he was disgusted with the crew, most of them pressed men and aching to be home again."

"He has a passion for good, sound, willing seamen, and pressed men drive him wild. I can sympathise. For even if the system was not iniquitous in itself, surely unwilling crewmen must be every captain's dread?"

They contemplated the sad fire. Summer had come and the drawing room grate was rarely lit, but a chilly morning, rather grey and windy, and then Charlotte's visit in the early afternoon, quite alone and unexpected, in the Upgate carriage, had induced Ann to think of buttered toast. The sky had cleared now, the sun was out again, and the fire refused to draw.

"I wish that he would write to me," said Charlotte suddenly, brushing crumbs from her bodice. "He could enclose a letter with the Doctor's – and who would know?"

"He would never do that, he is very strict. And in any case the Doctor would not allow it. He is strict too, in his own way."

"He never spoke of marriage, not once." A small voice, painfully resigned. "I am sure I mean nothing to him."

"I would say he is very fond of you."

"But that is not enough, not quite enough."

"Perhaps not." Experience was teaching her love came in many guises, and sometimes slyly, sometimes slowly, and was not often the convenient, malleable commodity she had once thought it.

There was a scuffle outside. Hollin's face looked in, lugubrious beyond the usual. "A message come by Pashman. Could you go to Priddy's Barns at once, the Doctor needs you."

"What for?" Ann rose.

"Accident most likely. He said to bring his bag which is on the table by his writing desk."

The chestnut, still lathered from his journey back from Tivetshall, was turned round, Charlotte's offer of a ride in the carriage firmly dismissed. High Common and Priddy's Barns were out of the way from Upgate and who knew how long she might be? It had happened before recently that the Doctor had asked her to be his messenger or his nurse, he seemed to think such activity would keep her occupied, would restore her to her old self, stop her thinking about Harry. For she did still think of him. How could they dare pretend she did not? She would be all right, she assured Charlotte, who kissed her warmly; she would be all right, quite safe.

Charlotte smelled of lavender and butter, had toast crumbs on her cheek. "Will Tom go with you?"

"Oh no, there are the cattle to be fed, the oxen, the horses."

"But you cannot go so far alone," protested Charlotte, with an anxious glance at the hot chestnut between the shafts.

"It is something important or he would not send. Why, any scrap of a boy could have run to High Common to fetch his bag. Depend on it, I am in for an interesting evening."

Hollin grunted from his stance by the horse's head. Tom helped her in; if they all had doubts about the wisdom of letting her drive herself to bleak and isolated Priddy's Barns with dusk already licking about them and the horse raging with hunger and spite, he at least did not. In everything but the matter of Harry Gerard he trusted her good sense implicitly.

Up on the Gorse the wind was strong, sheep huddled beneath the trees. Ann, turning for High Common, saw for a moment the whole of Thorn – or what was left to her – spread out in green glory under the blurred blue sky. And over there, hidden by the oaks, Blackow, its gardens thronged with workmen, with gardeners, with heaps of lime and piles of bricks and discarded slates and tiles. The new owner was to dredge the lake too. The news was all over the district as if, in a dull, bucolic way, it was some kind of melancholy joke.

In High Common the Lascar was caught in the act of throwing a carving knife at half a dozen hens discovered scratching up the flowerbeds; presumably, Ann thought, the choice of weapon was symbolic, an awful warning of what was to come. It had not, however, achieved its purpose – the hens were pecking round it with complete unconcern – and terrible, incomprehensible curses were now rising in preparation for a second assault. But the bag was found, that most special bag, packed for every emergency, and inadvertently left behind. In another twenty minutes

Priddy's Barns came in view, a remote group of cottages and tumbledown farm buildings some miles beyond High Common near the Ipswich road. Several inquisitive and cheeky children ran out to greet her, pointing and hallooing at the chestnut horse. The Doctor, they said, to Ann's mild enquiry, was in the malthouse cutting off Jim Polruan's leg.

It was not an impossibility. Like *Sable Island*'s surgeon the Doctor was forced to improvise in times of crisis. But in a malthouse? And could she face such a thing, wondered Ann; broken bones, cuts, fevers, childbirth, yes, but amputation? And in such a squalid place? She put the chestnut in a broken-down shed out of the wind and took the bag from the gig. The cluster of children had thinned a little as some were hurried away indoors by older sisters and the grey-faced mothers. There was a light drizzle beginning, like a sad mist over the far fields. The land was flat and open here, great tracts of common and sheep-cropped upland, a windy plateau above the Waveney.

The malthouse was in general disrepair, tiles slipping, door off its hinges. Inside it was dark, smelled rancid – something decaying perhaps – smelled of blood. It had not been used as a malthouse for many years and its deterioration was evident even in such light as there was, filtering through the ivy-covered window holes.

"Ann? I knew I could depend on you. The bag at last! I have sore need of it. Could you press here, and here. I have a mortal horror of his bleeding to death."

The patient was a young man, lying on an old door that had been supported precariously by some worm-eaten trestles. In the inadequate glow of four rushlights Ann could see that one leg was in a perilous condition, to her inexperienced and horrified eye apparently half severed just above the knee. But she put her fingers where directed and smiled into the dead white face looking up at her so earnestly.

"Why did you send for me?" she demanded after what seemed an interminable age.

"Because no one here has the competence, the good sense. And half the children are thieves. They would have opened my bag and spilled half the bottles before reaching me and might have delayed too long. It was quicker to send Pashman at the gallop to Thorn – he knows every yard of the country and that old vanner of his can leap like a cat. I knew he would ride as straight as he could and damn the consequences."

"But how fortunate he was passing."

"That was a dry remark; I do not think I like the tone. To be sure he is an old gossip but this time we might have causes to be thankful for it. This lad will, if he lives. It was Pashman who came for me at home, having taken his horse from its shafts the moment this happened," and he indicated the bloody mess beneath his careful hands. "Lucky Priddy's Barns was on his round today."

He worked in silence after this, issuing only essential orders. The light was execrable, the blood prodigious. It had been high spirits with an axe, the Doctor said, a lot of larking about in the yard, someone swinging a chopper with good-natured abandon; young men likely to be careless about such things etc. He looked up at Ann over the long, thin form of his patient, seeing her pale face and wide, shadowed eyes.

"I cannot save the leg," he said.

"Pray do whatever is necessary. If I faint you will have to carry on unaided."

"To begin with," he said genially, "you could fetch another glim. How is a man to work in this sort of light? And then go outside and see if the men are home yet. We need someone to hold him if he breaks the straps."

She hesitated. "Why could they not have carried him into one of the cottages?"

The Doctor bent over his task. He had discarded coat and wig and had rolled up his sleeves. The smell from his bottles, Ann realised thankfully, was slowly overcoming the smell of blood.

"They did. I had him carried out again. Except for lack of light this place is considerably superior, and twenty times cleaner at least."

The evening was indigo, fresh and damp. There must have been a rose bush somewhere for a sweet, heart-stirring fragrance greeted them as they stepped from the malthouse and breathed deeply.

"A sorry business," said the Doctor, "but he will live a while yet. And he has one sound leg after all: it is more than I expected. It cannot be roses, dear girl, is it not too early?" And then he turned and caught sight of her ashen face, her bloodstained dress. "Are you feeling ill? I had forgot it was your first operation. You acquitted yourself admirably, admirably. I knew when I sent Pashman I could rely on you completely."

"You imply this is the first of many times I shall be witness to such a ... a business."

"I imply nothing. It is good to know I can call on you for ungrudging help, that is all."

They walked together to the nearest cottage, and instructions for the care of the patient were given, several times and with absolute firmness. "Tomorrow he will be moved to the infirmary," the Doctor told them, "but tonight you must all do your best for him."

An old woman and her daughter volunteered to nurse the young man, the young man whose right leg, Ann remembered, was still lying next to him, though quite detached, in the malthouse. She found herself being offered bread and dripping, all they had. Her stomach heaved. She excused herself, fled for the shed where she had left the chestnut.

"I am half afraid to leave that boy," she said as the Doctor joined her. "He will die."

"Your sitting all night by his side will not keep him alive: time, cleanliness and God will do that, and maybe not in that order. And maybe not at all. Who knows? Stand! Get over!" This to the horse who was in a fret to get home to his supper. "You cannot deal with this wretch yourself, here, give him to me."

The Doctor, whom all horses regarded as a fool, all horses distrusted, and all horses disobeyed, laid his hand on the bit. The chestnut gave him a stare, nostrils distended, eyes luminous.

"See," said the Doctor, "he backs up like a saint. No wonder Brandt had no trouble with him."

Ann fastened the traces. "He is more cunning than you think. He knows he must be harnessed before he can get home to his oats."

The Doctor was loath to let it go at that. Perhaps his cheerful disagreement was a way of taking her mind off the boy in the malthouse, off the severed leg. He tied on his pony — he had ridden to save time and had nearly lost his life twice in foolhardy short cuts, his seat being the least secure in the county — and climbed up to take the reins. For a while they expended a great deal of energy without achieving much in the way of forward motion, the Doctor and the chestnut apparently at violent odds. But then the Doctor gave a blood-curdling yell, the horse turned in an instant in the direction of High Common, and they set off at a canter.

By this time a thin moon was riding high above them and the sky was deep blue, though still troubled by cloud.

"It will be fine tomorrow," the Doctor said as they saw the lights of the village. "No, stay and have something to eat, to drink. I owe you a share in my supper at the very least, dear girl. Surely it would not be considered improper?"

Of course it would — not that either of them cared for that. But Ann was too tired to protest for any reason. The evening had been long and terrible, the smell of blood, the boy's piteous cries still with her. She let the Doctor lead both horses to his stables with sudden thankfulness.

The Lascar produced a roast chicken and a rabbit pie, some strange stuffing, an interesting plum pudding. But Ann had lost her appetite the moment she had stepped inside the malthouse and ate so little she was subjected to one of the Doctor's most ferocious stares.

"No doubt he will live, foolish lad. He will do well enough."

"But what work will he find? He will end up a one-legged beggar."

"Would you rather he had died then? I assure you I had grave doubts about him, very grave. And if he is not taken into the infirmary as quick as may be, what is left of the leg may mortify and he will not have cheated death after all."

"You speak so lightly."

"It is a sort of professional levity, dear girl, it means no disrespect. In ninety-three I was in the Indies, soldiers dying all round me of diseases I could not even name — could I weep for each of them? In three years we lost how many? Thirty thousand? Forty?"

"I can see it would harden a man, how it must do so if he were not to run mad."

"Oh, I am not hardened yet, and half of High Common is convinced I am mad. You must eat something — or here — try some of this. William gave me a bottle before he left."

They drank. Ann saw the candle flame in her glass, amber in a ruby glow of wine. She thought of the boy at Priddy's Barns; she thought of William on board the *Petrel* suffering just such an operation, sweating and screaming on the surgeon's table.

"My dearest Ann, I beg you go upstairs and lie down. You are white and shaking. It is reaction, sweet, and it will pass. I shall drive you home myself in a little while, you are in no state to do so."

Ann murmured it was not so, was overruled. At the door, almost to herself, she said abruptly: "Thank God William was not at Copenhagen."

"They claim it was a victory," in the dry tone of a man who has seen too many bloody encounters so named. "Certainly it was a bold stroke." He saw she had closed her eyes. "Go up and rest for an hour, go, go. But I am glad to see you worry about William. I sometimes thought there was some kind of dislike, distrust between you two."

"There is none, I assure you."

The Doctor stroked his lean, bristly chin. His eyes gleamed. "I hope not indeed," he said, "but I am sad to say experience has taught me that the assurances of women are as the air."

Richard Saufret and Luke Brandt stepped off the London coach at Scole and hired a whisky to take them the last miles to Thorn. They reached it in less than an hour, breasting the hill at a racking trot, bones shaken, livers churned. The horse was pathetically willing but hard-mouthed, whip-shy, and with terrible, knocked legs. Luke had his work cut out keeping him in check. Saufret, unlike Miss Pennyquick, felt at a complete loss on dry land and only the most unavoidable business ever persuaded him to leave the ship. He clung to the seat with a pained expression and then: "This horse is a demon," he remarked as they plunged down the lane to Thorn.

"Say rather he is a victim of the Press and of innumerable indifferent commanders."

"That is sympathetic and poetical. But how I hate him! Pray, pull on that rein and see if he will turn to starboard. I shall only feel safe when I have my feet on the earth again."

It was a golden evening, a drift of bonfire smoke over by Hollin's cottage, a scent of roses. It was July; Tom was out in the cornfields, a critical eye on everything, a hand ready for any weed. They would soon be harvesting.

The horse was not acquainted with port and starboard; he veered sharply and scraped the gatepost. But they reached the back door without mishap and found Miss Pennyquick there, staring, and shading her eyes from the westering sun.

"Ann is in the garden," she said. "Shall I call her?"

"No, no," Saufret swung down, his eye like a beacon, his pigtail flying, "the garden will be excellent, the garden is the place." And he strode off round the corner of the house as if he knew the way exactly.

Luke smiled, secured the horse, bid Miss Pennyquick put on some coffee perhaps, or tea. She looked at him once, and read his face, and knew what they had come about, and she said nothing, only went inside and called for the kettle. Luke walked slowly across the yard and through the little wicket gate. The scent of roses was overpowering here, a vast climber tangled up an entire wall and smothered it in cream blooms. Ann was on hands and knees plucking out weeds with patience if not enthusiasm. Saufret had stopped at sight of her and did not move until Luke caught him up, then gave a shrug, another, slowly advanced.

Ann looked up and her face broke into a smile as she saw them. She was wearing a muslin dress, too pretty, too fine for gardening, but round it she had tied one of Miss Pennyquick's immense white aprons, and on her head was an old-fashioned straw hat tied under her chin with a pink bow.

"But what a pleasure! And why did you not let me know you were coming?"

Saufret took her hand and raised it, laid it against his cheek for a moment, a foreign and dramatic gesture. He looked grave and kind, not at all himself. Luke shuffled behind, hat in hand, two days' growth of beard darkening his square jaw and his eyes everywhere but on her face.

"I have received news," Saufret said. "It was waiting for me in Guernsey when we returned there a week ago. I made haste to sail to Dover and then went to Mr Liveman in the City. We are all agreed it is best you hear it from me, not from him."

"About Harry."

"About Harry," and he took a flat packet from his coat and handed it to her; it was a letter, several pages long, and by its appearance had travelled far and in low company; it was addressed to Richard Saufret, St Pierre, Guernsey. "Read, read," he said, seeing her hesitate, "it is for you. You will understand when you read it."

She opened out the pages and then, looking about for a suitable place, chose to sit on the low brick wall by the steps to the front door, where a strange old rose, red and white together, had scattered petals that still scented the evening air. There, tucking a stray curl behind her ear, she began to read.

Sir,

It is my sad duty to bring you news of the death of Sir Harry Gerard of Blackow in the county of Norfolk. He begged me to write to you since he was unable to do so, and finding this the last service I can render him, I shall try to give a clear account of his last weeks on earth. He spoke of you often, as a friend and a gentleman, and wished you to remember him only with affection.

I was a lieutenant in the *Monarch* when I first met him. I had noticed one of the seamen in my part of the ship seemed strikingly different from his fellows. This is not very unusual; I thought perhaps he was a debtor released for service or else a man pressed accidentally, having no one at hand to speak for him at the time he was taken up. It happened he could not bear the motion of the ship, and although he had served well enough in his fashion upwards of two months, he was generally sick and appeared to be wasting. Shortly before we sailed for the Baltic in March he was taken miserably ill and removed to the sick bay. It was there I came to know him better, partly through the surgeon's intervention. His affairs were unsettled, he told me, his mind in torment; he feared he would never see England again. Consequently I visited him to see what might be done, and little by little came to know him, and his history.

The first sheet dropped from Ann's fingers to the grass. She looked up a moment, at the distant fields, at the wild heights of the Gorse, and then bent to read the second.

Harry Gerard told me he was in debt, and in debt to such rogues that threats had been made against his life. Also he had deceived a poor innocent and trusting girl, to whom he had promised much in an idle moment, afterwards regretted; she, however, left home and family to join him. Unwilling to keep his word, equally unwilling to abandon her, he devised a mock marriage ceremony in a fit – or so I should guess – of either madness or drunkenness. He said he could not bear to distress her but was resolved only to marry money. And it seems he still supported her and was fond of her, a strange state of affairs and much to his discredit. He told me that, his debts so pressing, he had thought of suicide, but instead had fled to Deal, hoping to escape the country. There, while waiting for his servant to join him, he had, in a drunken stupor, been taken by the Press. He was carried off to Dover and, hands being required immediately by the frigate *Rapid*, was sent aboard her instead of the receiving ships. When sober he protested forcibly but nothing could be done, the *Rapid* already under way. Some time later he was transferred, at sea, to the *Monarch*, in the hope our own captain might look on his case more kindly. Unfortunately the *Monarch* was under orders to sail for Yarmouth at once in preparation for the journey to Copenhagen only a few days later. Harry Gerard's misery naturally increased. He fell ill, as I said, and while lying in his cot asked me to inform you of his whereabouts, in turn to inform his wife, and his legal adviser, a Mr Liveman. He was desperate for news, especially regarding his shares in a certain island — I do not know which — and whether their value was helping the settlement of his debts.

In the action off Copenhagen our ship took the fire of two Danish vessels besides being the most exposed to the great shore battery. We lost more than two hundred men. Harry Gerard left his sick berth and resumed his place on the gundeck with his fellows, and there was hit by splinters, most dreadfully wounded. The young midshipman in charge, knowing my feeling for the man, sent for me.

His last words were of you, of his hopes of being square with the world once more, of his home. He wished to be remembered to his wife. I think you should know he was always most cheerful, even in what to him must have been great adversity, and he always, in spite of rough and sometimes criminal company, contrived to remain a gentleman. On the lower deck, indeed, he was much liked and is greatly missed. He told me that I must instruct you to be certain Mr Liveman goes to a house called Thorn in Norfolk and that there, in the green calf-bound edition of Shakespeare, would be found his will, drawn up only recently and signed by reputable witnesses.

He had an easy, generous nature, perhaps rather too boyish and open, but endearing, full of charm. In spite of his faults he won many hearts beside my own, and I am sorry this letter must bring only bad news.

H.M. brig *Salome*

Saufret, who had steered Luke across the lawn to gaze unhappily at the blown roses and the massed daisies, turned back to find Ann sitting exactly where he had left her, tears running down her cheeks.

"My dear, my dear, he died well! How much worse it could have been!"

Ann looked up, and the tears still ran unchecked and silently. It was almost as if she did not see them, Luke thought, standing awkwardly to one side, aching for her, for whatever kind of loss it was she suffered. He had no idea how much she had loved the man, or even if she had sincerely loved him at all. But Harry Gerard had charmed everyone, everyone. Even he, level-headed, suspicious, could remember quite clearly those blue, innocent eyes, that low, pleasant voice, and remembered them with a slight, involuntary affection. He had been a fool, Harry Gerard, a creature of whim, but a generous fool, he had never stinted his friends.

And what did Ann remember, Luke wondered? Some brief happiness? He supposed she had had that, at least. He saw her eyes lift to where the hump of the Gorse showed through and above the leafy masses of the oaks.

"You must come in," Saufret was saying firmly, taking her arm, "you must come indoors. Luke, run for the old woman."

And Ann allowed him to lead her, quite docilely, until they reached the front door, where she turned and held out the letter.

"it is for you to keep," said Saufret unhappily, "if you so wish."

She shook her head, and when she spoke her voice was soft, stubborn, clear as glass. "Mr Liveman," she said, "must send it to Harriet Stratford. I think ... I think in all conscience it is hers, not mine. Only take out and destroy," and here she did it for him, crumpling the paper viciously, "the middle page."

"I understand; it reads sensibly, yes. But here on the last sheet it mentions his wife, Harry's wife."

"She will think it is herself."

"And is it?"

"We shall never know." And then, turning back to put her hand to the doorknob: "Does it matter?"

18

THE VIEW from Warren Hill was depressing. The river was in flood after a week of rain and all the meadows were under water. Ann wrapped her cloak more comfortably round herself and sighed.

"It is something to do with the mill," she said at last, "with the sluices and how they are operated. The land is not nearly so wet further up river."

Tom gazed blankly at the drowned willows, the crumbled banks, the sunken grass. They had been talking of Blackow, its new occupants the Houghtons, and a projected ball of Mrs Palmer's.

"Why do the Houghtons not call?" he demanded.

"Mrs Houghton objects to scandal – my marriage, I suppose – and to 'disorderly households'."

"It makes us sound like a pot-house. What is disorderly about Thorn?"

"I very much fear you are," Ann said with a laugh, tucking her hand through his arm and propelling him down towards the house.

"But we are received at Upgate."

"Ah, but then Mrs Houghton enjoys being in possession of keener morals than the family of the local squire."

From Thorn came the noise of altercation: Mrs McGinly was back, exhorting them all to wipe their feet and mind their language, shaming Hollin into Sunday best whenever he put his head round the door.

"Houghton has money, no doubt," said Tom.

"A great deal according to Mrs Palmer, who has examined him and his circumstances as minutely as posible. And the house is unrecognisable, she says, everything new-painted and new-furnished, workmen all over the place, hammering, polishing, pulling out weeds."

"And William," Tom swung her easily over the mud, "what of William? Why have we had no letters at Thorn when they have received any number at Upgate?"

"Perhaps ours were lost overboard, or mislaid."

"But where is he? What is he doing?"

"Well, Mrs Palmer is determined he will be in Norfolk for her ball. His ship was damaged in some brush with French frigates and must put into port for repairs."

"Which port?"

"Ah, there is the mystery."

The smell of autumn was in the air, of decay, rotting leaves. Was it really true, Ann was wondering, that William was coming to Norfolk? To see the Doctor, of course. To see Charlotte? She drew closer to Tom until her head was in the protective curve of his shoulder, her hair in springing curls under his chin. I do not care whether he comes or not, she thought, I do not care for him. And she looked back to Warren Hill and deliberately remembered Harry charging down its rolling slopes, remembered that bursting vitality she had loved, that childlike humour. Had she ever been so ridiculous as to think she would cross England barefoot for his kiss? Yes, but how long ago it seemed, how very long ago. And William was nothing like Harry, William was ...

"The Doctor is here," said Tom.

He was. He was sitting poking the fire in the drawing room, moody and irritable.

"The boy whose leg we chopped is doing well," he said to Ann. "He has learnt to walk on crutches and by all accounts is — what are the words they always use? — ah, yes, he is industrious and sober. The parson attached to the infirmary is trying to find him employment."

There was a pause. Then he pulled off his wig and threw it in the coal scuttle. "A guinea to remake it, can you believe? A guinea. And it is still a cursed weight and itches like the devil."

"Why must you wear it? It is only convention. Other conventions do not bother you."

"To remind me I am now and henceforward a country doctor, that I have finished with the world beyond High Common, that all my battles and voyages and extreme discomforts are over; it is a symbol of my submission, my return to security and sense."

Tom had left them to find refreshment, the room was very quiet. The clock ticked, the ginger cat in the chair stretched but did not wake. Ann crouched by the hearth, picking up the curled petals of the blown roses that had fallen from their vase, absorbed, at peace.

"No," she said at last, "you must not settle for High Common. There are still adventures to be had."

He had leaned forward; he was twelve inches from kissing her, six ... Her hair tickled his chin as she turned.

She drew back. "You look quite fierce," she said. "What has happened to upset you?"

He straightened, cleared his throat. "Nothing. Nothing at all. I have news of William. He hopes to be with us by the end of the week."

"Mrs Palmer will never forgive him if he misses the ball. She is hoping to divert his attention from Charlotte, I believe, especially now Mr Houghton has turned out to be so disappointing."

Ann had risen. She spoke brightly but it was a false brightness. The Doctor resumed his desultory poking of the fire.

"What are you going to do with the *Sable Island*?" he asked.

"Keep her, if I can."

Harry's will, so short, so explicit, so incontestably just perhaps, had left her the ship, that splendid ship; and everything else he had owned or had any interest in – apart from Thorn – to Harriet Stratford. The everything else, somewhat ironically, had amounted to a little over five thousand pounds. Ann was scrupulous in attending to its distribution. Liveman was no champion to the poor girl, considered her a loose woman – this his description during a stormy meeting with Ann in his office. He saw no reason at all why she should inherit even a penny. Ann herself had need of money, and he could guess how badly; it was absurd to become sentimental over a girl willing to turn her back on everyone for a wastrel. If it came to that, Ann told him, it was only what she had done herself, was it not? Blushes, apologies, a glass of strong sherry appeared simultaneously; Liveman declared himself prostrate. Then Harriet would have the five thousand? Yes, yes of course, there would be no objection. And then afterwards the irritating little man reported Miss Stratford overwhelmed, tearful, exultant – but he hoped never to have to do with such a business again.

"Yes, do keep her," the Doctor said abruptly. "Keep her. As you say, there are still adventures to be had."

Tom entered. "It is duck pie and saddle of mutton. Will you stay?"

The Doctor's smile was rather wan. "I would be delighted."

"Did you know the Houghtons will not call?" Tom was saying genially. "We are not sufficiently respectable."

"I can understand it, I sympathise. How could you expect a lady to entertain a man who walks behind his own oxen, who bathes in the horse trough?"

"Tom cannot tolerate being ignored," Ann said, "and he considers fifty acres unquestionably enough to make him a gentleman."

The Doctor snorted. "Is not one hundred the magical figure? A hundred acres and he could call himself a yeoman and thumb his nose at whom he liked."

Tom drew himself up, a blond giant. "A hundred acres is nothing," he said, "before I'm done I shall own a thousand."

The *Sable Island*, now riding easily at anchor in Falmouth Bay, water to which she often returned in deference to the staunch West Country smugglers who made up half her crew, had

rovided the wherewithal for a dress of oyster silk, cut in the
atest fashion by the best dressmaker in Norwich, as simple, as
attering as such a dress could be. It was a scandalous
xtravagance. Tom would not let them hear the end of it,
alculating the expense of his seed corn, his cocksfoot, his
ucerne. He had become by now the man of the house, and he
vas constantly trying to keep his women in order. How, he
emanded across the breakfast table the morning of Mrs Palmer's
all, would they pay for a hundred South Downs if every spare
hilling went on frills and Spitalfields silk? And for his part he
ould not see why the thing had cost so much, it seemed so plain,
o unpretentious. Why, there was nothing of it – certainly too
ttle for modesty's sake! He could have bought half a dozen
ullocks for the price.

"You are growing too much the farmer," Ann said, "you will
rudge us our petticoats next and say that for the price we could
ave bought a rook-scarer. If you lose your sense of humour,
om Forsie, I shall turn you out to live in a wattle hut on your
eloved fifty acres. So take care!"

He grinned across his plate of ham. Mrs Palmer, hoping to
ave as many young men as girls for the first time in living
memory, had included him in her invitation. This was a bold
tep, she felt rather pleased with herself for having the courage –
hough he was accepted at Upgate and in other houses. Her
aughters would never have forgiven her, in any case, had she
eft him out. He was going to be impressively tall, was always
miling and pleasant, never paid compliments he did not mean
nd spoke with disingenuous bluntness. In short, he did not care
vhat the world thought of him provided he thought well of
imself. Mrs Palmer liked him – she would never have admitted
– and unlike Mrs Houghton, who was far too proud, she could
wallow nine tenths of her moral objections to anything in an
ppropriate cause. :

"I have only the blue coat to wear," he said with mock misery,
and the waistcoat don't do up any more."

"That is because you grow an inch a day."

He sat looking at her for a moment, apparently lost in thought.

He saw her between the coffee pot and the muffin dish — it wa one of Miss Pennyquick's peculiarities to eat nothing but muffin for breakfast — and he saw a delightful young woman in lace cap — how he detested that cap! — and flowered cotton high to the neck.

"Why do you wear that awful thing?" he demanded with stab of his fork.

"Because I am a widow." She had worn mourning for month and then cast it off, for how, she had asked Miss Pennyquick, could it benefit the dead for the living to make martyrs of themselves? If Heaven existed and was indeed Heaven then better to put on white and dance for joy. Miss Pennyquick had thought this sounded blasphemous. Ann told her she had mistaken the nature of blasphemy, which Miss Pennyquick was prepared to admit, never having thought deeply on the subject. "I do not mourn for Harry," Ann had said, "I would be hypocrite to say I do. Yes, I am sorry that he is dead, but I canno weep for him. Not now, not any more, I think. And the world may say what it wishes about that."

Tom had approved this sentiment, he had advocated the throwing off of the cap as well. He said, rather petulantly, that i spoiled her hair; he meant that it reminded him she had onc been married to Harry Gerard. He had the good sense thi morning not to pursue the subject however, and turned to others the certainty of meeting the Houghtons at Mrs Palmer's, th Misses Palmer and their respective merits, the question of how h was to fasten his waistcoat. And then: "I would like to meet Luk Brandt again, become better acquainted. I would like to see you privateer. May I, if she returns to Dover?"

"A farmer at sea? It is all this strange information in William letters, is it not? Gunwales and gigs and mizzens, and all that stu about shot and powder. He will make you thirst for a life at se and I shall find Thorn gone back to rack and ruin."

"Never! I could not bear a life at sea. I took a ride down th Yare once on a flat-bottomed trader and nearly drowned mysel I prefer my feet on solid ground."

"Very sensible," said Miss Pennyquick, entering with he

eheated muffin and more butter, and flushed from her first
ncounter of the day with Mrs McGinly.

"But I would like to see this *Sable Island*," Tom continued. "I
would like to know ..."

"There is scarcely enough money to keep her afloat another six
months," Ann interrupted, picking up the newspaper by her
plate and finding it a week old – had it been in and out of every
le-house in the district before Pashman delivered it? "She must
atch enemy ships and valuable ones or I shall be forced to let the
Navy have her."

"No, you could not! But talking of the Navy, is William to be
here tonight? Is he arrived yet? It is something he hates, you
know, a party with dancing. He is not a sociable man. And I
gree with him, it is all a great waste of time and energy."

Ann, who had just thought that if she ever had to leave Thorn
o Tom she would leave it in unquestionably good hands, gave a
ittle cry of laughter and reached for the coffee pot. "Then why
re you going? And why worry so about a tight waistcoat? Have
more coffee, you rogue, and tell me about the lucerne. I did not
hink Mr Fowler recommended it? And why are the new beasts
brought yesterday so ferocious looking and so large?"

"They are Longhorns, most carefully bred. They are good
cattle, hardy and docile. You see, I shall do very well out of
hem."

Ann met Miss Pennyquick's pained glance across the muffin.

"I have no doubt," she said.

He was making a great noise with the toast. "I do hope
William is there tonight," he said, "I have so much to ask him."

Ann was silent. She hoped nothing of the kind. Human nature
being what it is, she hoped never to see William Claverden
gain.

Even smarting with the indignity of only being able to fasten
wo buttons of his waistcoat – and these if he stopped breathing –
Tom readily admitted the oyster silk was unsurpassed. The
implicity he had scorned was its very virtue, of course. Ann's
igure, so very far from voluptuous, was revealed as perfect. Or

revealed too much? She was in a daring mood though, certainly carried it off, moved with all her former grace and energy. Her hair, cut off to just below her ears only a day or two ago, was a mass of curl, chestnut in the candlelight. Mrs Palmer's exclamation on greeting her was, for once, the whole truth.

"My dear, you look lovely! And Mr Forsie – I declare you are broader every time we meet! Come, come, there is a young man over here related to the Townshends, visits frequently at Holkham too. You may talk agriculture with him all evening if you wish."

Lord Barsham had Ann's hand, was bowing over it.

"I am glad that dreadful business is over, glad you have come out of it so well. I understand from Claverden you own a ship, a schooner did he say? I wish her luck. This war has the look of an interminable struggle, ugly, very ugly. Thank God we have the Navy! But may I speak more personally, more as a friend? My old companion the Doctor is not himself, and though he does not admit it he is very sore on the subject of Thorn. Dear Lady Gerard, I do hope you have not quarrelled."

"It is impossible to quarrel with the Doctor."

"I fear it is only too easy. I have done it a thousand times, I assure you. He does not show his deepest feelings, his dearest convictions; one offends him and is at a loss to know why."

He could not tell her that this time he had made a more accurate guess at the Doctor's deepest feelings; he did not consider it his business. But he was a bluff and hearty man, open and honest, and he hated to see two people he liked fall out over nothing. In his opinion love was nothing, or was rather the most natural thing in the world – why, he had been happily married twenty-five years, there could be no state more comfortable. He did not understand the Doctor's reluctance to declare himself, to own to an interest.

"Is he here?" Ann asked.

"Indeed. And I do believe he is to dance with my wife. It is remarkable! In nearly twenty years he has not been known to stand up with anybody!"

"Then he is not himself at all!"

They laughed together. But they were both uneasy, and both without knowing why. Lord Barsham led her away with cheerful greetings to friends and neighbours on all sides, introduced her without hesitation to the Houghtons: "Lady Gerard from Thorn. You are neighbours, you know each other well." He was completely innocent, he had not listened to a word his wife said. He even misinterpreted Houghton's deep blush as a very natural reaction to Ann's entrancing décolletage.

He swept her on, he had had instructions from the Doctor

"There," stopping at last, "does he not look uncommonly fine? I wish I could have swaggered in such a coat when I was a young man. Ah, you look surprised, Claverden! It is Lady Gerard. Surely there is no likelihood of your not recognising her?"

William, his eyes only for Charlotte's face until that moment, found himself distracted by a vision of thin cream silk, by cropped dark curls under a ridiculous little cap, by a pair of beautiful eyes. He was speechless – from what emotion poor Charlotte could only guess, and guess wrongly – and Ann too stood unnaturally still and without her usual smile.

"I have been hearing about your ship, Ann," Charlotte felt compelled to deal with this awkward silence. "William tells me her captain has only one eye and looks like a Barbary pirate. Oh, here is Mrs Beckenham – I suppose I should go and prise Olivia away or she will be stuck to her mother all evening and not be allowed to dance with anyone. Papa, will you not help?"

Lord Barsham had been trying to remember the Doctor's directions. He frowned. "What? A stratagem? Must I?"

"It is for poor Olivia's sake."

William watched her weave her way through the throng on her father's arm, and then turned reluctantly to Ann. "You look well," he said bluntly, "but thin. You need a change, another week or two in Brighton perhaps. This place has too many memories."

"They are not all unhappy ones." It sounded provoking. She was altogether provoking tonight, he thought, scandalising everyone with that dress and that crown of curls, daring them all to do anything but admire her, for she had never looked lovelier.

He was obliged to nod to a passing acquaintance. Across the intervening heads he could see Charlotte talking to a tall, angular girl in deepest pink, Olivia Beckenham presumably.

"I was going to call at Thorn." It was not strictly true; he had been in two minds about it. "But I only arrived in Norwich yesterday."

"I did not know you had arrived at all. I did not expect to see you here." Her face had already told him as much, her white look on finding him in front of her. "Are you staying with the Doctor?"

"Yes. And have you seen Alex tonight? He is in the most contrary mood, has been in a foul temper all day, and never spoke a word between High Common and bidding Mrs Palmer a frosty good evening."

They were forced to step closer together to let others by, and while Ann looked about her with a false and wavering smile, William looked only at Ann.

"You are not well at all," he exclaimed. "You are wasting away and you have great shadows under your eyes. This business has upset you more than you let us know. Dammit, he's dead, it's over, you must learn to ... You must make a new life for yourself."

She started, stepped back instantly, but her voice when she spoke was quite normal, light and cheerful. "Perhaps I ought to take a voyage on the *Sable Island*. The sea air would do me good."

"You would get too much sea air on the *Sable Island* – and some French grapeshot into the bargain. Yarmouth, Brighton would be much the best."

More acquaintances, more nods, and a neighbouring conversation expanding briefly to include them, to make them laugh politely and cast about for witty replies. Someone asked William about his ship, and several more ladies drifted in his direction, hoping for a glance from those dark, dark eyes.

"Two French frigates almost knocked us to pieces," he admitted tonelessly, disliking being the centre of attention. "We were saved by fog and darkness together, nothing more heroic

he ship will be a while refitting. But I sail in the middle of next
eek, a cutter bound for Gibraltar carrying post, orders, things of
at nature. I am not to be left idle a moment."

"A cutter?" came the query.

"So insignificant a vessel it is hardly visible at any distance," was
Villiam's reply, and suddenly: "Is that the Doctor standing up to
nce?"

It was. He had Lady Barsham on his arm and he looked very
rious, in black tonight and nothing out of place, all quiet
egance. And he danced well, there was no doubt of it. A great
any people peered and manoeuvred to see it, and there was some
icy speculation on where he could have danced before, and with
hom.

Mrs Palmer bore down on Ann with a sandy young man,
armingly freckled, who had expressed a desire to meet Lady
erard; he had heard her name mentioned in connection with the
orfolk Agricultural Society. He looked startled to find Lady
erard a small, slim person in pale silk and lace. With irrepressible
al Mrs Palmer then led William away to meet half a dozen
itable dancing partners – no girl in the room, she said, would be
le to resist him. He followed her hesitantly, turning aside at the
ghtest interference; at one point it was Lord Barsham with some
quest, at another Charlotte's huge, pleading eyes, and then Tom
ucking at his elbow, having crossed the whole room with great
fficulty to reach his side. Each time Mrs Palmer, like an escorting
gate, tacked on the instant and was alongside, chivvying him on.

Ann did not dance, though not for want of partners. She took up
matronly stand near the supper table, well out of the way, and
lked farming to the young man with freckles until they were
th sick and tired of the subject. Tom accosted her as soon as she
as alone, demanding to know why she was stuck away in the
oom when everyone else was dancing, and to her reply that it
as only the young people who were dancing, he told her stuff
d shame, look at the Doctor and Lady Barsham and Houghton
ith Julia Palmer, and all in the voice he generally reserved for
astising the oxen, a fine, clear, carrying voice that reached the
r side of the room and caused a great craning of necks.

"Even William is dancing," he said more gently, seeing he ha
embarrassed her, "and he is neither very young nor does he car
anything for it. Come, dance with me. I have no partner for th
or the next."

"I do not want to dance, you foolish boy! Look, there is Mi
Beckenham gazing longingly in this direction. Go and make he
happy and stop plaguing me."

"You mean the gawky one in pink? Annie, how could you
Now, what is that? A great whispering at the door. Do yo
think the coachmen have fallen to fighting?"

A scarlet Mrs Palmer appeared as the last note of music die
away and the dancers broke into clapping and excited chatte
before regrouping for the next with a great many bobs and bow
"Ann, Ann dear, here is the most extraordinary thing – a youn
man to speak to you, rang the bell at the front door and asked t
speak to you! The impertinence of it! A great rough fellow
Dawes said, in dreadful clothes, no proper coat ... But that is b
the way. Of course he was not allowed in but he insisted o
leaving something for you."

"But why was I not called?"

"Why? But so unsuitable! I could hardly ask such a person int
my hall and could not expect you to step to the kitchen."

"Why not?" struck in Tom with that air of unabashe
innocence he often used when being most aggravating.

Ann trod lightly on his foot. "Excuse me," she said, "I will g
and see Dawes."

He was still in the hall, a small man and wiry. He reminde
Ann forcibly of Praed, but his voice was sonorous and genteel.

"The young man left a message, my Lady, said that he ha
been so bold, hearing from the Doctor you were to be at th
house tonight, as to step across with a nosegay by way of .
hmm ... a small gift for being so kind. I hope I have it right, m
Lady. The lad was very broad in the speech, not local. I coul
not catch all he said."

She stepped past him to the side table where a little posy o
creamy white roses lay discarded, filling the place with the
fragrance. They were prettily arranged, each perfect, each just o

the point of opening. They were late blooms, the last breath of the long-lost summer, and someone had taken infinite care with them, plaiting pink and silver ribbons between the stems.

"Was he … Did he have anything to distinguish him?"

"I cannot say, my Lady. He was not ill to look at, but of course only the one leg …"

To see Lady Ann Gerard dissolve into racking sobs directly in front of him unnerved even Dawes, the imperturbable domestic. He signalled frantically and a footman rushed away on slippered feet for assistance. In a minute William was there and had taken her arm and drawn her into the morning room, lighting two candles, and then turning to pull her against him, improperly, comfortingly, as impersonally as he could.

"You gave Dawes the fright of his life," he said. "He was as white as a new sail."

She was brushing ineffectually at her tears. "Are all your similes to be nautical from now on?"

His hand cupped her chin. "What is it? I never thought to see you cry in public."

"It was … it was the flowers. The boy must have walked miles on crutches to bring me these and they would not let him in."

"The boy whose leg the Doctor chopped? Tom told me you were there. But surely …" Surely such abandoned weeping had not been for a nosegay and a kind deed? "Ann, why are you crying?"

She could not tell him. The scent of roses and the sight of the delicate buds had brought back the memory of another such gift, of a summer that seemed so long ago now it might have been in another life. She could hardly say she was crying for Harry, for a love that had never existed, for misplaced affections and abused trust and all the sad confusion of her marriage. With a great effort she drew a steadying breath, heard her own voice speak from miles away, small and calm and sensible.

"I do so wish they had not turned him out like a thief."

"Not everyone is as broad-minded as you and the Doctor. I have no doubt you would both have asked him to the party."

She did not hear. She was staring at his dark chin, his shorn black head. She had stepped back to a safe distance but her heart still raced. She had thought so often of their next meeting since the moment he had turned away on that wet quayside, had tried not to think of it, had tried to subdue all the new, urgent desires. She had been in love with Harry and look what it had brought her, what confusion and hurt, what frustrated desire and unsteady affection, what misery. The Doctor had been right, damn him, damn him! She had not known what love was. And now ...

William took a step forward, she took one back. He looked fierce enough for anything. Was he going to kiss her again? No, no, anything but that. She would never be able to resist him. In this dress, in this dark, he would think her a wanton. And she could not bear his contempt, could not think of it. Another step back. She had come up against a chair.

"Ann, Ann ..." And his hands were there, warm on her bare shoulders.

"Why so few candles? Ah, Mr Claverden, I am so grateful. How prompt you were!" It was Mrs Palmer blinking in the doorway. "Is Lady Gérard quite recovered?"

She was quite recovered, though pale and inattentive. She walked out in front of them back to the ballroom, her face dry, the rosebuds in her gloved hand. And there was Charlotte looking a little anxious, and freckled Mr Gilbert plucking up courage to take her to supper, and the Doctor ... The Doctor was alarmingly sober, and thoughtful, deeply thoughtful.

And then there was Tom, large and comfortable, elbowing them apart.

"But how lovely! They are just like the roses on those funny little bushes at Blackow."

He was aware at once he had said the wrong thing, aware of William's dark face charged with sudden understanding, of Mrs Palmer's widened eyes, of a general silence in their vicinity.

But Ann appeared normal. She took his arm.

"They are, just like them. They are a present from an admirer. Dear Tom, take me to supper, I am so very hungry. And look," in a whisper, "the parson is approaching. Quick! Or I shall be

308

forced to listen to a whole sermon on Miss Pennyquick's iniquities!"

The carriages were being called, Mrs Palmer saying energetic and effusive farewells. Ann had no carriage, having come in the gig with Tom – a most disgraceful spectacle according to Mrs Houghton, who had seen them arrive – and Tom was at present pursuing some jocular business with Charlotte down by the deserted supper table. She could see Mr Bennet from Scole bearing down purposefully to talk threshing machines, and from another direction the parson, with whom she was bound to quarrel – and there was William, though he had not seen her yet, stalking through the idlers. Where could she hide? Only the library offered sanctuary – if Mr Palmer had not already fled there – for the library was large, private, comfortable and well lit.

She ran there, entered, leaned back against the door with a sigh.

"You did not dance," said a voice she knew. The Doctor emerged from the depths of a vast hooded chair through a cloud of pipe smoke.

"I must pay some lip service to convention. I am supposed to be in mourning."

"No one could expect it, no one would dare expect it! He used you too cruelly!"

She received the impression this was a man she did not know at all. There was no genial satyr's grin, no affectionate look. He walked angrily to the shelves, poked out a couple of volumes, brushed through the pages. "Dear God!" explosively. "You should have married William!"

There was a wretched silence, a gulf of misunderstanding, shock. Ann shrank back as if he had hit her. "What are you thinking of? William never … William would not …"

"No, he would not, more's the pity," very dry, "and by the time he would you were already Gerard's wife."

She crossed the room then. "What do you mean?"

She had both hands on his arm, he could not detach them. He

said a little desperately: "You know very well what I mean. And you must not leave tonight without saying goodbye to him. He is away to his ship tomorrow. You may not see him again for months, years," and he turned to embrace her, with discretion, with such discretion. "I would not lie to you, I love you too dearly. If you let William go tonight without a word about ... about your feelings, you will have let him go for ever. A dramatic statement but a true one, sweet girl."

She withdrew. The hooded chair reeked of his tobacco; she found refuge in it. After a while she said: "What are my feelings?"

A long pause. The Doctor was busy with his pipe. "You love him. You may deny it, but it is the truth."

There was no sound from the depths of the chair. Then: "You told me once I did not know what love was."

"Did I? How presumptuous of me. But you know now, do you not? And you and William have always been drawn to each other, from the first, the very first; this was inevitable ..."

"This? There is nothing between us. He thinks me a hoyden. If you could have seen how he looked at me tonight when we met ..."

The Doctor stopped smoking and waved gently to disperse the cloud that obscured her; she was still in the chair, a dim form pressed into the back, great eyes staring out at him.

"Perhaps you mistook the meaning of his look."

Was she blushing? He could not tell. She had retreated even further if that were possible. When she spoke again it was a bold attempt to change the subject. "What devil prompted you to stand up with Lady Barsham and astound the company?"

"A momentary mania, another act of defiance perhaps."

"Like your wig in the scuttle."

"Just so." He had walked to the door and opened it a fraction. "Bless me, it is Tom kissing Charlotte good night. This will never do! Should I not reprimand them, bring forth Biblical warnings?"

"Leave such things to the parson, he is full of impossibly good advice. No, I beg you," she had run to grasp his arm, afraid he would step out, "let them have their happiness."

He closed the door, turned to her. "Yes, let them. It is brief enough in all truth, is it not?"

"You speak with feeling."

"Oh, I am a cynic. Had you not noticed? But truthfully, do you think anything will come of it? Can you see Tom Forsie marrying a fortune?"

She smiled. "Most vividly. What about the thousand acres he swore he would own?"

The hall was empty, the faint babble of retreating guests fading and fading. It was time to leave. The Doctor took Ann's hand.

"Good night," he said, "dear girl, good night."

After she had gone he went back to the hooded chair and his pipe with the irritability of a man who finds – and perhaps not for the first time – that the rewards of virtue in practice fall sadly short of the expectation. He had done what he felt he must: he had spoken to her, he had brought them together. He had been debating all day whether to do so, had scarcely eaten, had been savage and taciturn; and then, on seeing her, he had known he must do it.

But he loved her deeply, and it had been painful.

He supposed, puffing out smoke until he vanished behind a fog bank of it, that he would survive.

William had brought the Doctor's gig to the front of the house and had waited with a seething impatience. God, to be away, to be on the ship, to be anywhere but here! If he saw her again he would tell her, declare himself, make a fool of himself ... He had nearly done so the moment before Mrs Palmer had opened the morning room door. And what would Ann have done, he wondered, what would she have said? She had looked quite terrified. And she was in love with a memory still, a memory of that fool Gerard ...

After a time he sent one of the footmen to find the Doctor, but the Doctor was not to be found. It would be like him to drive off in another carriage, William thought sourly. He buttoned his coat, undecided whether to stay or go. A quarter of an hour later he made up his mind to go. Only the stragglers were left to depart, only two more carriages grinding the gravel. There was a blanket of mist, a thin rain. Damn it, he would go! He took the whip from its socket, spoke to the horse.

And then, as he swayed forward, there was Ann at his wheel, calling.

He reined in. Her hand reached up. He grasped it, heaved her to the seat. "You will perish," he said, "your cloak is undone."

She had dragged off her little cap and her short hair was a damp mass of curl. "You must not leave ..." she gasped, clinging to the seat as the horse plunged, "... must say goodbye."

"Is that all you have scrambled up here to say? You are out of your mind! You have not even changed your shoes and your dress is muddy."

"The Doctor ..."

William had his hands full, the horse was wild to go. The gig twisted and rocked. "Damn the Doctor! And damn his horse!" and a second later: "He sent you. The Doctor sent you. Why?"

"He said you will be away years."

"Maybe. Do you care?" He was choking with resentment, with anger, with disappointment.

"More than you know."

"More than I know? Oh, blast this animal! I know there are only two things you have ever cared passionately for: Thorn and Harry Gerard. And now perhaps Thorn and *Sable Island*."

They were slewing across the drive; behind was shouting and a bevy of searching lanterns in the dripping dark.

"And you," she said; had he heard her? Her hand was on his arm. "William. I came to say goodbye."

She had thrown up her hood and it was so dark, almost too dark to see anything. William held the horse in a grip of steel, whip and reins in the one hand. With the other he dragged Ann to him, knocking his hat askew, knocking her hood back, bruising her mouth.

"Goodbye!" he cried, lifting his head. "I love you! I am going to marry you!"

A little later they found the Doctor wandering in Mrs Palmer's conservatory viewing the palms by candlelight, and they told him his gig was missing, it was feared the horse had bolted. And its driver, its passenger? Bolted too, gone careering off into the night.

312

For a moment the Doctor looked bemused, lost. They led
tenderly to the front hall, and there was Tom, casting round and
round for Ann, redder and more desperate by the minute.

"She is safe," declared the Doctor, "I am sure of it. Come,
drive me home, dear boy, and we will open a bottle together.
Come."

And he strode out and down the steps, whistling.

...is a leading paperback publisher of both non-fiction, popular and academic, and fiction. Below are some recent fiction titles.

- ☐ THE SERVANTS OF TWILIGHT Leigh Nichols £1.95
- ☐ A SEASON OF MISTS Sarah Woodhouse £1.95
- ☐ DOUBLE YOKE Buchi Emecheta £1.50
- ☐ IN HONOUR BOUND Gerald Seymour £1.95
- ☐ IN SAFE HANDS Jane Sandford £1.95
- ☐ SHARPE'S ENEMY Bernard Cornwell £1.95
- ☐ A WOMAN OF IRON Sheila Holland £1.75
- ☐ FAIR FRIDAY Peter Turnbull £1.50
- ☐ THREE WOMEN OF LIVERPOOL Helen Forrester £1.95
- ☐ FRIENDS OF THE OPPOSITE SEX Sara Davidson £1.95
- ☐ KNAVE OF HEARTS Philippa Carr £1.95
- ☐ THE SECOND SALADIN Stephen Hunter £1.95
- ☐ ECHOES OF WAR Joan Dial £1.95
- ☑ MAKING WAVES Liz Allen £1.95
- ☐ GLIDEN-FIRE Stephen Donaldson £1.25

You can buy Fontana paperbacks at your local bookshop or newsagent. Or you can order them from Fontana Paperbacks, Cash Sales Department, Box 29, Douglas, Isle of Man. Please send a cheque, postal or money order (not currency) worth the purchase price plus 15p per book for postage (maximum postage is £3.00 for orders within the UK).

NAME (Block letters) _____

ADDRESS _____

_____